ENCHANTING SARAH GREENBERG

JENNIFER INGLIS

CITY OWL
PRESS

ENCHANTING SARAH GREENBERG
A Paranormal Women's Fiction Novel

CITY OWL PRESS
www.cityowlpress.com

Cover Design by MiblArt. All stock photos licensed appropriately.

Edited by Tee Tate.

For information on subsidiary rights, please contact the publisher at info@cityowlpress.com.

Print Edition ISBN: 978-1-64898-137-1

Digital Edition ISBN: 978-1-64898-138-8

Printed in the United States of America

PRAISE FOR JENNIFER INGLIS

"Inglis has a light, comedic touch with this fantasy romance, *Enchanting Sarah Greenberg*… [The] slightly bonkers worldbuilding brings the fun without ever sacrificing genuine emotion; despite the magical backdrop, Sarah and Colin feel wonderfully grounded. Readers will be spellbound."
— Publisher's Weekly

"*Enchanting Sarah Greenberg* is funny, magical, charming and wonderful. I loved it!"
— Kristen Johnston, Actress & Author

"I'm so happy I stumbled upon *Girls Who Wear Glasses*. I absolutely adored it! I love reading books about women overcoming their inner fears. Rachel was such a relatable character to many women, including myself. I'm so happy she eventually found her voice!
— Lauren, happybibliophile

"Jennifer Inglis created a wonderful group of characters around Rachel and Nathan as well for a robust and humorous adventure. I enjoyed reading this delightful romance, *Girls Who Wear Glasses*, about a woman who learns to believe in herself and the man who believed in her all along. Great read!"
— Michelle Thorne, author of Both Darkness and Light

"I enjoyed *Girls Who Wear Glasses* from start to finish. I loved Rachel's wit and felt a real connection with her…She made me laugh and there was romance with a happy ending, so this one is a hit in my book."
— Shannon Stults, author of the Willow Creek series

For my father, James Inglis.

The World is full of magic things, patiently waiting for our senses to grow sharper.

– W. B. Yeats

CHAPTER
ONE

"And now, for my next trick…"

The street magician held court in front of a small crowd, the late summer sun behind him giving his lavender suit a slight glow. He stood in front of a card table covered in a black velvet cloth festooned with sparkling suns and moons. His gaze darted nervously, and he glanced at his donation bucket.

Producing a silver dollar from his hip pocket, he held it up for all to see. He rolled the coin through his right fingers, then his left. As he passed it back to his right hand, his face reddened as he dropped the coin, momentarily freezing as the crowd snickered. He wiped his brow with the back of his hand as he bent to pick it up, redeeming himself by vanishing the coin when he returned to upright. He let out a light stream of breath.

"That was a retention pass," Sarah Greenberg said to the man next to her. "It's a false transfer, relying on the short delay in the viewer's visual frame rate." She checked her phone for texts from her editor at the magazine. There were none, and she tucked the phone back in her jeans pocket. The stranger gave her the side-eye and grunted. "He'll put it in a secret pouch in his jacket," she added. The man turned to her and squinted. "It's called a topit. You know, if you're into that sort of thing." The man stepped away.

Sarah was into that sort of thing. She grew up around it, knew the ins and outs. Although she was gainfully employed as a food writer, a career that satisfied both her need to write and her love of food, she always had a soft spot for the whimsical. To be fair, she had no talent for magic tricks, as her hands always felt too clumsy and she always dropped whatever she had been trying to disappear, morph, or move. She just didn't have the knack.

She turned her attention back to the magician as he performed another series of simple coin tricks.

Too slow. I can see where your hand is going the whole time.

A couple in front of her turned and gave her a look, indicating to Sarah that she had actually said that out loud.

Hoping to retain the audience members who hadn't yet made a break for it, the magician dashed behind the table, sat, and pulled out a deck of cards. He did what Sarah knew to be a blind shuffle, which didn't change the order of the cards at all. Then she saw his hand dip slightly below the table.

"Amateur," she said, mindful of her volume.

While he was making a flourish with his right hand, Sarah saw him swiftly tuck his left hand under the chair, and she knew he was grabbing a secret duplicate card. She had seen this mistake before and was surprised he had made such a rookie move. The magician caught Sarah's eye, and more beads of sweat began to migrate from his forehead to the tip of his nose, moisture that couldn't be attributed to the current mild Midwest temperatures. Never breaking his rehearsed patter, however, he cut the deck and asked a lady in the front to pick a card.

"Ace of spades," she said.

With another flourish and a slightly better show of misdirection, he produced the named card. A few "oohs" and "aahs" rumbled among the remaining stragglers who hadn't yet made a run for their El train. But Sarah saw every move and caught each handoff. She wasn't impressed.

After he passed the donation bucket and the people dispersed, Sarah hung back. She sidled up to his table and dropped a dollar bill into the coffer.

"Your sight lines were messed up," she said. "And the handling was a bit convoluted. Card trick was okay. Decent misdirection."

"I saw you watch me," he responded. Up close, Sarah realized how young he was, probably not more than twenty. She threw in another dollar, just to be kind. "You saw what everyone else missed. You do magic?"

"No," she said. "But I'm familiar. My father owns a magic shop nearby."

"Which one? Rogers Park has a few. Or is it one of the ones in Ravenswood? Ooh, is it the one on Clark? With the gold ducks hanging in the windows?"

"Greenberg's. Just down the street a bit."

"Your father is Avi Greenberg?" The magician's eyes looked like saucers.

"Um, yes?"

He grabbed her hand and shook it so enthusiastically, her oversized purse fell off her shoulder. She grimaced slightly as the weight of her laptop and various notepads tugged on her elbow.

"You're like royalty in the magic community! Everyone knows Greenberg's! It's practically a Chicago institution! I mean, it *is* an institution. That's where the best of the best...is there really a secret meeting of top magicians in the back room of the store?"

"If it's a secret, how would I know?" She disengaged from his ongoing handshake and adjusted her bag back onto her shoulder. "Look, watch your sight lines and keep the transfers clean."

"I will. Are you sure you don't do magic?"

"Nope. Just an interested bystander." She smiled and turned to leave, intent on getting to her father's shop by lunch.

"Apple doesn't fall far from the tree!" Out of the corner of her eye, she saw him begin the process of drawing another crowd.

"An illusion for you, my friends, the best that magic has to offer..."

His voice grew fainter as she reached the end of the block. Forcing herself to look up from the short blades of grass pushing themselves through the cracks of the city sidewalk, she felt the heat of the sun warm the back of her neck. It had been a busy summer for her, with restaurants either opening anew or extending their patio services, showing off their freshly minted permits from City Hall. She always went into a place wanting to like the cuisine, but this summer had proved disappointing in many respects. Nothing felt new, so much felt uninspired. She loved being a food writer, but she had been doing the job for a while and was starting to feel that familiar itch.

Nothing up my sleeve, folks, nothing up my sleeve…

The buildings looked dingier than usual, as if they were thirsty for a late summer rain to wash them clean. Keeping her eyes sharp as she crossed the street, she then made a left while pushing a stray ebony curl from her forehead and moving her sunglasses back to the bridge of her nose. Catching a glimpse of herself in the drugstore window, she stood a little straighter, hoping to minimize the bit of roundness accumulating around her middle. Sarah had always been a little on the plump side, unlike her mother and her sister, who were always model-thin, although her mother had gained a bit in late middle age, which she always lamented. Her last words to Sarah, in fact, had been "Lose weight," which most people would take as harsh, but Sarah knew it was because her mother had felt that her weight gain had contributed to her cancer diagnosis. Sarah shook her head, dismissing the sad, passing thoughts, and focused her eyes on the street ahead.

"You have the day off, Sarahleh?" A deep voice resonated from just below her left hip. She gave a bit of a start, bringing her back to the present, and looked down.

She had, in fact, had breakfast at the new diner on Randolph Street and had several pages of notes scribbled into her notepad, but she decided to play along.

"On a nice day like this? How could I resist?" The man in the brown suit, slightly out-of-date but none the worse for wear, sat barefoot on a square rubber mat on the sidewalk. "Are you going to play something for me, Esra?"

The man chuckled. "Maybe, maybe. Depends."

"On what?"

"On whether I can win the disagreement I have been having with my brother." Esra twisted in his seat and waved through the open door of the pub.

Sarah waved as well. "Hi Nadav."

Nadav raised the white cloth he was using to wipe down the counter and waved in return.

"Nadav says I cannot play Bach on this instrument." Esra gestured at the box next to him. "I say, anything is possible."

Sarah tucked her hair behind her ear. "Well, how about something simpler? Not that I doubt your abilities."

"For you? Of course. Let us see what I have here…" Esra opened the small box and removed ten bands. He looped them around his toes, holding each one with the corresponding finger. His dark skin glistened in the sunlight as he pressed down with each digit, and a soft-toned vibrato sounded from each of the bands. It was both otherworldly and somehow familiar, and Sarah had never been able to figure out how he made the music. Esra continued to play, as if manipulating an invisible marionette, the soothing music dancing on the breeze. It was quick and light, the notes tickling her ear and weaving and pulsing through her head. It wasn't classical music, it sounded nothing like jazz, and though she had never heard the tune before, she instinctively began to hum along. Whatever worries she had been carrying lifted themselves and gently rolled away, and the usual sense of unease she typically felt with herself and the world in general suddenly seemed lighter. She glanced at the people walking past her on the street, who appeared oblivious to the sounds, and Sarah felt like running after them and asking them what their problem was.

Can't you hear it? Doesn't it make you want to sing?

She looked back at Esra, who began to play a little faster, his brow furrowed as he moved the flexible bands, which were now thinner and more transparent. She glanced back to the sidewalk, hoping to find anyone with whom to share this glorious melody, but discovered that people were no longer walking down the street.

They were dancing.

Sarah watched in amazement as old ladies pirouetted, businessmen tapped, and one teenager on a scooter jumped off and did the lindy hop with an equally fleet-footed mail carrier. Sarah's jaw hung open, her eyes laser-focused on the movement. Her heart beat in time with the drumbeat syncopation, and she felt as light as a leaf on the wind. Suddenly, the music stopped, and she returned her attention to Esra.

"Did you see that?" she said. "Wasn't that just amazing?"

"Well, I know my playing is good, but I do not know about amazing."

"No, Esra, the dancing! Did you see all the people dancing?"

Esra removed the bands, which had returned to their normal dull shades, and placed them back them in the box. "There was no one dancing, my *Zeeskeit*," he said, using the Yiddish endearment he reserved for when she was feeling low and needed cheering. "You were bobbing your head a bit, but that is it." He squinted his eyes from behind his dark, round glasses. "You saw them? People dancing?"

"Why, yes, I…" Sarah's voice trailed off. "I was just affected by the music, I guess." She coughed and straightened her shirt, tugging at the hem. She took a breath. "You *could* play Bach, I bet."

"It is all right, dear. My music affects people strangely sometimes. I just have a way, I guess." Esra chuckled and lowered his sunglasses. His eyes were dark green, the color of emeralds one might see in a museum or around Elizabeth Taylor's neck. It was a striking contrast to his burnished ebony skin, and he usually wore his dark glasses so as not to attract attention, even indoors. He grabbed his socks from the mat next to him and put them on, wiggling his toes as he did so. He got up from his seated position and unfolded a wooden chair that had been resting against the grey stone of the pub. Leaning on it, he put on his shoes, giving each foot a little tap as if to say to his footwear, "There you are."

"Next time you come by you can make a request of what you would like to hear." Esra smiled and tapped his temple. "I have got quite the catalog up here."

"I will." She smiled back. "You going to make up with your brother and have some lunch? Or I can run in and grab you something if you're not on speaking terms."

"No. We will be fine. Brothers quarrel. But I will prove him wrong. And I have snacks in my pockets." He patted his jacket, which Sarah thought was too heavy for the weather, but Esra appeared quite comfortable. "You tell your father I said hello. He said he would have a new trick for me the next time I come by." He packed up his things and adjusted his hat. "You saw right through that magician down the street, did you not?"

"Yeah, but it was no big deal. He wasn't very good."

"Not everyone sees so clearly." Esra raised an eyebrow. "They do not have the gift."

"I have no gifts, Esra. I just…saw what he was doing. That's all."

"Hmm. Well, you have a nice day, Sarahleh. Stop by maybe next week. We will have a drop of something, and you can watch me play *Toccata and Fugue in D Minor*." He waved his hat as he disappeared into the tide of passersby on the sidewalk.

That would be something. Bach on a toe piano.

Sarah continued down the street, the smell of dumpsters in the alleys alternating with the smell of fresh bread, candles, and coffee from the storefront merchants that lined this section of the neighborhood. There was a feeling of community here, but only in the sense that everyone put up with the same parking bans, traffic overflow from Cubs games, and constant road construction that all residents in Chicago did. No one really spoke to one another, except perhaps a quick nod now and again, but she knew everyone around her would be the first to defend their beloved city to the death.

Or at least until winter. Then it was every person for themselves.

Arriving in front of her father's shop, she took a deep breath, centering herself before stepping inside. She loved and loathed this place, this living, breathing entity that was both a business and a second sibling. Sometimes she felt her father paid more attention to it than to her, attending to its needs as if it were a petulant toddler, holding court for the stream of loyal customers who populated it between the hours of ten in the morning and five-ish at night, sometimes earlier, sometimes later—except for Fridays, when Avi Greenberg was always home by sundown for Shabbat dinner. And when they were children, it was her sister, Debra, younger by eighteen months, who had been his chosen companion there after school and on weekends.

Sarah pushed open the heavy, wooden door that had been in place since the store opened more than one hundred and fifty years ago. Her great-great-great-grandfather Benjamin Greenberg had bought the property and started the first magic store in the Midwest. Back then it was more of a general store with a special section for books, penny tricks, decks of cards, and the various odd ingredients. Some were distrustful of him, not only for his being a Jew, but because they thought he might be dealing in the black arts. But no one dared accuse him, and soon he was just Old Ben Greenberg, kindly merchant.

Over the years the sundries had changed as the shop passed from father to son again and again (with the occasional daughter in the mix), gradually reducing the bags of sugar and flour and adding more mirage billiard balls, locking rings, and magic kits for kids, as well as adding a professional section catering to the burgeoning theater scene. Greenberg's was considered top of the line. Avi saw to that, adding more exotic items like a Hindu basket illusion, psychic chest, levitation boards, and transformation cages—all special ordered—and some rare collectibles, such as the turn-of-the-century Okito Bowl of Gobi, which he had purchased at auction and displayed prominently behind the register. Every so often he would take it from the shelf and show it off to skeptical customers, appearing to turn confetti into water. Serious practitioners of the art knew to come to Greenberg's; if they didn't have it, Avi had the connections to find it. David Copperfield was so happy to find something at the shop that he sent Avi an autographed photo and standing tickets to any show he performed anywhere in the world, although Avi had never taken him up on it.

"Too showy," he once declared.

Sarah entered the store, taking in the familiar smell of incense and soap and warm pastry. She took a mint from the bowl by the cash register. Her father was most likely stocking the shelves in the storeroom, as she saw Raya enter the main area with an armful of scarves.

"Raya! Need a hand?"

"Nah, I have it. They're light." She placed them on a table in the middle by the Singing Silver Bowls and began to fold. Sarah decided to help anyway.

"These are nice." Sarah fingered the fabric and the hemmed edges. "Real silk?"

"These? No. Your dad saves those for the pros. These are for the Everydayers."

"Everydayers" was Raya's word for the casual customer, one who liked to perform tricks at their children's birthday parties and church talent shows. She meant no insult; the Everydayers were the store's bread and butter, and she never wanted to alienate a customer.

"How's school?" Sarah asked, as she continued to fold.

"Oh, fine. Teaching a pretty good class of undergrads this term. Although grading papers takes a lot of time away from my research." Raya had worked at Greenberg's since high school and had continued her employment through her post-grad work. They had known each other since childhood, her father Nadav being Avi's best friend, although even after all these years Sarah still wasn't sure what Raya studied. Most of it was over Sarah's head, but she surmised it was an experimental physics program with elements of women's studies and African history thrown in.

Her father finished shelving and joined the women at the folding table. He was wearing his usual argyle sweater vest, despite the mild summer weather, and his salt-and-pepper beard had a dust bunny lodged in it. He looked a bit like a jolly academic librarian, one who would shush you but then slip you a peppermint from his vest pocket.

"Hello, one of my two favorite daughters! To what do we owe the pleasure?"

"I told you I'd be stopping by to return the book you lent me." Sarah plucked the ball of lint from her father's beard. She placed the last scarf on the pile, which she thought had been green but was apparently blue. Her father regarded the loose fold on the scarf and raised his right eyebrow and pursed his lips. Sarah refolded it.

"It was an okay read," Sarah continued. "Not a page-turner or anything."

"Oh, yes, the book. Right, right."

"What did he have you reading this time?" Raya laughed.

"*The Philosophy of Natural Magic* by Heinrich Cornelius Agrippa." Sarah removed the huge tome from her bag and handed it to Avi. "Old Henry was a real hoot."

"At least he didn't make *you* read it in the original German," Raya said.

"And I thank you for that, Dad. I think I'm still scarred from Uncle

Gustav shouting at me every year at Thanksgiving." Gustav was her father's old college friend, who was now an antiques dealer. "Bring ze crezent rolls! Schnell! Schnell!"

Raya laughed and continued the imitation. "Vere ist ze butter?"

Avi placed the book on a shelf under the counter. "You can't fault me for trying. Just wanted to expand your horizons."

"I have a master's degree. I'm expanded."

"Yes. Yes, you're perfect, just as you are. Sometimes I forget that." Avi gave Sarah a light pinch on her cheek, then gave the pile of scarves a pat. "Okay, what's next?"

"Lunch?" Raya scooped up the pile of scarves and placed them on a shelf. "You haven't sat down since you got here this morning."

"Maybe later. A lot of new stock arrived today. So much to do!"

Sarah slapped her forehead. "Lunch! Crap! I'm meeting Colin at one. What time is it?" She opened her bag and started rummaging around for her cell phone. "Where is it? Where is it?"

The ancient cuckoo clock on the wall chimed. Sarah knew not to trust it. It had long since stopped keeping actual time and just popped out whenever it damn well felt like it.

"Twelve-thirty! Coo coo!" it croaked, flapping its small, wooden wings, its round, painted eyes darting back and forth.

"Is that the time or just a suggestion?" Sarah asked.

"It's twelve-thirty. Relax. You're fine." Raya shook her head, her long braids waving down her back. She went to the register and sat on the stool, watching the two customers who had just entered the store. "Browsers," she decided, and opened a book.

"I just don't want to be late." Sarah smoothed her curls. "Madison's going to be there, and it's the first time I'm going to meet her."

"Meeting the daughter, that's a big step." Avi pulled a stuffed rabbit out of a top hat. "Hello Stuart." He placed the rabbit on the top shelf next to the rest of the hats, which were artfully arranged by color, size, and potential contents. "Are you up for that?" He brushed the rim of a purple velvet bowler, smoothing the nap and straightening the bow on the orange top hat.

"It'll be fine. I'm looking forward to it, actually." Sarah could feel her stomach knot, and she put her hands on her hips. "Kids dig me."

"Remember," Raya said, looking up from her book, "they're like dogs. They smell fear." She placed the book down on the counter, then opened the register and took a stack of bills out and began to count them.

"She's fourteen. Should I bring something? What do kids like? Rye bread? Pokémon? How about money? Should I just give her money?"

"You'll be fine," Raya said. "Colin is a good guy, and he's lucky to have you." She put the money in a zippered pouch, then slung a canvas bag over her shoulders. Her toned arms seemed to barely register the weight. "I'm going to the bank, Avi!"

Sarah's father waved from behind a display of mannequins wearing rainbow tuxedos.

"You have anything in your car you need washed?" Raya said. "I'm going to the laundromat after the bank."

"You can do that at my house anytime, you know."

"I know. Thanks. I like the laundromat, actually. Something about the artificial smell of flowers, plastic baskets, and gumballs. It's comforting. Besides, I have a working theory on where the extra socks disappear to and I'm going to test it out. I'm thinking Cleveland. But not the Cleveland you're thinking of."

"All right then. Good luck with that." Sarah picked up her bag. "Dad? I'm going."

Avi had returned to the hat shelf and was engaged in an apparently one-sided conversation with the stuffed rabbit.

"Wait, what? Hold on a second, Stuart," her father said. "You're going? All right. Have a good lunch. Bring cash. Couldn't hurt. You need money?"

Sarah laughed. "I'm good."

"Told ya so," Raya whispered.

"Will I see you this weekend? Deb's coming by. She's making brisket."

Sarah shuddered at the thought. Debra's brisket was sadly like their mother's, which had the consistency of a leather saddle left out in the rain. And that was when it wasn't burned beyond recognition.

"I'll be there. We can order pizza if necessary." She pulled her sunglasses out of her bag, and almost on impulse, walked over to her father and kissed him on the cheek, patting Stuart on the head for good measure.

Raya pushed the heavy door open, which groaned with age. As the bell tinkled, they stepped out into the sun. Sarah popped on her sunglasses and blinked a few times, letting her eyes adjust to the brightness.

"You don't need sunglasses?" Sarah asked Raya, simultaneously pushing hers up the bridge of her nose.

"Nope. Doesn't bother me," Raya answered, her dark eyes sparkling in the summer afternoon sun, which gave them an almost iridescent glow. "Your car this way?"

"Possibly," Sarah replied.

Raya adjusted the heavy bag on her shoulders, shoving the money pouch in it, and they headed down the street.

"Oh hey, I forgot to tell you, I finally got my thesis topic approved," Raya said. "I wanted to do something with time travel, but my advisor put the kibosh on that. I finally settled on 'Programmable Synthetic Hallucinations: Toward a Boundless Mixed Reality.'"

"So something simple then." Sarah stopped and looked around. "My car's not this way."

"Okay. It's around here somewhere then. Off to suds! Later!"

Sarah zipped up her purse and turned the opposite way, which she was now pretty sure was the general direction of where her car was parked. She tried to leave it in the same place every time, but she decided she must have a very specific memory deficit when it came to parking spaces, because her car always seemed to be in a different place than where she thought she left it.

She walked a block and a half, spying the car down an adjacent street. "Aha. There you are. Found you." She got in, started the car, looked to the left, and then eased the car into the street.

"God, I hope this kid likes me," she said.

CHAPTER
TWO

Sarah had never dated a man with a child before. She'd dated several who could themselves have been categorized as a manchild, but that didn't count. None were long-lasting relationships. She liked to think she could chalk it up to high standards, but the truth was that she quickly got bored. Most lacked flash and possessed no sizzle, and while she knew to stay away from those who were *all* flash and sizzle, she also knew she wouldn't be happy until she found one with just the right balance of maturity and a splash of sparkle.

Or until she found a relationship as good as her parents had.

She held her mother and father up as an example of the perfect relationship, and that was hard to match. They had often existed in their own little bubble, complementing each other's strengths and weaknesses in a perfect balance of love, humor, and well-timed desserts. They brought Sarah and Debra into the bubble, of course, but Sarah always felt like she had one foot out of it.

And when her mother died, Avi was destroyed.

They had to close the shop for a while, opening it when Raya could cover a shift, but they spent most of their time with their father. He ate little, slept less, and spent his days slowly fading into the mists of what had been a forty-four-year marriage. She watched strange people stream in and out of her father's house, both while they were sitting shiva and afterward, odd types with big bags and small hats who Sarah could only assume were holistic healers of some kind—Debra was into that—and others bringing casseroles and various sundries, which were stacked in the fridge like bricks in an edible wall. It was a surreal time of black clothes, drapes over the mirrors, and people grasping her hand with that look of sadness and pity that Sarah grew to despise.

Eventually, Avi recovered, coming back from the brink with time, music, and a steady diet of corned beef. But she would sometimes catch him looking over his shoulder, as if he meant to say something to someone who was no longer there.

And at some point, Sarah decided she wanted nothing to do with this part of a relationship. So whenever things got even remotely serious, she bailed.

But then she met Colin. He was different—steady, kind, funny, and just ever so slightly sparkly. An accountant by trade, he had an interest in magic and had been stopping by Greenberg's sporadically for several months before Sarah worked up the nerve to talk to him.

"It's him again!" Raya would say whenever she saw Sarah staring wistfully. "Go ask if he needs help."

Sarah, no shrinking violet, nevertheless resisted the nudge. "I can't. He's too…yeah."

Something about him made her hesitate, as if he'd disappear in a puff of smoke if she actually spoke to him, like one of the Lovely Assistants in illusionists' acts. It wasn't his looks necessarily—he was handsome but not aggressively so. He just had a *way*. Debra said he looked like the dad at any random nine-year-old's birthday party who the moms like to hover around and refill his snack plate. Sarah didn't quite get this reference, but she got the gist. He was special.

Colin came in one winter day looking, in fact, for something for a birthday party.

"Okay," Raya whispered, "you're up." She gave Sarah a gentle-ish shove in his direction, and Sarah, caught unprepared, practically fell into him while carrying a stack of purple top hats. A dozen fake doves fell out and landed around his feet.

It wasn't a meet-cute, but it was definitely a meet-weird.

"Ta da?" he said, raising an eyebrow in amusement.

Sarah bit her lip. "Um, a bird on the foot is worth twelve in a hat?"

Pull it together, Greenberg.

Colin bent down and began to gather the doves. "Is it one dove per hat?"

"Oh yeah, that works." Sarah turned back to Raya, gave her a death stare, and was met with an enthusiastic thumbs-up.

"I'm looking for a trick I can do at my daughter's party. She's turning fourteen, so it's not a kid's party, but it's kind of a tradition. I need something with high impact that requires minimal skill."

Raya glided past and whispered in Sarah's ear. "See if he's married…"

Sarah coughed to cover Raya's question, then patted her chest. "Sure. We can find something. What were you looking for? Coin tricks? Spoon bending? Sawing a lady in half?"

"Maybe something in the middle? I'm trying to minimize risk. How about this?" He perused a shelf. "This looks cool." He picked up a set of silver interlocking rings.

"Classic, yes. But you'll lose the teens immediately. How about this?" She handed him a gold box. "This might be what you're looking for. It will take a bit of practice, but I think it's manageable."

"Acrobatic Silk in Glasses Tray," he said, reading the print on the bottom of the box.

"Yeah, it's fun. Inside the box is a tray with three glasses attached. When the illusionist holds the tray behind his back, the silk jumps from one glass to the next. At first the audience will think that they have caught you turning the tray around. But then they'll see that the silk jumped to the middle glass right before their eyes. Works no matter where the audience is sitting. I have an instruction booklet behind the counter. You read Mandarin, yes?"

"Of course," Colin replied with a laugh.

"I'm sure it will make your wife roll her eyes. Pull some flowers out of your sleeve to make up for it."

"*Smooth,*" Raya whispered, gliding back the other way.

"I'm um, well, I'm divorced, actually. And she's passed on."

Sarah felt a lump grow in the back of her throat and started to feel that itchy sensation on her earlobes whenever she found herself in an awkward position. "Oh, I'm so sorry. Bad case of foot-in-mouth disease."

"It's okay. She's been gone for eight years, and we were divorced for two years before that."

"Well, you're a good father for making the effort to entertain your daughter."

"It gets harder and harder. Mostly I just merit colossal eye-rolls." He squinted. "Have I seen you here before?"

"Probably not. I don't know. Maybe. I'm only here from time to time to help out my father. He owns this store."

"That must have been fun, growing up in a magic store."

"Less so than you'd think. I don't have much talent for it." She cleared her throat. "Do you want me to ring that up, or do you want to keep looking? That Head in the Box trick is still up for grabs."

"I think I'm good with this one. You've been very helpful." They walked to the cash register. "I'm Colin, by the way."

"Sarah." She rang up his purchase, then put the trick and the booklet in a purple paper bag with glitter-covered handles.

"This will be great. Thanks again," Colin said, placing his credit card back in his wallet. He turned to leave, the bell tinkling on the front door as he pulled it open. He looked at her again, smiled, and waved as he walked out.

Raya rushed the counter. "So that went…boring."

"You can write me a script next time," Sarah countered. "Or maybe just throw your voice like a ventriloquist."

"I can do that, you know."

"I have no doubt."

The doorbells tinkled again as Colin stuck his head in. "Hey, I'm kind of out of practice, so it took me a few minutes. Can I buy you lunch sometime?"

"She'd love that!" Raya volunteered.

And so she did. Colin and Sarah started seeing each other, usually meeting at the shop and going for lunch, dinner, movies, the usual fare.

Sarah worried about dragging her feet, but it felt so easy this time. She was happy with him, but it came with an ever-so-slight feeling of dread. She didn't know if it was a Sarah thing or a Jewish thing, but she sometimes felt she was waiting for the other shoe to drop. It had been five months now, and Colin had finally taken the big step—asking Sarah to meet Madison.

The feeling of wanting to bolt was minimal—a new first. That was encouraging.

She had worried about being late, but she was making good time. The traffic lights and construction schedules were cooperating—something that never happened any other time she had driven from the city to Oak Park—and she made it to Colin's house with five minutes to spare.

Why are we meeting here? Whatever happened to neutral turf?

She had been here before, of course, but always when Madison was staying with her grandparents.

It will be fine. She's probably more scared of you than you are of her. Wait, is that children or bears?

She tossed the keys in her bag and got out of the car. Straightening her shirt and taking a deep breath, she marched up the driveway. Truth was, she didn't have a lot of experience with kids. Even when she was one, she tended toward the adults in the room, as the other children often shied away from her, possibly due to her vocabulary, general interests, or just the steely glint that was often in her eyes. As a food writer, she knew foie gras and fine wine, not chicken nuggets and spicy tortilla chips.

Is that what kids eat? Do they like gum?

She knocked on the door and Colin answered, greeting her with a big smile.

"You made it! You could have just come in, you know," he said, stepping aside to let her enter.

"Well, with Madison here, I didn't want to look presumptuous," Sarah replied, hanging her bag on the coat rack. "Is she…around?" Her eyes darted back and forth as she stiffly craned her neck to look around the room.

"She's not a ninja, Sarah. She's upstairs in her room."

"Oh yeah. That sounds right. My dad says I went up to my room at age twelve and didn't come down until my high school graduation."

Colin laughed. "Nice. So much to look forward to. C'mon in. I've got some stuff brewing in the kitchen. You can supervise."

He wasn't kidding. The kitchen was enveloped in various food smells and the sound of bubbling pots, like some epicurean witch's brew. He had bread and a cheese plate out and a freshly made pitcher of iced tea.

"This is…a lot. I thought we'd just have a little deli or something," Sarah said, peeking under the lid of one of the pots.

"It's not as elaborate as it looks. Truly. Madison did most of it. She considers herself a budding foodie, whatever that means. She's eager to talk to you about all the restaurants you go to."

She moved in close to Colin and gave him a kiss. "I do more than go to restaurants, but if that's what she wants to talk about, I'm game. I'm just glad she wants to talk to me."

Colin tightened his grip around her waist. "She's a good kid. She wants to meet you. It will be fine." He kissed her this time.

"God, guys. Gross."

Colin and Sarah separated with a start. Madison stood in the kitchen doorway with a sheepish grin on her face.

"Sarah, this is my daughter, Madison. Maybe she *is* a ninja."

"Hi Madison, so nice to finally meet you." Sarah held out her hand. Madison walked up to her, looked down at Sarah's outstretched hand, and embraced her tightly. Momentarily caught off guard, Sarah wobbled slightly before gently patting Madison on the back.

"Oh, okay. You're a hugger. All right then," Sarah said.

Madison released her and jogged over to the stove. "I made French onion soup for you. Dad told me you had a really good one at some place on the north side. Maybe you can tell me if mine is any good?" Madison looked at her hopefully.

"Absolutely. It would be my honor. I'm sure it's very good."

Madison grinned again and brushed her long bangs from her eyes.

"Cool," she said.

"Would you two mind watching the food for a second? I left something in my car and need to run and get it," Colin said, grabbing his keys from a bowl on the counter.

"We've got it, Dad," Madison said, taking a couple of plates from the cabinet. "We can survive for two minutes."

Sarah watched Colin exit, then turned back to Madison. "You know your way around a kitchen," she said. "French onion soup is pretty sophisticated for a...what grade are you in? Fourth? Second year of college? I really don't know these things."

Madison laughed. "I'm in ninth grade. And I read a book. Some lady named Julia Child. Wasn't too hard. Plus I've been helping Dad with meals for a long time. You cook?"

"Not as much as I'd like to."

"I don't like the cleaning up part. But I guess it's part of the job." Madison chewed her lip. "Hey, can I ask you something? Woman to woman?"

The hairs on the back of Sarah's neck stood up. *Danger! Danger!*

"Do you think I should get purple streaks in my hair?" Madison held up her ponytail.

Oh, thank God.

"I'm just wondering if I can pull it off," Madison continued. "I mean, some girls at school have streaks, and I don't want to do it just because they're doing it, but I think it would be cool..." She looked at Sarah like she was the oracle at Delphi.

Sarah felt a wave of affection for this girl wash over her, and she knew everything would be fine. She smiled and nodded.

"Yes. It would look great on you. I even know someone who could do it for you." She passed her hand over Madison's head. "Just a couple of chunky streaks right here..."

As her hand glided down Madison's smooth, reddish-brown hair, the strands turned purple. Sarah pulled her hand back like she had been zatzed by electricity and examined her fingertips.

"Or maybe blue?" Madison suggested.

"Sure, sure, that would be great too..." Sarah's hazel eyes widened, and her heart began to race. She instinctively brought her hand back up to Madison's head and made an "erasing" gesture from roots to tip. The purple streak disappeared. Sarah let out a quick breath. Madison didn't notice anything had been amiss and began plating the salad on the counter.

What the hell was that?

Colin reentered the kitchen and placed a case of sparkling water next to the sink, where it landed with a soft thud. "Good to see you survived my absence," he said.

"Yup, yup, no problems, definitely nothing weird." Sarah grabbed a can of the sparkling water from the box, opened it, and chugged it in one long gulp, stifling a burp.

"Good to know," Colin said, eyeing his girlfriend. "Well, why don't we sit down and eat? I'm starving." He picked up the remaining plates and put them on the small table in the kitchen. When Sarah didn't move, he went to her, took her by the elbow, and guided her into a chair.

"Mad," he continued, "could you grab the napkins? We don't want to use our sleeves. We have company."

"Oh, Dad…" Madison rolled her eyes as she placed the napkin holder on the table.

After they had served themselves, Sarah poked at her salad. What had just happened? She thought about Madison's hair being purple and then…it was. Or at least she thought it was. It disappeared after she waved her hand over it, so maybe she was just imagining it. There was no way it had actually changed color. That's just not possible. Maybe her father had a trick at the store that could do that, but she certainly couldn't. One didn't do magic accidentally.

When they finished their salads, Madison brought the individual crocks of soup to the table. She had taken the time to thoroughly brown the cheese on the top, and she looked quite pleased with herself. She carefully placed the bowls in front of Sarah and her father and watched them expectantly as they broke the cheese with their spoons.

"Well? How would you write that up in one of your columns?" Madison asked.

"Hmm." Sarah took a sip, then another. "Very nice. Onions should be a little more browned, should be caramelized, actually, but I can show you how to do that. But the soup is well seasoned, nicely presented, and has an evenly browned layer of cheese. Attention to detail counts a lot. You even seasoned the toast, I noticed. Nice touch. Four stars."

"That's cool, maybe someday you'll write about my cooking for real." Madison beamed. "Let me get you an actual soup spoon. I put out the wrong kind." She leaned over the table, knocking Sarah's empty glass onto the floor. "Oh no! I'm so sorry!"

"No worries. I've got it." Sarah leaned over to examine the damage. As she reached to pick up the large shards, they began to reassemble themselves. She gasped and covered her mouth with her hands.

"Are you all right?" Colin asked. "Did you cut yourself? Do you need a tourniquet? I'll go get the broom…"

Sarah quickly leaned over again and saw that the glass was once more whole.

"No! I mean, no worries. It's actually not broken." She picked up the re-knitted glass and placed it gently on the table.

"How is that possible? I heard it break."

"Um, I don't know. But it didn't. Maybe it was…my cell phone. Yeah, I've got some weird alert noises on that thing." Sarah felt her forehead grow damp.

"That is weird," Madison concurred.

Colin frowned. "But I've never heard a sound like that from your phone…"

"Ha! Yes! Totally weird!" Sarah was starting to panic. "Listen, I'm suddenly not feeling well. I think I need to go…"

"Oh no, it's not the food, is it?" Madison picked up her bowl and sniffed it.

"It's not that, I just, uh, remembered something I have to pick up for Raya. Magic store emergency." Sarah got up from the table and placed her napkin over her glass. "Madison, it was so nice to meet you, and your soup was wonderful. Colin, I'm sorry. I'll call you later."

Colin stood. "Let me walk you out."

"No! I mean, that's not necessary. I know where the door is. Enjoy your lunch. Bye!"

Colin leaned in for a goodbye kiss, but Sarah spun on her heel and made a beeline for the front door. As she slammed it behind her, she jogged to her car. Remembering to breathe, she fumbled her keys as she tried to turn the ignition, finally getting the car started and backed out of the driveway. She wanted nothing more than to drive away and go somewhere—anywhere she could go and try to make sense of what had just happened. If it happened once, she could have chalked it up to fatigue and stress, but twice? That was no fluke. She was either losing her faculties or something deeply weird was going on.

I think the other shoe just dropped.

CHAPTER
THREE

S arah's head was spinning as she made the supreme effort to concentrate on the road. She was just an unremarkable writer from Chicago, and now—what? She was losing her mind? Had she somehow developed superpowers? Was she Spiderman? Madison's hair had turned purple. The glass had mended itself. She was sure of it.

But it's not possible.

Her scalp was itchy, and her elbow hurt. She had aches in her hip, nose, and feet. She blinked rapidly to keep her eyes in focus, and she was certain when she exited the car she would develop a limp and a pronounced facial tic. She rubbed her chest as she drove, trying to calm herself, and found what she was convinced was a lump, until she realized she had one on the other side and it was, indeed, her collarbone.

She was not well.

Once back in her neighborhood, she parallel parked her car, getting in the spot on the first try. This had never happened before.

I do have superpowers.

Sarah knew she had to talk to someone, but who? Everyone would think she was having issues, or had perhaps eaten bad mushrooms in her breakfast omelet. Who would believe her?

She hoofed it down the block to Nadav's pub. Maybe a gin and tonic was just what she needed. Or two.

Day drinking? Really? This is what it's come to? Developing superpowers and a slight drinking problem in the same day?

She spotted Esra in his usual spot outside the bar. He was playing something on the bands, and even with his glasses on she could tell that his eyes were closed. He was swaying slightly to his own music.

Toccata and Fugue in D Minor. I'll be damned.

She stopped to listen. Esra moved his fingers and toes so quickly they were almost a blur. But the Bach was unmistakable. She felt the tension drain from her body, each muscle tensing and releasing as if on cue. She imagined herself floating above the sidewalk, just slightly. She could actually visualize the vibrations rising from the bands as he played, each one producing its own shape, sound, and color. They danced around her, bouncing off her body, rising and falling with the music.

Suddenly, she was back on the sidewalk, feet firmly planted, and Esra had lowered his sunglasses and stopped playing. His emerald eyes regarded her carefully.

"See? I told you I could do it. Nadav owes me pie."

"I need to sit down."

"By all means. My brother will take care of you. I have something to finish here." He pushed his glasses back up his nose and began to adjust the bands on his feet.

She walked into the pub and sat at the bar. Esra commenced playing along with the song emanating from the jukebox.

Once upon a universe,
It's how the story goes…

"Is that The Spinners?" Sarah asked.

"*Mais non*, it's The Spiral Vogues," Nadav replied, placing a glass of water in front of her. "Sounds like them though. It's a recent favorite."

"Recent? It's got to be from the '70s."

"All depends on your perspective, my dear."

Take a trip, grab your hat,
Oh, how the time does flow…

"This is true." Sarah put her head down on the bar.

"Can I get you something else, sweetheart?"

"Gin and tonic. Please."

"Really? It's only two o'clock."

Sarah raised her head and gave him a stern look.

"All right, you're the boss. You want something to cushion the blow? I can make you a sandwich."

"Hit me."

Nadav poured her the drink, then pulled a sandwich from behind the counter.

"Take it slow, Sarah. You look a bit, how would your father put it…*fermisht.*"

"It has been a bit of a day, yes." Sarah sipped her cocktail. The drink was bitter yet refreshing, and it left a trail of warmth as it traveled through her system. She took another sip, hoping it would relax her. It didn't. She looked at the Reuben sandwich with extra sauerkraut that Nadav had placed in front of her. "That was fast."

Nadav shrugged and smiled. "If you write about my pub, I don't want points deducted for slow service."

"Never. You're always top-notch in my book."

Esra appeared in the doorway, his box of bands under his arm.

"Did you enjoy my song? Thought I would try something different today."

"Yes. Very hip. Maybe we can get you to try something a little more current next time."

"Depends on your perspective," Esra replied.

"That's what I said," added Nadav, nodding.

"Ah, it is all the same to me, Sarahleh. All goes like this…" Esra snapped the fingers on his left hand, then moved the box under his other arm. "Or like this…" He snapped his right-hand fingers. He glided over to the stool next to Sarah, his round form easing lightly onto the seat. "Well, my young friend. You are drinking in the daylight. Tell me why."

"You wouldn't believe me if I told you, Esra."

"You would be surprised what I can believe, m'dear."

"It's just that I…" Sarah felt the words lodge in her throat. She took a bite of the sandwich to try to push them down. "This is very good. Is this Russian dressing instead of Thousand Island?"

"It's always Russian dressing," Nadav corrected. "You know the difference. And you're stalling."

Sarah took a deep breath. Esra had removed his glasses, and she could feel his eyes follow her as she swayed in her seat. The more she paused, the more intent his stare became.

"We are your friends, Sarah. You can trust us. Remember when you were little and mischievous? We always kept your secrets so you would not get in trouble."

"I can't even tell Dad. He'll think I'm nuts."

"Sanity is relative." Esra patted her hand. "It will be all right."

Sarah looked into Esra's eyes and knew this instantly to be true. "Well, it's just that I…I think I did a trick today. Two, actually." She took another sip of her drink.

"Trick? What do you mean? Like a practical joke? You hate those."

"It wasn't a practical joke."

"Good," Esra replied. "Because I do not think those are funny."

"Very low form of humor," Nadav agreed.

"I made Madison's hair change color," Sarah said.

"How?" Esra blinked, adjusting his eyes to the light of the sun coming through the front window.

"I don't know. She said she wanted purple streaks, and I was demonstrating where I thought the color should go, and there it was. Then I made it go away. Somehow."

"Go on," Esra prompted.

"And then later, she knocked a glass onto the floor. It broke, but when I went to pick it up, it fixed itself."

Esra furrowed his brow and stroked his chin. He and Nadav exchanged a short glance. "And this has never happened to you before?"

"I think I would have noticed."

"It's amazing what we don't see when we're not looking for something," Nadav said.

"Have you noticed other things recently? Little things you cannot explain? Things appearing where they had not been before?"

"Maybe." Sarah thought of her car, and of the usually unhelpful cuckoo clock. She noticed Esra waving his hand down at his side. "What's he doing?" she whispered to Nadav.

"He's calling your father."

Sarah cocked her head and gave him a quizzical look.

"Bluetooth," Nadav said quickly. "Very sensitive." He took some glasses from the shelf and placed them on the bar.

"You just sit there, Sarah," Esra said after a few more seconds of waving. "I have contacted..." Nadav shot him a warning look. "I mean, *texted* your father. He should join us momentarily."

"I'm getting a little nervous, Esra." She chewed another bite of the sandwich and looked at both men. "The corned beef helps settle my stomach."

"Good. Focus on the sandwich."

"That's my life motto."

Her father appeared at the pub in what felt like mere seconds. Sarah's mouth fell agape, as she was surprised he could make the trip of a few blocks so quickly. His brow was furrowed, and he nodded at Nadav and Esra before his gaze came to rest on his elder daughter. He gave her a hug and alighted on the stool next to her.

"So..." he started. "What's new?"

Sarah waved her hand dismissively, and out of the corner of her eye she saw Nadav flinch slightly.

"I'm fine. I'm probably just a little stressed out. Imagining things. You know how I get sometimes."

"Yes, yes I do. It's part of your charm," Avi said. "But maybe those things aren't imaginary?" He placed his hand on her forehead as if he were taking her temperature. Sarah felt drowsy, as if the gin had taken effect all at once. She heard the song that was playing earlier, the bass line booming in her ears in its syncopated rhythm.

Once upon a universe,
It's how our story goes...

The room around her began to tilt, just a little bit, as the music continued. Her father got up from his stool and began to tap his foot.

Take a trip, grab your hat,
Oh, how the time does flow…

Avi began to dance, gingerly at first, and then with increasing gusto. He rocked back and forth and waved his arms over his head in time with the music.

In this cool moment in time,
With nothing left to say…

Esra joined him, moving his feet in simpatico, and they danced their way to the door.

Mr. Skye flows through you and me,
We travel on his way…

They danced in tandem down the street. Sarah watched in amazement as, one by one, the passersby joined in, like a hybrid flash mob-chorus line.

Through the groove of space and rhyme,
Dancing Mr. Skye…

More and more people began dancing, as if everyone had been given the choreography in advance. The dancers formed lines behind Avi and Esra, moving in perfect sync.

Lose yourself and be found again,
Dancing Mr. Skye…

Sarah felt like she had landed in a Broadway musical. The crowd kicked and grapevined, shimmied and twirled. She realized that she, too, was dancing in place, her eyes wide and wild.

Happily ever after now,
The colors grow and sing…

She had never seen her father dance before. Even at her bat mitzvah he stood on the sidelines while everyone else, including her mother, danced with abandon. But now he looked like Gene Kelly. And Esra kept pace with him, his shorter legs keeping up with the taller Avi, light on his feet and as graceful as a dancer could be.

Mr. Skye will guide you on,
As stars before you sing…

The men made their way back to the pub as the crowd dispersed, moving seamlessly from dance routine to their daily routine, going about their business as if nothing had happened. Sarah thought she might pass out. She closed her eyes and felt herself sink to the ground.

"Sarah? Sarah? Can you hear me?" Her father's voice called her from across a great divide. She slowly opened her eyes and found she was sitting upright on the stool, her father and Esra in front of her, just as they had been before.

"She's coming around," Avi said. "Nadav, can she have some more water?" He gripped her hand.

Sarah felt woozy but oddly invigorated. The music had faded, but something still pulsed through her. Nadav handed her the refilled glass.

"Here, sip this, slowly," Nadav instructed.

Sarah did as she was told, and the lightheadedness passed.

"You feeling better?" Her father touched her hair, smoothing the curls, then her cheek, then tapped her playfully on the nose.

"You saw it, did you not?" Esra asked.

Sarah straightened up and took another sip of water. "Saw what?"

"She saw it," Avi declared. "Don't worry, *Sheifale*, we know what it was."

"What *what* was?" Sarah was trying to be nonchalant, although she found the use of her father's old pet name for her a bit unnerving.

"The dancing, Sarah. You saw the dancing again." Esra's voice was gentle but firm.

"What was it?" Nadav asked. "The Bee Gees? ELO? Taylor Swift?"

"It was The Spiral Vogues, that old R&B group," Sarah said quietly.

"Ahhh..." the men said in unison.

"Called it," Avi said.

"Can someone please explain to me what is happening here?" Sarah felt her stomach clench again.

"Why don't we go to the shop? We can talk about it there." Avi took his daughter by the hand and led her to the exit. "Esra, Nadav, I thank you."

"Of course, *mon ami*," Nadav replied.

"Always," added Esra.

"Shall I wrap up the sandwich?" Nadav added, before Esra gently shushed him and picked it up to take a bite.

Sarah allowed her father to guide her back to the shop, although she knew the route by heart. The neighborhood around her looked a little bit dim, as if a phantom artist had wiped the damp paint from his canvas. But she was light on her feet, the city sidewalk gliding smoothly beneath her as she walked. She heard the tinkling of the bells that signaled their entrance into Greenberg's, and while the noise outside was muted, the clink of the metal bars on the door was sharp and in tune.

Avi gestured to Raya, and she turned the Open sign in the window to Closed and followed them to the back of the store. They sat in the purple, overstuffed chairs in the reading nook.

"It's happened," Avi said, and Raya nodded.

"So are you going to tell me anything? Or am I going to just sit here and quietly go mad?"

"You're not mad. In fact, for our family, it turns out you're quite normal."

"Define your terms."

Avi chuckled. "Yes, we are a motley bunch. But this will hopefully all begin to make sense to you." He leaned in. "You see, this isn't just a magic shop." He waved around. "It's a shop for Magyck."

"I'm not hearing the difference," Sarah sighed.

"It's in the spelling," Raya added.

"Obviously, this is a magic store, where magicians—or should I say, *illusionists*—of all kinds come to get their supplies and tricks. But it's also a place for other folks who are in possession of a certain type of...ability."

"Did you know about this?" Sarah asked Raya, who nodded and put her finger to her lips.

"All of this Magyck is very much of this world," Avi continued. "What most people call magic is simply pushing the boundaries of perception. Good illusionists divert an audience's attention and manipulate their expectations."

Sarah tilted her head in confusion.

"People see what they want to see," Raya said.

Avi pulled his chair closer to his daughter and clasped her hand. "But people like us, we are holders of Magyck. We can access it, use it, and it opens to us a whole other realm of being."

"It's pretty cool," Raya said.

Sarah let go of her father's hand and slumped in her chair, rubbing her fingers on the crushed velour upholstery. "So you're a...magician? Like a real magician? Is this a joke?"

"Magycians," Raya corrected.

"I'm still not hearing it."

"I assure you, it's very real," Avi said. "The Greenbergs have been Magycians for hundreds and hundreds of years, even back in the old country. Old Benjamin found the location for this place, and we've been here ever since. It's a very powerful spot."

"Powerful?"

"Indeed. All around us are vibrations, like currents of energy. In some locations there are more than others, where they come together in sort of a mesh pattern. This convergence of vibrations is what makes a location more powerful for those who know how to use it. Every person, Magyckal or not, has a vibration that is unique to them. Plants, animals, even the smallest of organisms do too. There are some of us who innately know how to tap into those or similar vibrations. They use this energy to do Magyck."

"Are you saying you use The Force?"

Avi looked confused.

"Star Wars," Raya prompted.

He laughed. "Something like that. And some of us are a bit more tuned into the energy than other Magycians, and that's why the vessel of the Twelve Moonstones is here and entrusted to us."

Sarah put her head in her hands. "And that is…?"

"I'll fill you in later. It's a bit much for now, I know."

"Caviar on Froot Loops is a bit much. This is, well, I don't know what it is." Sarah looked up. "How did I not know all this before?"

"That's where it gets tricky, if you'll pardon the pun," Avi said. "You never showed signs of Magyckal ability before. We knew it was possible. Every six generations or so, it skips someone."

"Me."

"You. But not just you. It skipped your cousin Rachel too. Your Aunt Ruth was very disappointed."

Sarah thought of Rachel, now a college professor at a small school nearby. They used to play together as children; they naturally gravitated toward each other, and Sarah thought it was their shared affinity for food and dislike of their curly hair. Now she knew there was more.

"But it's looking like it didn't actually skip you," Raya said.

"Sometimes it kicks in later in life, near middle age. We don't know why," Avi said.

"But I'm not middle-aged! I'm nowhere near middle-aged!"

"You're thirty-nine," Raya said.

"Exactly!" Sarah could feel the panic rising again, her arms tingling. "So yeah, this isn't happening. Not happening. I need to go." She started to get up from her chair.

"I'm afraid it is, my darling girl." Avi gently led his daughter back into her seat. "And we have some learning to do."

Sarah pointed at Raya. "Her too?"

"I am Magyck, yes. Runs in my family as well."

"So Esra and Nadav…"

"Yep."

"So I've gone my whole life thinking I'm an ordinary person, nothing special, and now you're telling me I'm freaking magic?"

"Magyck."

"Magyck."

"There you go," Raya said.

"I don't know what to do with this information," Sarah said, getting up and pacing the length of the reading nook.

Her father got up and gave her a hug. "It's a lot to take in, I know."

Sarah looked up at him. "Was Mom Magyck too?"

"No. But she knew. She helped keep our secret when it looked like you didn't have the ability," Avi said. "Sometimes non-Magycians…we call them the Unenchanted—"

"How flattering."

"—have trouble accepting our reality. Your mother was special."

"She did a good job. I feel *fabulous*." Sarah disengaged from her father's embrace and turned to Raya. "Is that why you work here?"

"One of the reasons. I like it here. But it also helps keep our families close."

"Are we related?"

"Not by blood," Avi said. "We are *cousins du coeur*, if you will. Cousins of the heart. They are the teachers, and we are the keepers of the stories, the guardians of the Twelve Moonstones."

"I see," Sarah said, although she really didn't. "So all this…" She gestured around the store.

"Is a real business. Yes," Avi nodded. "Just one facet, however. No one outside the Magyckal community knows any differently. And it's very important we keep it that way." He nodded again.

"That's why your family didn't tell you," Raya said. "We can't risk non-Magycians learning who we really are."

Sarah spotted a few people lining up outside the storefront.

"We should really reopen. Can't afford to lose customers. Even the Unenchanted." Raya went to open the door.

"Is that it?" Sarah asked.

"No. There is a lot you need to learn. In time. But first I need to show you something." Avi guided her to the back room of the shop.

"What, you have a griffin caged up somewhere?"

"Oh, of course not." Avi laughed. "They don't live indoors."

"Wait, what?"

"Come, let's get out of sight of the customers." Avi opened the door to the back room, and they entered the kitchenette.

"Pardon me, dear." Avi closed the door behind them and pointed toward a large, ornate wooden door on the far wall. "Let me show you the Crystal Room."

"There's a Crystal Room? I thought that area was for extra storage."

Avi ran his fingers over a stack of books on the wall next to the door. "Where is that door opener? I can never remember which one it is... Houdini...Blackstone...Penn...Teller...Copperfield...ah, here it is! Henning!" He pressed a leather-bound book, and the large, carved door began to open, its hinges creaking with weight and age. "I think I can disengage the security system now." He replaced the Henning book on the end of the row of books and pushed them together, and they stepped through the door.

Sarah felt numb, as if her world had just been turned on end but she didn't know how to hang on. Her father might as well have told her they were from another planet. Her brain kept trying to assemble a coherent picture, but like a castle made of dry sand, it kept falling apart. She heard the heavy door close behind her, and she waited for her eyes to adjust to the dim light. And there was an unfamiliar smell, like lemons and incense, mixed with something floral.

The room was medium-sized, filled with shelves on each wall, with a small stone fountain in the middle and several doors around the perimeter. Rather than being filled with scarves, cups, and top hats, these shelves were lined with large jars containing vague shapes. On the opposite wall were crystal balls of varying sizes, some clear, some with a smoky haze. Next to them were small wooden and metal chests of different colors and sizes. Sarah tried to get her bearings, and then something on the shelf sneezed.

"Gesundheit," she said instinctively.

"Thanks," said a purple and yellow plant in the jar third from the end. It then put down what Sarah assumed was its head and went to sleep.

Sarah froze. "Did that thing just sneeze?"

Avi looked at the row of jars. "Yes. Allergy season. No worries." He put his arm around Sarah's shoulders. "How're you doing?"

"I have no idea."

"It is a storeroom of sorts, as we keep various items on hand for our Magyckal brethren. And beyond this room," Avi said, pointing to two other doors, "are some meeting rooms and what we'll call an office of sorts. That's where we receive and process some of our more *unusual* stock."

Sarah turned and saw a third door, large, ornate, and metal, just ahead of her and to the left. The frame was edged with colorful stones, each one a different shape, texture, and hue. "What's that? Another bathroom?" She thought about the little one off the first backroom, where Debra was always leaving scented candles that were supposed to smell like the ocean.

"That is…a special room. It's where we keep the Twelve Moonstones, the source of energy for this space. Don't worry about that now." He gestured to the two doorframes on the other side of the room. "Or those." Avi turned Sarah to him and held her by the shoulders. "I know this is overwhelming, and there is a lot to learn. But you'll have help. Don't worry." He kissed her on the cheek. "Actually, I couldn't be prouder of you. I knew you were special."

Sarah was about to protest that he had never said anything of the kind to her before, when the "office" door on the opposite side of the room opened and a two-foot-tall blue creature wearing orange overalls entered, the overhead lights reflecting off the fine scales that covered his compact frame like a glass prism. He handed Avi a clipboard.

"Need your signature, Mr. Greenberg. New shipment."

"Thanks, Dave. Let me formally introduce you to my daughter. She'll be joining us from now on. Sarah, this is Dave."

The little blue man held out his hand. "Hey, how's it going? New haircut?"

Sarah touched her head. "How…"

"I've seen you around." He took the clipboard from Avi. "Talk to ya later."

Sarah watched him march back into the other room, his long, forked tail closing the door behind him.

"And that was…"

"Dave. Handles the special stock."

"Of course." Sarah's phone rang. She looked at the caller ID and hit the accept button.

"Colin? I'll have to call you back." She put the phone back in her pocket. "Dad? I'm going to need help reacting to something…"

FOUR

A fter Sarah's "magical metamorphosis," as she had decided to call it, she began to feel like everything in her life had been moved three inches to the left. She had been drinking a little more than usual, depleting her stock of good Merlot and starting on the three-dollar bottles. She changed her clothes when she remembered, which was usually after the food stains and cheese puff dust started to crack and sprinkle into her wine glass. On one particular day, her only goal was to deepen the dent in the couch cushion that had developed through a lack of hard work and a lot of television watching. She was having, as Raya might say, a rough go. She felt like a mere suggestion of her former self, one that followed her new self like a shadow on an overcast day. In the abstract she knew she *was* different—she was Magyck—but the idea hovered like a determined mosquito refusing to be swatted away.

She stared at a small water stain on the wall. When had that developed? Her cozy house, older than most on the block and filled with wood floors, trim, and charming built-in bookcases, was watertight. She had seen to that. It had cost her a pretty penny, but in the spring, when northern Illinois was deluged with heavy rains, her basement never flooded. She had used a company owned by a friend of her father's, and her basement remained bone-dry no matter the weather while the neighbors bailed like Noah's Ark had sprung a leak.

Oh yeah. Dad's friend. That makes sense now.

She mindlessly clicked through the channels, trying to find something to distract her. She had always been a bit of an oddball, even within her own family. Her parents and sister were brilliant at anything they tried, and with their myriad hobbies and activities they had no time for things like television. Sarah loved her books, but had a soft spot for the TV, which was comforting in its determined sameness. She was not brilliant at anything. Debra had a shelf of trophies. Sarah had participation ribbons with "You Tried!" printed on them and pinned to a corkboard.

She shifted her attention to the shelf above the red brick fireplace. Focusing on a small decorative vase, she wondered if she could move it. She wiggled her nose.

Well, that was a long shot.

Sarah remembered what her father had said about "vibrations." She closed her eye and tried to focus on any energy she might feel around her.

It's like Reiki massage for the mind.

To her astonishment, she found them. They were like little strings of varying length, each with its own color and vibrating at a different speed. She zeroed in on the one closest to her, lifted her hand, and knocked the vase onto the wood floor. She opened her eyes in surprise and stared at the shards scattered on the floor.

Holy shit.

She went to the kitchen and poured a glass of wine, downing it in one gulp. Pouring another one, she left the open bottle on the counter, went back to the living room, and stood over the broken vase, unsure of what to do. She wanted to call someone, but her family had been giving her a wide berth recently, assuming that she'd need time to figure things out.

They were right.

Days were passing as they always had. She quietly did her job, writing her columns, although she found everything at each restaurant she reviewed to be a bit flavorless and pale, each topic in food culture bland and trite. The lack of life luster was showing, especially in her most recent column:

...*the chicken appears to have been cooked by a chef who has lost the will to live, and treated herbs and spices as optional, or things to be feared. The wait staff was listless, all seemingly pulled from a 1950s existential French film...*

Her editor wisely chose to delete that passage from her review. She tried to write an article about "The Great Chicago Bagel Renaissance," but it felt like she was just examining round bread. She soldiered on, spending time with Colin and fielding texts from Madison that asked her what to do when a particular recipe went "zonkified," which initially mystified Sarah until she used context clues and decided it probably meant "went bonkers." But through it all, she just couldn't totally absorb what had become of her life, so the Magyck just hung around like a musty smell.

The questions had come at her fast and furiously.

Can I levitate?

Get brooms to clean my house like in Fantasia?

Am I Samantha on Bewitched?

Wasn't she a witch?

Is there a difference?

Do I have more wine?

Her father had listened patiently to her list of her concerns during one particularly fevered phone call, but he cut her off after about twenty minutes of first-class *kvetching*, insisting that it would all become clear when she began her "lessons." Clear and normal.

Not that she knew what that meant anymore. She moved a large shard of ceramic with her toe, willing herself to clean up the fallen vase.

At first she had been furious with her family. How dare they keep something like this from her? Had they been laughing at her, or did they feel sorry for her? How much did she miss out on? She could think of a few times in junior high when Magyck would have come in handy—like when she had to play goalie in PE. Or when she had a mishap with a flat iron and her curls went rogue and stood on end, and she had to spend the whole day wearing a headband that was so tight it made her look continuously surprised. Was there a Magyck mirror that could tell her when an outfit didn't look good from the back?

Mirror, mirror, looking glass,
What does this skirt do for my ass?

Eventually, the anger faded, though the melancholy remained, and things began to fall in place, at least a little. Memories began to reassert themselves. She remembered being outside when she was maybe eight or nine, sitting by herself and reading Julia Child's *Mastering the Art of French Cooking.* Even with her nose in a book, she noticed her father and Debra on the side lawn of the house they used to have, the one with the green shutters and overgrown lilac bushes in the backyard, playing one of their made-up games. Sarah knew that her father loved her, but Debra was his "special pal," and their inside jokes and sing-song rhymes made her feel very much "The Other." Once she had tried to join them but was waylaid by her mother.

"Let's not bother them, Sarah."

"But I want to play too!"

"Papa is teaching Deb to…throw a ball. That's really a two-person thing."

"What about baseball? There's nine on a team. I can throw!"

"Leave them be, Sarah. You have your own talents. Let's focus on those, okay?"

Her mother knew. Knew that Sarah was different, just like she was, and wanted something else for her. It must have been difficult for her mother too. She was an Unenchanted in a Magyckal world, one foot in and one foot out, joined to it by love but never a participant, carrying this spectacular secret that she had to keep from the everyday world, her career, and especially people like Karen from Accounting.

And from her daughter.

It was for her own good, her father told her. People couldn't handle knowing about the Magyck around them, and especially about the practitioners of the art.

"People are afraid of what they don't understand. And most won't understand this," Avi said sadly. "They would want us to solve problems that we can't solve. It would be chaos."

He was probably right.

And now, she was part of that world.

The vase still lay in pieces at her feet. She tried to remember where her broom and dustpan were, then wondered if she could knit the pieces together instead. She had done it with the glass at Colin's house, hadn't she? She looked at the pieces, and as she closed her eyes, noticing a nice, bright-green vibration string that she was sure was willing to be quite helpful, she heard a familiar voice just over her left shoulder.

"I would not try that just yet, if I were you."

She almost dropped the wine glass she had forgotten she was holding. Getting a firmer grip on it, and on herself, she spun around to see who had snuck into her house. No one was there.

"Getting warmer."

She turned her head to the right and allowed her gaze to rise slightly, when she saw Esra's disembodied head, greeting her with a smile.

She jumped as if shocked by electricity.

"How in the hell? Where's the rest of you?"

"The same place where all of me is, if you will pardon the awkward syntax. Nadav's pub," Esra replied, floating closer to her.

"How are you…oh, right. Magyck." She looked at her empty wine glass, then gazed longingly at the bottle sitting on her counter.

"I sensed that you were playing around, and I wanted to pop in and suggest that you do not do that. You want to wait until you have a bit of an idea of what you are doing."

"I have Magyck now."

"You do not *have* Magyck. You let it flow throw you," Esra said.

"Whatever. It's like giving someone the keys to a Porsche and telling them they have to keep it in the garage."

"A Porsche does not do a person any good if they do not know how to drive."

"Point taken," Sarah said. "So you can just appear wherever you want? Can others see you?"

Esra shook his head. "Just Magycians."

She laughed. "You're like The Great Gazoo."

"I do not get that reference," Esra said, floating over to the lamp, his eyes glimmering in the light.

"It's from *The Flintstones*. An old television cartoon. The Great

Gazoo was an alien from the future who would help Fred and Barney—"

"I am assuming these are the protagonists?"

"Yes. But no one else but kids and animals could see him," she finished. "Never mind."

"I am not able to stay long," Esra replied. "I just wanted to remind you not to try any Magyck until you have a little training. You do not want to blow up your house."

"That could happen?"

"Do you want to risk it?" Esra floated closer so that they were nearly nose to nose. "Sarahleh, you have a lot to deal with. Cook yourself a nice meal and get some rest." He looked her up and down. "Maybe take a shower or wash that sweatshirt? Come by the store tomorrow. It is time."

"For what?" Sarah asked, crossing her arms to hide the mustard stain on her sleeve.

"Your training."

"Will you be my teacher?"

"No, I am just an interested observer. But you will be in good hands."

Sarah put the wine glass on the coffee table and flopped on the couch.

"I don't think I can do this. Maybe I should just take a trip or something."

"Stay in the moment, my friend. All will be well. By the way, you have a hard candy stuck to your trousers." Esra winked one green eye, then the other, and promptly disappeared.

"So what am I supposed to do now?" she said, glancing down at the candy, then deciding to leave it.

She closed her eyes, this time envisioning her mother. Sarah was eight again, and they were at the kitchen table. Debra was working with clay, and Sarah wanted to try too.

"No, sweetheart, you don't have that talent. You don't want to be disappointed, do you? Come, help me make the carrots for dinner." Her mother guided her to a place by her side at the kitchen counter.

She opened her eyes to mere slits and examined her hands, turning them over and back as if they belonged to someone else. She pressed them to her face and exhaled deeply.

You can't. You don't have the gift. Try something else. Don't get hurt.

Her eyes popped open.

"Oh my God," she said, her hands still on her face. "How am I going to tell Colin?"

She picked up her glass, marched into the kitchen, and finished off the bottle of wine, inhaling half of a brioche roll at the same time. She put her head down on the counter, the marble cool against her cheek. She pulled the hard candy from her leggings and tossed it into the sink.

"This is not my finest moment."

She poured herself a glass of water and removed the broom and dustpan from the pantry. She returned to the living room, ready to do a manual clean-up.

The vase was mended and sitting back above the mantel.

CHAPTER
FIVE

Sarah had a rough night. She slept fitfully, alternating periods of wakefulness with strange, exotic dreams full of wizards and fairies and spells. The idea of wizards freaked her out, and her only experience with fairies was limited to a pair of wings she gave her niece, Miriam, on her third birthday, which lasted a couple of hours before being replaced by a stuffed unicorn given to her by Debra's sister in law, otherwise known as "the fun aunt." Regardless, Sarah knew it would be an unusual day, but she also knew she wasn't one hundred percent on board with the whole thing.

When she entered the store, it was empty, save for her father and Raya. It was a weekday afternoon, a slow time to be sure, but there were usually some random shoppers milling about. But today, nothing. It was quiet and weird, and the hairs on the back of her neck stood up, and she felt like a gazelle at a watering hole being eyed by a tiger. A sixty-five-year-old tiger with acid reflux and a wonky knee, but a tiger nonetheless.

"You came!" Raya embraced Sarah, practically knocking her back out onto the sidewalk. "I was sure you'd run away and join the circus or something."

"Clowns creep me out more than whatever the hell this is," Sarah replied, gesturing vaguely.

Her dad kissed her on the cheek. "I don't blame you. They're off-putting, to be sure." He guided her to the back of the store, to the same chairs in the reading nook where she had learned about her new identity just weeks before. "How'd you sleep? You want some food?"

Sarah decided her father had been downgraded from tiger to mildly myopic elephant. "No, I'm fine. Not much of an appetite right now. And I slept oddly."

"Do you mean upside-down?" Avi said with a grin.

"Yes, in a closet," Sarah retorted. "Did you have a pastry this morning? You're a little too amped."

"I am. We're going to teach you to be a Magycian. Most people start much younger than you, so you've got a bit of catching up to do."

"Think of it like Remedial Magyck," Raya said, sipping a coffee.

"Will there be puppets?" Sarah raised an eyebrow.

Avi handed her a stack of books. "Most of it will come naturally, we hope, once you know what you're looking for. Esra told me you did a little experimenting last night. We don't want any mishaps."

"I know. He didn't want my house to explode." Sarah laughed. "A bit melodramatic, right?"

Avi and Raya looked at her, stone-faced.

"Right?" Sarah shivered.

"Most of this is practical application," Raya said. "But you do need to study the whys and wherefores."

"There are laws," Avi clarified. "A way of using the Magyck. It's important to know."

"Will we be practicing every day?" Sarah asked.

"You and I won't," Avi said. "But you and Raya…"

"Raya's my teacher?"

"You were expecting Merlin, maybe?" Raya put her hands on her hips.

"No, no, I just thought…you know, a father-daughter thing."

"Too close," her father said. "Remember when I tried to teach you to drive a stick shift? It ended in tears. For both of us."

"So you didn't teach Deb?" Sarah asked.

Sarah remembered her younger sister as a girl, full of sass, knowing everything and stubborn as they come. No one could tell her what to do. At her bat mitzvah, her Haftorah portion took over an hour because when the rabbi called her to read it, Debra suddenly decided to become mute.

"No, we had to farm her out. She was…challenging," her father said with a chuckle. "I'll leave you two to it. Let me know if you need anything."

"We survived Lilith Fair," Raya said calmly. "We'll be fine."

"That wasn't me," Sarah whispered.

As Avi turned and walked back to the register, Raya and Sarah headed for the reading nook.

"You have no idea what to expect, do you?"

"I'm a little at a loss, yes."

"One step at a time."

"I do have one question."

"Just one?"

"No, but they're all kind of jockeying for position right now."

"Okay, shoot."

"Do I get a wand?" Sarah asked.

"It's not standard issue," Raya said, sitting in an overstuffed chair and crossing her legs. "Why, do you feel you need one?"

"I think I want one." Sarah sat in the chair across from Raya.

"It's not really necessary. They're just for show, actually."

"It would give me something to do with my hands."

"Awkward Magycian. Nice." Raya took Sarah by the hands and stood her up. "I guess it might be helpful at first. But really, you can use anything as a wand. Just something to help you to concentrate and direct the energy. After a while, you won't need it."

"How about spells? Do I need to learn spells?"

"Boy, you really don't know anything, do you?"

"I have a master's in political science. I know some things."

"There is no Magyck in politics. Trust me. You'll learn a few spells —they do exist—but it's largely a 'think it, do it' thing. Picture what you want to happen, connect to the vibration, make it happen."

Sarah put her hand to her chin and paced around, stopping behind her chair. "What's the difference between energy and vibrations? Sounds like we're getting into physics territory."

"Sort of," Raya said. "The vibrations are made by the strings you tap into to make something happen. Energy is what fuels the strings and gets them to vibrate. No energy, no vibrations."

Sarah leaned on the back of the chair. "Starting to sound like a Beach Boys song."

"Can we focus, *please*?"

"Is that the Magyck word?"

"Sarah."

"Sorry. I'm fighting the urge to flee. Joking is the only thing keeping me here right now." She folded her arms and sighed.

"I know how you get. But this isn't Debate Club, and you're not sixteen. You'll be fine." Raya tapped her chin. "Okay, let's start with something easy." She looked around the reading nook. "How about that plate?" She pointed to a decorative wall hanging. "I want you to remove the plate from the wall. That's it. Don't do anything with it, just take it off the brackets."

Sarah made a face and made her hands look like spell-casting claws. "Hummmmmm…" She dropped her hands. "Yeah, I have no idea what I'm doing."

Raya gave her a friendly side-hug. "Because I haven't told you how yet." She patted Sarah on the back. "All right. Now I want you to focus on the feeling of energy in the room. You know that sensation you get when you rub your hands together, then hold your palms close to each other? Same sort of thing, but in the whole space. Quiet your mind."

"That'll be a first."

Raya shushed her. "Quiet your mind, regulate your breath, and just feel it." She lightly smacked Sarah on the back of the head. "Why are you closing your eyes?"

"Am I not supposed to?"

"Generally, it's better to see what's going on around you. Now focus. Do you feel anything?"

Sarah quieted herself and concentrated on the space around her. She felt a slight prickling on her arms.

"Good," Raya said. "That little twitch in your arm muscles and slight flush on your cheeks—I can tell that you sense it. Do you feel a little light-headed?"

"Just a bit. Not bad."

"Take a deep breath if you need to. It will pass." Raya slowly circled around her friend. "I know this sounds weird, but relax your eyes. Don't let them totally go out of focus, just relax. Look around the spots where you feel the most energy. Do you see anything?"

Sarah did as she was told. She began to see little floating strings come into her field of vision. Some were gently floating, some were tense little filaments buzzing about. She suddenly felt like she had to pee.

"How are you feeling?" Raya asked. "You have to pee, don't you?"

"Little bit."

"Totally normal. First time I saw them, I couldn't stop sneezing. Startled the hell out of my mother," Raya said. "Now picture lifting the plate from the wall. Which string do you find appealing? Sort of calling out to you?"

Sarah let her mind wander through the haze of threads. There were so many, she wondered how people didn't get caught in them all the time. It occurred to her that when people "trip over nothing," maybe they were actually tripping over a large vibrating string. She was about to tell Raya about her hypothesis when a short orange string caught her eye.

"There's a nice one right there," she said, pointing down and to her right.

"Yes, I see it too," Raya answered. "Now gently tap into its vibrations with your mind."

"How do I…"

"Just reach out. You can do it."

Sarah reached out to the orange string. She immediately felt it respond, and she could feel a bridge forming.

"There you go," Raya said. "Now look at the plate and lift it from its brackets."

Sarah stared at the plate, which then flung itself from its brackets and smashed against the opposite wall.

"Oops."

"Let's try again," Raya said, scooping up the shards and knitting them back together.

Sarah attempted the maneuver again and again, each time sending the plate flying with less intensity and velocity. She was able to touch the needed string more and more quickly and obsessing less about the process, which amazed her because even with walking she often found herself thinking, *Left foot, right foot, left foot, right foot…*and soon she realized it was less a matter of power and more about control. She didn't need to throw everything at the plate to make it move; she backed off a bit and just let it happen.

After mastering the plate, they switched to lifting vases from the shelf, rotating chairs, flipping coins in the air, and choosing on which side it would land. In no time, the afternoon was gone. And Sarah was suddenly very tired. She slumped into one of the overstuffed chairs, and a glass of water materialized in front of her.

"Drink it," Raya instructed. "Takes a lot out of you, doesn't it?"

"I didn't work this hard on my master's thesis," Sarah responded, downing the water in one gulp. "Of course, that doesn't say much about my thesis."

"Well, that's poly sci," Raya said, shrugging. "But this is like exercise. The more you do it, the stronger you get."

"That must be why you have such great triceps."

"No, that's from kickboxing," Raya laughed.

Sarah felt something inside her shift, ever so slightly. She had never been particularly talented at anything. Her mother had encouraged her to stick to things in her comfort zone so she wouldn't get hurt. She was a decent cook but was encouraged to stick to writing. "The culinary world is so tough," her mother once said. She had let Debra shine as an all-around superstar, while Sarah stayed in the wings. But now, she could do something Debra could do, which made her feel a little closer to her family. She was one of them.

I can do Magyck. Real Magyck. Take that, Donna from HR.

It was empowering too. Unlike other people, just going about their everyday business, she felt special, relishing the idea that she now had control of her environment. The world wasn't static. She could affect change. Maybe she didn't have to bolt just to protect herself from hurt. It was heady stuff, to be sure, and it was rattling to her core.

I shall change the position of that lamp.

I can pick up a table without having to lift with my legs.

I can change the temperature in a room.

All fun things, but Sarah knew it all to be more than just a charmed feng shui, although she was beginning to suspect that this was how Debra got so much housework done in a day. As she practiced, still using a wand that Raya had grabbed from a nearby display, she began to feel there was something more, something deeper that made her feel more connected to her life. There was a sense of power, of awesome responsibility, and she knew acutely that the idea of evil in society needed to be counterbalanced with control and faith and love. Ideas started to form, settling in her mind like pieces of a jigsaw puzzle, mapping out the place of Magyck among a society that valued the concrete, the knowable, and the solvable.

After a few hours she went home, thanking Raya for the day's lesson and promising her father she wouldn't blow up the house. She changed her clothes and poured herself a glass of wine. She decided to go online and buy herself a new wand, even though Raya said she didn't need it. But she wanted one. She found one on Amazon that looked straight out of *Lord of the Rings*—elegantly shaped with elfin-like script carved into it. Cheesy, but she loved it. She knew it was not Magyckal and that she would use it only to channel the energy she tapped into, and after it arrived she would carry it like a talisman, a reminder of what she was becoming.

Besides, it made her feel badass. She clicked "Buy Now."

For the rest of the week, she practiced the lessons Raya gave her, which included "reaching out" to her teacher. She would imagine Raya, with as many details as she could, think about making contact, tap into the appropriate string...and Sarah could feel a little "tap-tap' in her field of vision, an acknowledgement from Raya that her presence had been felt. She didn't know how to use the wand while doing this, so she just stood in her living room, reaching out to Raya while maintaining dramatic poses.

After doing this for a while one Saturday morning, she held a more outrageous pose to encourage herself, as she was tired and wanted the challenge. She held her arms up, head back, and lifted one leg to the side.

"That's fun. Nice way to be greeted. Is that what we're doing now? I dig it."

Colin was standing in the entrance to her living room, picnic basket in hand. Sarah gave a start and dropped her pose as well as her wand.

"Oh…no, hi. I was just…yoga," she stammered.

"Interesting form. Tornado stance?"

"More like Upward-Facing Dork." She picked the wand up from the floor, casually hiding it behind her back. "Are we ready to go?"

"What's that?" Colin asked. "The thing you're trying to hide from me?"

"I'm not hiding anything from you! Everything is normal!"

Colin pointed to the end of the wand, which was sticking out from behind her back.

"Oh, this? You mean this? This thing here?" She held it up. "Um, it's a…"

She paused, trying to make up a clever excuse.

"Wand."

Damn it.

Colin laughed. "Ah. I have one in red. Goes with my flowy robes."

"Back scratcher. I mean it's a back scratcher. In the shape of a wand. I've been…itchy."

"Okay, itchy. I'm going to get some napkins. I forgot to pack them." Colin headed for the kitchen. "Madison uses a ton, I don't know why."

"Where is she today?"

"She went to the aquarium with her grandmother and a few friends."

"Nice. Fish."

Esra's head appeared in the living room.

"Be careful when you tell him. Not everyone reacts well."

"Shh!" She tried to wave him away like an errant bubble.

"He cannot hear me, you know." Esra dodged her hands.

"But he can hear *me*, and he's going to come back in here and wonder why I'm having a really intense conversation with a lampshade," she hissed.

"No worries. I slowed down time in the kitchen. We have a minute."

"Wait, we can do that?"

"I can."

"Really? How do you…okay, not important right now. I know I need to be careful with him. Maybe I just won't say anything."

"You need to eventually. If he is going to be a part of your life—and I hope he is, because he seems like a very nice chap—he needs to be aware of this aspect of your, let us say, talent."

"I lived in a family of Magycians for thirty-nine years, and no one bothered to tell *me*."

"That was different."

"How? I mean, I thought you said the Unenchanted can't know."

"Your parents did not tell you because of a very specific safety concern. I will leave that to your father to explain. But if a Magycian marries an Unenchanted, they have to be told. And we bind them to secrecy."

"I'll get to it. Really. Just not yet."

Esra floated over to the window, and Sarah could imagine him holding a glass of scotch.

"To reach your full potential in Magyck, one must have an open heart."

"I'm not sure I have full potential, but thanks for the vote of confidence." Sarah heard the clasp on Colin's picnic basket snap shut. "Can you go? I'm sorry, Esra, I don't mean to be rude, but I don't know if I'm ready to deal with this right now."

"All right. I just wanted to check in. I am learning a new tune to teach to my students. I will play it for you the next time you stop by the pub."

"Giving private lessons these days?" Sarah's eyes darted to the doorway.

"Old Town School of Folk Music. Master class." Esra raised his eyebrows. "I do have a life apart from you and the others, you know."

"Of course. Sorry. I look forward to hearing it."

Sarah watched Esra's head slowly dissipate, the emerald eyes the last to fade. It reminded her of the Cheshire Cat.

"We're all napkined up and ready to go." Colin appeared in the entrance and gave Sarah a sideways glance as he grabbed her bag from the coat rack and handed it to her. "You all right?"

"Fanfrickintastic."

"You'll feel better when you get some cheese and crackers in you."

"Always do."

"That's my girl."

Sarah smiled and gave him a quick hug. She appreciated his kindness, and his willingness to deal with her occasional oddities, which he never pointed out to her in criticism. He also wouldn't stand for her putting herself down, which she both admired and found a bit annoying. If self-deprecation was her superpower, Colin's tacit support was her kryptonite, and she found herself doing it less and less. But it wasn't entirely gone. After a lifetime it was the glue that held her together, and without it she wasn't sure she wouldn't crack.

"Shall we head off?" Colin said.

"Let's boogie."

The park, just a few blocks away from Sarah's house, was lovely and green and had plants and benches and birds chirping.

Sarah instantly hated it.

It really wasn't the park's fault. It was probably very well-designed and easygoing as far as parks went, but it was perfectly laid out for picnics and Sarah hated picnics. She wasn't fond of the outdoors in general, but Colin was, so she put up with the occasional dining *al fresco*. Secretly, she counted herself lucky—he could want to go camping but had fortunately never asked.

"You know what lives in the woods?" her mother asked her once. "Bears. You want to share your dinner with a bear?" Sarah did not, so she didn't inquire further. Although she was pretty sure her mother could take on a bear. With or without Magyck she was pretty formidable, and within minutes the bear would probably be weeping and realizing that, yes, he needed to call his mother more often.

After navigating through a seniors' tai chi class and a game of Ultimate Frisbee, Sarah and Colin found a spot on the park lawn, and

Colin spread out the blanket. Sarah stood there, staring at it, until Colin finally motioned for her to sit down. It took her about six tries to get comfortable. Her waistband cut into her side a little bit and she winced and wished she could buy into the whole "yoga pants outside" deal.

"Iced tea?" Colin offered.

Sarah accepted the bottle and took a sip. Looking around, she decided that the park was actually quite nice and not nearly as bug-infested as she had feared, although on the way in she did notice a swan with a notch in his beak and a look that said "I could bite your face off and then laugh."

Shivering a bit, she looked at Colin, who was rustling through the wicker basket. He was kind. He didn't care that she was socially awkward or hated sports, or that she'd always be just a little bit plump. He made her call when she got home at night just so he'd know that she was safe. He sent her pictures of cats. He was tall, considerate, handsome, and he made her feel more like herself than anyone she had ever known. She felt the urge to brush a lock of his brown hair from his forehead.

She had to tell him.

"Hey, want to hear something bonkers?" she said.

"Can it wait just a second? I want to show you something."

He removed a dollar bill from his wallet and handed it to her.

"You want me to go get you a soda?" Sarah asked.

"No," Colin laughed. "Look it over and make sure it's real."

"Dabbling in counterfeiting? Unbecoming for an accountant."

"I'm trying to do a trick here."

Sarah made a show of inspecting the bill, then handed it back to him.

"Okay, madam, you can verify that this is a bona fide dollar bill. What I'm going to do now is levitate it using magical energy."

What?

Sarah took a long gulp of tea. Colin was trying to do a magic trick. And a cheesy one at that.

We're going to have to break up now.

He held the bill between his thumbs and first two fingers and folded it in half. Then he unfolded it from the back to show the other side of the bill.

"Just your average dollar bill, nothing unusual…"

He folded the bill in half lengthwise with his index fingers, then folded it in half again.

"Do you like my watch? See how shiny it is?"

This is painful.

He pinched the ends of the bill with his thumb and forefingers.

"And now, the magical energy I have so recently been able to harness, I give you…the levitating dollar bill!"

He looked at her expectantly, a proud grin on his face.

"Ta da?" Sarah said.

"Darn right, ta da! Took me a week to get that right. You like it?"

"It was…fun."

"I know it's tacky and all. I mean, magic? Who would want to spend all their time with that? It's kind of dumb, but I thought you'd get a kick out of it."

Sarah reached into the basket and grabbed a banana, peeling it quickly and shoving half of it in her mouth. Her cheeks bulged as she tried to smile and chew.

"I actually saw a professional magician at a birthday party once when I was a kid," Colin continued. "He made live birds disappear and then reappear in a cage behind us. Scared the hell out of me."

"Magicians scare you? That's…great."

Sarah swallowed the lump of banana, then reached out to Raya for moral support. They couldn't speak yet, but texting would be too obvious. Sarah felt a little tap on the left side of her head, which let her know that Raya had heard her.

"Where's that mustard?" Colin was rooting around in the basket again.

Without thinking, Sarah envisioned a bottle of stone-ground mustard, picked up a small branch, and gently pointed to the basket, focusing her energy through her fingers.

"Here it is," he said. "I thought I had brought the Dijon. Oh well."

He unscrewed the top and spread a bit on a slice of rye, then opened the packages of deli meat and commenced making himself a sandwich, indicating that Sarah should do the same.

"Dig in," he said.

Sarah picked up the mustard. It was becoming second nature, small spells like that. She was a long way from the bigger ones, which required more finesse and skill. She wondered if there were spells that affected people. Could a spell change someone's feelings or actions? If she could get Colin to say "I love you," maybe it wouldn't matter how she told him about the Magyck.

"That is some dangerous territory you are considering." Esra's head appeared just behind her right shoulder. She gave a start, then tried to act casual and ignored him. "Messing with the human mind—that is some dark stuff, Sarahleh."

She waved him off, and when Colin noticed, acted like she was waving away a bug. Then she popped a few grapes in her mouth.

"I'm going to fill up my water bottle over at the fountain, okay? Do you want any?" Colin got up from the blanket and put his wallet back in his pocket. When Sarah shook her head, he pointed to the food. "Don't wait for me. Enjoy. I'll be back in a flash."

Sarah watched him walk away, and when he was out of earshot, she turned to Esra. "I'm not going to do anything to his brain. I was just wondering. And how did you know? Can you read minds?"

"I saw the way you were looking at him. It was an educated guess." Esra floated into her field of vision. Instinctively, Sarah pulled the wand from her bag, and looking around to make sure no one was watching, tapped the vibrations and pictured the foodstuffs exiting the basket and arranging themselves on the plates.

"Mmm. Gouda. Nicely done." Esra eyed the food coming out of the wicker container. "However, you might want to be very careful about demonstrating your new talent in such a public spot." Esra's voice was soft, but clear and firm.

"No one is watching."

"Someone is always watching. Never forget that."

"You're right. Sorry."

"In the meantime, maybe you should figure out what you are going to say to that nice man."

"I'll figure it out!" With the momentary increase in emotion, Sarah let the energy control slip, and the strings darted away from her. The bag of bread flew and expelled its contents, while the bags of cold cuts expanded and popped, sending turkey and roast chicken into flight. Sarah dropped her wand and tried to catch the airborne food all at once. Colin came jogging back to the blanket, his eyebrows raised in alarm.

"What the hell happened?" he said.

Sarah stared at the bread and meat, now scattered across the blanket and partly on the side of the tree.

"I sneezed?" she said, peeling a leaf off of a slice of turkey. "Then I lost my balance and…"

"Wow. Well, I think some of this is salvageable. You all right?"

"I'm fine, you know, pollen." She gathered up the pieces of rye and a few pieces of sourdough that weren't covered in grass clippings. Colin picked up the rest, dumping some in the trash and declaring the rest edible.

"I think it is time. Tell him now…" Esra's voice was a bit louder.

"NOT NOW!" she hissed.

"What?" Colin asked.

"HOT DOG!" she improvised. "Wish we could, um, grill out."

"Next time, maybe. Although I'm a little worried about leaving you alone with fire. Here, let me make you a sandwich."

"Sarah…" Esra said.

"Please!" she hissed again.

"Come again?" Colin asked.

"CHEESE!"

"You got it. Cheddar or…"

"SWISS!"

"You can stop yelling about the food," Esra whispered in her ear.

When Colin's attention was on assembling her lunch, Sarah turned her head and gave Esra a pleading look. He shrugged his invisible shoulders and faded from her view. She let out a long, heavy sigh. Colin handed her a sandwich, generously filled, on a flowered paper plate.

She bit into it and nodded approvingly. It wasn't what she was used to, but the man did have a way with mayonnaise.

"Thanks for doing this," Colin said. "I know eating outside isn't your favorite locale."

Sarah smiled, releasing a touch of tension from her forehead. "I like being with you. The location is negotiable."

"Good. So next time we'll go camping."

Sarah threw a wedge of lemon at him.

"Kidding! I like being with you too."

Colin looked at her so earnestly, Sarah thought her heart might break. Would he still like her if he knew what she had become? Was Magyck a non-negotiable? Would she freak him out like the party magician with the birds? She had tentatively accepted her new reality but didn't want to consider one that didn't include Colin.

"You know, I've recently discovered something about myself...." Sarah thought that was as good a way as any to begin.

"Look, I think I know what you're going to say. You're worried I'm not like you. That the differences are too great. But it doesn't matter to me, and we can make it work."

How does he know?

"What? I, uh, what?" The lump of chewed bread got stuck in her throat.

"You know. Because I'm not Jewish."

Sarah dropped her sandwich. "Oh! Okay! Yeah, that's fine! Phew!"

"What did you think I was going to say?"

Sarah imagined the look of fear on Colin's face, of bewilderment, of betrayal. She saw him running away, leaving an empty space in her life. She saw this played over and over in her mind for what seemed like hours but was probably no more than a few seconds. The intensity took her breath away.

It was too much. Then she heard it.

Once upon a universe,
It's how our story goes...

"Wine gives me headaches!" she blurted. "So I won't be drinking wine anymore!"

"All right." Colin handed her another plate. "More cheese?"

He scooted over to her and placed his arm around her shoulders. "Speaking of cheese..." He shook his head. "Never mind. I just want you to know that...I love you."

Time slowed, and Sarah knew it wasn't of Esra's doing. She looked deep into Colin's gentle, kind eyes and felt a connection she had never had with anyone before. She wanted to wrap her arms around him and tell him she loved him too. Something was holding her back.

Like one of Esra's musical rubber bands.

Noting the irony, she stroked his arm and smiled. Saying the words would make them real, and right now, reality wasn't on the docket.

"I...am so happy to hear that," she said.

She saw the glint in Colin's eyes dim, but just for a moment. He pulled her in close.

"It's okay if you're not there yet. I'll wait."

She kissed him, gently at first, hoping her lips would say what she couldn't express out loud.

"Wow," Colin said after they had separated. "PDA. That's new for you." He clicked his tongue. "That is good Swiss cheese."

Sarah allowed herself to feel happy, an ever-so-slight emotional butterfly fluttering in her solar plexus. Since she had become aware of her powers, she had felt a new connectedness to the world around her, and her usual slog had changed to a tentative glide. Now, things had a bit more color and shapes were sharper, even though her glasses prescription hadn't changed. She had learned to manage some of her anxiety by tapping into the appropriate vibration and found that it eased. She could even make herself giggle by creating a little poof of glitter out of her elbow—when she was alone, of course. It wasn't elegant, but it was fun.

And it would have to stay a solitary activity. At least for now.

Colin spent that night at her place since his daughter was with her grandparents. With the lights dimmed, Sarah could sneak in a bit of Magyck without Colin noticing—connecting with a vibrating red string, for example, she could make the light warmer or give it slight blue tinge. His eyes drooped, and his arms relaxed around her.

"This is the most relaxed I've ever been. Did you change the light bulbs or something?" he said.

Sarah was undeniably pleased with that reaction. And she found the strings helped in other areas too.

They stayed in bed a little too long, ignoring the alarm several times. Consequently, the morning was a bit rushed, and Sarah remembered at the last minute that she had an article due that afternoon. A quick breakfast, a bit more kissing over coffee, and their separate days began.

"You're still coming to my father's house for dinner tonight, yes?" Sarah asked.

"Is this Shabbat dinner?"

"No, that's Friday evening. We don't always get together for that. This is just a regular family dinner. They happen occasionally."

"I'll be there." Colin gave her a final kiss, wiped a droplet of coffee from her lower lip, and departed. Sarah had a little more time to linger in her robe before throwing on some sweats, sitting down with her laptop, and putting together her article. Her notes were hard to read, but she could pull enough information from them, and the meal she was reviewing was memorable as well, although not in a good way. Sarah wished she could use the words "congealed floor paste" without sounding unprofessional, so she just went with "under-seasoned."

After hitting send on the email to her editor, she changed her clothes and headed over to the store. She was due for another lesson and was curious to see what Raya had planned for her. Her father usually closed the place on Saturdays, but occasionally, he'd have appointment hours for some professional magicians (as well as Magycians, she assumed) who came to Greenberg's not only for supplies but also to talk shop with her dad. Parking her car, and making a mental note of where it was, she slipped on her light grey hoodie. The morning air had a bit of a chill, although it was likely to become seasonably warm in an hour or two.

Opening the door with its customary chime, she saw that the place was empty, save for one woman. She was tall and of indeterminate age, with long, white-blonde hair swept back in a severe chignon. Her ankle-length blue velvet cloak was cinched tightly at her narrow waist with a gold belt, and she wore tailored white pants over impossibly high stiletto heels. Her grey eyes scanned the store like she was casing the joint. Sarah locked eyes with her, but the woman turned away as if she had just looked at an old piece of fish. Sarah saw the door to the back room crack open.

"Psst! Sarah! Over here!" She spotted Dave waving at her. The guest either didn't notice him or didn't care, and Sarah slipped by her quietly and very quickly.

"Come in here," Dave whispered. "Your father's busy."

Raya stuck her head out, standing above Dave's diminutive form, and after Sarah squeezed through the door, he quickly shut it behind her.

"You see her?" Dave asked.

"Hard to miss," Sarah responded. "Who is she?"

"We don't know," Raya said. "Never seen her before."

"Terrifying, isn't she? Gave me the chills from over here," Dave added. "Want a bagel?"

"Always," Sarah said, accepting the toasted bread Dave offered. "Cream cheese?"

"There's butter."

Sarah scrunched her nose.

"Sorry, I'm not Jewish," Dave said with a shrug, then popped a whole sesame seed bagel in his mouth. He licked his lips with a long, forked, purple tongue that reached practically to his eyeballs.

Her father entered from the back chamber, as Sarah had taken to calling the extra, mysterious rooms, and walked past them without acknowledging their presence. He pushed open the back room door and made a beeline for their unfamiliar guest.

"I have to know what's going on out there," Sarah said, swallowing a chunk of half-chewed bagel.

"Be careful," Raya said. "She might try to steal your Dalmatians and make them into a coat."

Sarah opened the door a crack and peeked out. Her father was behind the counter, as if using it as a barrier between himself and this strange woman. Raya handed her a small, cone-shaped piece of grey stone.

"It will help you hear," she said.

The woman placed her hands on the glass case next to the register and leaned in slightly.

"Dahling, I won't let you renege on a deal," she said, her voice lyrical yet cold.

"It wasn't my deal," Avi said.

"It was a family deal," the woman retorted. "And it is your duty to uphold it. Can you make me a martini? Never mind, you won't do it right." She waved her hand, and a martini with two onions materialized in her hand.

"I'm not giving you the store."

"Your eldest child is not Magyck. She cannot inherit. Subsequent children are inconsequential. If you don't have a direct heir by age sixty-five, which you are, the property reverts to my family, namely me, as the last surviving Bex."

The woman slammed a yellowed parchment on the counter, then centered herself and smoothed her hair. Avi pushed the parchment back to her. Sarah craned her neck to get a better view and switched the hearing cone to her other ear.

"I will not honor it. It is old and outdated." Avi said.

"And perfectly valid according to our laws." She tapped it with a long, manicured nail. "There is the signature of my great-great-grandmother." She moved her finger across the document. "And it is signed right there by your ancestor, Benjamin Greenberg. And that is his drop of blood. Do you deny *this*?"

"I do not. But it is not valid. My daughter *is* Magyck."

"Pfft. Her? The chubby brunette?" She pulled out a long cigarette holder from her sleeve, which featured a pink cigarette that she lit with a flick of her finger. "No, she isn't. You filed her as Unenchanted years ago." She took a long drag, delicately blowing the smoke into the shape of a dragon. "My family has been waiting a long time for this place."

"And you'll keep waiting, Zondra. It is true. She is a *ronichlent*."

Zondra laughed. "A late bloomer? Please."

"It is true." Avi pulled himself up to his full height, and to Sarah he suddenly looked quite formidable. But the woman was not deterred.

"Even if that is so, she will not be powerful enough to handle this place by the time spelled out in the contract."

"I'm not going anywhere anytime soon."

"Doesn't matter. This property and its contents—all of them—will be mine."

"Please leave now," Avi said. "There is nothing for you here."

"I will be back, Avi," Zondra said. "This is not over."

She turned on her heel and then glanced over her shoulder. "I'm sure that somehow we can come to an amicable arrangement. Like we should have done years ago, before you married that...woman." She shot a quick glance to the back room. Sarah ducked under her sightlines.

"Holy shit," she said under her breath.

Zondra swept out the front door, and Sarah felt the temperature in the place rise at least ten degrees.

She handed the hearing cone back to Raya. "I'm not exactly sure what's happening, but it sounds like some serious stuff is going down."

"You can say 'shit,'" Raya said.

"I already did."

After making sure the coast was well and truly clear, they descended upon Avi, who was leaning on the glass case. He let out a slow breath and straightened his shoulders.

"How much of that did you hear?" he asked.

"All of it," Sarah said.

"Who was that?" Raya asked.

"She wasn't Magyck Council, was she? I usually see the paperwork first," Dave said.

Avi gave another sigh. "That was Zondra Bex," he said, as if that answered their questions.

Sarah leaned over to Raya. "Sounds like a diabetes medication."

"That was her?" Dave sounded incredulous. "Seriously?"

"You know her?" Raya asked.

"You don't?" Dave said. "Well, I've never actually met her, but I've heard of her. I wasn't entirely sure she was real."

"Oh, she is," Avi said.

"She wants the store? Why? She can't have it. She's not family," Sarah said.

"And she won't get it," Avi assured her. "A Greenberg was entrusted with this place, and it will remain with us."

"But she said…"

"Don't get all *fermished*, sweetheart, I will take care of it."

"I'm not upset, I just…"

"Do as I say, please. Go practice your lesson with Raya, and don't give it another thought. I'll talk to you later at dinner."

Avi's smile was friendly, but the knot in his brow and the sadness in his eyes told Sarah otherwise. She was about to protest when she felt a tug on the hem of her hoodie.

"Let's go, kiddo. Your dad has it all under control." Dave took her by the hand, his small, blue fingers encircling hers. "Let's get you some more practice. And perhaps another bagel. I've grown quite fond."

"One of these days I will introduce you to pickled herring."

"Oh, is he a friend of yours?" Dave opened the door to the back room with his tail.

"Who?"

"Mr. Herring."

Sarah turned back to see Raya talking to her father and then conjuring a small figure in see-through armor, the image hovering over her palm. Her father shook his head and waved the image away. Sarah felt a fluttering in her mind, but quickly pushed it aside.

After a few minutes of watching Dave inhale bagels, Raya joined them in the back.

"All right! Who's ready to work? Dave, do you need a napkin?"

Raya's voice was light, but that nagging feeling in Sarah's brain returned. Things were changing, she felt it deep down. And she wasn't sure she liked where it was headed.

CHAPTER
SIX

"**S**top! Put that down! Put! That! Down!"

Debra was chasing after her nine-year-old son, Aaron, who was racing from the kitchen through his grandfather's living room ringing a crystal bell. Suddenly, the bell loosened itself from Aaron's grasp and flew in an elegant arc into his mother's outstretched hand.

"Told ya," Miriam said with a bit of glee, but frowned after her comment was met by her brother's outstretched tongue and crossed eyes. "You keep doing that, your face is going to freeze that way."

Aaron stuck out his tongue again at his younger sister and found, almost immediately, that it was indeed stuck and he could not retract it into his mouth.

"Mob! Sheesh doingk it magan!" Aaron blepped.

"Miriam, I have told you to stop playing with your brother's tongue." Debra placed her hands on her hips and gave Miriam a stern look, one that still held sway with her seven-year-old sensibility.

"Fiiiine…" Miriam waved at Aaron, and he was able to put his tongue back where it belonged.

Sarah sat on the couch, out of the line of fire, and tucked her legs under her, holding on to her glass of chardonnay like it might fly away.

Here, it actually might.

"I like how you have to be very specific as to the body part," Sarah said.

"You have no idea," Debra said, sitting next to her sister. "One time she gave Aaron horns."

"Where's Mike?"

"His mother fell and twisted her ankle. He drove to Rockford to help her out."

"How convenient."

The kids went into the den to play a board game, and Debra poured herself some wine.

"I'm so glad we can have everything out in the open now. It was hard not using Magyck around you," she said, brushing her bangs from her eyes. Her pixie cut was perfectly tousled, the dark brown hair highlighting her olive green, almond-shaped eyes.

Sarah opened her mouth to protest but gave it a second thought. "Yes, I suppose it would be."

"I know it was for your own safety, but I still hated keeping it from you. But you know what? I envied you in some ways." Debra picked up a picture of them when they were teenagers, one that their father kept on the end table.

Sarah choked on her wine. "Me?"

"You got to be 'normal.' You went to regular schools."

"Meh. You didn't miss much. Normality is overrated," Sarah sniffed, then grinned. "Funny thing is, even in the normal world, I never felt all that normal."

Debra put her arm around her sister's shoulder. "I'm glad Magyck came to you. How's it going?"

Before Sarah could answer, Debra snapped her head in the direction of the den. A rubber mallet came flying out, and she caught it in her right hand.

"Knock it off!" Her hand went up, and she aimed her palm toward the room where the kids were playing.

"Aww…" they said in unison.

"What just happened?" Sarah asked.

"I blocked their access to the strings in that room. If they want to do Magyck, they'll have to do it where I can see them."

"Parental controls. Nice." Sarah smiled warmly at Debra. "So this is how you do it all. Magyck."

"I honestly don't know how other mothers manage. They're freaking heroes." Debra went silent and cocked her head. "I hope Dad's all right in there," she said, nodding toward the kitchen. "Dad? Everything okay?"

"I'm fine," Avi yelled from the kitchen. "It's a brisket, not a nuclear reactor."

"I thought you were cooking tonight," Sarah said.

"Dad wanted to. He found Mom's recipe and wanted to give it a go. We can always order takeout," she whispered.

"I heard that!" Avi said.

"I think he turns up the volume on his hearing," she whispered again.

"Heard that too!"

"So *that's* how he always knew what we were up to," Sarah said.

"Listen, your mother and I had two teenaged girls in the house." Avi entered the living room with a bowl of mixed nuts. "It was the best way to keep you out of trouble. Or at least come up with a response plan." He pointed to the nuts. "I took out the hazelnuts. You said Colin doesn't care for them."

"That's very thoughtful. Thank you."

"Speaking of Colin, where is he?" Debra asked, looking at her watch.

"He texted me. He's on his way," Sarah said. "Look, you two know I haven't told him about my recent change of life."

"It's Magyck, Sarah, not menopause," Debra said.

"Regardless, he doesn't know, and until I'm secure with it, I'd like to keep it that way. So no Magyck this evening, all right?"

"So no…" Avi flicked his fingers and turned the room a pale shade of blue.

"No."

"And no…" Debra made tiny sequins rain from the ceiling.

"No."

Debra waved and made the sequins disappear, and her father returned the room to its original hue.

"You really don't think Colin can handle it?" Avi said. "Mike was fine when Deb told him."

Sarah looked at her sister levelly. "Mike was probably stoned when you told him. Sorry, Dad."

"This is not news," Avi replied.

"This all would have been easier if you had left Frick and Frack with him," Sarah said, pointing her thumb toward the kids' play area.

"They'll be fine. They wanted to go see their grandma, but we thought they might be too much for her."

"Lucky us," Sarah said.

"Hey now, you love them."

"I do. But *please* keep them in line tonight?"

"I'll go talk to them right now." Debra rose from the couch and refilled her glass.

"That's not where they are," Sarah shouted as Debra walked into the kitchen.

"I'm gathering bribes."

"Oh, good idea." Sarah turned to her father. "Can you help here?"

"Ah, no. I have found it best not to meddle in other people's parenting. Especially your sister's."

The doorbell rang, a chime reminiscent of The Byrds' "Mr. Tambourine Man." Sarah looked at her watch. It was too early to be Colin, as he wasn't due for another twenty minutes and he was always perfectly prompt.

"Did we give up on the brisket and order pizza?" Sarah asked.

"No, I invited some guests," Avi said as he walked to the door. He opened it and greeted his guests with outstretched arms and a wide smile. "My friends! Come in! Come in!"

Raya, Esra, and Nadav stood on the other side of the doorframe. Raya looked slightly sheepish, and Esra held what Sarah believed to be the largest fruitcake she had ever seen. They each touched a finger to the mezuzah in the doorway as they entered, and Esra handed off the cake to his brother. He embraced Avi warmly, kissing him on both cheeks.

"Thank you for inviting us, Avi. It is a good occasion to come together. And a reason to celebrate too!" Esra nodded at Sarah.

Nadav struggled slightly under the weight of the fruitcake.

"Um, *mon frère*, can you…"

"Oh yes, of course," Esra said, taking back the fruitcake. "This is for you. The most festive of all desserts."

Nadav shrugged. "I thought we should bring a nice babka, but Esra was insistent."

"It will be wonderful, I'm sure. Where is your lovely wife?"

"Nina couldn't make it, I'm afraid. She is setting up for a show at her gallery. It's a very busy time. She sends her love." Nadav held up his palm, and an image of a woman with dark, bobbed hair and sparkling eyes appeared. She blew Avi a kiss, then disappeared.

"She will be missed," Avi said. "Please, everyone, have a seat. Sarah, can you give me a hand?" He took the cake from Esra. "We'll put this in the kitchen for safe keeping."

Sarah left the couch, and after giving her friends a quick hug and kiss, helped her father carry the cake into the kitchen, where it hit the counter with a thud. It momentarily glowed with a pearlescent sheen.

"Using Magyck to carry it would have been rude," Avi whispered. "And I don't have a wheelbarrow handy." He winked.

They returned to the living room with a plate of cheese and crackers. Raya, perched on the bench under the bay window, passed on the snack but her uncle and father gladly partook, Nadav offering the fact that his wife rarely let him eat cheese.

Avi and Esra took out their pipes, filled them, and lit them without matches. The smell was light and sweet, like cherries, but with a woody note that Sarah found quite pleasant.

"I don't know that Deb would want you two smoking around the children," Sarah said.

"It is of no harm to them, and of great benefit to us," Esra said, inhaling deeply. As he exhaled, the smoke swirled in the air like two koi swimming in a small pond.

"Nadav? You're not a pipe smoker?"

"It's not Papa's thing," Raya said, gesturing toward Nadav, who was waving his hand over a crystal glass, filling it with an amber liquid. "He's fine."

Nadav put two more cubes of cheese in his mouth and gave Sarah a thumbs-up.

"Uncle Esra! Uncle Nadav!" Aaron and Miriam came flying out of the bedroom, making a beeline for their favored guests. The men gave them big hugs, and then Aaron sat at Nadav's feet while Miriam snuggled in her grandfather's lap. Avi and Esra began to entertain the children, each blowing smoke rings that started off circular before morphing into animals. Avi's was a rabbit, which hopped around Miriam's head, and Esra's smoke ring took the form of a parrot, swooping and circling around the coffee table. Aaron tried to maintain his cool, but soon his nine-year-old self could contain his delight no longer, and he started laughing so hard he accidentally banged his forehead on his knee.

"Uncle Esra," Aaron said, rubbing his head, "can you do a peacock?"

Esra obliged, giving the bird a tinge of color in its fanned tail feathers.

"Make a dog, Zayde!" Miriam clasped her hands and gave her grandfather a pleading look, with her eyes wide and hopeful.

"What do we say, Miriam?" Debra asked as she leaned against the dining room doorframe.

"Pleeeeeeease?"

Avi inhaled again and released the smoke in the perfect form of a basset hound, which loped about in the air above their heads.

"I think I can top that," Esra said, blowing the sweet, silver smoke into the form of a phoenix, which rose from its nest and glided around the room, its red-and-orange-tinted feathers glimmering like stars. Both children cheered.

Sarah was mightily impressed as well.

Above the din, she heard the doorbell ring. She turned with a start, realizing it must be Colin.

"Shh! Shh! Stop! It's Colin! Dad, can you…" She made an erasing gesture toward the smoke animals. Avi waved his hand, and the figures disappeared into a puff of shiny streaks.

"Aww!" Aaron said. "Why did you have to do that?"

Debra sat on the arm of the couch and touched her son lightly on the shoulder. "We talked about this. Colin isn't Magyck, and Aunt Sarah doesn't want him to know about it right now."

"Well, that's just *sad*," Miriam said with a tiny pout. "Magyck is awesome."

"It is awesome," Sarah said, walking to the front door. "I'm just not ready for him to see it, especially since I'm pretty new to it myself."

"Oh yeah, I forgot. Okay." Miriam nodded and folded her arms, as if giving her tacit approval to the plan.

"Remember, no Magyck at all while Mr. Colin is here, okay? Not even a little bit," Debra said, pointing a finger at Miriam, then at Aaron.

The children nodded, and Aaron got up from his seat on the floor.

"Then I better go put Albert back in his box," he said, taking a small dragon from his shirt pocket and cupping him lightly in his hands. It was teal green and no more than six inches from nose to tail. "C'mon, Al. Bedtime."

Sarah gave a wide-eyed look to her sister, who merely shrugged and watched her son walk away.

"They're very clean animals," Debra said.

"Kind of not the point, Deb. Are there any other surprises I need to be aware of?"

Raya, still on the window-box seat, peered in her backpack. "Nope, we're good."

Sarah smoothed the front of her shirt and took a deep breath. "Okay, everyone. Be on your best behavior, please. I'd rather not have a Colin-shaped hole in that wall from him freaking out. Promise?"

Everyone held up his or her right hand.

"Promise," they said in unison, although Miriam was a beat behind.

"Showtime," Sarah said under her breath.

Albert flew through the living room and landed on Sarah's shoulder. She gave a start, then turned around and pointed at the dragon.

"What did I just say?"

"Sorry," Aaron said. "He got out." He scooped the mini-dragon from his aunt's shoulder.

"Make sure he stays in, please."

Sarah never could have imagined just three months ago that a dragon landing on her shoulder wouldn't rattle her. Yet here she was. Colin, however, was another story. He might not adjust so easily.

I can't lose this one.

"Sarah? You going to open the door?" Raya said gently.

"Oh yeah. Right." She opened the door with a wide smile plastered on her face.

Everything is fine.

She was greeted by Colin's equally wide but slightly more sincere smile. He had a bouquet of flowers in one hand and a bottle of Glen Livet in the other.

"Hi," he said, kissing her on the cheek and handing her the flowers. "Did you know there's a huge chunk of fruitcake on your front porch?"

"There was *more?*" Debra whispered to her father.

"Was it glowing?" Sarah asked and then slapped her hand over her mouth.

"What?"

She slowly put her hand down. "Or…is that Rudolph I'm thinking of? The nose? Ha, ha. Christmas stuff. Comes earlier and earlier, am I right?" She kissed him full on the mouth. "WOULD YOU LIKE SOME WINE?"

"In a minute. Let me give this to your father."

"Oh, of course. Let me take your coat."

Please be normal, please be normal…

Esra, Debra, Nadav, Avi, and Miriam greeted Colin as he entered the living room. Raya, who was for some reason holding Aaron upside-down by his ankles, gave him a perfunctory nod.

Sarah chose not to engage.

"Colin, this is my family. Our friends Esra and Nadav, my sister Debra, her children Miriam…"

"I'm seven!" Miriam exclaimed.

"…and, um, Aaron."

Aaron waved from his upside-down position.

"And you know Raya…"

Raya raised Aaron up and down in greeting.

"…and my father, of course."

"Hello, Mr. Greenberg. Nice to see you again." Colin extended his hand.

"Avi, please." Avi shook his hand firmly.

Aaron waved excitedly.

"Are you a bat?" Colin asked.

"I was just showing him a combat move," Raya said. "Let's just say he zigged when he should have zagged."

"I zigged!" Aaron added for reinforcement.

"I think you can put him down now," Sarah said.

"Aww..." Aaron responded.

Raya carefully placed Aaron back on his feet. "Watch your back, friend-o." She poked him lightly on the forehead.

"Oh, I'm sorry, I completely forgot. This is for you, Avi," Colin said, handing the bottle to his host.

Nadav intercepted. "This is a good label. *C'est bon.*"

"Nadav owns a pub. I have lunch there a lot," Sarah said.

"And I play music there on occasion," Esra added. "When the mood suits me."

"Are you a musician?" Colin asked.

"Of sorts."

"What do you play?"

"Well, it's a special instrument..."

Sarah shot him a look.

"Banjo. I play banjo," Esra said. "And I teach."

"Why don't we all have a seat and get comfortable?" Sarah interjected, not sure how she would have explained the body-length magic rubber bands Esra used as an instrument.

"We're having bisket for dinner," Miriam said shyly.

"Brisket," Debra corrected, touching Miriam lightly on her head. "Speaking of which, how's that coming along, Dad?"

Avi closed his eyes and cocked his head. "Five minutes," he said, nodding and opening his eyes. "Then it has to rest."

"Don't we all?" Colin said, while the others laughed politely.

Something whizzed past Sarah's head. She followed its path with her eyes and saw Albert perched on the edge of the lampshade. She felt a lump in her throat. She signaled to Nadav, and as Colin turned to Sarah, he wedged himself in between them.

"So you're a banker?" Nadav asked as Aaron dashed across the room and grabbed Albert. Debra waved her hand, turning the mini dragon into a chinchilla.

"Accountant," Colin said. "Mostly tax work." He noticed Debra's gesticulation out of the corner of his eye. "Hey, what's that?"

"That's Albert. My drag—"

Sarah shot her nephew a look.

"—chilla. Dragchilla. That's a fancy chinchilla," Aaron finished, looking quite pleased with his save.

"Well, hey there, buddy," Colin said, leaning over and giving Albert a little rub on the head.

"I need to put him to sleep," Aaron said.

Colin's eyes widened.

"He means to bed," Debra quickly added. "Honey, take Albert back to his cage, okay?"

"Okay. Sorry 'bout that." As Aaron walked away, the chinchilla burped a tiny purple flame. Aaron quickened his pace as Sarah poured Colin some wine.

"How's Madison?" she asked.

"Great, thanks. She talks about you all the time, you know. I thought about bringing her, but she's got a slumber party."

"Maybe next time," Sarah said, giving a silent sigh of relief.

"Your lunch? Wasn't that the time when something suddenly came up?" Raya asked.

"What does that mean?" Colin said.

"Raya's being funny."

"She's not wrong," Avi said. "That was a big day for you."

"Why was it…" Colin started.

"WHO WANTS MORE CHEESE?" Sarah stood up, almost tripping over Miriam.

"Sarah's very into cheese these days," Nadav said. "*Vive le fromage.*"

"I can get it. I'm assuming the kitchen is that way?" Colin pointed.

"Yes. That would be great. Thank you." Sarah gestured vaguely.

Sarah watched him walk to the kitchen, then turned on her heel to face her family.

"What did I just say?" she hissed.

"You asked for cheese," Aaron said as he re-entered the living room. "I heard you from all the way back there."

"No. I mean, yes. But I meant before."

"You said no Magyck," Miriam said as she plopped on the couch.

"Right. That includes no talking about it too."

"Easier said than done, Sarah," Debra said. "We're trying."

"Really? It's so difficult? You did it for thirty-nine years. And every function you and Mike go to, do you just walk up to people and say, 'Hey, nice to meet you, would you like to be turned into a frog?' It just pops out?"

"We rarely turn people into frogs," Esra said. "The mammal-amphibian change is very complicated. More likely to try something like a vole."

Nadav leaned over to his brother. "I think you might be circling the perimeter, *mon frère*."

"Look, I will tell him soon, but I think now, with everyone here, it might be a little overwhelming. So everyone just cool it for one night, okay?"

As Colin came back with the cheese, everyone assumed what they thought was a relaxed position, with Esra smoking his pipe, Nadav pretending to whistle, and Debra trying to wet down Aaron's cowlick. Avi examined the Glen Livet label.

"I found the cheese. Why does everyone look weird?"

"We are looking natural," Esra said. "How are we doing?" He blew a smoke ring—which, to Sarah's relief, remained a ring.

"Great. Very lifelike." Colin placed the plate of cheese on the table. "Um, Avi? There's a bit of smoke coming from the oven. Is it supposed to be doing that?"

"I would imagine it means the brisket is done," Avi replied. "Why don't we make our way to the dining room?"

As the rest of the group moved to the dining room, Sarah remained in the living room and hovered over the cheese plate.

"Lay off that," Debra said. "You look like a demented mouse.

Which, by the way, I have encountered, so I know what I'm talking about."

"I'm stress eating."

"You've been stress eating since 1987."

"You're right." Sarah stopped mid-chew. "When did you see a demented mouse?"

"Thanksgiving, 1996. Cousin Ira got sloshed and kept turning himself into a rodent." Debra took a piece of cheese from her sister's hand. "You spent most of that holiday in your room listening to The Cranberries. Oddly appropriate, I thought."

"Must be where I get my dairy obsession. I've always thought…"

"You're stalling. Get in there." Debra pointed her finger at Sarah. "Hand over the cheese."

"I like the cheese," Sarah replied, her mouth full.

Debra waved her hand, and the tray disappeared.

"No Magyck!"

"He didn't see it. I had to cut you off. Go." Debra gave Sarah a little shove.

"I think I was happier when I didn't know about any of this."

"Ignorance is not always bliss." Debra brushed past Sarah and took a seat at the table next to her children, stopping Aaron from dropping an ice cube down Miriam's back.

"Ah, family," Sarah sighed, slipping into the empty dining room chair next to Colin, who was sipping a glass of the whiskey Nadav had passed him.

Avi entered from the kitchen, carrying a large brisket. Sarah saw he was not using potholders and was about to protest, when she noticed that the roasting pan was hovering about half an inch above his hands. She glared at her father, who quickly placed the pan on the trivet.

"Um, ow. Hot." Avi pretended to shake the heat from his hands.

The brisket joined a myriad of other dishes, from glazed carrots and mashed potatoes to a bowl of spinach sautéed in garlic. There were two kinds of rolls, three kinds of wine, and steamed broccoli—for Debra, of course. Sarah was sure her father hadn't cooked all of it on his own and wondered how he got it all done. Just then, Dave poked his blue head into the dining room, looked at Colin pouring himself some water, and wiggled his non-existent eyebrows at Sarah. She waved him away, and when he didn't get the hint, Sarah excused herself and slipped into the kitchen.

"Why are you here?" Sarah whispered.

"Nice to see you too, Sarah." Dave put his hands on his hips. "I helped with the cooking, if you must know. I've been taking lessons."

"I don't mean to be rude, but you're not planning on, you know, joining us?"

Dave rolled his yellow eyes. "No worries, dear heart. Your father told me there was to be no trace of Magyck tonight, because of your guy. I'll be out of here any minute." He picked up a small piece of brisket from the cutting board and popped it into his mouth. "Perfect, if I do say so myself. Good thing I made a backup. Your father is always losing track of time." He took another piece and then licked the spoon from the mashed potatoes. "I'm gaining a fondness for human food, that's for sure. All right, I'm off."

Dave waved and snapped his fingers, disappearing in a puff of vanilla-scented fog. A second later a slit opened up in the fog, and Dave poked his head through.

"I forgot. The meringue is in the top oven. Don't let it overbake." He blinked twice, smiled, and was gone once more.

Everything will be fine.

She reentered the dining room to find Esra playing his rubber bands. She gasped in horror, but Colin appeared to be taking it in stride.

"I thought we were eating," she said.

"Esra told me about this strange instrument he plays, and he insisted on demonstrating. It's pretty incredible." He turned back to Esra. "Is that Elton John?"

"Good ear, my friend. From his earlier catalog. He was such a pleasure to work with." Esra's fingers gently plucked the gold and silver bands, pulling out a tune Sarah instantly recognized. He looked at her and nodded. "But I think my Sarahleh is right. It is time to eat." He gently eased the bands from his fingers and toes, placed them in his pockets, and eased his feet back into his velvet slippers.

"I want to go barefoot too!" Miriam exclaimed, passing her hand over the floor beneath her.

"Shoes on!" Sarah hissed. Her niece pouted, whined a barely audible "harrumph," and then passed her hands over her feet again. Fortunately, Colin was busy putting a napkin on his lap and didn't notice.

She sat, her stomach too clenched to eat. Avi stood and held up a glass of wine.

"I'm so glad to have you all here in my home tonight. The company of family and good friends is always the best tonic. Here's to a…magical evening."

Why can't my family just play nice?

Avi carved the rest of the roast, and the slices were passed along with the plentiful side dishes. Sarah's stomach began to feel better as she enjoyed the food and genial conversation. Moments like these, few and far between, were the ones she enjoyed the most—the easy camaraderie, the lack of pretense, and except for her sister, a minimum of competition. She thought of her mother and how she would have enjoyed this dinner and meeting Colin. She felt a pang of regret as she watched Colin listen to Avi in rapt attention, as he discussed his one and only meeting with The Amazing Randi.

She would have loved this. Though she would have told me to lay off the potatoes.

She looked around the table. She finally felt like one of them, wiping away the lifelong, nagging feeling that she maybe had indeed been found under a cabbage leaf as an infant. Maybe it would be okay. Maybe her mother was wrong. She could do this. She almost smiled to herself, then noticed Aaron and Miriam playing with their food.

Literally. They were hunched over, having turned the glazed baby carrots into tiny orange men with sticks and playing a clandestine game of hockey on their dinner plates. The figures glided smoothly over a round rink made of mashed potatoes. Sarah panicked. Her eyes grew wide, and she nudged Debra, who was having a rather animated conversation with Raya about some designer's spring line. Sarah's gaze never left the children's plates. They got very excited when Aaron scored a goal with his carrot. She nudged her sister again, who gave her the "just a minute" finger.

Sarah couldn't wait. Closing her eyes, she pictured the vibrating strings of energy, picked the one closest to where the children were sitting, and waved her butter knife.

The carrots went airborne.

Everyone watched the vegetables shoot upward and hit the ceiling fan.

"Children! What did I say?" Debra shouted.

"It wasn't us!" Aaron said, defensively.

"Yeah, we were just playing carrot hockey," Miriam added, not realizing she wasn't being helpful.

Sarah leaned over to her sister. "It was me," she mumbled.

They watched Avi stand on a chair and wipe the mess with a napkin. Colin assisted by holding the chair steady while Nadav and Raya supervised.

"I had to stop them," Sarah said into Debra's ear. "I tried to get your attention, but you gave me the finger."

"What did you do?"

"Just as Raya taught me. I closed my eyes, reached out to the string that felt right, and channeled the energy through the butter knife."

"Why the knife?"

"I didn't have my wand."

"Who are you, The Great Fantastico?"

"It helps me."

"Whatever. Did you remember to open your eyes?"

"I forgot."

"You have to open your eyes. Otherwise, the energy just kind of goes pfft," Debra said, making a little explosion gesture.

"Noted."

Colin held out his hand for Avi, who climbed down from the chair.

"I'll get the rest of it tomorrow," he said, looking at his grandchildren.

"You should have let me get up on the chair," Colin said.

"It's fine. I have good balance." Avi looked again at his grandchildren. "I might have to repaint that spot, and I'll need some helpers."

"We'll help," Aaron said, nudging his little sister. Miriam gave Aaron the evil eye, as she was none too pleased to share the blame.

"No more playing with food, please," Sarah said. "I don't think Zayde wants to replace the carpet too."

They all sat back down at the table. Sarah reached for her water glass and took a sip, relieved that the fracas was over. The liquid dribbled out of the glass and onto her front. Aaron giggled quietly.

"You little stinker," she mouthed.

"Sorry about that," Debra said, checking to make sure Colin's attention was diverted before waving her hand and drying her sister's shirt. "I'll talk to him." She waggled her finger at her son.

Aaron looked at his mother with his "But she started it" face at the ready. Debra wasn't having any of it. She pulled her son close and talked into his ear.

"I know you're bored and you didn't think anyone would notice. But we told you, no Magyck."

"But…" Aaron said, pointing to Miriam, who was balancing a piece of meat over a fork that was itself hovering over her plate.

"Miriam!"

The fork clattered to the plate, and Miriam glanced at her mother.

"Sorry," she said.

The noise, however, had caught Colin's attention.

"Hey, how'd she do that? Great trick!"

"Just one of the more advanced illusions I can do," Esra interjected. "Some people do close-up magic, I do…across-the-table magic."

"Always needs to be different, my brother does," Nadav added.

"I consider myself a student of magic," Colin said. "Maybe one of these days you can teach me that trick."

"We can do Magyck now?" Miriam said brightly, waving her hand over her water glass, refilling it to the top. "Look what I can do!"

"Wow, that's great!" Colin said. "Did your grandpa teach you that?"

"Raya did! I can also —"

"Yes, it's a fun parlor trick," Sarah said, cutting her off. "Family business, you know."

"But we can—" Miriam started to protest, before Aaron waved his hand and muted his sister. Her eyes grew as big as saucers, and she flicked her hand and a dinner roll went flying.

"Hey, how'd you…" Colin said.

"Stop!" Debra yelled. "Or no interdimensional travel videos before bed!"

"If she gets to throw something..." Aaron said, before levitating in his chair.

"Oh my God," Sarah said, placing her hand on her forehead. She slumped in her seat before noticing something whiz past her.

Albert, now half-dragon, half-chinchilla, landed expertly on Aaron's shoulder. He gave himself a shake, and the rest of him reverted to scales and talons, his fuzzy tail the last to return to normal.

Colin was starting to sweat.

"What is going on here?" His voice trailed off as he grabbed the sides of his chair.

"I can explain," Sarah said. "It's just that we..."

"Hey, did you guys ever check on the meringue?" Dave stood in the doorway of the dining room, all two feet of him covered in sparkly blue scales and orange overalls. "I'm just concerned it's going to dry out, and I didn't make a backup dessert." He blinked his yellow eyes.

Colin's mouth opened and closed several times, as if it were trying to come up with something to say independently of his brain. His eyes rolled back in his head, and he hit the floor with a thud.

"So is that a yea or a nay on the meringue?" Dave said as everyone rushed to Colin's limp form on the floor. He looked at the group. "You want I should get some ice or something?"

Sarah held Colin's head in her lap. When he woke up, she had some serious explaining to do.

"**W**hat was that?" Colin said, finally regaining consciousness. Dave handed him a glass of water. "Thank you." As he reached for it, he noticed the small, scaled hand, his eyes traveling up to the bald blue head with the reptilian eyes looking back at him.

He promptly passed out again.

"Oh, for Pete's sake," Raya said, waving her hand over Colin's face. His eyelids fluttered, and he awoke again, shaking his head. He sat up, looking at the group staring down at him.

"I'm Dave." The demon held out his small but strong hand. Colin looked at it, looked up at Dave, looked at the hand again, and gingerly shook it.

"I'm going to need a little context here," he said.

"Dave works for me at the store," Avi said, giving Colin a hand to get him to his feet.

"Nope," Colin said. "Doesn't help."

"He works in the special section," Raya said.

"He'd have to," Colin said. He looked at Sarah. "Did you know about this?"

"Not until recently," Sarah said. "It's kind of new to me as well."

Colin took a swig from his wine glass and leaned on the dining room table.

"Sorry, Colin. We didn't mean to freak you out," Aaron said.

"Kids, why don't you go play in the den," Debra said, ushering them out of the room. "Good luck," she mouthed at her sister as she exited.

"I don't mean to be difficult here, but I'm not quite sure what is going on. You own a magic store, but you actually do magic? Like, *magic* magic?"

"Yes," Avi said. "But it's Magyck, actually."

"That's what I said."

"You said magic."

"Wait, what?"

"Magic is an illusion," Avi said, trying to clarify. "*Magyck* is a way of harnessing energy, of making changes to the reality we think we know." He put a hand on Colin's shoulder as if to steady him.

"Oh, that's much clearer now, thanks." Colin took a deep breath. "And you can all..." He gestured vaguely.

"Yes," Esra said.

"Can you do, how did you say it? Magyck?" Colin addressed Sarah directly.

"Sort of," she replied. "I couldn't before. Then I found out I can."

"How long were you planning on keeping this from me?"

"I'm sorry. It's so new. I'm just figuring it out myself. I didn't want to frighten you."

"Frighten me? It's not like a roller coaster or a face tattoo. This is…I don't know what this is."

Avi gripped Colin's shoulder again. "Son, let's go have a seat in the living room. We'll straighten this out."

He guided Colin to the couch, everyone else trailing behind.

"Sarah was doing this for you," Avi continued. "She thought it might be too much for you to deal with." He gently sat Colin down.

"Not everyone handles the idea well," Raya said, sitting on the other side of him. "She needed to get her head around it first. I mean, can you imagine?"

"So the whole family is in on it?" Colin asked.

"Well, it's not a criminal plot, but yes." Avi nodded. "We are a Magyckal family. Debra and Sarah are my daughters. Esra and Nadav are brothers, and my brothers in spirit. Raya is Nadav's daughter."

"We are a Magyckal family as well," Raya said.

"Our family, the Bachars, have been intertwined with the Greenbergs for generations." Nadav put his arm around his daughter. "Teachers and historians. Both have equal importance."

"Are you a good witch or a bad witch?" Colin said. "Sorry, that was rude."

"Magyck is not meant to harm. We live our lives as you do. We just have an extra layer of existence, if you will," Avi nodded.

"Kind of an added bonus," Raya said.

"Colin, look, I'm sorry to have kept this from you. I was going to tell you, really." Sarah knelt in front of the couch and took his hand. "But think about how I felt. I had no idea about my family. None. They felt it was best to keep it from me."

"So you wouldn't feel bad?" Colin asked. "That would be tough, not having an ability everyone else around you has."

"That was partly the reason," Avi said. "It would have been very frustrating for her. And knowing is not without risk. If Sarah accidentally told the wrong person about her family, she risked harassment, even physical harm. If we kept it secret, it was more likely that no one would notice."

"I didn't know that, Dad."

"There are always bad apples, in any community."

Colin leaned back in his seat. "And you didn't have powers until now? That's odd. I mean, odder."

"Late bloomer, I guess," Sarah said. "They tell me it happens."

Colin stood up, lost his balance for a moment, and then righted himself. He looked around the room, then at each person in front of him. "I don't know, Sarah, I just don't know. This is a lot to take in."

"I'm sorry."

Colin took his keys from his pocket.

"Look, everyone, I have to go. I just…yeah. Thank you very much for dinner. I…" Colin watched Dave cross from the kitchen to the dining room.

Dave waved.

"Yeah. Okay. I need to go." Colin ran his hand through his hair and turned toward the door.

"Will you call me tomorrow?" Sarah asked, standing.

"Yes. No. Maybe. Just let me process this, all right? I'm going now."

Colin walked swiftly out the door and didn't look back. The family remained in the living room, looking at each other in silence.

"Who's up for dessert?" Dave appeared in the living room with a tray. "Forget the meringue. I made individual flans!"

"Read the room, Dave," Raya said.

"Sorry. Did that Colin guy leave?" Dave handed her a plate of dessert, but Raya declined.

"Yes." Sarah accepted a ramekin of the custard. "It was too much for him to take in." She stared at her flan and frowned.

"Too bad." Dave scooped a whole piece of flan into his mouth. "Well, what can ya do? Some Unenchanteds can't handle it. Want me to wipe his memory?"

"Not yet, Dave. Let's see how this plays out," Avi said.

"Sure thing, boss. Hey, Sarah, if you're on the market again, I've got a cousin you might like. He *is* a demon, but he has his own business and a time-share in Boca."

"Thanks. I'll keep you posted."

"All right, I'm off. Got a hot date." Dave winked and disappeared in his usual puff of smoke.

Sarah had her third bite of her second helping of dessert when Raya took her plate away.

"It's out of your hands now, Sarah. And so is this flan."

"That's right. He'll come around. Or he won't." Avi leaned back on the couch.

"How comforting," Sarah said.

"Look, there's not much you can do," her father continued. "If it's meant to be, he'll return. If not, move on." Avi scooted over to the cushion next to Sarah and gently touched her hair. "Colin is a good man. But the Magyck life is not for everyone. Come." He stood and offered his hand. "Let's clear the table and you can help me with the dishes. We'll do them manually. You always liked the bubbles."

"I did always like the bubbles." Sarah took his hand and followed him to the kitchen.

CHAPTER
SEVEN

Sarah awoke the next morning feeling hungover, although she hadn't had more than one glass of wine the night before. The evening could not have gone worse, and everything she had feared would happen, did happen. Colin knew she was Magyck. But he was no Darrin to her Samantha; he had fled her father's house as confused as Mrs. Kravitz. She debated calling him, but what would she say? She hadn't lied, except perhaps by omission. How does one bring up being an honest to God, real life Magycian in casual conversation?

"Hi. I'm Sarah. I like walks on the beach, a nice Merlot, and oh yeah, I can make a lampshade turn inside out."

She wondered for a minute if she actually could make a lampshade turn inside out, then spent another minute wondering why that might be necessary. And also, that she disliked the beach. She realized she might be focusing on the wrong thing, pulled her pillow over her face, and groaned for one more minute.

It was not helpful.

Truth was, she wasn't even sure how she felt about the whole thing. She had accepted it rather matter-of-factly—it was kind of an "okay, sure" reaction. But she hadn't taken the time to really digest it, to think about what it truly meant. Her world had been turned on its ear, and she was thinking about how to get the laundry to fold itself. Her family had kept this entire, huge thing hidden from her.

For my benefit.

With the dark from the pillow still encompassing her face, she let the new reality sink in. It had been several months of training and learning, but it still wasn't truly real. But Magyck was real. There were strings, vibrations of energy that allowed people like Esra, like Debra, like Raya, to make what appeared to be miracles. Hell, even seven-year-old Miriam could do Magyck, and she hadn't yet figured out how the bank drive-through worked. And for most of her life, Sarah had no idea this world existed.

For my protection.

A single tear ran down her cheek, instantly absorbed by the pillowcase. She lifted the pillow, taking a breath of fresh air, and dropped it next to her on the bed. She wiped her cheek with the back of her hand. It appeared that the single tear was merely a scout for the rest of the drops lying in wait, as they now came freely and her hand was no longer enough to manage them.

She thought of her mother, always trying to protect her, to keep her from hurt.

"It's okay," she'd say. "It's not for you. Move on. Don't get invested."

Except now, her life was forever changed, and Sarah realized there was no place to move to. This was it.

I'm a food writer. And a Magycian. That's weird.

She waved her hand at the lamp, and it turned on. Getting dressed, she felt the weight of Magyck on her shoulders. The responsibility. The repercussions of what a life without Colin might mean. She hoped he would come around, but if he didn't, there was nothing she could do about it.

A man ran away from me this time. That's new.

When she got to the shop, it was quiet. She let herself in with her key, slowly opening the front door and trying to avoid the chimes. It wouldn't open for another two hours, so the quiet was to be expected, but it was still disconcerting. Usually there was someone milling about—

her father, Raya, sometimes Aaron—but everything was still. She spotted Raya in the back, sitting in one of the purple overstuffed chairs, her foot over the armrest and a large book in her hands. She saw Sarah and waved, closing the book and floating it back onto the shelf.

"Your dad's in the back room," Raya said. "He's trying to talk Dave out of ordering a cappuccino machine. I never should have given him that Nigella Lawson cookbook. We've created a monster. In a manner of speaking." She gave Sarah a hug. "How are you? Did you hear from Colin?"

"No," Sarah replied. "Maybe he just needs some time, like he said."

"It'll work out."

"Are you psychic too?"

"I have my moments. Okay. You're here. Let's teach you levitation."

"Well, you know what they say," Sarah said. "Levity is the soul of wit."

"How long have you been sitting on that one?"

"I've had it in my pocket for a while." She went to open her bag. "So I need my wand?"

"Need? No, not really, but if you want it…"

Sarah shoved her hand in her bag and grabbed the wand. She felt the weight of it in her hand and considered what it represented. It was fake, she knew, and she probably didn't really need it, but she liked it. Made her feel like she knew what she was doing. One didn't mess with a girl with a wand.

"Okay, let's fly," she said, hoping she sounded more confident than she actually was.

"Hold on a sec, Buzz Aldrin. We have some skills to practice first." Raya pulled a feather from her pocket. "Let's start with this."

"A feather? That's a little on the nose, don't you think?"

"Ha, ha." Raya dangled the feather in front of Sarah's face. "This is super light. You'd think it would be easy to levitate, right? Actually, the lighter the object, the more control you need. Anyone can do brute force. You've sent things flying across the room, right?"

"One or two times," Sarah admitted.

"Sure you have. Tap the energy and fling. But control is vital. When you don't have control, that's when things can go pear-shaped."

"Sounds logical."

"Good. Now focus on the feather. Just like always, find the string, focus on it, tap into it, and picture it around the feather."

Sarah did as she was instructed. She closed her eyes and wrapped the energy around the feather. She raised her wand and gave it a slight "push."

It flew straight up and plastered itself against the ceiling.

"That's a good start. But think elegance, think ease. And open your eyes. Helps to see the thing you're trying to levitate." Raya held out her hands. "Now let go of the feather, please."

Sarah pointed her wand again and released the energy around the feather. It drifted casually into Raya's hands.

"Let's try again," Raya said. "Hold the energy in place. It's a feather, not a missile."

Sarah began the process again, finding the energy and wrapping it around the feather.

"Eyes open, please," Raya instructed.

"Sorry."

She held her wand steady and tried to keep the energy in check. To her surprise, the feather didn't fall after Raya removed her hand from underneath it.

"Good. Very good. Hold it there." Raya placed her hands on Sarah's face and touched her forehead with hers. "Relax a bit. You're straining."

"How can you tell?"

"Your face is all scrunched up. You look like one of those dried apple dolls."

As Raya stepped back, Sarah relaxed her face along with her shoulders and arms. The feather stayed in place.

"There you go," Raya assured her. "You're not working so hard. Feels better, right? Excellent. Keep it there…good." She sat down, draping one leg over the arm of the chair. "Now rotate it. Picture what you want it to do." She gestured in a circular manner. "Then do it."

Sarah moved her wand in a circle, just as Raya had demonstrated. The feather complied with her command, rotating slowly in a clockwise direction.

"Now the other way," Raya said, watching the feather with laser-like intensity. "Good. Now on the Y-axis, please."

"Huh?"

Raya moved her finger up and down. Sarah nodded.

"Now move the feather over to me and ease it into my hand."

Sarah glided the feather over, gently moving it, tracing the path with her wand. Just before depositing it in Raya's hand, she gave it a little horizontal spin.

"Show off." Raya smiled.

"What's next?"

"We're going to levitate something a bit heavier. You."

"I'm going to fly now?"

"Well, the aerodynamics are a bit different from flying, but you will be off the ground. You're not winging it to Pittsburgh."

"I'm not sure how I feel about that," Sarah admitted.

"Most people are pretty sure they don't want to go to Pittsburgh."

Sarah laughed. "No. About...you know…" Sarah mimed flying with her hand and arm.

"Haven't you ever dreamed of flying?"

"Only in first class."

"This will be different," Raya said. "No hot towels or warm cookies."

"That's disappointing."

"Sarah does enjoy the cookies." Avi reentered from the back room, wiping his hands on a towel. He stood with his hands on his hips, watching his daughter.

"All right, no fooling around anymore." Raya wagged her finger at Avi, who wagged his finger back. "Basically, levitating yourself is not much different from levitating a feather, except you're dealing with a slightly larger object."

Raya positioned herself on the rug.

"We're going to start from a seated position," Raya continued, pointing to a spot in front of her. "Sit. Now start like you did before with the feather. Visualize the strings, reach out to them, feel which one will be right for you, and tap into it. Keep your eyes open."

Sarah sat cross-legged on the rug in front of Raya and tried to see the strings without closing her eyes. They appeared, and she tapped into a calming blue-green one that didn't look like it was vibrating too aggressively.

"Good," Raya said. "Now, just like the feather, gently push away from the ground. Keep control. We don't want you plastered on the ceiling."

Sarah watched in amazement as Raya demonstrated the technique, hovering about a foot off the floor.

"I knew I picked the right teacher," Avi said. "Raya, you're a natural." He wandered to the front of the store, humming to himself.

"Now you," Raya instructed.

Sarah found that nice blue-green string again and let the energy fill her torso. Then, with her mind, she pushed ever so gently away from the floor.

It worked! She no longer felt the rug on her rear end. She was flying! She waved her hand under her to make sure, then looked down. Just as she did so, she landed with an undignified thump.

"Ouch," she said, rubbing her hip.

"Yeah, you remembered gravity. Don't do that."

"And if you ever find yourself falling again," Avi shouted from behind the register, "notice where the ground is and...don't go there."

"Thanks, Dad."

Raya touched down, then stood up and reached out a hand to Sarah.

"I think you have the gist. Let's try again from a standing position."

Sarah stood up but lost her footing, fell forward, and wound up standing nose to nose with Raya. She took a step back and steadied herself.

"Yeah, it takes a second to get your land legs back," Raya said. "All right, it's the same process as before, but it's even more important to maintain tight control so you don't start spinning."

"That can happen?"

"Oh yeah. Once I got so excited that I forgot what I was doing and started spinning like a pinwheel. I had just had lunch and barfed everywhere. From then on, my dad always made sure I levitated on an empty stomach."

"Good call." Sarah touched her stomach and hoped her breakfast would hold.

Raya shuddered. "Still can't look at a croque monsieur without getting a little nauseated." She shook her head. "Now, we're limited in space because of the size of the room, but that's okay because it will limit height, and really no one flies outside much. Too many potential witnesses." She laughed. "Mostly, I use it to reach the top bookshelf at the library."

They held hands and tapped into the vibrating energy. Sarah felt herself once again leaving the ground and made sure not to be surprised by it. She felt strengthened by Raya's grasp and inched higher and higher. She felt Raya let go of her hand, and Sarah was able to support herself on her own power. It was an amazing feeling, being both solid and weightless at the same time.

"Excellent," Raya said, alighting. "You've got it. Now try to move over to the door back there."

Sarah gently pushed away from her current position and floated to the door of the back room, touching the frame lightly with her hand. Then she moved back to where Raya was standing. For effect, she posed like Peter Pan.

"Second star to the left and beyond!"

"I appreciate the enthusiasm. I want you to practice moving about the room. Pick things up off tables, put them back, that sort of thing."

Sarah spent the next hour flying around the room, moving displays, pushing chairs, swapping books from one shelf to another. She felt awkward at first, trying to figure out what to do with her arms since flapping them wasn't an option. But within minutes she felt like she had been doing this her whole life, despite bumping her head several times on the chandelier in the center of the store. Raya then upped the ante a bit, throwing things at Sarah so she could learn to work on her speed and agility. Then she pulled a short, thick baton from her backpack, which she extended into a five-foot-long pole.

"Let's make this more of a challenge." Raya held the pole like a broadsword, cutting into the air around Sarah.

"Move!" she said after Sarah allowed herself to be bonked on the arm. "Anticipate my actions!"

The next swing caught Sarah squarely on the thigh. She winced from the pain and felt herself falling.

Miss the floor.

She caught herself and swept upward in a quick arc. Raya's pole kept coming at her, landing to her left, her right, above her and below. Each time she dodged the blow. Raya spun the pole like a martial arts master, which Sarah quite quickly realized she was. The rotation made her a little dizzy, but she cleared her mind quickly when she saw the pole coming straight for her head. She spun ass-end over teakettle, as her mother was fond of saying, avoiding the blow and landing on her feet on the other side of the room.

Raya stopped in her tracks and looked at Sarah with admiration.

"That was great! There you go! Excellent!" she said, dropping her weapon and gathering Sarah up in a big hug.

"I didn't think you'd come after me with a stick," Sarah gasped. "What the hell was that?"

Raya held Sarah's shoulders and looked at her sternly. "You need to be prepared for anything. There are some shady characters in the Magyckal community. It isn't all feathers and tiny dragons."

She handed Sarah a handkerchief from her bag. Sarah wiped the sweat from her brow.

"Thanks," she said. "That was intense."

Dave brought them a pitcher of ice water and two glasses.

"Well done," he said. "You're a natural."

"Maybe a few more lessons like that and I'll have arms like Raya," Sarah said, finishing her water in two gulps.

Dave looked Sarah up and down. "Yeah, sure. Why not." He turned to Raya and shook his head. "You want I should get the fire extinguisher now?"

"No, I think we'll be fine. We've got the water pitcher," Raya replied.

"You sure? When I taught you sparking skills, you set your uncle's hat on fire."

"Shh!"

"Wait, Dave was your teacher too?" Sarah asked.

"You'll have more than one teacher, especially when you know someone who's especially skilled in an area."

"I'm good with fire," Dave said. "And summoning charms. And coq au vin. Who knew?" He saw Sarah's confused look. "What, you thought I was just a shipping clerk?"

"No, of course not, I…um…" Sarah's cheeks felt hot.

Dave let out a light chuckle.

"Newbs." He snapped his fingers as he wrapped his tail around his legs and disappeared in a puff of smoke.

"Just for the record, I was pretty sure he wasn't just a shipping clerk," Sarah said, her body vibrating with energy and her eyes bright. "So are we going to do this?"

"Yes, yes. Chill. You've got the adrenaline going. You don't want to work with fire when you're hopped up. The Great Chicago Fire? Wasn't started by a cow, let's just say." She cracked her neck. "Okay, fire. Hmm. Maybe I *should* get Dave back here…"

"Raya, you're stalling. If I want a caramel flan, I'll call Dave. You can teach me fire spells. I trust you."

Dave's head appeared in front of her, midair.

"Hey, you'd be lucky to get the caramel flan, lady-girl."

Sarah waved him off, and he popped out of view.

"It is very good flan," Raya nodded. "Let's do this. Fire can be a bit tricky because you're not just pulling from energy lines. You've got to connect two specific strings, and this is one of the few cases where you have to verbalize." She looked around the store. "What can I use, what can I use…"

An old-fashioned, black-and-white magic wand, the kind amateur magicians use to wave over a top hat, appeared in her hand.

"Thank you!" Raya said.

"Welcome!" Avi waved from the front of the store.

"Okay, so what I'm going to do is light the tip of this stick." Raya focused on a far-off point. "I'm gathering energy from around me, and I'm searching for the two particular fire strings I need. They're usually ice blue and vibrating so tightly they'll almost look like they're not moving… There they are. Now I'm tapping into both of them. Now I focus on the end of the stick and…*esh chaaya*."

The end of the stick started to glow, and a small flame began to grow, until the magic wand looked like a black-and-white birthday candle. Raya held her hand perpendicular to it, controlling the flame.

"*Esh chaaya*? That sounds Hebrew," Sarah said.

"Close. Same origin, adapted a bit."

"Fire…life? That's what it sounded like. Interesting."

"Want to give it a go?" Raya waved her hand over the wand, and the flame extinguished. She handed it to Sarah. "Here, I've warmed it up for you. Literally."

Sarah took the wand. The end was slightly charred; it wasn't an illusion.

"Now, one step at a time, just like I showed you," Raya continued. She watched Sarah intently as she got her own wand from her bag and walked through the steps, making sure she didn't close her eyes.

The wand was lit. Sarah felt both surprised and confident, like a neophyte scout creating fire for the first time at a campsite.

Magyck.

"Excellent!" Raya said. "Now put it out."

Sarah looked around for the pitcher of water, then wondered if she should just blow on it and make a wish.

"Just feel it. It's there," Raya said calmly. "And keep your eyes open."

Sarah waved her wand over the light, willing it to disappear. Just as she felt the fire lick her palm, it was snuffed out, the smoke merely a ribbon in the air.

"See? You've got this," Raya said. "After you get really good at that, I'll show you how to do this…"

She held her hand in front of her, palm facing the ceiling. She gave a little intake of breath, whispered the charm, and a round, blue ball of flame, the size of a baseball, appeared in her hand. Sarah's eyes widened in appreciation.

"Oh my God, that's so cool!"

Sarah and Raya both gave a start and turned to the source of the exclamation. Madison was standing in the middle of the store, mouth agape. She rushed over to the women.

"How did you…oh my God, that's just SO COOL!"

Raya extinguished the flame ball, and Sarah dropped her wand.

"Madison! How did you get in here? Dad, did you see Madison come in?" Sarah said, looking for her father.

"She slipped by me," Avi said. "I was sorting doves."

"The door was unlocked," Madison said. "I figured it would be okay." She looked around. "Is this your store? Awesome."

"It's my family's. That's my dad," Sarah said, pointing to Avi, who was holding an armful of grey, stuffed birds. He waved with his elbow.

"How did you get into the city? You don't drive yet," Sarah said.

"I'm here with my friend Bethany. Her mom drove."

"Where are they?" Raya asked, craning her neck to look around.

"They went to the stationery store down the street. Wedding invitations. Bethany's sister is getting married. Ow, that hurts."

Sarah realized that she was gripping Madison's arm a little too tightly and let go.

"Your hands are really warm," Madison said. She turned to Raya. "You're a really talented magician. Do you do parties?"

"Magycian," Raya corrected.

"Yeah, that's what I said."

"Raya, Madison. Madison, Raya," Sarah said quickly. "Raya works here and studies physics at U of C. She's…teaching me a few tricks."

"That was a good one!" Madison said.

"Hey, does your dad know you're here?"

"No. I mean, he knows I'm in the city with Bethany, but not here specifically. But he'd be okay. Even though he's been acting kind of weird. Won't tell me why." Madison furrowed her brow and pouted slightly. "He says it's one of those 'I wouldn't understand' things. I understand things."

"There's a bit more to it, Madison. I wish it was easy to explain."

"Well, try. I'm not a little kid, you know."

"Actually, that might make it easier," Raya said.

Dave opened the back room door and came barreling into the store, carrying a box of cookies.

"Hey, I heard some racket coming from you here. You set something on fire again, Raya? Should I call the fire brigade?" He noticed Madison and held out his hand. "Hi, I'm Dave."

Madison took one look at Dave's blue face and passed out, crumpling into a heap.

"For Pete's sake, what is it with your family and fainting?" Sarah said, catching Madison as she fell.

"She's coming around."

"Thank goodness."

"Does she want a cookie? Some pâté? What do small humans eat?" Dave waved his hands around.

Madison was lying on the velour couch in the back of the store. Her eyelids fluttered, then she blinked. Sarah thought Madison might vomit, based on her pale, slightly green pallor, and looked around for a bucket. Madison continued to blink determinedly, looking from one face to another, first Sarah's, then Raya's, then...

"Sandwich?" Dave offered. "Cucumber and cream cheese?" The iridescent, lizard-like eyes blinked back at her.

She started to faint again.

"No, no, no, no, no..." Sarah patted Madison's hand. "Honey, come back. It's okay. Dave, could you, you know..." She motioned for him to leave.

"How about this?" Dave morphed into a young human man with red hair and freckles.

"The eyes," Raya prompted.

"Oh yeah. Sorry." Dave shook his head, shifting his eyes from reptile slits to almond-shaped green ones.

"This is your human suit?" Sarah asked. "I always thought you were the UPS guy."

"Glad I passed. This body always weirds me out." Dave shook his rear end. "How you all get along without a tail I'll never understand."

"Hey, guys?" Madison whispered. "A little help here?"

"Sorry." Raya handed her a glass of water.

"Thanks."

Madison sat up and sipped slowly, holding the glass carefully with both hands.

"So, uh, Sarah?" she said.

"Yes?"

"What the heck just happened?"

"It's kind of hard to explain."

"Duh," Madison said, taking another sip. "Is that why my dad's been acting so weird? Because you're a witch?"

"Magycian. With a Y," Raya clarified.

"Probably," Sarah nodded.

Madison pointed to the sandwiches Dave had placed on the coffee table.

"If I have one of those, I won't turn into a frog, will I?"

"Oh no, no…" Sarah paused, then looked at Dave for confirmation. He shook his head.

"Why don't Dave and I check out some stuff in the back?" Raya motioned for the two of them to leave.

"Sounds good." Dave morphed back into his short, blue self. He hiked up his overalls and jogged to the back room and held the door open for Raya.

"So that's…" Madison pointed to them.

"Dave."

"And he's a…"

"I have no idea."

"Okay," Madison said, taking a sandwich from the tray. "These are good."

"It's a new thing for him. Raya told me he used to be into wine tasting. A lot of stuff got broken." Sarah took a sandwich for herself. "Apparently, when you're a two-foot-tall demon and you don't spit out the wine, things go south pretty quickly." She rubbed Madison's arm. "Are you okay?"

"I think so. I mean, it's weird. But kind of cool." Madison swallowed her last bite. "Dad's last girlfriend was into astrology. This at least makes a little sense."

"Glad it does for you. I'm still working it out. It's new."

Madison's cell phone dinged, and she read the text and typed a response.

"Bethany and her mom are headed back this way. Don't worry, I didn't say anything. I just typed the unicorn emoji and a door. That's not code, is it?"

"No, there's no code. You're good." Sarah attempted to hug Madison, halting and starting, then halting again, as if she had forgotten how. Madison leaned away.

"Not yet," she said quickly. "I mean, I'm okay but I need to process."

"That's very mature," Sarah replied. "I get it."

The chimes on the front door tinkled, and a gust of cold wind blew the door fully open.

"Is that Bethany?" Madison whispered. "I told her I'd meet her outside."

"When?"

"The door emoji."

Sarah stood up to look. A tall figure in a white fur coat stood in the doorway with two hulking shadows behind her.

"Definitely not Bethany." Sarah gathered Madison's things and put them behind the couch. "Stay here. Don't go near her."

Madison looked at the woman in the coat. "Who's Cruella de Vil over there?"

"Family acquaintance."

From the corner of her eye, Sarah saw Raya and Dave peeking out from the back room. They quietly walked out and stood near the bookcases.

Madison was still staring at Cruella. "She's scary. And her friends are creepy."

"Go stand over by Raya," Sarah said, giving her a gentle nudge.

Sarah slowly walked to the front counter, rubbing her arms as if she were suddenly cold.

"Hello, Zondra. Nice to see you. And you brought friends." Her voice was calm, but her stomach felt like a rock.

"Assistants," Zondra replied. "They help with the…unpleasant." She waved her hand at them dismissively. "Still here, I see? I thought you'd be packing up the stock by now."

"My father made it clear that we aren't going anywhere." Sarah could smell Zondra's perfume, spicy and thick.

Zondra rested her hand lightly on the glass counter. "Where is he, by the way?"

"He stepped out. " Sarah could feel acid in the back of her throat. "What do you really want, Zondra?"

"I think you know. Or maybe you don't. You don't seem all that bright, actually." She glided her fingers over the glass and rubbed them together as if they had been soiled. A handkerchief appeared in her hands, and she dabbed at her fingertips.

Sarah felt Raya and Dave's presence behind her. She hoped the three of them appeared at least slightly intimidating.

The handkerchief disappeared from Zondra's hand and reappeared in Raya's.

"Take care of that, won't you, dahling?" Zondra purred.

Raya did a quick fire spell, and the handkerchief disappeared in a brief flash of light.

"You heard my father," Sarah said. "You have no claim. We're done with this."

Sarah noticed a brooch on Zondra's suit jacket. It was an opaque, green stone about three inches across, set in a gilded, gold base. The stone itself appeared to be lit from within, flickering as Zondra spoke.

"I will not be ordered about," Zondra said, the stone gleaming. She noticed Sarah's gaze, and she placed a hand over it.

"Why do you want the store so badly? You're not the retail type," Sarah said.

"Oh, I have no plans to run a *store*." Zondra's smooth face suddenly flashed with anger. She brandished her arm like a sword, and before anyone could react, Sarah was flung back with intense force, landing on her back. She gasped and held her chest. Dave lurched forward in her defense, but Raya held him back.

Sarah struggled to get to her feet. She felt as if the room was tilting, and her eyes wouldn't quite focus. As she turned to Zondra, the two "assistants" sprang forward. Raya stopped them, throwing up a translucent wall. They both hit their heads and stopped. The slightly larger one rubbed his forehead. Raya removed the wall.

"Sorry, dahling. But as I told your dear father, you do not meet the terms of the contract. It is cut and dried. The person who inherits the store must be a Magycian."

"I am a Magycian," Sarah said, her voice soft and unsure.

"Hardly," Zondra replied. "I remember when you were born. It was obvious even then. Your poor mother must have felt rather guilty, I should think. Although I can't imagine what she expected, being Unenchanted herself. I don't know why your father settled for her."

Sarah's mouth felt dry. "You knew my mother?"

"Oh yes. We were great friends, she and I. Well, maybe not great, but she knew how to make an excellent martini, and that's always good for something."

Sarah took a step closer, feeling the acid in her throat start to burn in her chest.

"I am a Magycian. I'm a little late to the party, but it still counts."

"Latecomers are a myth."

Zondra waved again, but Sarah was ready this time, nearly dodging the wave of energy Zondra threw. It knocked her on her rear end, but she was quickly back on her feet, springing with surprising energy. Zondra hissed, and a bolt of light flew from her right hand. This time Raya was by her side, and she deflected the light with her staff.

"The hired help has to protect you," Zondra said. "You don't even have the skills to protect yourself. You. Are. Nothing!" She waved both her arms, and Raya and Sarah were tossed up to the ceiling and held in a field of crackling energy. Sarah's lungs were frozen, and she struggled to escape. She saw Raya hold her hands together as if in prayer, then raise them up and outward. She broke the beams and held herself aloft as Dave spun in place like a whirlwind, bolts flashing from his tail and hands. Raya then tossed a golden rope of light around

Zondra's henchmen, holding them in place. Zondra stumbled backward, and the fields holding Raya and Sarah vanished. Sarah felt herself fall.

"Sarah! Fly!"

Without thinking, Sarah grasped the energy around her, pushing against the floor that was fast coming up to meet her. She stopped midair, hovering about a foot off the carpet.

"Yes!" Sarah said to herself. "Wait, where's Madison?" She craned her head to look for the girl.

"I'm here!" Madison waved her arm and poked her head up from behind a velvet chair in the back. "I'm okay!"

Sarah landed softly on the floor and turned to Zondra, who was still struggling to catch her breath and furtively touching the green stone of her brooch.

"Am I supposed to be impressed by this little display?" Zondra said. Her voice was even, but her eyes flashed. She smoothed her white-blonde hair. "Your father knows the terms of the contract, Susan."

"Sarah."

"Are you sure?" Zondra waved her off. "Regardless, I know the agreement backward and forward. You are not the heir, and the place will be mine."

Zondra fastened the top button of her coat and threw an ornate scarf over her shoulder, obscuring the green decorative stone.

"But there is another way, of course. Why don't you ask your father?" She practically cooed, and it gave Sarah a creepy feeling in her spine. "We would make an exceptional team."

"You and me?" Sarah said.

"No." Zondra turned on her heel. "First thing I will do is up the standards for the Magyckal community. Too many..." She turned her head and looked Sarah up and down. "You know."

Zondra exited the store in a wave of hairspray, angora, and condescension. Her assistants followed, slamming the door behind them and causing the chime to fall to the ground.

"She'll be back." Raya touched down easily to the floor and retracted her staff. "We need to be more prepared for next time."

When Dave landed, he leaned over and placed his hands on his knees. "Whoo! I am out of shape," he said, standing up and placing his hands on his hips. "Good work, kid."

"It wasn't enough," Sarah said. "I need to know why she wants this place so badly. I know Chicago real estate is at a premium, but this is a bit much."

"I want to know what she meant by 'another way.'" Raya cast a furtive glance at the back room.

"I need to call my dad," Sarah said. "Like, right now." She glanced at her watch. "Shoot, I'm supposed to meet my editor for coffee. And I need to get Madison home. Damn. Okay, I can walk and talk."

"Yeah, you really can't." Raya patted her arm. "Be careful. In the meantime, let me see what I can uncover. That woman is bad news." She picked up some cards that had fallen to the ground in the scuffle. "I didn't know she knew your folks from way back. Interesting. You sure you've never met her?"

"I think I'd remember." Sarah wiped some perspiration beads from her forehead and picked up her bag. "Madison? Come on out, hon."

Madison came out from her hiding place and looked around her in amazement. She looked both scared and exhilarated.

"OMG. What's going on here?"

"I'm not sure, exactly," Sarah replied, putting her hand on Madison's cheek. "Honestly."

Madison's phone dinged. She looked at the screen and read the text.

"Bethany and her mom are still waiting."

"Are you sure you're all right? I can take you home if you want."

"No, it's okay. I'm fine, really." The teenager paused for a moment, then gave Sarah a quick hug. Sarah was so surprised she forgot to move her arms to hug back. "I don't think I'm going to tell Dad though. He might, you know, freak out a little."

Madison turned to leave, then stopped.

"Sarah?"

"Yeah?"

"You're pretty cool. I just wanted you to know that. And not just because of..." She gestured vaguely around the room.

"Thank you."

"I bet you hear that all the time, with your job and all."

"Literally not once."

When Madison was at the door, she turned to look at Sarah.

"Hey, you think you can teach me some of that magic?" Madison said.

"Magyck," Raya corrected.

"I still don't hear the difference."

"You get used to it," Sarah said. "See you soon?"

"I hope so."

Madison waved, picked up the door chimes, and placed them on the shelf next to the door. Sarah let out a heavy sigh and turned around. She went to her bag and pulled out her phone. Tapping out a text, she hit send and put the phone in her pocket.

"What *is* going on, Raya?"

"Your father is obviously protecting you from something. I think we need some answers." Raya rubbed her neck and shoulder.

"You hurt?" Sarah asked, pulling her phone back out from her pocket and looking at the screen from the corner of her eye.

"No, I'm fine. Let's go to the pub." Raya squinted as Sarah tucked her phone back into her bag. "Wait, didn't you have to meet your editor?"

"I texted and told her I need to reschedule. She does it to me all the time. I think I can do it once."

"Sounds good. Dave, you want to come?"

"You two go, I'll stay here," Dave said, materializing a broom and dustpan. "I'll straighten up a bit and probably open the store for a few hours."

This declaration was met with a look of skepticism from Sarah. Dave nodded and morphed back into his redheaded young man persona.

"Ta da," he said.

"Thank you, Dave. For everything."

"No sweat, kid. Go and do."

"Let's go," Raya agreed. "We need info. My dad might not know anything about this, but I know who will."

"Esra," they said in unison.

CHAPTER
NINE

The pub was busy with the lunch rush, and Nadav was pulling double duty filling drink orders and bussing tables, but even though he was hustling, he remained calm and sweat-free. He waved at Sarah and Raya as they entered and nodded at two open stools at the end of the bar.

"Maybe we should come back?" Sarah said, hopping into her seat. "Besides, I don't see Esra."

"He's around, I'm sure. Even if he's out teaching a class, he'll be back soon," Raya said. "He wouldn't miss lunch. Let's give it a few minutes and see if the crowd dies down."

Nadav placed a couple of iced teas in front of them. "Be right back." He gave his daughter a quick peck on the cheek. "A large business meeting and two tour groups. Whoo, what a day, what a day!" He glided away, raising the tray confidently above his head.

"Your dad looks like he's ice skating," Sarah said. "Looks so effortless."

"Check his feet."

Sarah looked down to catch a glimpse of Nadav's feet as he placed drinks in front of some patrons at a side table. His shoes, newly shined and without a scuff, floated almost imperceptibly above the waxed hardwood floor.

Raya squinted her eyes and looked at Sarah. "Hey, how are you doing? I haven't actually asked you that."

Sarah's shoulders slumped. "It's a lot to deal with."

"It is. Especially at your advanced…"

"Watch it."

"Super-young age. It's like learning a new language. Takes a while to get it to sink in."

"Did you ever feel sorry for me?" Sarah took a sip of her tea.

"Honestly? A little. Not because you couldn't do Magyck. Lots of great people can't. But it made you a little isolated from your family. I would have told you, but your parents felt differently." She took the paper straw from her drink and placed it on a napkin on the bar, then took a large gulp. "On the other hand, I kind of envied you."

"Me? Sheesh. You can create fire. Like, with your mind."

"I can. That's cool. But you were free in a way. The Magyck community is awesome, but there are countless rules and restrictions. You have to work within the guidelines, and there's a ton of unspoken rules that you can't break. Lots of people working on the honor system, you know?"

"That's sort of true for everyone."

"Yeah, I guess. I think that's one of the reasons I like physics. There are rules, of course, certain principles, but the uncertainty of physics and the randomness just make it all the more beautiful and exciting. It's kind of liberating in a way."

"Plus you get to wear the cool goggles."

"There is that," Raya laughed. "Look, just remember that you've got this. And I'll always be here for you. We're *cousines du coeur*, remember?"

"Yes. And I'll need it, because I just don't know if…"

Esra appeared between them, placing a hand on their shoulders. "My favorite niece! And my favorite honorary niece! So good to see you!" A barstool materialized between them. "Mind if I sit?" He plopped down on the seat with as much flourish as his round physique could muster.

Nadav glided by and placed an empty beer stein in front of his brother. "Be careful, Esra. Don't alarm the locals."

"Oh, they are not paying attention to me," Esra replied.

"I thought you said that someone is always looking," Sarah said.

"I am particularly skilled at the art of misdirection." He pointed at the chilled mug, and as he raised his index finger from bottom to top, the glass filled with an amber liquid.

"A little something special for me," he explained. "Nadav does not keep it on tap." He grasped the handle and raised it to his lips, humming as he did so. He drained the mug in one swallow.

Nadav held up one finger, and Esra nodded. "My brother is reminding me to keep a clear head. Sometimes, I forget." Esra smiled impishly. "What can I say? I am a musician." He wiggled his fingers and produced a musical *glissando*, each note easing up the scale as he delicately pressed each digit in the air. It made Sarah think of butterflies, and she smiled back.

"We've met Zondra," Raya said, snapping Sarah back to reality.

"Ah, the redoubtable Ms. Bex," Esra said, clicking his tongue.

"I'd go with Battle-Axe Extraordinaire," Sarah said. "Do you know her?"

"By reputation," Esra said. "She tends to appear when she needs something from the 'peasants.' I used air quotes. Did I do that right?"

"Or wants something," Raya said. "She wants the store. And yes, you used them correctly."

Esra shook his head. "I knew she would eventually come to collect. But it is not the store she wants. It is the location." He rubbed his forehead, trying to smooth out the creases that had collected there. "Has your father ever told you about why the store is located where it is?"

"Old Benjamin got a good deal?" Sarah asked.

"Well, he did, but at the expense of the Bex family. It was a contested transaction. They only came to a resolution because of the contract." Esra inched his stool closer to them. "You understand the concept of strings, yes?"

"We've been working on it," Sarah replied.

"Good. Well, on this earth there are areas where the strings tend to concentrate—collection pools, if you will. Located under the store is one of those areas—quite a strong center, actually. Benjamin was in charge of connecting the energy strings of air, water, and earth. He also built a special holder where the energy could come together in a stream without being contained. Others have done the same, but Old Benjamin's was—is—the strongest. You could call it a circuit board for Magyck."

"Sounds powerful. Wait…did you say *this* earth?"

Esra waved his hand. "It has strengthened the Greenberg family, helping a family of powerful Magycians become more so. Fortunately, you come from an honest, wise family, and the power has not been abused. But Zondra…"

"Has other intentions," Raya said. "That's pretty clear."

"I fear those intentions," Esra said. "We all should."

"Is she a supervillain, or something?" Sarah asked. "How afraid should we be?"

"I do not know what that is," Esra said, "but my answer would be 'very' to 'a lot.' We have been fine so far because it has stayed in the family. You have all been good caretakers of the energy, and my family has helped."

"But now the contract has been voided because Sarah wasn't born Magyck," Raya said.

"She does have grounds to contest it," Esra said. "We would have to have a solicitor with a background in birthright bonds look at it."

"I'm not Magyck enough," Sarah said. "I have no idea what I'm doing." She rested her chin on her hand. "Why isn't Dad telling me any of this? He just tells me, 'Don't worry about it.' I'm almost forty. He's still keeping things from me."

"Fathers always want to protect their children." Esra placed his hand gently on Sarah's cheek, and she could swear she heard tiny bells.

"So what should we do, besides get a lawyer?" Raya asked. "Zondra isn't going to give up, that's obvious."

"Keep up your Magyckal studies, Sarah. But be discreet. The less Zondra knows, the better," Esra said. "I will keep my eyes and ears open." He stood and waved his hand over his stool. It winked out of view just as a woman from one of the tour groups was approaching.

"Excuse me," she said. "Are you still using your…" The woman looked down to where the stool was. "Oh, I thought you were sitting on a bar stool. Wow, okay. I need to lay off the pinot in the afternoon! Sorry!" She brushed the bangs from her forehead and turned to leave, her gaze remaining on the spot where the stool was. She exhaled loudly and went back to her group, her gait slightly wobbly. Nadav picked up Esra's mug and shook it at him.

"I told you to be careful!" he said.

Esra waved his hand dismissively. "She was, how do you say, day drinking. She will not remember."

"Still…"

"Shh, brother. All is well. People see what they want to see." He tugged on his vest. "So, Sarahleh. What are you going to do now?"

"I don't know, Esra. I'm a little freaked out." Sarah felt her breath quicken and placed her hand on her chest.

"Well, do not be freaked out, but a little concern is fine. The answers will come. Perhaps have a nosh, listen to some music. I have been hearing good things about this young Carlos Santana fellow. Have you heard of him?" Esra placed his cap on his head, securing its usual jaunty angle. "I bet he could play a mean toe piano. I mean, anyone can play guitar." He touched the brim of his cap and turned on his heel. He pushed open the heavy door of the pub, holding his hand up against the bright, early afternoon autumn sun. He stepped outside and disappeared into the foot traffic on the sidewalk.

Raya turned back to the bar. "Wow. This got real."

"You can say 'shit.'" Sarah smiled slightly, her lips tight and closed.

"What do you want to do? Practice some spells? I have some time before class."

Sarah felt a weight on her chest and had to remind herself to breathe. "No, I don't think I can right now."

"But Zondra…"

"I know about Zondra! But I just can't wrap my mind around this right now. I have to go. I'll call you later, okay?" Sarah picked up her purse from the bar and slung it over her shoulder.

"Sarah…"

Sarah walked out the door and managed to locate her car on the third try. Sitting in the driver's seat with her hands in her lap, she felt numb. Her head felt like it was wrapped in wool flannel, and she could feel hot, wet tears form in the corners of her eyes. She imagined her mother looking at her worriedly and advising her to run away. And she wanted to. A few months ago she was a middle-aged food writer with a lovely boyfriend, few responsibilities, and no real discernable talents. Now she was a burgeoning Magycian with a secretive father engaged in a century-old blood feud. She worked up the strength to start the car and drive away.

Where's my TED talk on THIS?

CHAPTER
TEN

A fter driving around the north side for a while, then taking a jaunt down Lake Shore Drive, an image popped into Sarah's head and she knew where she needed to go.

She drove to Colin's house in Oak Park with a mission. She wasn't ready to throw in the proverbial white towel on their relationship and didn't want to let being a Magycian stand in their way (it's not like she was a *mime*, she reasoned). She decided it was up to her to plead her case. It was the only thing that made sense.

She glanced at her watch as she turned into Colin's driveway.

It's too early. He won't be home from work yet.

But as she pulled up to the house, she spied Colin's car in the garage, which was partially open. She lightly knocked on the front door, suddenly half-hoping he had carpooled to work. After a few seconds, she turned back to her car when the door opened, revealing Colin in his bathrobe, clutching a box of tissues and what Sarah assumed was a mug of tea.

"Oh hi," he mouth-breathed. "I'm sick."

"Wow, yes you are. We need to talk. Are you up to it?"

Colin sighed, then coughed, a deep, wet cough that made Sarah wince. "I might be dead in an hour. Sure." He stepped aside to let Sarah enter.

"How very Jewish of you. I appreciate it," Sarah said.

The air was moist from the industrial-grade humidifier running in the living room, and a few tissues dotted the floor, as if Colin wasn't sure he'd make it back from the front door and had left the tissues to mark the trail. Sarah felt the urge to smooth his hair and make him some chicken soup.

"Have a seat," Colin said. "Would you like some tea?" He sniffed and then sneezed into a tissue.

"No, no. I'm fine. You sit."

Colin put down his tea and crumpled onto the couch. He looked at her, his head hung low, and wiped his nose with the tissue still in his hand.

"So?" he said. "Learn any new tricks lately?"

"A few."

"Can you fix my cold?" He raised his eyebrows hopefully.

"I don't know how to do that, unfortunately." Sarah thought of her mother and shifted to the edge of her chair. "Have you had time to, you know, think? About all this?" She waved her hand vaguely.

"Tons. I still don't know *what* to think though."

"If it's any consolation, neither do I."

"It's like everything I thought I knew about the world just got chucked out the window. I mean, tiny dragons? Flying carrots? *Dave?* It's a lot." He cleared his throat.

"I get it. I mean, I thought I was this one person my whole life, and suddenly I'm another. It's a different kind of awkward."

"I would imagine."

"And I can levitate now. That's new."

"Cool. Cool. So, are we breaking up?" Colin pushed his hair back.

"I think the ball's in your court."

"Are you allowed to be with a regular person?"

"I can be with a regular person, not that I consider you regular. You just have to decide if you want to be with a Magycian."

"Better than a mime."

"That's what I thought!"

Colin sat up and shoved the tissues in his pocket. He picked up the mug from the side table and held it in both hands. "Does this change how you feel about me? About us? I can't levitate, you know."

"That's the thing," Sarah said. "When you left my father's house a few weeks ago, I was devastated." She looked down at her feet. "I would give it all up for you, Colin, if I could. You're my Magyck. It doesn't work without you."

With much effort and not a little groaning, Colin got up from the couch and walked over to Sarah. Bending over slightly, he lifted her chin so she was looking up at him. "Good. I've missed you. You're my Magyck too. I'm not one hundred percent on this whole situation, but I will try to deal."

Sarah stood and hugged him. "I really want to kiss you right now."

"Me too. But probably not a good idea. This is some monster-level yuck. I think the dragon may have sneezed on me."

"I'll risk it." She raised herself on her tiptoes and kissed him lightly on the lips. He leaned in for another kiss, and she ducked. "Hey, I don't have a death wish here," she smiled.

"Great! I guess you guys are back together."

Madison appeared in the living room, her backpack still on her back. She wore a red flannel shirt tied around her waist and had a chain around her neck that featured a small, silver witch's hat.

"Yes, I guess we are," Colin said.

Madison dropped her bag and joined them in a group hug. "Excellent. I'm glad you came to your senses, Dad. I mean, Sarah couldn't help that woman being all crazy in the store and stuff."

"What woman?" Colin asked. "And when were you at the magic shop?"

"Last week. When I went into the city with Bethany and her mom."

"I didn't know you went…"

"Madison?" Sarah interrupted. "Can you give us a minute?"

"Oh, it's all right, Dad. I mean, it got really scary with those, like, magic lasers flying around, but Sarah, Raya, and Dave protected me."

"Protected you?" Colin said, releasing Sarah from his embrace.

"Totally. I hid behind a chair. That evil lady never saw me."

"Magic lasers? Sarah, what the hell is my daughter talking about?"

"Madison stopped by and there was a minor kerfuffle."

"With lasers."

"Technically, no."

Colin blew his nose again and wiped his forehead with the back of his hand. He glared at Sarah.

"There's this woman who wants to take my dad's store, but we won't let her. She got a little...snippy."

"Snippy?" Madison exclaimed. "She was shooting bolts of lightning from her hands and Raya was hitting them with a stick, and this lady shot one at Sarah and Sarah went flying, and then Raya put up this wall of light to protect them, but later she put Sarah in this invisible box, I think, but Sarah got out and...it was *so cool*!"

Colin paced the length of the living room several times, then stopped and covered his face with his hands. "I can't believe this."

"It's okay, Dad. Like I said, they protected me. I'm fine."

"It's not fine! You could have been killed!" He pulled a handful of tissues from the box. "Christ, Sarah, I was all right with the water glasses that refilled themselves and the disappearing cheese. Even flying I can deal with. But this? Putting my daughter at risk?" He started to pace again. "And now there's someone who wants to kill you?"

"She doesn't want to kill me. I think. She just wants the store."

"But it sounds like she was trying to go through you to get it!"

"Madison was in no danger, I promise. I didn't know all this was going to happen."

"You live in a world where people shoot lasers out of their hands! That's not normal!" Colin wobbled a bit, and Sarah tried to steady him. He pushed her away. "I knew this was a bad idea."

Sarah took a few steps back, no longer steady on her feet either. Colin glared at her, his cheeks flushed. He wiped some beads of sweat from his forehead. He opened his mouth to say more, but just plopped back onto the couch.

"I can't deal with this right now, Sarah. Just go."

"Colin, no. I promise..."

"Madison's safety was the red line. Your lifestyle put her in danger. We're done."

"My *lifestyle*?"

"Dad, it wasn't her fault!" Madison rushed to her father and sat next to him. "She was amazing. You don't want to do this."

"Madison, go to your room. We'll talk about your part in this later," Colin said quietly.

"Dad, I…"

"*Go.*"

Madison slowly got up from the couch and went to her room, stopping to hug Sarah on the way.

"I'm sorry," she whispered. "We made a promise to never keep anything from each other. I had to say something."

"It's all right. Everything will be all right."

Madison gave Sarah a sorrowful look before leaving the living room. Sarah knotted her hands in front of her, the worry and dread congealing her insides as she faced Colin. If only she knew how to fix this, what spell to cast, how to somehow touch the right strings and find that perfect energy to make this all better. She closed her eyes for a moment, searching for an answer, but came up empty. The strings were gone.

"I think you need to go now." Colin had lost his burst of energy and was back to looking sickly and defeated.

"Is there anything I can do?"

He turned away from her, the room going silent and cold. Sarah liked the shape of him, how wide his shoulders were, how strong his hands felt when he touched her. The memory thickened the cold in the room. Sarah picked up her purse, chancing a look back at him.

"Colin…"

"No."

Slowly she walked to the front door, each limb like wet cement. The tears built up behind her eyes.

"I'm sorry," Sarah said, swallowing hard. She had never cried in front of a man, and she wasn't going to start now.

She could barely see her keys by the time she got to her car. Fumbling, she struggled to start the engine. The street ahead of her was blurred as she wiped her face again and again, moving carefully into traffic. Street after street became the expressway, then the hazy red lights of cars in front of her. The numbness was a salve, distracting her from the tightness in her chest, making her almost miss the exit that would take her to her own neighborhood.

"Where's the spell for this?" she yelled, hitting the steering wheel.

She marched up the front porch of her house, entered, and made a beeline for her bedroom. Dropping her bag, she threw herself face-first onto her bed, like a toddler having a tantrum. She leaned over and pulled down the shade, then kicked off her boots and wrapped herself in her heavy, floral comforter. In the dim room, she cried until she felt dry, then drifted off into a fitful sleep, lasting the rest of the afternoon and the whole night, dreaming of bolts of energy, fallen flan, and the beautiful, sneering face of Zondra Bex.

CHAPTER
ELEVEN

The next morning Sarah woke up, opened her eyes, and found herself staring at Nadav's kind face, which presently was approximately three inches from her nose. She jumped about six inches to the left.

"*Bon matin*," he said. "Soup?"

In the sunlight, the sprinkling of grey in his short, black hair shone, and the lines around his eyes were crinkled with his gentle smile.

"What?"

"I brought you soup. We didn't hear from you yesterday and thought you might be feeling poorly. I heard Colin had a cold."

Sarah winced slightly at the mention of Colin's name. "Who's *we*?"

"Hey," Raya said, waving from her perch atop Sarah's dresser.

Sarah sat up, smoothed her hair, and coughed.

"Now that you mention it, my throat feels a bit sore."

"Did you talk to Colin?" Raya asked.

Sarah waved her off. "Later."

Nadav raised the bowl of soup. "Chicken matzo ball. Not made by a Jewish mother, but it has Magyckal properties nonetheless."

"Literally," Raya added.

Sarah sniffed and felt her nasal passages swelling. "Well, my mother never made me soup, so I have nothing to compare it to. Bottoms up." She gingerly took the bowl from Nadav and reached for the spoon in his other hand.

The soup was warm and rich, with peppery notes, and the carrot slices floated on the top like little orange lily pads. The matzo balls were fluffy and comforting, and as the broth coated her throat, she could feel the scratchiness fade away and her breathing become easier. Perhaps her symptoms were psychosomatic, but Sarah didn't care. She felt better, energetic almost, like the caffeine boost from a good cup of coffee.

"Wow, that's some good soup," Sarah said, finishing the last few drops. "The steam really cleared me up."

"No, you're actually healthier. Dad worked some Magyck on it," Raya said. "He can do some light healing. Nothing major, just things like colds and the errant scraped knee and such."

"It's a gift," Nadav added. "Although the matzo balls are from a mix."

He took the bowl and spoon from Sarah and placed them on a tray on her nightstand. With a wave, the tray disappeared and was replaced by a cup of tea.

"Now that you're on the mend," Raya said, jumping down from her seat on the dresser, "can I ask why you're still dressed?"

Sarah looked down at her clothes, sighed, and took a sip of the tea. Raya and Nadav waited, their expressions neutral.

"Sweetener?" she asked.

Nadav pulled a small, tan packet from his vest pocket. Sarah tore it open and emptied the contents into her teacup, stirring the contents slowly and deliberately.

"Any time now," Raya said.

"Why don't I go to the kitchen and give you two a chance to chat?" Nadav said. "I'll straighten up a bit in there too, if you don't mind. I don't understand your organizational system and it's making me a little tense."

After he left, Raya sat at the foot of the bed.

"So?" she said.

Sarah pulled off her jacket with great effort and fell back onto her pillows. "Everything sucks. Colin dumped me."

"Bastard. He needs to ovary-up. You want me to turn him into a lemming or something?"

"No, no, it wasn't that. I think he was okay with the Magyck. But when he found out Madison was in the store during Zondra's visit, he lost it. I don't blame him. She's his child."

"But that wasn't your fault. You didn't do it deliberately."

"I know. But it was his 'red line.' I get it." Sarah closed her eyes. "Did you know that I'm tired all the time? Seriously. And I have the strangest dreams. Like, really vivid, intense dreams with smells and sounds and everything, and I remember every detail. I spend half my time feeling like I'm walking through water and the other half very aware that I know things other people don't, and it makes me very anxious. I mean, like, 'Go postal on the barista' anxious."

"That's natural," Raya said, patting Sarah's leg. "You've had a lot thrown at you recently."

"And I don't have the hand-eye coordination to catch any of it."

"It takes time." Raya put her hand on Sarah's forehead. "You feel a little chilled. You want a blanket?"

"I want my old life back."

"How about another pillow? Maybe a cookie?"

"I'm not kidding." Sarah got out of bed. "I don't want to do this anymore. I want to go back to being the Sarah who didn't know anything."

"Sarah—"

"Seriously, can't you or your father or Esra do something? Say a spell or touch the right bands or something? Take this stuff away from me? My dad won't do it. He's so happy I'm actually Magyck, he's absolutely *kvelling*. He's never *kvelled* before. At least about me." Sarah was pacing, taking off her sweater and scarf and dropping them on the floor. Raya followed her, picking up the items and handing them back to her, which Sarah dropped again.

"You just need some more training. You're doing very well, really. It's coming very easily for you," Raya said, handing her the scarf for the third time.

"But I don't want it to come easily. I don't want it at all!" Sarah threw her sweater across the room, which Raya caught with a wave of her hand and deposited gently on the back of a chair. She gathered Sarah in a hug, but her friend immediately pulled away.

"I'm serious. I'm done. Done." Sarah started to cry. "Done."

When Raya hugged her again, Sarah didn't pull away. She waited until Sarah's breath normalized, holding her tight. Sarah, for the first time in a while, felt safe, like when her mother would sing her nursery rhymes when she was small. But instead of her mother's perfume, she could smell the scent her oldest and dearest friend had worn in her hair since they were children: lemon, vanilla, and something faintly warm and herbal. Her mind flashed back to them playing marbles, which Raya always won, and trying to learn the elaborate card games Nadav and Esra played. Now she understood that there were elements of Magyck in those games. How could she not have seen it then? What did Esra say? *People see what they want to see.* But she hadn't. She couldn't.

But she did now.

Raya looked at Sarah, her amber eyes peering deeply into her friend's muddy hazel. Sarah felt a soft cloud enter her mind, calming the storm and easing the anguish. She took several deep breaths and felt the tension in her back ease.

"Are you okay?" Raya said softly.

"I just don't—"

"Shh. I know. But you're in it now, sister," Raya said. "You're going to have to deal."

"How are we doing in here?" Nadav stood in the bedroom doorway, teapot in his hands. "I made more tea. This one came in a box with a bear on it. I thought that was encouraging."

"Dad, you do know that you don't work here, right?" Raya said.

"I make myself at home wherever I am," he replied. "So, tea? Yes? No?"

"I'm good," Sarah said. "Raya?"

"No thanks. I do not find the bear encouraging."

"Alrighty then," Nadav said, making the teapot disappear.

"So you two, what do you suggest I do now?" Sarah said. "I'm kind of at a loss here."

"Esra thinks you should go to the library," Nadav said. "He said there would be some helpful information for you there."

"Really?" Sarah said. "The library? Now?"

"The books he's thinking of will be very helpful. Go to the fifth floor and look for a custodian in a pea-green jumpsuit. Goes by 'Larry.' He'll help you."

"But the library only has four floors," Sarah replied.

Raya raised her eyebrows and lowered her chin.

"Ohh," Sarah said. "Gotcha."

"Find Larry. He knows those bookshelves better than anyone." Nadav checked his pocket watch. "All right, I'm off. I have some errands to do before I open the pub. Will you stop by for lunch?" He kissed his daughter on the cheek and pinched Sarah's chin. "I'll make something special."

"Something to make me younger? Taller? Maybe something to make me into a superhero?" Sarah said.

"Oh no," Nadav laughed. "I can't do that. Well, not *anymore*." He waved them off. "Never mind. I'll make gumbo." He chuckled to himself as he left.

"He does make good gumbo," Raya said. "Studied with Paul Prudhomme."

"When did he...never mind."

"I'll make us some coffee while you get showered and changed. Then we'll go. I have a class at two, but we should have plenty of time."

"That's fine. I have some writing to do."

"Perfect. Go."

"Okay." Sarah grabbed the robe that was draped over the foot of her bed. She turned toward the bathroom and then stopped. "Larry?"

"That's what he said. Go shower."

"Those books aren't going to bite us or anything, are they?" Sarah asked. "Or sprout legs and run away?"

"Oh no, no." Raya paused for a second. "Probably no."

Sarah let out a growl as she went into the bathroom. She hoped she could find her library card, but then she decided the people on the heretofore unknown fifth floor wouldn't care.

CHAPTER
TWELVE

B y the time Sarah showered and dressed, Raya was halfway through her second cup of coffee and sitting on the couch, drawing words in the air with her finger. The silver letters hung in perfectly formed lines, glowing in a neat, flowing script. Raya noticed Sarah and made an upward sweep with her arm, erasing the writing.

"What are you doing?" Sarah asked.

"Sending a text," Raya replied. "There's some coffee left if you want to take some with us. I've arranged for a ride to take us to the library."

"I could drive. We don't need an Uber."

"Oh, it's not an Uber. Really not."

Sarah didn't have it in her to argue. They went outside and waited on the driver. The air was still crisp, not terribly cold, and the morning dew had evaporated from the leaves that were blushed with orange and red and falling at a rapid rate. Sarah shivered a little. She adjusted her bag and shifted her weight from foot to foot, again and again, until Raya had to put her hands on Sarah's shoulders to get her to stop. Raya went back to her silent watch, standing tall and still, her braids piled neatly on her head in a large bun. She wore a turquoise and purple bead necklace over a dark grey, scoop neck T-shirt and a fleece-lined denim jacket. Her large hoop earrings glinted in the sun, and she had several rows of bracelets stacked on her right arm. People paid stylists thousands of dollars to look this effortlessly chic—for Raya it was just another thrown-together outfit. She squinted slightly and put her hand up to shield her eyes.

"There they are," Raya said, pointing to a car about two blocks down the street.

"They?"

"Slenn uses the pronouns they and them. Just FYI," Raya said.

"Understood. Thanks."

Sarah turned her attention back to the oncoming car. She could barely make out its shape, catching a glint or two off the front headlights. As it moved closer, she could make out thin tires and a large grill. The headlights themselves looked like lanterns, and Sarah could see a hand crank by the hood.

"Is that a—"

The car made a loud "AaaOOOgah!" as it pulled up in front of Sarah's house.

"—Model T?" Sarah finished.

"1928 Ford Model A Tudor Sedan, actually." The driver got out of the car and walked around the front. They pushed up the sleeves of their green leather jacket. "But just to you. To everyone else, it's a Toyota Prius. Disguise spell." They waved and smiled broadly. "Hiya, I'm Slenn."

Slenn opened the passenger door, and Raya and Sarah climbed into the back seat. The fabric on the seats looked brand new, despite the apparent age of the car.

"It smells like cupcakes," Sarah said. "Did you just come from the bakery?"

"Nope. Gotta love that new car smell, right?" Slenn closed the door behind them.

"Slenn is an old friend of mine. We went to university together, until they dropped out to do some travelling." Raya nodded at her friend as they walked to the driver's side door.

Slenn slid into the driver's seat, draped an arm over the seat back, and ran their hand through their short, rainbow-colored hair, knocking their thick-lensed, black frame glasses slightly askew. "Yeah, I had the wanderlust, I guess. But it's nice to be home."

"Do you work for a taxi company or limo service?" Sarah asked.

"Neither," Slenn replied, playing with the rings on their right hand. "I just work within the Magyckal community, helping out here and there. It pays the bills." Slenn took off their glasses and wiped them with a handkerchief.

"Slenn's an artist," Raya said.

"Yup. I work mostly in animated metals and ultra-dense sentient oil paint. It's cool, but those materials do tend to argue about the artistic vision. Kind of like making art by committee except you're by yourself." Slenn grinned. "Oh, I hope you don't mind. I brought my support animal with me." Slenn pointed to the back of the car, where a small, teal green dragon in a little orange vest sat by the rear windshield.

"He looks like Albert," Sarah said, remembering her nephew's renegade flying lizard.

"That's Alvin. They're probably from the same clutch," Slenn said, holding up one black nail-polished finger. "Okay, where did you say we were headed today?"

"The library," Raya said. "Ours."

"Oh, you going to see Larry?" Slenn said. "Tell him I said hi and that he still owes me a fire scotch."

"What's a fire scotch?" Sarah whispered.

"It's a regular scotch," Raya said, "But you set it on fire and drink it while suspended upside-down in midair. It's an acquired taste."

"All right, belt yourselves in!" Slenn said.

Sarah looked at the bench seat but saw no seat belts. "How do we…?"

Slenn waved their hand, and two hot pink straps appeared over Sarah and Raya's shoulders and laps, clicking into the seat. "Safety first!" Slenn pulled away from the curb, narrowly missing a blue Volkswagen with a dent in its front bumper.

Slenn drove a little faster than Sarah was comfortable with, but they were obviously adventurous and adept behind the wheel. After a few gasps and inadvertent ducking, Sarah got her "sea legs" and settled in for the ride. Alvin, the mini-dragon, made a little "eep" sound whenever

Slenn levitated the car over the potholes in the road, and an "urp" sound whenever they hit them and he banged his little head on the roof of the car. Eventually, he flew to the back of Slenn's seat and settled on their shoulder, although Sarah noticed his talons dig pretty deep into Slenn's jacket. Down the city streets they flew, sometimes literally, weaving in and out of traffic like a downhill ski slalom.

"Shortcut!" Slenn announced, making a sharp turn into a narrow alley.

"We can't possibly fit!" Sarah shouted.

"We're good!" Slenn hit a yellow button on the dashboard, and Sarah felt the air around her condense until she could barely breathe. The bricks of the buildings on either side of them looked distorted and full of static. Just when she thought she might be squeezed into oblivion, they came to the end of the alley, took a sharp left, and the original dimensions of the car were restored. Sarah caught a glimpse of herself into the side mirror; she felt positively green around the gills.

Raya put her hand on Sarah's arm. "Freaky, right?" She pulled a wrapped candy out of her pocket. "Here. It will make you feel better." She unwrapped it and popped it in Sarah's mouth. It tasted like root beer. "Better?"

Sarah nodded.

Finally, the world outside the car windows came back into focus, and Sarah saw that they had all made it to the library in one piece. Taking a deep breath and grabbing her bag, which was now wedged under her seat, she looked to Raya to open the door so they could exit. Raya, however, sat still and quiet.

"Raya? We're here," Slenn announced, perhaps a bit more loudly than was necessary. Sarah winced. "Sorry. Shifting into dimensional overdrive sometimes clogs my ears. Hold on." They pinched their nose and blew out, then shook their head. "There we go. Helllooo?" they said in a normal volume, waving their hand at Raya.

"What?" Raya said with a start. "Oh, sorry. Lost in thought."

"About what?" Sarah asked.

"Condensed matter physics, mostly. And a little bit about solid-state intelligence. Also, marshmallows." Raya smiled. "You ready?"

Raya opened the door, holding it while Sarah slid down the large bench seat. Raya signaled for Slenn to open the passenger window, then leaned in.

"Thanks, Slenn. We appreciate the ride. Just put it on my tab. See you later for a pickup?"

"Whatever you need, friend. Just send me a text, and I'll be here. I think I'm going to take Alvin to the vet now. He looks a little peaked."

The mini-dragon burped a puff of glittery smoke and looked at Slenn through lowered eyes. They patted Alvin on the head and gave him a small, brown, lumpy treat.

"See ya!" Slenn gunned the engine and took off like a shot. Poor Alvin practically hit the back windshield before presumably alighting back on the passenger seat headrest.

"Poor little guy," Sarah said. "He's going to need his *own* emotional support dragon." She looked around at the parking lot, which was deserted. "Is the library even open yet?"

"No. Doesn't matter though." Raya walked to a spot next to the main doors. She ran her hand over the exposed brick on the left side. "Where is it, where is it...there!" She made a fist with her right hand, then quickly opened her fingers, splaying them about a half-inch from the wall. Sarah saw a yellow energy stream emanate from Raya's palm, and the outline of a door began to emerge. When it had fully materialized, Raya pulled it open and stepped inside. Sarah hesitated.

"Come in, Sarah. It's okay."

Sarah stepped over the threshold of the newly revealed door, watching the floor, then the door, which disappeared behind them. She followed Raya down a long, gold corridor lined with triangular windows, from which she could see the main floor of the library. She ran her fingers over the etchings in the wall, intricate lines creating flowers, trees, and large bear-like creatures with even larger wings. The walls were so highly polished she could see her face reflected in them.

Raya stopped midway down the hall in front of what looked like elevator doors. She tapped her finger on the rosewood trim, and the doors opened with a quiet hiss. Stepping into an empty space, she motioned for Sarah to follow her, but Sarah felt glued to the floor.

"Is there anything actually supporting you? Or are we supposed to float upstairs?" Sarah said.

Raya tapped the invisible wall next to her, which sounded like someone clinking a spoon on a crystal goblet. "It's ultra-clear glass. It's safe. Get on."

Sarah took a small step into the elevator, gingerly placing a toe on the ornate carpet.

"Oh, for Pete's sake," Raya said, pulling Sarah by the arm.

Raya got them to the fifth floor by placing her palm on the gold plate where the floor numbers would usually be. The ride up was quiet and smooth, and Sarah was gladdened by the lack of elevator music.

The doors opened, and they stepped into the oldest-looking room Sarah had ever seen. It wasn't dingy or dusty, but there were countless books on enormous shelves made of wood so ancient-looking, they looked like they could have had roots. The floor was covered in an expansive rug, worn slightly here and there, but the pattern was still sharp and vibrant. Iron and crystal chandeliers hung in rows from the ceiling, emitting light that was less electric in intensity and more like a soft, warm, candle-like glow. It even smelled old, but pleasantly so, with notes of wool and vanilla and apple, much like the pipe tobacco Sarah's grandfather used to smoke. And the books—so many books of varying sizes, some with gold lettering on the spine, some embossed with silver, but all of them coming together to produce that wonderful book smell that she always found so enticing and at times wished she could bottle. She inhaled deeply.

Raya took a few steps forward, looking down the first row of bookshelves. She scanned the room carefully, taking in the layout and nodding when she found it to be all in what Sarah presumed was its usual place.

"Let's find Larry," Raya said. "He should be around here somewhere."

"Well, well, well," said a voice behind them. "I step away to get some coffee, and I come back to visitors."

The women turned to find a middle-aged man in a dark green jumpsuit, the patch over the left breast pocket indicating that he was, indeed, "Larry." Sarah was startled. Not that his appearance was so odd —in fact, she thought he looked quite like her seventh grade social studies teacher. But given the apparent advanced age of her surroundings, she expected its caretaker to be similarly antiquated.

"Nadav let me know you'd be coming," Larry said. "I was glad to hear it. Don't get a lot of visitors these days. Old people think they already know everything, and young people prefer to get their information zlonlyne."

"You mean online?" Sarah said.

"No, zlonlyne," Raya said. "Magyckal internet. It's a thing."

Sarah opened her mouth to question further, but Larry cut her off.

"You'll probably be wanting the recent history section, given your family background," he said.

"Well, we need to go back to at least 1850," Sarah said. "Not that recent."

"Matter of perspective," Larry said. "Anyway, the Greenbergs have had that property for a long time, and it's quite valuable as I'm sure you know. There should be a fair amount of info just over here." He motioned for them to follow him, like a Magyckal sherpa, his mop trailing behind him. Sarah noticed he wasn't actually holding the handle —rather, it was following him like a devoted puppy.

They walked down the main aisle and turned left twice, landing in a section that felt slightly newer than the others, with the bookshelves less worn and the smell more apple-y than old book-y. The books looked newer as well, their spines straight like little soldiers and the silver embossing bright and shiny. Sarah felt the urge to run her fingers over them, and as her hand got closer she felt a faint hum of energy from the leather covers, and she drew back her hand in mild surprise.

"All right, the volumes you want would be here through…here." Larry ran his hand down a section on the third shelf from the top, indicating a set of tall, blue leather volumes. The books slid themselves off the shelf, and Raya and Sarah did their best to catch them. "And maybe this one." Larry tapped another one, which flew in a straight line, rose about two feet, then landed gently on top of the stack in Raya's arms. "There's some tables over there, make yourselves comfortable. Leave the books there when you're done. They'll re-shelve themselves when they're ready." He touched the brim of an imaginary hat, which suddenly materialized under his fingers, then disappeared when he put his hand down. "If you need me, I'll be around. Yell loud though. I've got to polish some of the heart wood."

"Is that a euphemism?" Sarah whispered to Raya.

"Nope," Larry winked. "Real floor polisher."

Sarah blushed.

"Thanks, Larry," Raya said.

Larry smiled and turned to leave. Sarah looked down and saw that the mop was still hovering next to her.

"Um, Larry?" She nodded to the mop.

"Oh yeah. Here, Dusty." He whistled at the mop, which trotted back to his side, and he left the women to their research.

Sarah and Raya lugged the books over to the table and dropped them, producing a small cloud of dust and, Sarah thought, a faint "oof" sound.

"Okay." Raya pulled out one of the tall-backed chairs and positioned herself on the cushion. "Let's start with some background on the property. I'd love to try and find any loopholes in the contract."

"Shouldn't we wait until my dad calls a lawyer?"

"Yeah, I don't think he will. You know how he is. He's going to try to fix this himself."

"That's what I'm afraid of."

They settled in at the large table, arranging the old books by topic. Sarah pulled a large volume toward her, opened the thick cover, and began to flip through it, impressed by the ornate color drawings of natural scenes and portraits of long-dead Magycians and scholars. She knew a bit about the myth and mysticism of her culture but assumed it to be just that—stories and fables. But it was becoming clear to her that these legends were based in fact, including a chapter heading that confirmed what she already had come to believe. The main principle of Jewish Magyck, beginning in the medieval ages, at its core relied on the Powers of Good. There were those who deviated from Good, but they were the exceptions rather than the rule. In its beginning, the framework of Magyck existed within the laws of Judaism, which by its very nature disassociated itself with the Forces of the Dark.

Well, that's comforting.

She read on. As her father had said, Magyck was not some

supernatural force. It was generally believed that all things are imbued with Magyckal properties, and it was possible to access that energy from the specific to the general and back again by manipulating the energy inherent in not only living things but the natural elements all around them. A little more descriptive than "feel the strings," but it made sense. And it touched on some of the Eastern European fairy tales she had heard as a child. Not all Magycians were Jewish, of course—in fact, the majority weren't—and they lived in all parts of the world, but much of the history was entwined with them.

"Hey, listen to this," Raya said, pointing to a paragraph in her book. "There's an element of geology to the whole basis of Magyck. That's cool, I didn't know that."

"Yeah, I think I remember my father telling me something about that."

"Apparently different minerals are compatible or incompatible together, and they combine strength. You'd be able to tap into a whole different level of Magyck if you have the right rocks put together."

The Twelve Moonstones.

"What about the incompatibles? What happens if you put a couple of those together?" Sarah asked. "Do they explode or something?"

Raya laughed. "Oh, I'm sure they don't…whoops, nope, yeah they do," she said, running her finger to the next paragraph. "Noted."

"Which ones will explode?"

Raya held up her index finger and placed it to her lips.

"What was that?" Raya whispered. "Did you hear that?"

"What? No, I didn't hear anything. Maybe it was Larry…"

"Shh!" Raya held up her hand and cocked her head. "I hear a hum." She narrowed her eyes and reached for her bag.

They didn't have much time to react. The thugs from Zondra's entourage appeared at the end of the bookshelves and sent bolts of light over their heads. Raya and Sarah ducked under the table.

"Stay here!" Raya mouthed. She rolled backward, crawled to the shelf next to them, and returned fire, intense light emanating from her palm as she aimed at the men. Sarah looked at the floor and summoned the energy from the strings she found and widened them, causing them to vibrate with a bit more intensity. She carefully peeked around the table legs and caught the eye of the taller thug, who sent a bolt of light at her. Sarah shot up a window charm, deflecting the bolt, which the tall man dodged. Raya scurried back to their table and upended it to provide a barrier. She ran her hands down the middle of it, adding a coating of energy, which she said would act like a shield.

"Nice work deflecting that bolt," Raya said as they both flinched from an energy arrow that went over their heads.

"Is it wrong that I thought of the old saying, 'I'm rubber, you're glue?'"

"Whatever works, my friend," Raya said. "All right, we need to go on the offensive here. They are not messing around. But they seem like midlevel Magycians so far, nothing top-notch."

The room was eerily silent, with only thin streaks of light periodically whizzing past them.

"Let me distract the big one," Raya continued. "If I can get him under control, I'll come back and help you with the little guy."

"You sure you can do that?"

"You bet," Raya said, flexing her bicep. "Pilates." She pointed at the "little one," who Sarah estimated to be about six foot five and two hundred fifty pounds.

Raya chose her moment and leaned around the table. She set off a few flares of her own, which were met in kind, and Raya was nearly singed. Under different conditions, Sarah thought, she would find the lights pretty, if she didn't know they could vaporize her in a second.

As Raya shot back, like a sheriff in an Old West shoot-out, they suddenly heard "Barracuda" by Heart.

"What is that?" Raya said, dodging another bolt.

"Oh God, it's my phone!" Sarah said, frantically digging into her bag.

"You're going to answer it *now*?"

"Hello?" Sarah hissed into the phone.

"Hi Sarah. It's Colin. How are you?"

"Oh fine, fine, nothing exciting going on at all," Sarah replied, as Raya threw another barrier spell over their heads.

"Listen, I'd love to talk about what happened the other day."

"Yeah, that's great, me too."

"Are you okay? You sound distracted."

"No, I'm great," Sarah said, flinching as an energy bolt hit the table's barrier and crackled like a small firecracker. "Raya and I are at the library."

"Tell her I said hi," Colin said.

"Colin says hi."

"Hi Colin!" Raya shot out a blue beam that knocked the smaller man backward over a chair.

"Listen, I'd like to talk more, but I can't now. You know how libraries are about noise. Can I call you later?"

"Sure. Hey, can I tell you about something Madison said real quick?"

"Colin, really. Later, please?"

"Well, I..."

"Great, thanks, you're a doll, byeee!" Sarah threw the phone back in her bag. "Sorry."

"No, that's fine, I'm glad you two are talking again. That's *super* important right now." She raised her eyebrows. "Okay, I'm going to go over there..." Raya pointed to a spot about ten feet away. "...and try to separate those guys. Unless you're expecting another call."

Raya ran over to the other table, stood up, and waved at the thugs.

"Whoo-hoo! Hello! Over here!"

The bigger man followed Raya, crouched like a panther about to attack. The other assailant was conspicuously silent; he hadn't sent out any bolts since Raya moved. Sarah thought maybe he had been hurt and took a chance by peeking out from behind her table.

"Ding, dong," a deep voice said.

Sarah looked up and into the craggy face of the smaller thug. He raised his hand to shoot, and Sarah instinctively threw out a shield charm. Taken aback, the man stumbled backward as he absorbed the force of the light. Sarah took the opportunity to scramble away from the table, finding a safe spot behind a display case of taxidermied lizards. Doing her best to remember her lessons, she focused her energies, threw out another shield, and shot a beam from her hand. She missed the man by a couple of feet, but both of them looked stunned. She stared at her hand as if it were a foreign entity, then tried again. This next shot was closer, but the man was more prepared this time and easily sidestepped it, quickly returning fire. Sarah realized she could visualize what he was going to do and anticipate where the beams would land. She made herself as small as possible, and the shield absorbed the bolts.

"Sarah! Stay there!" Raya shouted from the other table.

"No worries! I'm not going anywhere," Sarah called back, flinching and crouching in place. "I need my wand! My energy is all over the place! It's in my bag right there! Just throw it!"

A white stick, about five inches in length, came sailing over the lizard case. It landed on the floor and rolled a bit, and Sarah reached to pick it up.

"Thank you, this will do just…a tampon? You threw me a tampon?"

"It's the first thing I grabbed! It's fine. Just use it."

Sarah gripped the tampon in her left hand and channeled her energy, touching on the strings she saw in her mind's eye as the strongest and most vibrant. She didn't sense any incoming hits, so she gingerly peeked over the top of the display case and aimed the energy at the craggy Magycian.

"Nice hit!" Raya performed a forward roll that got her from the far table and next to Sarah behind the glass case. She placed herself into a crouch. "He's down." Raya held a foot-long, black, wooden baton in her hand. She tugged on the ends, extending it into a five-foot staff. "If you can keep doing that, I'll be able to get us out of here."

"The tampon is a little singed," Sarah looked at the wrapper. "Super Plus. I'll say." She shuddered slightly and took a deep breath. She knew she should feel nervous, scared even, but the adrenaline must have kicked in because she had begun to feel unusually calm and confident. "Let's end this."

"You sound like a badass. Good for you." Raya patted her on the shoulder. "Now stay behind me and slightly to my right. Don't get hit by the staff. Things are going to move fast."

Sarah widened her eyes and took another deep breath. "Ready."

As Raya stood up, she began to spin the staff so quickly it was immediately a blur. Sarah kept her eyes on the two Magycians and prepared to deflect any shots of energy that might get past Raya's weapon. It wasn't necessary. Raya handled the weapon like an extension of her arm, moving it up and down, scooping underneath them, and then arcing it upward and bringing it down like a lever, ensuring that each light beam was deflected back at the enemy. She moved like a panther, practically weightless, and Sarah was so entranced by her movements she momentarily forgot about the two goons trying to kill them.

She snapped back to reality when an errant energy arrow streaked by her arm. She felt the heat graze her skin, and she gasped. Raya performed a somersault in front of her, and Sarah remembered to concentrate on the strings. They moved past her, and she touched on each one no matter their size or color, directing their energy, sending it out ahead of her, away from Raya, and more often than not, getting close to her target. Raya moved faster than before and spun, forcing Sarah to keep pace, sending out energy as fast as she could.

"Yes! That's it! Good!" Raya sounded like she was calling from a great distance. Time slowed, and she could see each rotation of Raya's staff, each beam of light from her own hand inching away from her. Sarah gathered her strength inside of her solar plexus, and with both hands up, sent a wave of energy from her whole body, slamming into both thugs and suspending them about a foot off the ground.

Sarah gasped for air and fell to her knees. Looking up, she saw Raya standing over her, staff at her side, while Larry held the two men in a shimmering net.

"Well done, ladies!" Larry grinned at them. "Well done!"

"Thanks," Raya answered. "Where the hell you been?" She pulled a handkerchief from her back pocket and dabbed at her forehead.

"Sorry. I told you that I was using the floor polisher. It's really loud."

Larry looked around at the state of the room, loose sheets of paper covering the floor, books upended, and the large wooden table pockmarked with charred holes.

"Could be worse, I guess," he said. "How are the boys?" He pointed to the glass case with the lizards.

"The boys?" said Sarah, getting to her feet. "They're dead, Larry."

"Oh no! Tim...Barry..."

"They were dead already. Taxidermied. Right?"

Sarah looked down at the case housing the two lizards, who were now standing on their hind legs, one of them waving at her.

"Or not," Raya said.

"Could have used the help, guys," Sarah said to the lizards, who merely shrugged and went back to sitting on their branch.

"Who are these fellows?" Larry said, pointing to the men in the gold, shimmering net.

"Zondra's goons," Raya said. "Did she send you?" She pointed at one of them, but they both remained expressionless.

"This is insane," Sarah said. "I'm sure if we just sat down with her and explained the situation…"

"We're beyond a casual chat. She's out for blood. Let me show you what I saw in one of the books, before we were interrupted."

"I'm going to go take out the trash, if you don't mind," Larry said, picking up the rope attached to the net and dragging the men away.

Sarah and Raya climbed over the piles of books and papers and reset one of the overturned tables. Raya scanned the floor, picked up a large book, and placed it on the table. She thumbed through the pages until she found the information she was seeking.

"There," she said, pointing at a black-and-white photograph. "Chicago, 1855. Opening of Greenberg's Mercantile."

"I thought Old Benjamin opened it in 1850."

"That's when he arrived in Chicago. Took a while to acquire the property, it says, and even longer to get the store ready to open. But that's not important. Look at this. Anyone look familiar?"

Sarah peered at the grainy image. "That's Old Ben."

"Yes, it is. But look over here," Raya said, moving her finger over to the image of a woman standing in the back row behind several men in ceremonial robes.

"That looks like…it can't be. It must be her great-great-grandmother. The Bexs were probably at the opening, since they had contested the sale."

"It could be her ancestor, sure, but from what I've read today, I think it's actually—" She thumbed in the direction where Larry had disposed of the thugs.

"Zondra? No. Impossible." Sarah looked at Raya, her mouth agape.

"There have been stories of immortals in the myths. It's not common though," Raya said. "You give up a lot."

"I would imagine."

"You said your dad told you about the geological elements of Magyck."

"A little bit."

"There are twelve foundational stones that come together in various combinations to concentrate the energy we use." Raya flipped the book to another chapter. "While not exactly like the gemstones we commonly use as fine jewelry, they have similar properties and names. *Odem,* a ruby, *pitdah,* which is a kind of topaz, *bareket,* an emerald, *nofech, sapir, yahalom, leshem, shebo, ahlamah, tarshish, shoham,* and *yashfeh.* All have their individual uses, but put ones with the same energies together, which is hard to do, and you have the Moonstones. Very powerful, very coveted by certain individuals."

"The Twelve Moonstones. That's what Zondra wants."

"Yup. Looks like it."

"That's why she's trying so hard. You know, I saw Zondra wearing a very interesting green stone—"

Sarah's phone rang. She dashed over to her bag to retrieve it and answered it quickly.

"Hey, Sarah, it's Deb," her sister said before Sarah could issue a greeting. "Where are you?"

"Library. With Raya."

"You sound tired. You okay?"

"Had a bit of a run-in with a couple of Zondra's men. We're fine."

"You need to get to the store right away." Debra's voice sounded thin and reedy.

"Why? What's the matter?"

"Dad's missing."

CHAPTER
THIRTEEN

"Hold on!"

Slenn slammed a large, green button on the car's dashboard, and Sarah felt herself turn inside out, as if her body had disappeared and she was merely a collection of thoughts. Then she flipped back, taking up more space than before, feeling like a beluga whale being squeezed through a keyhole. The blur in the driver's seat gripped the steering wheel as they flew.

Then, just as suddenly as they had started, the car flipped again, and they were in a parking lot on Clark Street. Sarah let out a breath that sounded like she was being punched in the stomach. She looked out the window and realized they weren't at the store yet.

"Why'd we stop?" Sarah said.

"Let's say we hit an interdimensional construction zone." Slenn adjusted a couple of levers next to the steering wheel. "Sorry. We'll have to drive standard for the rest of the way."

"I know a short cut," Raya said, pointing to another alley.

"We can't go there," Sarah countered. "It's all alleys and stairs."

"On it," Slenn said.

Slenn sped out of the parking lot, veered right, and headed for the top of a cement staircase. Sarah braced for a bumpy ride, but it was like riding a sled. She looked around to see if anyone noticed them, but per usual, if the Chicago drivers and pedestrians did notice, they just didn't care. They landed at the bottom of the stairs, turned left, and got back on their route.

"You levitated the car, didn't you?" Sarah said.

"Yerp. I need to replace the shocks on this old thing. If I didn't levitate, I'd be scraping you two off the awnings of that building."

"Thank you," Raya said.

"No prob," Slenn said. "Can I do anything to help? Send out the Bat Signal or something? I have people who know people. We can find Mr. Greenberg."

"We think we know who's behind this, but I appreciate it," Sarah said.

"Boy, if I ever see those two guys who attacked you, they won't know what hit 'em." Slenn propped their foot on the dashboard as they took another sharp turn, their lime-green Doc Marten leaving an imprint by the speedometer. "Why did they try to hurt you?"

"Retail dispute," Raya said.

"Ever heard of Zondra Bex?" Sarah grasped the handle by her seat to avoid toppling over onto Raya as Slenn changed lanes.

"Oh yeah. Bad news. Watch out for her. She got sued by some group for illegal surveillance and some shady business dealings. But the whole thing just went away. Very suspicious. Well, here we are!"

Slenn pulled up in front of the store. Sarah's stomach took a moment to catch up with her, and she swallowed hard.

Slenn turned in their seat to look at them. "Hey, if you need anything, you contact me, okay? I'm good at healing spells, and my Krav Maga teacher says I'm about six lessons away from being somewhat intimidating."

"Thanks, Slenn. We'll keep you posted." Sarah looked around the cab. "Hey, where's Alvin?"

"Spa day. His nerves were shot."

"I know the feeling."

Raya opened the door and got out, holding it open for Sarah. She waved at Slenn, who nodded and drove off, a cloud of yellow smoke enveloping the back end of the car.

They entered the store to find Esra, Nadav, and Debra huddled around the cash register.

"Oh good, you're here." Debra rushed to her sister and embraced her.

"What's going on?" Raya said.

"I came by to drop off some leftover meatloaf for Daddy. The store was empty, but his hat and coat were slung over the chair and the register was still open. And there was this note." Debra handed Sarah a scrap of paper.

"*Mazzikin*," Sarah read her father's uneven scrawl. "I don't understand."

"Demons," Esra said. "Avi did not leave on his own accord."

Sarah's hand covered her mouth as she gave a small gasp.

"There, there." Esra patted her arm. "I am sure he is all right. He is a powerful Magycian, and he is worth more to Zondra alive."

"You think this is her doing, Uncle?" Raya asked.

"It has to be. The *mazzikin* were banished from this world a long time ago. They would not be here without a little help."

"Someone opened a door for them, that's for sure," Nadav agreed.

"Isn't Dave a demon?" Sarah asked. "Wait, where is Dave?" She looked around the store for their blue friend.

"Yeah, I am, but not that kind," said a voice from above. "Um, a little help here, please?"

There was a large, gold cage hanging from the ceiling. Inside it, Dave was suspended upside-down, hanging from his ankles with a golden rope.

Esra raised his hand and slowly lowered the cage to the ground. With a flick of his fingers, he undid the ropes and opened the lock with a small spark.

"Thanks," Dave said. "I just now got the gag off my mouth. Bit clean through the damn thing. That was something else, I'll tell you."

"Are you okay?" Debra spun Dave around and inspected him like one of her children. "Oh no!"

"What?" Dave looked behind him, then down. "Well, shoot. I was afraid that had happened." He turned around to show the others. "They got my tail."

"Who did?" Sarah asked.

"The demons who came for your father. He's okay. They didn't hurt him. They came into the store and ambushed him. He got off a few defense spells and knocked two of them on their asses. Sent a few bolts their way too. I tried to help, but one of them sucker punched me and shoved me in that cage. It's a barrier, you know. Once you're in there you're without power." Dave growled. "It was that woman. I know it."

"We figured it was Zondra," Raya replied. "Are you in pain? Is there someone you can see about your tail? I can call Slenn…"

"No need." Dave placed his thumb in his mouth. "Hold on a sec."

He put his lips around his thumb and began to bear down. Within seconds, a new tail appeared in a puff of shimmering blue smoke. Sarah's eyes widened in surprise, until a noxious smell overcame them a few seconds later.

"Whoo, Dave, give us some warning, would ya?" Raya waved her hand in front of her face.

"Sorry. That happens sometimes." Dave grinned, showing all four rows of teeth. "Must have been the flan." He hopped onto the stool next to the front display case.

"So we have to go get him, right?" Sarah's voice was high-pitched and reedy. "Why are we standing around? Let's go!"

Sarah felt a hand on her shoulder. "Not yet, *Sheifale*. We have some planning to do."

She turned to Esra, his face calm and smooth. He had just called her a "lamb," which she usually liked, but now she felt irritated, his light touch feeling like a vise.

"What do you mean not yet? It's my father. Your friend. We have to go get him!"

"That would be unwise," Esra replied. "First of all, we do not yet know exactly where he is. Secondly, Zondra is counting on you to rush blindly to his rescue."

Esra took some stones from his pocket and shook them like dice. He opened his hand and examined the gleaming pieces in his palm. At first, they appeared to be lighting up in a random pattern, but as Sarah looked at them, she heard them produce faint tones. It was *music*. Esra stared at them, his brow furrowed over his round, dark glasses. He grunted and placed the stones back in his pocket.

"If you will excuse me, I need to check on a few things." He straightened his hat and left the store without another word.

"Is that it?" Sarah threw up her hands in exasperation. "He has to check on a few things? What, did he leave the oven on?"

The front door chimes rang, and Colin peeked his head through the door.

"Oh good, you guys are here," he said, entering the store. "Debra left me a message, but she didn't say where to go. Oh hi, Deb."

"Sorry," Debra said. "Mom brain."

Colin walked over to Sarah and gathered her in his arms. "It will be all right. "

"You're speaking to me now?"

"I was being an idiot."

"I won't argue. But I understand." She looked up at him. "How do you know it will be all right? You have no idea what we're dealing with." She sighed. "Neither do I, for that matter."

"I just have the feeling that everyone in this room is worthy of your trust," Colin said, meeting the eyes of the others.

"Hey thanks, man," Dave said, jumping up and punching Colin on the arm. "I think you're pretty cool yourself." He looked around. "Anyone want a sandwich?"

When no one responded, Dave shrugged and went to the back room.

"Esra will be back. He knows what to do. He will not let anything happen to Avi," Nadav said reassuringly.

"How do you know? He's a good Magycian, but Zondra is not kidding around." Sarah disengaged from Colin's arms and began to pace. "She wants this store, and she's not going to let anyone get in her way."

"Everyone has something they want and something they're willing to settle for," Nadav said. "And Esra is special. You know he's my adoptive brother, yes?" He cleared his throat. "He found me. He saved my life."

"I didn't know that, Papa," Raya said.

"Oh yes," Nadav replied. "I was very small, maybe six or seven. I wanted to play with some older boys. My mother didn't like them, said they were up to no good. But one day I couldn't resist their allure. I followed them to an abandoned lot just a few blocks from my house. They didn't know I was there. They were shooting bows and arrows at paper targets, but then one of them decided that wasn't exciting enough. He started aiming at squirrels, birds, whatever was small, alive, and moving. I inched in closer to get a better look, and apparently I sounded like a little animal, because when I looked down there was an arrow squarely in my chest."

"I never heard about this! *Mon dieu!*" Raya gasped.

"Yes," Nadav continued. "The older boys saw what happened and ran away, fearful of getting into trouble. I lay on the ground, and every breath was agony. But all I worried about was missing the apple tart Mother had made for dessert that night." He chuckled. "The things children think about."

"Then what happened? How did you survive?" Sarah asked.

"Esra." Nadav leaned on a table and crossed his legs. "I felt a presence about me. I opened my eyes and looked into the wide, kind face of a child with the greenest eyes I had ever seen. He didn't appear to be much older than me, but his hands worked quickly and expertly over my wound. He placed three stones over my heart. I could feel the warmth penetrate my body, and after a minute I felt brand new. He saved my life. He said he didn't have any family, so I brought him home. He has been my brother ever since. It was *beshert*, as you might say. Meant to be."

"Where did he come from?" Colin asked.

"He never said. And I never asked." Nadav looked levelly at Sarah. "Esra is a different kind of Magyck. He will help us."

"Do you want something to drink, Papa?" Raya looked concerned. "You look tired."

"No, I'm just thinking." Nadav smiled at his daughter. "Zondra is a formidable opponent. She may not be who she seems. We must approach fully armed."

Raya grabbed a weapon and stood at the ready.

"Put down the sword, Raya. It was just a figure of speech." Nadav wagged his finger at his daughter.

"Fine." Raya sighed and placed the large, curved sword back on the wall where it had been hanging as a display.

"I don't know if this is relevant," Sarah said. "But when Raya and I were at the library, we found a book that had a photo from the day Old Benjamin opened the store. I didn't get a good look at it before we were..." She looked furtively at Raya. "Interrupted. I know it sounds crazy, but there was a woman in the picture who looked a hell of a lot like Zondra. Great-grandmother, I hope?"

"No, it was not a relative. It was she."

Everyone turned to Esra, who had returned to the store unnoticed. He held a long staff, similar to the one Raya used, but with gold tips on each end. Even with his short stature and round physique, he looked quite formidable.

"The stones reacted strangely when I asked them a question a few minutes ago," Esra said. "That music you heard, Sarah? It was about her."

Sarah hadn't realized she was the only other person who had heard the music.

"I had to consult...some books. And things." Esra ran his hand over the staff, which then shrunk to the size of a pencil. He placed it in the front pocket of his jacket. "However, I do not know if she used time travel or if she is...long-lived, shall we say." He started to walk to the back of the store and motioned for the others to follow. "Let us make ourselves comfortable. Raya, you and Sarah go in the back room and... grab some supplies. The rest of us will stay here and make some plans," he nodded. "Everyone, please sit."

The group arranged themselves on the couch and overstuffed velour chairs.

Dave opened the back room door with a flourish.

"I made nachos!" he exclaimed, holding up a large tray.

"How nice." Esra waved him over. He nodded at Raya, who guided Sarah to the back room, taking the door from Dave, who had been holding it open with his tail. They turned to look at the others, and stood in the doorway. Nadav materialized a teapot and cups on the coffee table, pushing aside some books. Esra gestured to Colin, who was still standing in the middle of the store, looking lost.

"Come, Colin, sit with us. I am sure you will be of great assistance."

Colin joined them, sitting on the arm of the couch.

"What is it that you do, Colin?" Nadav poured milk into his tea.

"Accountant. Cost accountant, specifically. I'm responsible for examining every expense associated with a company's supply chain to conduct a profitability analysis and budget preparation."

Colin was met with blank stares. Dave coughed and shoveled some nachos in his mouth, crunching loudly.

"Yes," Esra said. "Indeed. Well, you look strong. Perhaps you can... hold things." He nodded at Raya, and she and Sarah stepped into the back room and closed the door behind them.

Sarah felt her hands grow numb. This was happening quite fast, and it was putting her new skills to the test much sooner than she ever could have expected. The knot in her stomach tightened, and a growing sense of foreboding felt like a weight on her shoulders, dragging her down. This is not what she had planned for the day. She had a column due. Her editor would be pissed.

But Colin's here. Thank goodness. But if he thought it was weird before...

She felt a smile play about her lips. He could have been done with her, could have easily walked away, writing her off as an oddity. And he had been mad, but it was more about his daughter's safety than anything else, and rightly so. Did Madison say something to change his mind? She decided she should probably buy the girl a gift regardless, although she didn't know what it would be. Pokémon? Municipal bonds? She'd find something, because she herself had been given the best gift she could have hoped for. He came back. Into a strange and difficult situation, to be sure, but he was there.

Might have been worse. I could have tried to take him to a class reunion.

She sniffed, then shrugged.

I'd never go to a class reunion.

The knot in her stomach relaxed, and she felt a wave of warmth come over her.

I love him.

"Sarah? Where'd you go?"

Sarah realized that Raya was speaking. "Oh, sorry. Just having a moment."

"Yeah, Colin's a good one," Raya said. "C'mon, let's go." She handed Sarah a lollipop, a spiraled yellow confection on a pink stick. "Put this in your pocket. You might need it."

"I thought we were just getting plates and napkins," Sarah said.

"We're going to do a little fact-finding while we're here," Raya said. "Zondra wants this place, and she's been here before. Let's try to find some clues."

"Okay, Nancy Drew. This is a kitchenette. How long could it take?"

"It's more than that, Sarah," Raya said, pointing to the carved wooden door in the back of the room. "You father told you about that space, right?"

"Some."

"There's more to it. The Crystal Room you've seen. Kind of normal, relatively speaking. But you remember all those doors? You know where they lead to?"

"The music store next door?"

"No. There's a whole space you can't see. Sort of exists off-dimension. There are places even I wasn't allowed to go. There's a reason Zondra is so crazed to get a hold of this place. It's not the Chicago real estate market."

She opened the door to the Crystal Room and motioned for Sarah to follow her. They entered, and it was much as it was before—the stone fountain in the middle, crystal balls and jars and potions lining translucent shelves on the walls, and bowls with different types of plants, several of whom were playing cards. Sarah instinctively waved at them.

"Now, you know what that room is," Raya said, pointing to a small door to their right.

"Meeting room, a few cots."

"Yes. The rest of it…that's what your family are the gatekeepers for." Raya scanned the bookshelves next to the larger, ornately carved wooden door. "We're just going to look around. But be alert. And be careful. You just never know."

"She's right, you know," said a voice from the shelf. They turned to one of the larger jars, where its inhabitant was watching a tiny television.

"Hey Brad," Raya said. "Anything good on?"

"Nah, just channel surfing." The small, gnarled being pressed his face and leafy arm against the jar. "Can you tell Dave to take his cooking forays down a notch? Just now he was making such a ruckus in the kitchenette that the walls in here were literally shaking. Had to do three defense spells just to keep from falling off the shelf."

"I'll tell him," Raya said. "Notice anything else unusual?"

"Maybe," Brad replied. "Earlier today there were a few strange shadows moving through here. Normally I wouldn't think twice about it —you know, could have just been some strong vibration echoes or whatnot. But the weird thing was that we all got really sleepy, including Farley over there, who I'm pretty sure has been awake since the '70s."

"Wow, the 1970s?" Sarah asked.

"Probably more like the 1670s," Raya whispered.

"We were all out for a good while. Didn't think anything of it until just now when we heard about Avi."

"Okay, thanks, Brad."

"No problem." The creature sat back on his leaves and picked up his tiny remote control. He waved his small, leafy arm as the women turned away.

Sarah looked around her. She heard a hum, almost imperceptible, that changed tones at regular intervals.

"Do you hear that?" Sarah said, walking farther into the Crystal Room, near the fountain. "That's kind of annoying."

"What is?"

"You don't hear it? That humming sound? It's a B if I'm not mistaken. Okay, now it's a C-sharp."

"I don't hear anything, Sarah. Maybe it's tinnitus."

Raya's attention was now focused on the wall to their left. She approached it, holding out her hand, and gently traced the outline of an invisible door.

"What are you doing?" Sarah asked, now humming in D-sharp.

"I'm trying to find the entrance to the Other Way," she answered. "What are you humming?"

"Now? I think it's changed to a B-major scale. You sure you don't hear it?"

"No, I…got it!" Raya kept her hand on the wall as a door appeared in front of them, glowing with a grey haze. "Put your hand up next to mine," she instructed.

Sarah put her hand up, and as she did so, the door itself disappeared and they stepped through the arch. Sarah fought to catch her breath as she realized how vast a space they had entered. It was a dim, grey courtyard, in the middle of which was another fountain, this one with three tiers and bubbling with a mercury-like liquid cascading down each tier like sheets of foil. Sarah had a strong urge to touch it but felt Raya's hand grab her arm.

"Not a good idea," she said.

Sarah was beginning to feel light-headed. "Where are we?" She blinked a few times, hoping it would help her find her balance. "Shouldn't this be the music store next door?"

"Yes and no. We're playing a bit fast and loose with space here."

"Okay." Sarah was feeling downright woozy. She imagined herself as Alice just having stepped through the looking glass and not knowing if she were large or small. "I don't feel well."

"Have your lollipop."

Sarah fished the candy from her pocket and popped it in her mouth. Amazingly, she felt immediately restored, her equilibrium coming into balance. And it tasted like lemon and lavender.

"Better?" Raya asked, and Sarah nodded. "Good. Look, I don't know quite what we're looking for here, so we're going to have to keep our minds open. Zondra wants this place, but she's not a legacy proprietor."

"Power trip?"

"Maybe."

"But why did she take my father? From what you said he's pretty powerful, and he owns the place by birthright. She'd have a hard time overtaking him, and I doubt he'd go willingly."

Raya was distracted, her eyes scanning the room from portal to portal, which were set up like kiosks against the far wall. Her gaze landed on one small doorway with metal spikes scattered over the top third of it.

"Maybe Avi let her kidnap him. Maybe they have a past."

"That's crazy. He was devoted to my mom. And Zondra couldn't be less like her. No. No."

"You never know, Sarah. People have lives before their children."

"He didn't go willingly. Besides," Sarah said, shaking her head, "he knew I'd come looking for him. He wouldn't put us in danger."

"I think he was counting on it. And I think Zondra knew it too." Raya ran her hands over the wall, feeling the bas-relief carvings with her fingertips.

"So you think she's here somewhere?"

"Not in person. But she may have left some traps."

"But Dad…"

"I could be wrong, but I think Avi knows the only way to get rid of Zondra is to prove that you're the rightful heir to the store. Otherwise, she's going to try to get you out of the way by any means necessary."

"I still don't know if I want the place."

Raya turned and took Sarah by the shoulders. "That's kind of moot right now. We have to deal with the problem at hand. Then you can consider stewardship of the store."

"I thought you meant ownership."

"No one really *owns* this place. The Greenbergs just take care of it. But there's only one steward at a time. You can't take over until he's passed on, but if he's not around…"

"It creates a gap. Maybe that's the loophole she was looking for."

"Maybe." Raya put her hands in her pockets. "She probably won't kill him, at least we have that."

"That's good. Why not?"

"Too big a risk. Killing a fellow Magycian is the ultimate crime. They send you to a place from which you never return. She wouldn't risk it. Avi's too high profile. But you? Hmmm."

"That's comforting."

Raya closed her eyes and put her hand up perpendicular to the ground. She flexed her wrist up and down.

"There's something here."

They heard a cough from across the room. They turned to find Colin holding some rope and a small rubber mallet.

"I wanted to help," he said. "I didn't know what to bring."

"You shouldn't be here, Colin. How'd you get in anyway?" Sarah asked.

Colin turned and pointed to the main door with his thumb. "It was open."

"Still," Sarah said. "It could be dangerous."

"Look, where you go, I go. I'm not leaving you alone, even though I'm pretty sure Raya could kick both our butts seven ways 'til Sunday."

Raya nodded, then took his rope and put it in her bag. "We haven't really found anything yet. If Zondra's been in here, she didn't leave much in the way of tracks. Just stay close and don't try anything macho."

"Got it," Colin held up his mallet like a broadsword.

Raya rolled her eyes.

Sarah heard that hum again, louder this time. It was coming from the doorway with the metal spikes.

"I don't feel well," Colin said. "This is weird."

Sarah spun around and popped the lollipop in his mouth, and before he had a chance to protest, he smiled.

"Thanks."

Sarah inched toward the metal door. "The sound is coming from here, I'm almost sure of it."

"That room hasn't been opened in a while. The door is almost rusted shut," Raya said. "You sure?"

"Yes."

Raya shot a narrow, pale beam from her palm, tracing the edge of the door's hinges. When she finished, she gently opened the door, scanning the entry for anything suspicious.

The three of them cautiously stuck their heads in. Sarah found it hard to breathe, the air dense and acrid with a damp, earthy smell.

They stepped inside the room, and the metal door closed behind them.

"What is this place?" Sarah asked as Raya produced a lamp-like orb in her hand and held it out. It was a huge space, with broken pots strewn about, rotting plants lining the walls, and thick, rope-like vines hanging from the ceiling.

"I think it used to be a garden," Raya replied.

"Used to be?" Colin said. "What happened?"

"Shh!" Raya put her finger to her lips. She cocked her head and took another small step forward, motioning for the others to stay behind her. Raya slowly pulled her staff from her bag, but before she could open it, she pushed her companions against the wall. She tried to open the spiked door, but it wouldn't budge. They were trapped.

Sarah realized the pounding noise she heard wasn't her heartbeat. The sounds grew stronger, and the noise became a buzzing in her ears. She couldn't tell where the sound was coming from; it emanated from all around them.

Then they all saw it.

Whatever it was, it was massive. It was about seven feet tall and lumbered toward them from the back of the old garden room. It was vaguely humanoid, with a head, two arms, and two legs, but that's where the similarity ended. It had dark holes where its eyes should have been, and it looked straight ahead as it moved, as it had no neck, its head attached directly to its torso. It was unaware of their presence, seemingly unable to hear their breathing, which for Sarah was coming in ragged, shallow waves.

"*Golem*?" Sarah whispered. The hulking mass gave no indication it heard her, as it continued to pace around the anteroom.

Colin pulled on the door handle. "I can't open it either. It's really stuck."

"I don't think it's quite a *golem*," Raya responded quietly, ignoring Colin. "It's a humanoid mass brought to life by Magyck—dark Magyck. But it's not *golem*."

"What the hell is it then?" Colin hissed.

"I'm not sure. But look at its forehead. Instead of the name of *G-D*, it has two lines of text. Do you still read Hebrew?"

"Not well," Sarah replied.

Raya looked at Colin, who held up his hands.

"Episcopalian."

"Okay," Raya said, herding Sarah and Colin away from the door. "The first line is the word *Nezach*. Loosely translated, that means 'everlasting' in biblical Hebrew. And the second line is *Olam*, which literally means 'beyond the horizon.'"

"So what does that all mean?" Sarah asked.

"It's complicated." Raya looked over her shoulder. "The Hebrew word for 'space' is also used for 'time.' It gets a little hinky, because it's also used for time of the distant past as well as the distant future. Basically, it's a time that is difficult to know or perceive."

"Much like this conversation," Colin said, his eyes darting back and forth across the anteroom.

"No, I get it. Zondra is keeping some of her energy in that thing, using it as a guard. She wants to live forever."

Raya stopped suddenly and looked at the monster. "It knows we're here."

They turned to face the golem-thing, who was taking long strides toward them. If it hadn't been aware of them before, it was now. Raya put up a window shield, but it passed through it as if it was water. Sarah felt her chest and scalp tighten, and her feet wouldn't move. The creature was nearing, its arms outstretched, searching for them, reaching closer and closer...

"Sarah, now!" Raya waved her arms, sending beams of light and vibrations at the hulking mass, some landing on their target, others being waved away like errant mosquitoes.

Sarah didn't have time to think. She summoned the energy from around her, focusing on the red strings. The silver fountain was glowing brighter, so she pulled some energy from that as well, its flowing cascades turning darker as she did so. She put her hand out, and the first beam she issued landed squarely on the monster's chest. Its face was expressionless, a smooth slate of grey. Sarah hit it again, this time with enough force to send it rolling backward.

"Good one, Sarah! Yes!" Raya turned and pumped her fist. Out of nowhere, the creature rose to its feet, found a burst of speed, and in an instant was heading straight at Raya.

The creature's arm lashed out, striking Raya and sending her across the room. Her staff landed with a metallic clatter on the stone floor. She wasn't unconscious, but she looked dazed.

The creature turned its attention to Sarah. It was moving slower now, lumbering toward her, inching step by step. Sarah held her ground, searching for energy strings. It reached out for her, and she felt Colin's hand touch the small of her back.

Then her mind went blank. She saw nothing but strings and colors, bobbing and weaving around her like a kaleidoscope. She moved her arms by instinct, the vibrations radiating through her one after the other. The creature was slowed, but not stopped. It was impervious to her firepower, absorbing some and waving away others. More and more she fought it, blue then red then yellow then green, each string of vibrating energy moving through her like waves. She felt her own energy drain from her body, and her vision began to dim. Out of the corner of her eye, she saw Raya get up and grab her staff, but there wasn't time. The creature continued inching forward, and Sarah could feel the power it contained as it held out one massive arm.

She saw something fly past her, and the creature stumbled backward and fell. Sarah spied Colin's mallet lodged firmly in its forehead, obscuring the words imprinted there. Its body hit the ground, and it disintegrated into a pile of dust. The air grew cold, and a breeze circled around them, whipping the ashes into a green cloud that then disappeared.

Sarah turned to look at Colin, his eyes like saucers and his arms cemented to his sides. Raya ran over and hugged him.

"That was brilliant, Colin! Why didn't I think of that? Destroy the words, destroy the creature!"

"I…just…threw it," Colin stammered.

"Whatever, man. Good work." Raya joyously punched him on the arm.

Sarah's eyes darted quickly around the room, from wall to wall and door to door, then at the silver fountain. "We need to go now." She felt herself start to tremble.

"Agreed. We don't know what else Zondra's got here. Better let Esra take a look." Raya put Sarah's hand in Colin's. "Let's go."

This time Raya was able to pull the metal door open with a spell, and they practically sprinted out of the interdimensional room into the Crystal Room. The smaller fountain was now trickling with gold water, but the sounds it made when the falling rivulets hit the holding pool were softer and less metallic. The creatures in the glass jars were all pressed up against the sides, their leaves waving.

"Way to go, guys," Brad said. "Everybody okay?"

"Thanks. We're good," Raya said, reaching the exit first and finding it unlocked.

As Sarah walked past the fountain, she heard a faint voice calling to her. She stopped and looked around, but there was no one else in there with them. She felt the voice from within her, calling her name. She looked at the fountain and felt an overwhelming need to sit down.

"Guys, I'm going to rest for a moment," she called out.

"I thought you wanted to leave?" Colin asked.

"I do, but I need to sit here for a second." She alighted on the edge of the fountain, placing her hands on either side of her. Raya nodded and guided Colin out the door in front of her.

"If you're not out in five minutes," Raya said, "I'm coming back for you."

They exited quietly through the door, and Sarah turned to look at the fountain, now gilded and flowing. The pool was smooth, even where the water cascaded into it from above, save for one set of concentric circles that appeared and disappeared. The voice in her head grew more distinct, and she heard it say her name again. She looked into the pool of gold liquid, and the face of her mother slowly appeared in the rippled surface. Sarah wiped her eyes, then squeezed them shut, willing them to focus. She looked again, her mother's face clear and distinct as if she was looking at her own reflection. Sarah leaned from side to side, and her mother's gaze followed her.

"I'm really here, Sarah. Stop with the leaning. You're making me dizzy."

"Mom? How is this possible?"

"Haven't you figured it out yet?"

"Obviously not," Sarah said, slightly annoyed. She felt like the stone underneath her was beginning to dissolve, and she gripped the edge tightly.

"I just wanted you to know that everything is going to be all right," her mother said, her voice soft and cool like a breeze at sunset. "I've spoken with your father…"

"Is he okay?"

Her mother's image scowled. "What? Yes, he's fine. He's with Zondra. We knew her years ago. She's actually quite charming when you get to know her."

"I'll take your word for it," Sarah said. "So far, I'm not impressed."

"Don't frown. It will give you wrinkles." Her mother's face softened. "You don't have to do this, you know."

"What do you mean?"

"Well, you didn't grow up with Magyck like your sister did. I just don't want you to be disappointed. And you're such a perfectionist. If you can't do something perfectly right out of the gate, you tend to—"

"Give up. I know. That's why I can't roller-skate."

"It's just all a bit beyond you. Maybe you should just try something more your speed. You sister can't take over—it's not in the contract. Besides, she's so busy—with her husband, her children, her travel agency."

"Deb's a dentist."

"Oh, yes. Of course. Sometimes things get a bit hazy for me." Her mother held up her hand. "I'm dead. Cut me some slack."

"I miss you, Mom."

"I miss you too, darling."

Sarah cocked her head. Never in her life had her mother called her darling.

"Do you remember when I was seven and I fell off my bike? I broke my arm, and you drew a bunny on my cast." Sarah leaned in.

"Of course I remember," her mother nodded. "I remember. Bunny."

Sarah's stomach tightened. She had never broken her arm. She felt a cold, prickly feeling creep up her neck.

"Look, Sarah, I don't have much time. But let me tell you this—walk away. You're not strong enough to handle this. Sign off your rights to the store, and Zondra will release your father. That's what you want, yes?"

Sarah slowly nodded, her throat tight and dry.

"You don't want the store. So much to learn, so much responsibility. Just walk away, your father will be fine. And when the time comes, Zondra will take over. She's really quite clever. Just go back to your little magazine job, and your nice boyfriend, and everything will be fine. That's what you want, yes?" her mother repeated. "Just walk away."

It felt like the stone basin was swaying. Sarah put her hand on her cheek, willing herself to stay still, but she grew faint and weak. Maybe it would be easier, maybe she should just walk away. Maybe…

She sensed a hand on her shoulder, and as she turned away, she saw the image of her mother being drawn back into the pool of gold water. Then everything went black. Then green. Then purple. Then a horrid shade of neon orange. Colors swirled behind her eyelids, keeping Sarah in a place between consciousness and awareness, between reality and a place where she floated yet still felt that strong hand on her shoulder, guiding her along like a small child.

"Drink this," the voice said. She put her hands out and felt a large cup placed between them. She brought it toward her mouth and sipped, the warm liquid enveloping her tongue as a warm ray of light made its way toward her brain, washing away the multihued fog and bringing her back to what she hoped was real life.

Sarah awoke to find herself on the purple couch in the back of the store, her feet propped up on several cushions. Her family surrounded her like Dorothy in her bed after her journey to Oz. Dave handed her a mug, and she sipped it.

"This is not the stuff from before," she stated. "What is it?"

"Swiss Miss," replied Dave. "Good, huh? I made it with two-percent milk. Oh, and there's some *herdulam* in it too."

"What?"

"It is an herb," Esra explained. "Used to make potions, for lack of a better term. It is what helped you back, along with the first drink."

"I saw my mother. But it wasn't her, really."

"You are right. It was Zondra's doing. She enchanted the pool. You fought it very well though." Esra scratched his head, shifting his hat to a precarious angle. "I believe the spell had an amnesia feature, a fail-safe measure in case you could not be persuaded."

"What would have happened if you hadn't come after me?"

"Yeah, you would have had your brain pretty much wiped, and you would have walked out of there in a daze, eventually forgetting who you were." Raya squeezed her hand.

"It almost worked. I was close to giving in, even though I knew it wasn't my mother. I'm sorry." Sarah looked around at her family and Colin. "I'm a screwup, I know." She sat up, but then leaned her head against the back of the couch. "This is so beyond me." She closed her eyes.

"We are here for you, Saraleh. And you are not, how did you say, a screwup. What a peculiar term." Esra sat next to her and put his hand on her cheek. She looked up at him, and he lowered his sunglasses to meet her gaze, his emerald eyes sparkling even in the store's dim lighting. "I had a friend look over the contract. He thinks she might be able to enforce it, because your Magyck was dormant at birth. All is not lost, but you have a challenge ahead of you."

Something shifted in Sarah's soul. Everything she thought she knew and thought she was had been turned upside-down. She wanted so much to be brave, to rise to the occasion, but she couldn't find her footing. And now she was expected to save the store, her father, and basically the whole Magyckal world and keep a malevolent leader in a Chanel pantsuit from ushering in an era of darkness.

Sarah had been a Magycian for a few months. It didn't seem like a fair fight.

Suddenly, she snapped. This was beyond her pay grade, she thought. It wasn't going to happen. She looked around at her family and friends and felt the urge to bolt. Fast. Far. She made a lunge for her coat and bag, sweeping them up in her arms like she was gathering piles of cash from the floor. She tried to think of something to say, something that would properly explain her fear, her absolute panic, but all she could think about was running away as far as possible where no one knew Magyck and no one expected her to save anything. She had no idea where she could go. Peru? Omaha?

She grabbed Colin by the arm. "Let's go." She pulled him toward the door before anyone could stop them and made a beeline for her car, which was only three spaces away from where she thought she left it.

"Get in."

Without a word, Colin slid into the passenger seat next to her. She fumbled for her keys, started the car, and drove away as fast as she could, with no destination in mind. She just drove.

CHAPTER

FOURTEEN

S arah gripped the steering wheel so hard her knuckles were white. She saw an exit sign and merged onto I-94 West. Lake Geneva. It would be a bit of a trek but not too bad; hopefully, it would be far enough away to hide. She could start a whole new life—as what? Butcher? Baker? Candlestick maker? She'd find something, anything that was as far removed from being a Magycian as possible.

She looked in the rearview mirror but only saw her mother's face. Was it really her face? She couldn't remember now. She only remembered her eyes. The eyes that blazed when she told Sarah she wasn't good enough. That she should just walk away. She knew it was Zondra, but their faces had begun to blend, and all Sarah felt was a nagging sense of inadequacy, of feeling like the family schlub, different without knowing why.

Now she knew.

Her whole family had watched her struggle and had done nothing. She spent her whole life feeling like she was playing a game of catch-up, trying hard and falling short. And yes, walking away.

What exactly had she accomplished anyway? She wrote about appetizers and food trends for a second-tier regional magazine. She had a house where the sink always dripped in three-quarter time and the

radiator hummed in B-flat. She was almost forty years old—when did
that happen? And she was suddenly an awkward Magycian and heir to
a Magyck store that might very well be the key to keeping the Magyckal
world safe from destruction.

Or not. Maybe Zondra was just misunderstood.

Maybe she could just lean into it and get a ferret, because things
weren't weird enough. Maybe they came in blue.

Maybe, maybe, maybe.

Out of the corner of her eye, she watched Colin drum his fingers on
the door.

He makes sense.

But he must have thought he was getting involved with Normal
Sarah, not Pull-a-Rabbit-out-of-My-Hat Sarah. She wondered how long
it would be until he ran for the hills. He was probably debating jumping
out of the car.

She had a feeling shit was about to get really, really weird.

They had just crossed the border into Wisconsin, and neither had
yet to say a word. Sarah stopped at a roadside diner for a rest and a bite
to eat.

The Copper Coffee Pot. That sounds safe. Maybe they have blueberry pie.

As they waited to be seated, Sarah stopped at the dessert case and
practically pressed her nose up against the glass.

They had blueberry pie.

At the table, the blue gingham-clad waitress brought them menus, a
bread basket, and two glasses of water. Sarah downed her water in one
long gulp, then reached for Colin's and finished that off in short order.

"What can I get you folks?" The waitress pulled an order pad from
her starched apron. "Or do you need a minute?" She smiled, showing a
dimple in her right cheek, but regarded Sarah with the wary gaze of a
woman who had seen it all within the confines of a twenty-four-hour
roadside diner.

"Pie," Sarah said. "Blueberry pie. Please."

"All rightie. How about you, sir?"

"BLT please. Thank you." He handed her the menus.

Sarah watched the waitress walk away and then leaned toward
Colin. "I could materialize the pie right here, you know. Just bring it on

over with my superpowers. I can do that. It might fall on the floor and knock over this table or possibly explode, but I could totally do that."

Colin leaned back. "But you won't because that would call attention to something you don't want to call attention to, and I don't know how much experience they have with Magyck in southern Wisconsin. They might run us out of town and over the lake to Michigan. You don't want to go to Michigan."

"No. No, I don't."

"So why don't you take a minute to tell me the real reason we drove all the way up here."

"I love—"

"Nope." Colin shook his head.

"The scenery is beautiful this time of year."

"Sarah, I'm a forty-two-year-old accountant, and I know a small, blue guy named Dave who served me kugel. I fought a clay monster. I think I can handle the truth."

"You can't handle the—"

"Nooo."

She sighed. "All right. When I was sitting by the fountain, I saw my mother."

"How?"

"I heard her calling me. I looked into the water, and there she was. And the weird thing is," she whispered, "she always hated swimming."

"No wonder you were dazed."

"She told me to walk away. Give up. That I wasn't good enough. That it just wasn't for me. All the things she said to me when I was growing up."

"She said those things to you?"

"Not in so many words. Well, she used a lot of those words, but she was much nicer about it." She raised her glass and caught the waitress's eye. "It wasn't her though."

"Zondra."

"Yup. Pretty sure."

"Is that what upset you?"

"Maybe. But I think I was still under the effect of the spell. Kind of a Magyckal hangover."

The waitress refilled her glass and winked. "Been there, honey. Been there."

"Thank you!" Sarah tensed her shoulders and reached for the water.

The waitress came back a minute later with their food. Sarah picked up a fork and hovered it above the pie. Why blueberry?

I like blueberry. But I think there's something with chocolate over there.

"Hello? Where'd you go?" Colin took a bite of his sandwich. "Needs mayonnaise."

"Bacon *and* mayo? You earning points to renew your gentile card?"

Colin laughed. "And she's back."

"It's the pie," Sarah said, taking a large bite. "Good for the nerves."

"So what are we going to do? We can't stay in Wisconsin forever."

That was the million-dollar question. She couldn't go back to her family, at least not yet.

"While we were waiting for you to wake up, Esra told me that Zondra is holding Avi in a picture frame. Art jail, if you will. I can't imagine that," Colin said.

Neither could Sarah. Her father had been there through everything —teaching her to ride a bike, drive her car, repair a table leg. He rescued her when she got her jacket caught in a swing, and when she got stuck in a tree, which happened more often than she cared to admit. But she wasn't there for him. And she felt helpless.

She looked down at her plate. Her pie was gone. She wiped her mouth with a napkin and slid out of the booth.

"I'm going to use the restroom. I need to floss."

"Don't need to give me a reason. I believe you," Colin said, tucking into the other half of his sandwich.

Spying the ladies' room in the back, Sarah weaved through the half-empty tables and looked both ways before pushing the restroom door open. She listened to determine if there were any occupants, casually looking under the doors for feet.

She was alone.

Rummaging through her purse, she decided that she really did have to floss. Sarah wound the waxed string around her fingers, looked into the mirror, and opened her mouth.

She was looking into a face that wasn't her own.

Sarah jumped back in surprise and momentarily lost her footing. Righting herself, she pinched her cheek and made a face.

"I am here," Esra said. "Easier than teleporting. Although I almost caught an old lady quite by surprise. That would have been quite hard to explain."

"What are you doing here?" Sarah hissed.

"How is the pie?"

"Good. A little too sweet." She gripped the sides of the sink. "Never mind the pie. You should be figuring out how to rescue my dad."

"We have come to the irrefutable conclusion that we need you." Esra noticed a smudge on the mirror and tried to wipe it away from his side.

"I am useless. I can levitate three feet off the ground and spin a feather. I could probably set something on fire, but I wouldn't be able to specify what. I am of no use to you and never will be."

"That, my *Zeeskeit*, is patently untrue. You just do not trust yourself."

"I can't do it! I can't get him back. My father needs me, and I can't do anything about it."

Esra's face disappeared in the mirror as the bathroom door opened, and a lady and small child entered. She looked at Sarah and nodded in understanding.

"Pep talk. One of those days, right?" The woman led the toddler into a stall and closed the door behind her. "In the potty, Claire. Just like at home." The toilet flushed, and the girl cried. "I know, it does that by itself. It's okay."

"But I wasn't done," the girl wailed.

"For the love of God, just pee! It will flush again!"

There was rustling in the stall and then mother and daughter emerged, none the worse for wear.

"Don't worry," Sarah whispered to the girl. "I don't like them either. I like to decide when I'm done."

The girl giggled as her mother held her up to the sink to wash her hands, only to be re-startled by the automatic hand dryer. She cried, and her mother ushered her out of the bathroom, letting out a long sigh as they left.

"I do not blame her one bit." Esra reappeared in the mirror. "Those contraptions always startle me too." He scrunched his nose. "Where were we?"

"I was failing my father."

"Ah, yes. And I am here to tell you that there is nothing at which you can fail. He is back."

"Dad? What? How?"

"Zondra released him. He will not give us the details unless you are here. That is why we need you. Come home."

"Is Zondra giving up?"

"No. Things have changed," Esra said, his normally placid face betraying a flash of worry. "Also, when you come home you can help me learn the opening chords to a song called 'Jumpin' Jack Flash.' Even on the rubber bands I cannot get it to sound right. I do not know how Mr. Richards does it. I will have to ask him at the next meeting."

"Keith Richards is…? You know what? Never mind." She waved her hands around. "Are you sure everyone wants me there? I did have a bit of a meltdown."

"Everyone will be glad you are all right. We all have our moments. You earned yours," Esra reassured her. "Just come home. You still have much to learn."

He tipped his hat and disappeared from the mirror. She threw the floss back in her purse, sucked the pieces of blueberry from her teeth, unwound the waxy string from her finger, and tossed it in the wastebasket.

Grow up, Sarah. It's time.

She went back to the table.

"We need to go home," she said, sliding into the booth. "There's been a development."

"Are you sure? We can live here. We can pitch a tent and this place will keep us stocked in dry BLTs and pie."

"Jews don't camp. We make reservations." She scraped her plate with her fork. "I can do this. I need to do this."

"Let me go pay." He got up from the table and picked up the check.

"You're not going to ask why I changed my mind?"

"I know why." Colin turned on his heel and walked to the register.

"Do *not* have the patty melt," said a voice under the table.

Sarah looked down and saw Dave's yellow eyes.

"Hello, Avon calling." He smiled. "That kitchen is an embarrassment. Good pea soup though. You done with your little temper tantrum?"

"It wasn't a tantrum. I was affected by Zondra's spell."

"Please. I've seen demon toddlers who missed their nap hold it together better than you. *Hungry* demon toddlers." He reached up from under the table and snatched a dinner roll. Sarah looked around without moving her head. "Relax. People see what they want to see, remember?" He speared three butter pats with his forefinger claw. "If you want my advice, order some more pie to go. The fructose will neutralize any last remaining traces of Zondra's enchantment nonsense. I recommend razzleberry." Dave winked and disappeared in a small cloud of blue sparkles.

On their way out, Sarah purchased an extra slice of pie for the road, substituting cherry for Dave's prescription, and they headed back to Chicago. The sky was more overcast, the late autumn chill being given free rein. As Colin drove, she clicked the heater in the car up a notch until he complained that he felt like he was in a mobile sauna.

"Sorry," Sarah said. "Body temperature is out of whack."

She opened the clamshell container and smelled the pie. It was fresh out of the oven and took the edge off her consternation.

"You want some?" she asked, holding up a forkful of pie to Colin's face.

"No thanks. I think you need it more than I do."

"Fair enough."

Sarah watched the scenery, the trees hanging on to their last few leaves in a crowd of red and orange. Rosh Hashanah was late this year but approaching fast; Yom Kippur would follow, and she'd have to atone for her sins. Did killing a golem count? She knew that Magyck itself wasn't on the list, and although not exclusive to one faith or group, it was rooted in the history and lore of Judaism as a way ancient Jews could keep themselves alive in places where they weren't always welcome. Through time, Magycians were able to keep their abilities secret, disguising themselves in carnival shows and as street performers, some becoming known as "master illusionists," thrilling audiences who would never know the tricks were real.

In truth, Sarah wasn't quite sure what she was returning to. Her "little tantrum," Magyck-induced though it was, had left her feeling unreliable and unstable, and she worried her family wouldn't totally trust her. Her father was in jeopardy, and she had flaked. One look at the danger that loomed in her safe little life, and she had bolted. How could she even consider becoming the caretaker of the Grand Central Station of the Magyckal world? She was never hall monitor, always played far left field in PE class, never stood out, never spoke up. How was she supposed to fight the forces of evil? She was Sarah Greenberg. The best she could hope for was to merely annoy the forces of the moderately rude, and maybe they'd just shuffle away.

But Zondra Bex was not of the moderately rude. She was mean and ruthless and possibly immortal. She wanted the Greenberg store and wasn't going to be intimidated by Townsperson Number 2 in the Little Tykes Passover Pageant at Temple Beth Shalom.

"You want me to put on the radio?" Colin asked. "You have NPR on preset, but I can turn to whatever. Or play the music on my phone."

She picked up his phone from the cradle on the dashboard and examined his playlists. "This is your workout jam? You're the only person I know who can get pumped up by Phish. No thanks. The radio is okay."

"Phish is awesome."

"They're fine."

"They're very improvisational, so it keeps you on your toes."

"Are you trying to convince me or you?" Sarah asked.

"Okay, here's an oldies station."

"If they play 'Brandy' I'm jumping out the window."

"Noted."

Colin turned up the volume so they could hear it over the blast of the heater, the sound of the car, and—Sarah felt—the beating of her own heart. The last strains of something electronically orchestral played out, fading into silence. Then she heard a familiar staccato bass line and immediately closed her eyes.

Once upon a universe,
It's how our story goes…

As it had before, the world swirled, seating Sarah in a place between reality and elsewhere, and she bobbed her head almost imperceptibly as the beat of the music wrapped around parts of her mind long dormant.

Take a trip, grab your hat,
Oh, how the time does flow…

The road ahead began to sway, the white, dashed lines rotating and building in color until it filled her field of vision.

In this cool moment in time,
With nothing else to say…
Mr. Skye runs through you and me,
We travel on his way…

And then she saw it. Zondra, in a white, billowing dress, conducting the vibrating strands of Magyck like a crazed Maestra—blue and red and green, like whirling dervishes dipping and diving and stretching the bands of space and time. Her family came in and out of focus, reaching for her, their faces sad and drawn. Images of her grandparents and great-grandparents appeared, then began to fade like old, worn photographs left too long in the sunlight. And Zondra was there, spinning and laughing and waving the Greenbergs out of existence.

Through the groove of space and rhyme,
Dancing Mr. Skye…

And then she saw Esra, only Esra, his sunglasses off and his hat askew, with eyes no longer vibrant green but a clear pink, reach out his hand to her.

Lose yourself and be found again,
Dancing Mr. Skye…

Sarah tried to take Esra's hand, but he was too far away, being pulled back by the strings. She reached and reached as he grew smaller and smaller…

"Sarah? Sarah, we're here. Wake up." Colin's hand gently shook her shoulder, and she awoke with a start, her hands balled up into tight fists. "Whoa, whoa, are you angry or sleepy?"

She looked at her hands and unclenched them. "I don't know. I… where are we?"

"We're at the store, remember? We were summoned back here." Colin looked concerned. "That must have been a hell of a dream."

"I hope it was. A dream, I mean."

The store was at half-light and vaguely hazy. Debra was gone; she probably went home to take care of her children. Raya, Nadav, and Esra sat casually on the sofa and chairs. She was glad to see Esra safe and sound. She smiled, and Esra nodded in return and gave her a short wave as he sipped his tea. Raya and Nadav each had a cup and saucer in front of them, and Sarah noticed one more place setting. She looked to the back room.

"Papa!" Sarah ran to her father, practically stumbling over Dave, who darted out of the way just in time. She hugged her father close. "You're here!"

"You haven't called me Papa since you were ten. You must have really missed me." Avi kissed his daughter on both cheeks. "I am indeed here."

Sarah turned to her companions. "You got him back? How?"

"Zondra placed him in a holding spell, in a mirror of all places," Raya said. "Hung him on the wall of her living room."

"It wasn't a strong spell, to be honest. I could have gotten out of that mirror sooner, but I took some time to reflect." Avi grinned slyly at his daughter, obviously very proud of his pun.

"Does Zondra know you're gone?"

"Yes. I let her think it was her doing. We had a lot of time to talk, she and I."

"I'm just glad you're back and all right." Sarah hugged her father again.

They sat down, and Sarah poured herself some tea. Everyone

appeared calm, but Sarah felt an undercurrent of tension. Raya was picking at her scone, and Nadav drummed his fingers on the arm of his chair. Only Esra was unperturbed, happily dropping a second sugar cube into his cup and popping a grape in his mouth. He was humming softly, and Sarah realized that it was the theme to "The Partridge Family."

Avi addressed the group. "All right, now that Sarah's here…oh, hello Colin, I didn't see you there, do sit down. I have some things to discuss with you all."

"After that," Raya interjected, "I think Sarah and I should make a quick trip to the library. Uncle Esra mentioned something called a *bareket* stone, and I think we should look into it."

"Good idea," Sarah agreed, remembering the green brooch that Zondra wore. "Do you want to come, Colin?"

"I think I'd better head home. I want to call Madison and make sure she's doing okay at my parents' house. I'll be around if you need me." He kissed her, although chastely, as he knew they had an audience. He put on his coat, wrapping his scarf tightly around his neck and grasping his car keys.

"All right, would you all come over here?" Avi waved his family toward him. "I have a—"

"Do you remember where you parked?" Sarah called out.

"Yup, I always park in the same spot," Colin said, the front door chimes tinkling as he waved and exited.

"Now, about what I need to discuss with you all—" Avi rubbed his beard.

"Sarah, we better get to the library before dark," Raya interjected.

"Wait, everyone, please. I know we're all excited, but this is important—"

"Five minutes, and we'll go." Sarah looked at her watch.

"I've come to realize that the contract with Zondra is valid, and we've made a bit of an arrangement. I need you to listen closely—"

"What are you saying, Dad?" Sarah looked out the window, then back to her father. She felt a coldness on the back of her neck, and she shivered. "Raya, do you have the notes I gave you?"

"This is something that concerns all of us." Avi's voice grew louder, a sharpness honing his words. "It's important that you—" His eyes landed on the front door as a ray of light edged the floor.

"Yes, I have them in my bag." Raya rummaged around her backpack.

"You really should clean that out." Nadav pointed to her. "Tsk, tsk."

"Leave her be, brother." Esra patted his arm. "She has a system."

"Ahem." A velvet voice floated over the din and dissipated.

"Okay, good, that was my only copy," Sarah said.

"I wouldn't lose that," Raya replied.

"You should back stuff like that up on the…what is it called?" Dave scratched his chin and snapped his fingers. "The nimbus?"

"Ahem!"

"I know you wouldn't, I was just checking—"

"Greenbergs!"

The door slammed, the sound reverberating around the room like a snapped rubber band. Everyone stopped talking and, as a unit, spun around to face the entryway and the tall figure looming there.

"Hello, everyone. I hope I'm not interrupting." Zondra waved her hand, adjusting her fur coat that was draped over one shoulder. "Dahling." Zondra's face softened as she addressed Sarah. "Come give a kiss to Mummy."

Zondra sashayed into the store, dropping her coat on Dave's head, who immediately dematerialized it. She was by Avi's side in the next instant, holding his arm like a coquette, batting her eyelashes and patting his hair. Sarah felt acid in the back of her throat.

"It's so nice to be here, surrounded by *family*, to make this marvelous announcement," Zondra practically cooed.

"Now, we don't have to make this into a major event—"

"Make *what* into a main event? Dad, what's she talking about?" Sarah felt beads of sweat on her upper lip. She looked around for a wastebasket in case she vomited.

Avi cleared his throat. "As I was trying to tell you all, while I was trapped in the mirror—"

"When he was away," Zondra corrected.

"Zondra and I worked some things out. I realized that the contract couldn't be broken—"

"Avi wants to keep the store in the family, which of course I completely understand. Bloodlines, blah, blah, blah."

"We came to an arrangement that appears to be mutually beneficial." Avi tugged on his shirt collar.

"We're getting married. Isn't that just wonderful? Of course, this was something I hoped for when we met forty years ago, but better late than never. And at my age…Sarah, dear, you know what that's like, yes?"

The ringing in Sarah's ears took on symphonic proportions.

"Married? But you had a golem try to kill us when we went into that old garden room!" Raya said.

"Oh, pooh. You're exaggerating." Zondra squeezed Avi's arm.

"And the *mazzikin*?" Dave said.

"Those boys? Harmless. They just get a little overexcited, that's all," Zondra said.

"You masqueraded as my dead mother and tried to get me to run away and abandon my family." Sarah was seething.

Zondra slid into the nearest chair and crossed her long legs. "That wasn't me. I'm not exactly the maternal type."

Sarah lunged at Zondra, fists out. Raya caught her and held her back as Avi dashed to her side.

"Not now," he whispered. "I have a plan."

"Well, aren't you…spirited," Zondra said as she materialized a martini. "We're going to be *family* now." She practically spat the word. "And you no longer have to worry about taking over the store."

"It would come to me after you're dead."

"The Bexs are very long-lived." She fingered her large, green brooch.

"Is this really what you want, Dad?" Sarah worked to catch her breath.

"It is for the best. Now why don't you and Raya head off and take care of that errand?" Avi kissed his daughter on the cheek and squeezed Raya's hand.

"Do as your father says, sweetie," Zondra said. "We have so many details to plan before the wedding. Avi dear, how do you feel about ivory and ultra-biomarine as a color scheme?"

Sarah started to protest, but Avi stopped her before she could speak. "Please." His voice was soft but firm.

Sarah nodded, and she and Raya left the store. Sarah let out a long stream of air, as if she had been holding her breath underwater.

"I know," Raya said. "What the hell was that?"

Sarah looked at the heavy, wooden front door, engraved with a large, ornate G. "He's not marrying her. He can't."

"I hope you're right, Sarah. Talk about an evil stepmother."

"Let's go find out about that *bareket* stone. There's more going on here than we know."

"Agreed. Where's your car?"

"It was right here…oh, there it is." Sarah pointed to a space three spots down.

Raya opened the car door and slid into the passenger seat. "In the meantime, if she offers you any fruit, don't eat it. It never ends well."

CHAPTER
FIFTEEN

The library was technically closed, but Sarah knew that didn't matter. They used the special entrance for the fifth floor and got on the elevator. Raya casually placed her hand on the gold panel next to the doors. The ride was uneventful, except this time Sarah felt like they were travelling sideways. They stepped onto the now-familiar worn carpet and waved to the lizards in the glass case.

"Tim. Barry. How're you doing?" Raya said.

Barry grunted, and he and Tim went back to playing gin rummy.

"They're a little more animated this time," Sarah said. "Less taxidermied."

Larry was nowhere to be found, so Sarah and Raya made their way to the reference section they had perused briefly before their Magyckal run-in with Zondra's "assistants." Sarah pulled the largest book off the shelf and plopped it on the table, where it landed with a dusty "oof."

"I'm going to go over to Geology." Raya pointed to a nearby shelf. "I think it's one row over. I want to see if I can find that stone Zondra was wearing on her suit."

"You noticed it too? Good. There's something to that thing. But it might not be a stone per se. Might be a gem. I remember there's a repository of sorts on the property, in that interdimensional room. Might be what she was trying to keep us away from."

"Agreed. I'll find it."

Sarah sat down on the intricately carved, dark wood chair and opened the book to the first page. The cover was heavier than it appeared, leading her to believe that it was made of more than paper. She ran her fingers over the ornate script on the title page.

The Hystorie of the Chicago Magyckal Community 1833—1895

Sarah already knew that her great-great-great-grandfather arrived in Chicago in 1850 and started the store shortly thereafter, and that it had managed to survive the Great Fire of 1871. She flipped through the pages carefully, scanning for mention of her last name or any mention of the location itself. She didn't have to look long, as her ancestor was quite prominent and involved in many aspects of the community, or at least as much as the community allowed a foreign-born Jew to be. She recognized his picture immediately—Avi was a dead ringer for Benjamin, salt-and-pepper beard and all. There were pictures of him standing stiffly next to George Pullman, accepting a wrapped gift, attending the groundbreaking ceremony of the new department store called Marshall Field's, and shoveling debris with local workers after the fire. She finally located a picture very similar to the one she saw before, of the opening of Greenberg's Mercantile. She moved her finger along the row of men wearing dark suits and beards until she spotted Old Benjamin. Then she saw that familiar face again, the tall, blonde woman standing off to the side of the main group. She looked closely at the image and realized the woman was wearing a brooch similar to the one Zondra wore now, but there was no stone. Sarah had no doubt this time. It was Zondra.

The picture began to blur. Sarah wiped her eyes lightly and blinked. The lines waved and undulated, and she felt dizzy. As she closed her eyes, she felt herself being pulled into a tight tunnel, falling for what felt like several minutes. Her body jerked as she landed softly, and the pressure eased. She opened her eyes to find herself floating above the street of her great-great- great-grandfather's store. She realized that she was now inside the photograph. Benjamin Greenberg was shaking hands with city officials, and as he held up the scissors the camera's flash popped. At that exact moment, Sarah spied Zondra slipping behind the front door of the business. Sarah tried to follow her but was unable to move. A minute or two later Zondra emerged from the store, unnoticed by the crowd around her.

Sarah's body was jerked again as she was pulled back through the tunnel and out of the photograph. She opened her eyes and realized she was sitting in the exact same position as before. Except this time Raya's hand was on the collar of her shirt, which was noticeably damp.

"Take a little trip, did we?" Raya raised an eyebrow.

"Not intentionally, believe me. I didn't even know we could do that!"

"Yeah, sometimes photos have a travel spell embedded in them. Really gives you a bird's-eye view."

Sarah tapped her finger on the photo. "Zondra was there. I'm sure of it. That was her. And she snuck into the store when no one was looking."

"I think I know why. You know that stone she wears? It's a *bareket*."

"And I think she stole it from the store," Sarah said.

"Let's go see your dad."

A vi filled the kettle with water and placed it on the stove. "Do you want tea? I'm making tea." He turned on the flame. "Chamomile. Very soothing."

"No, I'm good, thanks." Sarah tapped her finger on the counter. Her father's kitchen was neat and orderly, just like her mother had kept it.

"I'll have some," Raya said. "Do you have cookies?"

"Oh no. Debra says I shouldn't eat them. She's the expert."

"Right-hand cabinet, third shelf, toward the back," Sarah said. Her father raised his eyebrows. "Please. You always have a stash. Don't worry, I won't tell Deb."

Raya went to the cabinet and easily found the cookies. "Chocolate chip, cool," she said, grabbing two from the package and setting it on the counter. "Now I need some milk."

"Second shelf in the fridge, on the left. There's Lactaid in the pantry if you need it."

"Thanks. Sarah and I found some interesting things at the library," Raya said, her head still in the fridge as she rummaged around. She grabbed the milk and poured a glass.

The kettle whistled, and Avi poured the hot water into the mugs, dunking the tea bags up and down.

"Really? Interesting how?" he said. He sniffed the tea, and deciding it wasn't strong enough, set the mug back on the counter and stared at it. A flower of color bloomed on the surface, and he nodded and put the tea bags in the sink. "Did you find anything about the *bareket*?"

"You know about the *bareket*?" Sarah raised her eyebrows in surprise as she sipped her tea.

"I figured that's what it was. There are a few stones that look similar and have their own Magyckal properties, but a *bareket* would probably be at the top of her list." Avi leaned against the counter.

Raya sat at the table and crossed her legs. "We're pretty sure that's what it is."

Sarah cocked her head. "I'm assuming you're going to tell me it's functional as well as fashionable."

"Yeah. It's kind of an emerald, but a super-charged one." Raya munched on a cookie. "If you wear it, it's supposed to make you wise, opens your heart, and 'lights up your eyes,' whatever that means." She dunked the rest of her cookie in the milk and held it there for a few seconds before finishing it in one bite. "Oh, yeah. Here's an interesting bit. If you grind it into a powder and ingest it, it 'rejuvenates the old.'"

"That's how she did it!" Sarah exclaimed.

"I'm familiar with the stone. It's one of the Twelve Moonstone gems." Avi joined Raya and Sarah at the kitchen table and sipped his tea. "Together, they're a source of great power in the Magyck world."

"Dad, I think that's the stone Zondra has—her brooch."

"There are one or two other stones that have healing properties…"

Sarah waved him off. "I was looking at some pictures of the store's opening, and I saw someone who looked exactly like Zondra. I wasn't sure at first, but I got pulled into the picture and—"

"Oh, I love that," Avi said. "You get such a good perspective that way. Once when I was at university—"

"Dad, focus. Please." Sarah leaned in. "When I was in the photo I got a good look. It's her, Dad. Zondra. Not an ancestor. And when everyone was busy shaking hands and getting their picture taken, she snuck into the store. She was only in there for a short time, but when she came out she was wearing a brooch just like the one she has now, but bigger."

"Interesting. That explains quite a bit. This is helpful." Avi reached for a cookie. "Very helpful."

"You seem very relaxed about this, Uncle Avi," Raya said. "I mean, your fiancée might be almost two hundred years old."

"And she doesn't look a day over a hundred and fifty," Avi said, biting into his cookie. "Yes. I am concerned. But things are starting to make sense."

"You don't think she's going to kill you after you get married and just take the store?" Sarah asked.

"No," Avi replied. "No, if there's an heir, even a contested one, the widow doesn't take ownership. She needs me around."

Sarah put her hand on her father's shoulder. "Dad, why are you marrying her? Is it really just for the store?"

"No," Avi said, taking her hand and giving it a kiss. "I mean, that has something to do with it. I've known Zondra a long time. We…have a history." He gave Sarah's hand a little squeeze. "Trust me. I know what I'm doing."

Sarah took a deep breath and let it out in a long, hard stream. "All right. You know I trust you. What do you need me to do?"

"Keep Zondra busy. Maybe get to know her a little bit. I have some things I need to get done in the store and ideas I need to discuss with Esra. That would be a big help to me." Avi stood up and went to the front hall closet. He pulled out a grey container the size of a shoebox. He removed the contents and brought it over to Sarah. "Here."

Sarah took the object from his hands. It was humanoid-shaped, with half a dozen geometric patterns on the front and back. It felt lumpy and heavy for its size.

"Hold onto this," Avi continued. "It's filled with bits and pieces of

Zondra's possessions that I've been able to nick when she wasn't looking
—a cigarette butt, hairpin, lipstick, a button from her cape, and even a
small lock of hair. It will help you, how do I put this, keep a rein on her?
It's not very powerful, but you may even be able to modulate her
behavior slightly by using it."

"So, it's like a…JewDoo doll?" Sarah said.

Avi laughed. "Of sorts. Like I said, it won't do much, but it might
help in a pinch."

Sarah put the doll in her bag. "I'm not happy about any of this."

"So *nu?*" said her father, using the Yiddish expression, a shortened
version of *So what else is new?* "I know you're not. But I need you to keep
your eyes open and take one for the team, so to speak."

"More like take twelve," Raya said.

Her father gave them each a hug. "You two should go. You have
things to do, and so do I." He pointed to the cookies. "Raya? A few for
the road?"

"I'm good," she said. "Thank you though."

Avi smiled and gave them a quick wave as they left. They could hear
some rustling about behind the closed door—and then, silence. Sarah
felt the weight of the figurine in her bag increase twofold.

"That was weird, wasn't it?" Sarah said, as they walked down the
front path.

"Yeah. He's way too cool about all of this. He must have already
known everything we told him."

"I don't know if that makes me feel better or not."

"I know. The next few weeks are going to be interesting, I'm
guessing. Very interesting."

CHAPTER

SIXTEEN

A vi signed for a large package and started dragging it to the
back of the store. Raya left the pile of large, interlocking rings
she was sorting and helped him carry it to the back.

"You're getting wedding gifts already?" Sarah said, barely looking
up from her laptop. "How do people know?"

"Zondra put an announcement in the *Daily Tell.*" Avi brushed his
hands together.

"Fun, right?" Raya put a ring over her wrist and spun it around like
a Hula-Hoop.

"That wasn't a gift, actually," Avi said. "It's a special order. Mitch
the Magnificent needed a new Saw-a-Lady-in-Half box. He's picking it
up Thursday."

"What happened to his old box?" Sarah asked.

"Mitch sawed his assistant in half but accidentally sent the lower
part of her to Des Moines. They got her back, obviously, but it was still
this whole big thing. She was not happy. Went after the box with a
chainsaw."

"I would have gone after Mitch," Raya said.

"Well, she still had to earn a living," Avi said. "Thanks for helping,
by the way." He pointed to the box.

"Hey, I don't work here." Sarah gestured at a yellow legal pad full of scribbled notes that she was transcribing into her laptop. "My column is due tomorrow. My editor ran a 'Best of' column last month and gave me an extension this month, but I don't want to press my luck."

Avi kissed his daughter on the head. "You're right. And I appreciate the time you've spent with Zondra the last few weeks. I know she's…"

"High-maintenance? Yes. She is. You can still call it off, you know."

"I know. It will be okay."

"Your family says that a lot," Raya said.

"Generally, it's true." Avi walked to the counter to ring up a customer, a little boy and his mother purchasing a beginner's magic kit.

Raya leaned over Sarah's shoulder to read her screen. "What place is this?"

"That little bistro over on Halsted. And…save." Sarah hit the icon on her screen with a flourish. "I'll give it a read-over tonight and then send it in."

"How was the place?"

"The chicken was a little bland, the lettuce a little limp. I survived."

"Some people do not know how to season their chicken."

"Amen." Sarah shut her laptop. "I'm going to get some coffee from the back. You want?"

"I'm topped off, thanks."

"Dad, you want coffee?" She looked around for him. He had finished ringing up the customers and was nowhere to be seen.

"No thank you," a muffled voice responded. "I am currently neck-deep in faux pigeons."

"I better go help him," Raya said. "The feathers make him sneeze."

"ACHOO!"

"I thought the pigeons were fake?"

"I have a deeply rooted belief that it's psychosomatic," Raya said over her shoulder. "He tends to sneeze when he's unpacking any stock he doesn't like."

"He did the same thing when I was in school. He sneezed all the way through my seventh grade band concert. He added a whole percussion section to 'Rock Around the Clock.'"

"I remember. That was epic."

Sarah went to the back room for her coffee. Picking up a mug from the mug tree, she glanced over to the door of the Crystal Room. It was ajar. Dave entered from the storeroom and gave Sarah a perfunctory nod as he munched on a pear.

"Hey, is that supposed to be open?" she asked.

Dave shrugged. "Maybe Avi left it open. He usually locks it with the book keys though." He pointed to the shelf, then walked around the table and shut the door with his tail as he morphed into his human form and went into the store.

Sarah poured her coffee, stirred two sugars into it, and stared at the door. She took a sip of the coffee and winced when it burned her tongue. She decided on a glass of water instead.

"Your father didn't leave it open," said a voice. "It just kind of opened on its own."

Sarah turned to the shelves to address the purple and yellow plant in the third vase from the left.

"What do you mean, on its own?" She held up the water glass as an offering. The plant waved no thank you.

"It just moved. Weird. I've never seen that happen. I'm Simon, by the way. This is George," it said, pointing with one of its leaves to its companion, who was snoozing.

"Hey. Are you related to the guys in the Crystal Room?"

"Nope. Different genus. Those guys think they're such hot stuff." Simon shook its head. "Anyhoo, that thing is sealed pretty tightly most of the time. But there's been some strange sounds coming from there lately."

"We crossed paths with the golem. It's not that, is it?"

"No, it's different." A leaf fell off of Simon's torso, and it picked it up and stuck it back on. "The only people who I've seen go back there are Avi and Esra. I think."

"Msphdhtshmmm…" The other plant, George, rustled its leaves.

"Oh yeah, how could I forget?" Simon slapped what was probably its forehead with its right branch. "That creepy lady snuck in there one night, real late. That's when the sounds started. Sorry about that. Sometimes I have the memory of a tulip."

"Happens to the best of us," Sarah said reassuringly. "Was she here just the one time?"

Simon put its leaf on its "hip" and stared at the bottom of the vase. "Hmmm…"

"Rhsdmnphss…" George mumbled, then went back to sleep.

"Oh, yeah yeah yeah, you're right. Yes, she came in a few more times. Last time was two nights ago." Simon paused and let out a big sneeze.

"Gesundheit," Sarah said. "Still allergy season?"

"I live in a vase surrounded by other plants. It's *always* allergy season."

"Fair point. Thanks for the heads-up. I'm going to check if my coffee's cooled down yet."

"Enjoy," Simon replied, settling into a pile next to George. "I shall take a nap. It's my thing." It put its top branches down and was soon snoring in concert with its roommate.

I will never get used to having a conversation with a plant.

She looked at the heavy door. Why had Zondra been back there? Was she laying more booby traps? If she was a time traveler, is that where she caught…what? The seven-fifty train to the nineteenth century? That had to be what she was doing.

Magycians aren't immortal. Right?

Oh, but they can time travel?

She remembered her father telling her about a special room. Well, not really telling her about it, more like letting her know it existed. The Crystal Room was like a weird version of an Advent calendar her sixth grade best friend had, except there wasn't chocolate behind each door.

She took a fortifying sip of coffee—the right temperature this time —and gingerly turned the ornate brass handle. Meeting no resistance, she turned the handle fully and carefully opened the door.

The "foyer," as she had taken to calling the Crystal Room, was quiet and still. Even the fountain was turned off, the water unmoving in its basin. She looked around, and seeing no one else, stepped inside and gently closed the door behind her.

The air was humid and thick and had a slight metallic tang. As she took a few steps, the air changed and began to smell of lilacs. It reminded her of her mother, and she glanced furtively at the pool of water in the fountain.

As before, there were several other doors on the far side of the room, each as intricately carved as the one she had just walked through.

Except for that one with the metal spikes. Stay away from that one.

She instinctively headed for the fourth one, then stopped and looked again at the fountain. She walked over to it and sat on the edge, placed her mug down, and tapped her fingers on the surface of the cool, silver water.

Gradually, an image appeared, the small details filling in, colors becoming brighter. It was her childhood home in Oak Park with the white fence and purple shutters on the windows. Her parents sold it when she was in high school and downsized to the house where her father still lived. How she missed that place. As she took in the image, she saw herself reading a book on the front steps while her father and sister played ball in the side yard. She watched her father control the ball, making it dip and spin, then allow it to drop gently into Debra's hands. Her sister giggled with delight as she replicated her father's actions, with an added flourish of turning the ball into a sphere of pink cotton candy. Young Sarah didn't even notice. The front door of the house opened, and Sarah's mother came out and sat next to her daughter on the step. She put her arm around Sarah as she glanced at her husband and younger daughter, happily "playing ball" merely twenty feet away. She kissed Sarah on the head, ruffled her hair, and went inside the house.

It was happening all around me. And I had no idea.

The image dissolved and was replaced with Colin's living room. The fire was blazing, and Colin was stretched out on his couch, balancing a bottle of beer on his stomach while Madison sat on her yellow, faux-fur beanbag. They were watching a movie. Sarah saw herself enter with a bowl of popcorn and hand it to Colin, who sat up, cupped her face in his hands, and kissed her. Like an actor in a silent melodrama, Madison gestured her unconvincing repulsion at their PDA and settled back into her chair. Sarah and Colin shared the popcorn as he held her close, and she nuzzled her head on his shoulder. Sarah felt a rush of warmth at the sight but was confused. This had never happened.

"Feels real, does it not?"

Sarah quickly turned to find Esra hovering just behind her. He landed gracefully and sat next to her at the basin. He pointed at the image. "Do not worry. You are not forgetting anything. This has not happened yet."

"This thing can tell the future?"

"Future, past, it is really all the same."

"Is this actually going to happen?"

"I believe it depends on whether you view time as linear or cyclical."

"What's the difference?"

"Well, if it is linear, a time will come, then move along, never to come again. If it is cyclical, things will come and go and come again. Peace and war, feast and famine, winter and summer, the Cubs losing and... I guess that is a bad example."

Sarah looked back at the image. "What do *you* think time is?"

"Me? I think time is just time. Now Raya, she thinks time is shaped like a line drawing of Freddie Mercury. Who can tell?"

"Was Freddie...you know...like us?"

"Oh yes. Definitely."

"What about Prince? I mean, c'mon..."

"Surprisingly, no. He was just very talented."

"How about Dolly Parton?"

Esra placed his hand on her arm. "Let Dolly be Dolly. Do not overthink it."

"I like this," Sarah said, gently running her fingers over the image of her and Colin in the pool.

"Then you will make it happen." Esra shrugged. "Or you will not. Who knows? But I would never bet against you, Sarah Greenberg."

Sarah got up from the basin and began to pace. She stopped and faced Esra head-on.

"What is going on here?"

"That is a loaded question, my Sarahleh. Can you narrow it down a bit?"

"You know what I'm talking about. Why is he marrying her?"

Esra sighed. "Oh, that."

"Yes, that. She's a nightmare. She doesn't love Daddy. She just wants this store."

"She wants more than that. She wants..." He gestured around them. "This."

"This?"

"This is a special place. A place of True Magyck. Your family has been entrusted with it for almost two hundred years, with good reason. It is important that your father keep it in the family. Even with the contract."

Sarah took Esra's hand. "I understand that. What I don't understand is why he has to *marry* her."

Esra gave her hand a squeeze. "Have you heard the expression, 'Keep your friends close and your enemies closer?'"

"So Zondra's the enemy?"

"Maybe. Your father knows what he has to do."

Esra dragged his index finger along the surface of the silver water. The image of Colin and Sarah in domestic bliss disappeared, and a black-and-white image of the store's original opening appeared. It began to animate, as it had at the library. Sarah quickly spotted the tall, blonde woman off to the side who so resembled her future stepmother.

"What are your instincts telling you, Sarah?"

Sarah stared at the image. "That's Zondra."

"And?"

Sarah tried to form the words, but they wouldn't come. She watched the woman in the picture. Then she knew.

"Zondra isn't a time traveler, is she?"

"Has your father ever told you about the Twelve Moonstones?"

"He's mentioned it."

"The Twelve Moonstones are a collection of the most powerful stones in Earth's Magyck field. They harness great energy, and much of the vibrations that we use to work our Magyck emanates from them. One repository for the stones is here, in this spot. And a stone is missing."

"The *bareket.*"

"Yes."

"Zondra's brooch is the missing stone?"

"Possibly."

"She's been in and out of this place several times. Why doesn't she just take the rest of them?"

"She cannot. I am not sure how she got the *bareket*, as only the guardian of the Moonstones can remove them. She must have gotten it before Benjamin put the protections in place."

"The *bareket* is what's keeping her alive."

Esra nodded.

"Raya said it rejuvenates the old."

"Zondra is no spring chicken, as they say." Esra touched the water again, dissolving the image. "Right now, Zondra thinks that by marrying your father, she will get close to the Twelve Moonstones. But it does not matter. Only your family can influence them." He stood up and held out his hand. "Come with me."

They approached the fourth door, opened it, and entered the room. There was an obelisk in the center, glowing faintly with a soft, incandescent light. Esra sighed softly and placed his hand on the glass bubble contained within it, and the Moonstones began to glow brightly and floated around more rapidly. Sarah could hear a distinct hum. It was the same sound she had heard before, the one only she could hear. Esra closed his eyes and began to sing, his tune in perfect harmony with that of the stones.

The sound was overwhelming and beautiful. Strings of energy began to fill the room, dancing and vibrating with the music. Deep, soul-aching music that saturated her being with a joy she had never felt before. She watched the strings float, going over her and through her. She, too, closed her eyes and felt her body drift away, higher and higher until it seemed she was no longer of this world. She was in a night sky full of strings: blue, red, green, yellow, plus colors she had never seen, yet they somehow felt completely familiar. She was both as big as the universe and small as an atom, and the vibrations held her and moved her up, down, around, and through the space. The space between. She felt the incredible power pass through her as she moved stars and planets—and perhaps even the tide of time.

And then, just as she had begun to lose herself in the vastness of the *between*, indeed, almost come to understand it, she was back in the room with Esra, holding on to him for dear life.

She was crying.

"What was that?" she asked, wiping the tears from her cheek.

"That was the Source of Magyck, Sarahleh. Up close and personal."

"I thought a stone was missing."

"It is. I have…certain abilities to compensate. But with the twelfth stone in place, the ability to control time and space is limitless. Zondra has one. She wants the others. We must not allow it."

"I understand." She sat on the cool, stone floor. "Wow."

"Wow, indeed." Esra sat next to her, and they stared up at the Moonstones. They sat quietly, wordlessly. Esra sighed again.

After a few minutes, Sarah could feel her foot falling asleep, and she shifted positions, tapping her foot gently on the floor.

"I don't know if I'm up to this," Sarah said, finally breaking the silence. "I studied political science in school."

"It might have been better if you had studied interpretive dance, but we play the hand we are dealt." Esra winked, raised himself to his feet, and offered Sarah a hand. "You want a piece of candy?"

Esra dug around in his coat pocket and pulled out a small disc wrapped in yellow cellophane.

"Does that have Magyckal healing properties?" Sarah said, accepting it.

"No, I think it is just a butterscotch." He pulled out another one. "They are tasty though."

"Thank you." She unwrapped it and popped it in her mouth. She felt her body relax and a wave of happiness pass over her.

"Never underestimate the powers of a little sugar," Esra said. "All right, then. That is enough for now. Let us go back."

Esra led Sarah out of the small room, touching the glass bubble as he passed it. They walked through the Crystal Room, and Sarah gave a wistful glance at the silver fountain. Entering the kitchenette in the back room, Sarah had to shade her eyes against the fluorescent lighting. As she started for the sales floor, Esra stopped her.

"We have much to do," he said, looking over the top of his dark glasses, his emerald eyes glinting in the harsh light.

"Yes, we do," Sarah nodded. "And we have a wedding to plan."

Z ondra spat out a bite of chocolate cake into her napkin. "Ugh! Did they make this with spoiled dragon milk? Disgusting. I knew we should have gone to a Magyck-owned bakery."

"Shh! The owner will hear you!" Sarah practically hissed.

"I like it," Colin added. "Moist."

The bakery owner returned with another plate of samples.

"Maybe one of these will be to your liking, Ms. Bex. The red velvet is quite popular."

Zondra sighed as if the weight of the world rested upon her slim shoulders.

"I can't take another bite. I just can't. My palate is too refined. Sarah, you choose. You'll eat anything…I'm guessing."

Sarah swallowed hard, choosing not to engage.

"The vanilla was very nice," she said. "Classic."

"Also very moist," Colin said. He noticed Sarah giving him the stink eye. "Sorry. I know you hate that word."

"Every woman hates that word," Sarah said.

Colin looked at Zondra, who reluctantly nodded.

"How about carrot?" he said.

"For a wedding cake?" Zondra raised a perfectly arched eyebrow.

"Dad hates it."

"Who hates carrot cake?"

"My father, apparently."

The owner waited nervously, drumming her fingers on the metal tray. "So…"

"We'll go with the vanilla," Sarah said. "Is that all right with you, Zondra?"

Zondra waved her hand dismissively.

"We'll take that as a yes," Sarah said. "Zondra, please give the lady the deposit." Sarah and Colin stood up to leave.

"It would be my absolute pleasure," Zondra replied, dropping a wad of bills on the table and throwing her fur cape over her shoulder. As she approached the door, she wobbled a bit, and Colin grabbed her by the elbow to steady her. "I'm fine, I'm fine. Hands off, sailor." She looked at the bakery owner and smiled as sweetly as her taut face would allow. "Might I trouble you for a glass of water?"

"Are you all right, Zondra?" Sarah said as the bakery owner scampered to the back.

"I'm fine." She sat back down at a table. "Just the whirlwind of wedding planning. You know how it…never mind." She suddenly looked quite pale and wan.

"You know, I'm going to go warm up the car," Colin said. "Do you think it's even remotely near where we left it?"

"Who knows? I'm starting to believe it has a mind of its own."

"I'll go hunt." Colin zipped up his jacket against the early winter wind and left, looking one way down the street, going the other way, then coming back to where he started. He pointed, nodded, and then proceeded the opposite way down the sidewalk.

"Have you been married before, Zondra?" Sarah cautiously sat down at the table across from her.

Zondra studied her warily, then softened her shoulders. "Once," she said, looking out the window. "A very long time ago."

"What was his name?"

"Why do you want to know?"

Sarah panicked. She hadn't expected to get this far in the conversation and found herself looking for a mental road map.

"Um, uh? Because…family?" she stammered.

"Trying to get to know your new mummy, are we?" Zondra gave the merest hint of a smile. "His name was Gideon. We were married very briefly when I was younger. For a time we were very happy."

"What happened?"

"We wanted…different things. He…left."

"I'm sorry."

"As I said, it was a long time ago. And of course, I met your father many years later. I thought he might be the one, but as you know, your mother had other ideas."

"As did my father, obviously. They were quite devoted to each other."

"I'm glad he found happiness. Hopefully, he will find it again." Zondra looked around, then held up her hands in exasperation. "Where is that infernal woman with my water? Did she have to go pump it from a well?"

As if on cue, the owner appeared with a large glass of water.

"I'm sorry it took so long, Ms. Bex, I—"

Zondra looked at her, then at the table. When the woman did not get the hint, Zondra reached out and grabbed the glass.

"Oh, for Cain's sake," Zondra said. Condensation formed on glass as she grasped it, and tiny, diamond-shaped ice cubes appeared in the water. "Thank you!" Zondra said, shooing the woman away. She removed a small, green capsule from a carved mother-of-pearl pill case and swallowed it with a tiny sip of water. Within seconds the color had returned to her face. She gently placed the glass on the table and made it disappear with a wave of her hand.

"Well now," Zondra said. "Vitamins make everything better, don't they?" The green stone in her brooch began to glow, pulsing briefly before fading back to its normal color. "I feel like a new woman." She stood up and adjusted her cape, and without another word, swept out the door.

"Is she gone?" The owner popped her head out from behind the double doors of the kitchen.

"She's gone. You're safe," Sarah said.

"Wow, she's terrifying. She reminds me of someone…"

"I'm sorry."

"Ooh, ooh, who was that sea witch who stole the mermaid's voice in that movie?"

"Yeah, the character was based on her."

"And she's going to be your stepmother?"

"Ostensibly."

"Good luck there."

Sarah shook the woman's hand and left. She looked around for Colin, who waved from about a block down from the bakery.

"Did you see Zondra leave?" Sarah said, approaching the car. "She flew off on her broom, I'm guessing?"

"She has a car. The driver looked about a hundred years old."

"He's probably only thirty-five." Sarah pointed at the vehicle. "This isn't my car."

"I know. I found it a few blocks down."

Colin offered his arm as they set off down the sidewalk.

"Do you ever think about this stuff?" he said. "For you, I mean?"

Sarah turned back to look at the bakery. "I think about cake almost daily."

Colin laughed. "No, I mean wedding things. You think about it?"

"Do you?"

"Well, I, um…"

As Colin stammered, Sarah felt the weight in her tote bag increase. They stopped, and she pulled out the Zondra Doll her father had given her, held it in her hands, and closed her eyes. In her mind, she saw an image of Zondra holding the *bareket* stone. Sarah instinctively knew Zondra was planning something, but she couldn't tell what. Suddenly, the stone in her mind turned red, then blue, then yellow…

She stuffed the doll back into her bag and pulled Colin's arm. "Let's go."

"Zondra up to something?"

"Oh always, I'm sure."

They spotted the car, and Sarah tossed Colin the keys. He opened the driver's door and unlocked the passenger side, then looked at Sarah from over the top of the car.

"I think about those things. Wedding things."

"You do?"

"From time to time."

Sarah dropped her bag, then scrambled to pick it up. She slid into the passenger seat and slammed the door shut.

"Who do you see yourself doing these things with?"

"Sometimes Sandra Bullock, but I'm pretty sure that's not going to work itself out. The rest of the time it's you." He got into the driver's seat and turned the ignition. "You okay with that?"

"Sandra? Sure. I wish you guys well." She fastened her seat belt.

"I mean us." Colin sighed. "It's okay to turn down the sarcasm once in a while."

"I'm sorry," she said, leaning over and giving Colin a kiss. "I am okay with that."

"But not now."

"Noooo," Sarah said, shaking her head.

"Noted."

Colin looked carefully behind him and pulled out onto the street. After about two blocks, they came to a stoplight. He turned to Sarah. "I thought spring might be nice, or summer when Madison's out of school…"

"Not now."

"Okay."

The light turned green. As Colin accelerated, a small, blue head popped out of the air vent, and Sarah practically backpedaled into the back seat.

"Sorry, sorry," Dave said as Sarah tried to catch her breath. "You're wanted at Nadav's place."

"Who are you, Western Union?" Sarah said. "What if I had been driving? I could have wrapped this thing around a tree!"

"Nah, you'd be more likely to hit that thing," Dave replied, gesturing at the overpass behind him. "Besides, you weren't driving. He was." Dave pointed his thumb at Colin. "I'm not a maniac."

"I don't know, Dave, you scared the hell out of me too," Colin said.

"What's going on at Nadav's?"

"Magycian town hall. Raya said you should come."

"We'll be right there," Sarah said.

"Nah, drop Mario Andretti over there off first. He'd stick out like a sore thumb. No offense."

"None taken." Colin shrugged. "I'm not even sure if that's an insult or not."

Dave adjusted the vent, then pulled his head back into the slats and disappeared.

"I guess you're going home," Sarah said.

After dropping Colin off at his house, Sarah took the wheel and drove back into the city, probably faster than was wise, and parked her car outside the pub.

"Stay," she ordered her car.

Raya was sitting at the bar, her toned arms showcased in a sleeveless AC/DC T-shirt, her legs crossed languidly as she reached for the bowl of pretzels, her bracelets jangling. She put three of the mini-pretzels in her mouth before noticing Sarah had arrived.

"Hey." Raya coughed and reached for a stein of beer. "You got my message."

"You could have texted."

"I figured you were driving."

"Oh yes, Dave in my heating vent was much less jarring," Sarah said.

"Telephone, telegram, tell-a-demon. It works."

"Hello, *ma chérie*," Nadav said, appearing behind the bar. "Want something to drink? I have that iced tea that you like."

Raya glanced at the back door. "I think she's going to need something a little stronger."

Nadav nodded and reached under the bar, pulling out an ornate, amber-colored bottle with a silver stopper. He poured the green liquid into a shot glass and pushed it gently toward Sarah.

"What is it?" She gave it a sniff.

Nadav looked at the bottle, swirled it around, and smelled it. "It is green."

"Got it." Sarah downed the shot. It felt both warm and cold going down her throat. The sensation was not altogether unpleasant; it was much like being zapped with a taser and hugged by a grandma at the same time.

"How do you feel?" Raya knocked back the rest of her beer and dabbed her mouth with a napkin.

"Fortified."

"Good. Because there's something you need to see."

Raya and Sarah went to the back of the pub, weaving among the occupied tables and the waitress who was intent on not noticing them. Raya pushed open the black, carved door, which glided noiselessly on invisible hinges. They stepped quietly into what Sarah realized was a surprisingly large space and closed the door behind them.

The room itself was filled with about two hundred people of every age, size, gender, and ethnicity. Voices rumbled among the crowd, some people arguing in languages Sarah could not understand. Under the wrought iron chandelier, which hung in the center of the room but was not attached to the ceiling, Sarah saw a young woman with pink hair having a very animated discussion with a small man wearing a hat that was almost twice his height. Two other men, both wearing shirts with swirls of metallic fabric that changed color as they moved, passed a gold ball back and forth, each one insisting it belonged to the other. And she saw a woman with the palest skin she had ever seen sneaking sips from a wooden flask with a picture of a witch on it. She spotted Avi on the dais with two elderly men, one of whom was banging a gavel with as much strength as he could muster, which at the moment was not enough to rise above the din. Avi released a firework from his palm, which exploded in a puff of sweet-smelling smoke as it reached the ceiling. The crowd got the hint and made their way back to their seats, some by foot and a few hovering a few feet above the floor.

"So we're here, Greenberg," a bass voice boomed from the audience. "What are you going to do about this?" The crowd murmured in agreement.

"Look, you all know the situation. Some of you even know Zondra personally," Avi said. Sarah sensed he was nervous, although his shoulders were broad and square, his voice strong and steady. But there was a look in his eyes...

"I thought she was gone for good. We sent her away years ago!" A man with a grey tinge to his skin shook his large fist.

"She left willingly," Avi said. "You know as well as I do we couldn't force her to stay away."

"After the circus she made at your first wedding?" A tall woman wearing a hat with a live bird stood up. "That was beyond the pale."

"Yes, yes, I remember."

"She's a *shellal*!" another person shouted.

"She's not immortal," countered another. "She's just mean."

"What's going on here?" Sarah whispered.

"They're talking about Zondra," Raya whispered back.

"They know?"

Raya put her finger up to her mouth to silence Sarah, then pointed to the dais.

Avi put his hand up. "The situation is more dire than I feared. She had a legal claim to the store. I could not let her have it. And yes, she is a *shellal*. I believe she has the missing *bareket* stone and has been using it to prolong her life."

"*I knew it!*" Sarah hissed.

The crowd erupted again, but the two elders on the dais with Avi quickly regained their focus.

An older woman stood up. "Avi, why are you marrying her? You could fight the contract in court. If you're lonely, I have a binder full of eligible women."

"She's a bit of a yenta," Sarah whispered.

"Yeah, she's the resident busybody," Raya replied, her voice hushed. "Knows everyone and everything. She makes a killer brisket, but you can never let your guard down around her."

"It's not just the contract," Avi said. "She wants the other Moonstones. I can't risk her working against me."

A man in a blue velvet bowler waved his hand. "Why don't we just have her arrested?"

"I can't prove she actually has the missing *bareket*, and she hasn't made another move," Avi said.

"Yet," said one of the elders.

"It's clear she did. She's a danger to us all. Use the *moshalen*!" A giant man in the back gave a little hop, and Sarah felt the resulting vibrations in the floor.

"No!" boomed a voice from overhead. Sarah, along with the crowd, turned her head as Esra descended from a beam in the ceiling. "We cannot use the Death Spells against another Magycian. Or anyone. You know they are against the law!"

"But—"

"That is not the way it works, Yasirit Smith. You know this," Esra said. "Do not let your fear get the better of you." Esra's feet landed softly on the stage. He looked around the room, taking in all the expectant and worried faces looking back at him. "She will not get the Twelve Moonstones."

"But he's making her a part of their family!" Philsalaro Brooks, her father's accountant, approached the stage. "Why don't you just bake her a cake and throw her a party before she takes control of the Source?"

"I have no choice, Phil! Don't you understand?" Avi boomed. "If I honor the contract, she gets the store. If I don't marry her, she will kill my daughter!"

At that moment, Avi and Sarah locked eyes. Avi grew as white as a sheet and reached out for a chair. He sat down and put his head in his hands.

All Sarah heard at that moment was a low buzzing sound. She felt Raya's arm reach around her waist to steady her, but Sarah brushed it away. The entire room turned to look at her, and she could feel the stares of the congregation bore into her being. Avi raised his head, and she saw the faint traces of tears on his face, even from across the room. She wanted to go to him, hug him, tell him it would be all right, just like he had when she was small and afraid of the thunder.

The crowd began to move as one. The room was closing in on her, the wall of people inching closer. Their muffled voices became clearer as individuals started reaching out to her.

"Poor dear…"

"She must be so overwhelmed…"

"I didn't think she had it in her…"

"She can't face Zondra Bex alone…"

Sarah turned and ran. She bolted through the hall door, through the pub where she nearly knocked over a busboy, and out to the street. Gasping for air, she dashed down the street as fast as she could until she reached the corner. Unable to decide where to go, she instinctively turned right and instantly tripped over a corgi out with its owner for a late afternoon walk.

"Sorry! Oh, he's so cute…" As she fell, she landed between the building and an old newspaper machine, scraping her elbow on the exposed brick. "Ow!"

The owner dashed off, the corgi giving her a resigned look as it was led away. She waved at the dog, then rubbed her arm. Her sleeve was ripped, the skin beneath it raw and bleeding. She sat on the sidewalk and tried to pick the small pebbles from the wound. A man walking by dropped a dollar at her feet.

"Hey, I'm not…never mind," she said, stuffing the bill in her pocket. She put her head in her hands and took a few deep breaths.

"Well, that was a show," Raya said, standing over her. "I didn't know you could move that fast."

"Me neither."

"It was impressive."

"Don't feel you have to take notice of where I'm sitting, please." Sarah looked up at her.

"Okay." Raya looked down the street, as if trying to locate a ship at sea.

Sarah pulled herself up by grabbing the newspaper machine and then leaned on it, brushing the street debris from her backside.

"Oh good, you're up." Raya grabbed Sarah's arm and ran her hand over her elbow, mending both the scrape and the ripped fabric. "Nice little freak-out you had back there. Definitely in your personal top ten." She took Sarah by the arm. "Let's walk."

"I think I was justified," Sarah replied curtly. "Dad's trying to avoid my death by marrying an immortal sociopath bent on domination of the Magyckal world. It's not like you can hear that and think, *Oh well, that's nice, anyone want a stick of gum?*"

"Why gum?"

"I always have gum. If anyone ever says, 'Does anyone have gum?' I can say, 'I do.' It's a thing."

"Odd thing to be smug about." Raya picked up her pace, forcing Sarah into a jog.

"Where are we going? I need to talk to my father."

"No, you don't. He has stuff right now. You need an advanced Magyck lesson. I've been lax."

"Now?"

"Now."

EIGHTEEN

R aya broke into a full jog, her braids bouncing as she gripped her messenger bag tightly. She made a sudden turn down an alley, which Sarah didn't anticipate. She double backed toward the alley, where Raya grasped her arm and pulled her along.

About halfway down the alley they stopped in front of a nondescript doorway, the door itself blending in with the rest of the stone building. Raya pulled her staff from her bag, and without extending it, rapped on the door. It echoed, the sound traveling as if in an expansive cave, and in short order Sarah could hear hollow footsteps inside. A small window opened, and they found themselves looking at a pair of beige eyes under very bushy grey brows.

"Kookamunga," Raya said.

The window snapped shut, and the heavy stone door opened quickly. They stood face-to-face with a rather odd-looking gentleman in a tank top and a pair of tennis shorts. He could have been anywhere between forty and ninety years old, and he had a slightly crooked smile that beamed as he greeted Raya.

"Helllloooo!" He bowed and swept his hand to the floor.

"Sarah Greenberg, meet Kookamunga Jones. He's the manager of this gym."

"Oh, I thought 'Kookamunga' was a password. Okay, cool. Nice to meet you," Sarah said, extending her hand.

"Common mistake," he replied.

"Really?"

"No, not really." He grasped her hand, pumped it once, and dropped it. Kookamunga turned and gave Raya a huge hug.

"Been a while, Raya! How's school? Doesn't leave a lot of gym time, I'm sure."

"Going well, thanks. I've been working out on my own, and I haven't had time to come by. Busy with this one," Raya said, pointing at Sarah.

"Oh yeah, I've heard. Quite a little situation going on there." Kookamunga squinted at Sarah. "She doesn't look like much. A bit soft." He squeezed her bicep.

"Hey, watch it there, pal," Sarah pulled away. She wanted to feel offended by the insult, but remembered she often had trouble walking without thinking, *Left foot, right foot, left foot, right foot...*

"Is the Box available? Need to do a little sparring practice." Raya craned her neck to see if she recognized any of the members walking around the club.

"Box?" Sarah said, but Raya waved her off.

"It's free," Kookamunga replied. He nodded at Sarah. "She up for it?"

"She's tougher than she looks," Raya said with a smile.

Left foot, right foot...

"It's yours. Conjure a *solarapring* lamp to hang outside the Box and no one will bother you."

"Thanks. Owe you one."

Kookamunga nodded, then sat on a stool by the door, picking up a newspaper and opening it with a flourish.

Raya and Sarah walked down the long, stone corridor, their footfalls echoing, and Sarah was momentarily startled by the various pops, bangs, hoots, and hollers from the rooms on either side of them. Puffs of pink smoke curled out from underneath one of the doors, its tendrils forming geometric shapes before dissipating into the cool air.

"Are we really going to work out?" Sarah asked. "I don't have any gym clothes. Or the right bra."

"Won't need 'em," Raya said. "I mean, you will need clothes, it's not that kind of gym, but what you're wearing is fine." She glanced at Sarah's feet and waved her hand to transform her shoes to black sequined sneakers.

Sarah examined her new footwear. "Will these help me?"

"Nah. Those are just snazzier."

They stopped in front of a room fronted with smoky glass doors. Raya conjured a *solarapring* lamp as Kookamunga had suggested, and hung it on the wall. Sarah reached for the door handle, but Raya stopped her and stepped easily through the glass. Sarah followed. It felt like she was passing through a cold, damp fog, and she shuddered. When she was over the threshold, she rubbed her eyes and looked around.

"We're playing racquetball?" Sarah looked at the lines painted on the floor of the court, which undulated in succession around the room.

"Sort of." Raya put her hand on a dark, glass panel on the wall, and the lines on the floor transformed into fluorescent beams of light. "No rackets though." She put on a pair of round goggles and smiled. "This is your racket." She held up her hand and waggled her long, elegant fingers.

"So, handball."

Raya sighed. "Has it not registered where you are?"

"I try not to think about it too much," Sarah replied. "I find it's best just to go with it."

"Fair enough. Okay, we're going to do a workout of sorts. I come here from time to time to polish my fighting skills, but that's a bit above your skill level at the moment. Given the recent developments, I think we need to work on some foundational skills. Primarily your reflexes."

"What's wrong with my reflexes?" A hairbrush, wallet, and granola bar flew through the air and hit Sarah in the arm, leg, and torso. "Ow, my boob."

"That's what I thought." Raya gathered up her things and plunked them back into her messenger bag, which she then tossed to the side of the court. "We'll start at Level One."

Raya held her palm upward, and a gold ball materialized above it. "Watch the ball," she continued. "Don't try to hit it, just dodge it."

"Should I pretend it's Zondra trying to kill me?" Sarah giggled nervously.

"No."

The ball floated away from Raya and gracefully bobbed and weaved between the pillars of light that had materialized on the court. Sarah eyed it cautiously, hypnotized by its languid orbit around the room. Suddenly, it zoomed directly at her and grazed her arm, leaving a faint red mark.

"Crap! That hurt!"

"You got lulled into a false sense of security. Just because something seems slow doesn't mean it can't change on a dime. Let's try again."

Raya guided the ball upward, then let it float away. It changed speeds several times, first coming at Sarah at a high speed, then slowing down as it neared her head. She reacted too soon, dodging it before it actually reached her, and bonking her head on it as she stood up.

"Now you're anticipating. Don't think too hard. Just be casually aware of where the ball is," Raya said.

"I am very tense right now."

"I know. I've met you. Just loosen up and think of cake."

Raya sent the ball flying again, making an irregular path around the court like a drunken bumblebee. Sarah tried to relax, and when the ball came near her, she easily sidestepped it.

"I was thinking about a Black Forest gateau," Sarah said.

"Whatever works, babe."

The ball came at Sarah faster, spinning around the room, spiraling among the columns of light, but Sarah grew more confident in her abilities, dodging, ducking, and weaving around it. Raya upped the game and added two more balls, one red and one blue, and varied the speed to keep Sarah on her toes.

"They'll come faster now! Try thinking of cheesecake!"

The balls increased in speed, never going in the same route twice, but Sarah kept up, finding that the less she thought about it, the easier it was.

I wouldn't be picked last for dodgeball now, that's for sure.

Raya called the balls back to her and left them hovering in the air by her side. She materialized a towel and handed it to Sarah.

"Thanks." Sarah dabbed her forehead. She hadn't realized how hard she had been working.

"Now we're going to up the ante," Raya said. "Instead of dodging the balls, I want you to hit them away."

"I've done something like this." Sarah recalled the shoot-out at the library, the bolts of light and the menacing assailants vivid in her memory.

"Yes, kind of. You were working blindly then. We're going to focus your energy. No, you won't need your wand," Raya said, stopping Sarah before she could get to her purse.

"What do I use then?"

"Most of us use our hands, but I had a classmate back in the day who liked to deflect energy with his elbows. He was very flexible."

"So how do I do this?"

"Same kind of thing that you've done before. Reach out to the vibrating strings, focus the energy on your hand, and build up a little cushion. That will repel the ball." Raya gathered her hair into a bun on the top of her head and wrapped it with a scarf. Sarah noticed that she was perspiring too, actively training as if she were in a boxing ring. "You don't have to hit every one, but do the best you can."

Sarah started slowly, pulling the strings' energy and concentrating it in her palm, adjusting the color and strength of each string to match the velocity and trajectory of the gold ball. She hit most of them back, like a game of shiny handball, moving around the court, avoiding the columns of light, and ducking and weaving as necessary. After a few minutes, it became second nature, and Raya adjusted the game accordingly, adding back the blue and red balls, which Sarah found were different in size and weight.

Her body felt lighter as she moved, taking in the energy and dispersing it as needed. For the first time in her life she felt agile, almost powerful, instead of the slow girl who always got placed in the made-up position of very far left field. Raya was nodding and smiling, her words encouraging and positive.

The room dimmed. It was hazy now, the balls glowing and leaving slight trails of light as they careened around her, coming faster and with more force. Dodge, weave, repel. Sarah's breath came in jagged rasps as she struggled to keep up. As the haze thickened, she spotted a new figure in the Box with them. She made her way forward, battling back the glowing balls that threatened to block her path. She inched around the nearest column and saw the figure of a man dash to the back corner of the court. She inched closer, and Colin, with eyes like two pools of ebony, stared back at her. She opened her mouth to call out to him, but before she could make a sound, the figure hurled a black disk at her, missing her head by inches. She whirled around in surprise, almost forgetting to reach out to the energy strings to defend herself.

She couldn't find any.

The sound of another disk whizzed past her ear, and she leaned away. She tried to deflect it, but her energy reserve was gone. The room began to fade to black, and Sarah reached out for Raya, who was in the corner of the room waving her arms and creating colored vapor trails in their wake. Sarah fell to her knees and reached out, willing the trails to come to her as the figure of Colin approached.

She crawled backward, trying to fill her mind with thoughts of color, light, energy—whatever might take her back to the strings. The dark figure grew closer and closer, until it loomed over her. It reached back with its arm, a larger disk in its hand, and threw it down. With one last gasping breath Sarah found a string, and without thinking, used both hands to push the energy up toward the familiar face now looking down at her.

"I'm sorry, Colin."

Boom! The energy string made contact with the figure, and it flew backward into one of the pillars of light, winking out of existence like a burned-out bulb on an old lamp. She scrambled to her feet and away from the middle of the room, again reaching out for Raya, who had collapsed on a chair in the far corner.

"Raya! Are you all right?" Sarah tried to wave away the haze as she embraced her friend.

"I'm fine," Raya replied, giving Sarah a squeeze. "What the hell was that?"

"That wasn't you?"

"God no," Raya said, reaching out with one arm and dissipating the fog. "I wouldn't do that to you. That was some weird-ass stuff."

She sat up straight and looked intently at the main door of the Box. She pointed at a small, shadowy figure lurking just outside the doorway, its figure outlined in the backlight of the smoky glass.

"Kookamunga! I see you! What the hell, man?" Raya dashed to the door. The shadow tried to run, but Raya was quicker and grabbed the man by his tank top. Pulling him through the door and into the court, she tossed him into the chair. He sat with his arms folded, a grim look on his face.

"I didn't do nothin.'." He gave Raya a steely glare. "Can't prove it."

"Yeah, totally can. You're the only one with access. What's going on?" Raya said.

He said nothing and turned away. Sarah slid down the wall and sat on the floor, wiping her face with a towel.

"You used the Black Sphere, Kook. That's some advanced level dark Magyck. We didn't ask for that." Raya stood next to him, hands on her hips. "What's going on?" She looked ready to wait as long as it took for an answer, and Kookamunga was prepared to oblige.

Raya stood in silence, the faint sounds of other Magycians' bangs and booms echoing down the corridor outside. Their host merely tapped his foot, either in impatience or in time to some orchestration in his own mind.

"Who's paying you?" Sarah's voice broke the quiet.

Raya and Kookamunga turned their heads in unison, his mouth gaping in surprise. He opened and closed it several times, hunting for an answer that wouldn't incriminate him. He hung his head and sighed.

"Zondra Bex."

Raya looked surprised, but Sarah felt strangely calm. She got to her feet and walked slowly toward him.

"What did she promise you?" She stood tall, lowering her head slightly to meet the man's gaze.

Kookamunga stared at them blankly.

"C'mon, Kook. What was it?" Raya asked.

"I don't know what you're talking about."

Raya grabbed his chin. "I heard you've been trading in some illegal Smoke Beasts."

"Untrue." He pushed her hand away.

"Hmm." Raya folded her arms. "Maybe I can grab one from your office and materialize it in here."

"You'd die," Kookamunga sniffed. "You can't outrun a Smoke Beast."

Sarah leaned in and kicked the leg of his chair, causing him to flinch. "We don't have to outrun *it*. We just have to outrun *you*."

Kookamunga's eyes darted back and forth between the women. He licked his lips and squeezed his eyes shut. "An interdimensional room!" he blurted. "She said she was going to get her hands on the store one way or another and said if I helped her she'd transfer one of the interdimensional rooms to my facility. Can you imagine the business I'd do if I had that here?"

"So you sold out."

Kookamunga tried to stand, but Raya pushed him back into the chair.

"I wouldn't have hurt her!" He grabbed Sarah's arm, but she pulled away. "Maybe wound her. Just a little!" He ran his hand through his slicked-back hair. "And so what? Her family has had stewardship of that place for too long! Zondra said she'd share. Make us rich. How could I say no?"

"You really think she's going to share anything with you?" Sarah asked, bending down again and putting her face close to his. "You really want us to die? Because that's the only way she'd get anything."

"No! I just…I mean…she promised. And she said she wouldn't hurt Avi. Or you. She just wanted you out of the picture, she said."

"That's what she told you, huh?" Sarah could feel Kookamunga's hot breath, and it made her queasy. "She lied."

"But…but…" Kookamunga sputtered. "She wouldn't do that, would she?"

"What have you been smoking, Kook?" Raya laughed.

Kookamunga covered his face in his hands. "Oh, geez. Please don't tell Avi what I did. You won't tell him, will you?"

Sarah felt a wave of pity and mild revulsion. She stood up. "I won't tell my father if you do one thing for us. Tell Zondra that you were successful, and that I was frightened. Tell her I talked about taking off. You can even tell her you wounded me. Just a 'little bit.'"

"Yes, yes, I'll do whatever you want," Kookamunga said. "Let me get you ladies some water. And some free T-shirts. Wait here, all right?" He ran out of the Box and down the hall, ordering people out of his way. "Samli! Get some shirts! And those hover sticks! Do we have any smoothies?"

"You were much kinder to him than I would have been." Raya packed up her bag and hoisted it over her shoulder.

"Zondra can think she won this round," Sarah replied. "Maybe she'll let down her guard. Hopefully, it will give us a little more time to figure out what to do." She picked up her purse and tucked it under her arm. "It would be easier if we could just have her arrested."

"Technically, she hasn't done anything yet. Well, nothing we can prove."

"We need to get that *bareket* from her."

"If it is indeed the missing Moonstone."

"It has to be." Sarah pointed to the door. "Let's go. I need a shower, and I want to call Colin."

They called Slenn for a ride back to the pub, although it was only a few blocks away, and as they got into the car Sarah felt a wave of fatigue overcome her. After belting herself in and patting Alvin the mini-dragon on the head, she closed her eyes, her lids heavy. Slenn took it easy on them, driving carefully and at a reasonable speed. As Sarah listened to the hum of the engine and Slenn and Raya's quiet conversation, she dozed off and dreamed of strange, dark figures and balls of light. But this time she wasn't afraid. In her mind, she followed the light down a glowing green path, past vibrating string and Black Spheres, past small demons with glittering blue skin and plants that played gin rummy. At the end of the path was a pair of emerald-green eyes, warm and kind, and the music of The Spiral Vogues playing on rubber bands let her know that this was the right path to be on—and for the first time in a long while, Sarah knew that everything would be all right.

Slenn dropped them off at the pub, and Sarah found her car and drove home. As she closed the front door behind her, she stared at her living room, everything just as she had left it this morning. Outside, a light snow was beginning to fall, and she took her robe and went to the bathroom to take a long, hot shower. Afterward, she sat on the edge of her bed and picked up her cell phone. She scrolled through her address book and tapped the desired name, humming to herself as she listened to it ring. Life was too short, she figured, and she knew how she wanted to spend her time.

A familiar voice answered the call, and she smiled.

"Hi Colin. Want to come over? Bring cheesecake."

CHAPTER
NINETEEN

T he bridal shop was small and smelled a bit like patchouli and paprika, and the storefront was covered in ivy. Debra, sitting in a chair upholstered in ivory silk damask, nibbled on a protein bar she had stashed in her purse while Miriam played with a toy truck and Aaron chased Albert the mini-dragon around the storefront mannequins.

"I don't know why we couldn't just go to a regular bridal salon," Sarah said.

"After the cake-tasting debacle, Zondra said she 'just didn't want to work with the Unenchanted.'"

"It was hardly a debacle. She didn't eat any cake and then made the owner cry. Considering who she is, I'd give the whole thing a B-plus."

Debra raised her eyebrows and accepted a glass of champagne from a small, prim, slightly grey shop assistant. She took a little sip, then a longer one.

Sarah walked up to the rack and picked out a dress.

"Okay, who would wear this?" She waved her hand through the garment. "It's made exclusively of mist."

"It's pretty."

"It's condensation."

Sarah put the dress back and grabbed another.

"What is this?" she said, holding up a short, sheer, multicolored shift.

"Oh, that's the latest thing," Debra said. "Simple really. Light from the sun strikes a drop of water on the wearer's body, and some of the light is reflected and some is refracted. Then the white light is split into a spectrum of colors, the light is reflected inside the back of the original drop of water, it's refracted again as it leaves the droplet, and the colors are further dispersed."

"So it's a rainbow. You'd be wearing a rainbow."

"Basically, yes."

"Has no one heard of Vera Wang?"

"Oh, she and I had a falling out years ago."

Zondra glided into the bridal shop wearing her usual white tailored ensemble, stopping to take a champagne flute from the dour assistant. "She said that my ideas were too 'over the top.' Me, over the top? Please. But I suppose she's done all right for herself."

With a flourish she downed the champagne in one swallow and set the glass in the outstretched hand of a nearby mannequin, which placed the flute on the table next to it before returning to its original position. Sarah was pretty sure it scowled.

Miriam, noticing the new member of the shopping team, rushed to Zondra with all the requisite energy of a seven-year-old and wrapped her arms tightly around Zondra's waist. Zondra looked at her and frowned.

"What is it doing? And why is it a bit sticky?" She disengaged herself from the girl's grip and wiped her hands on a napkin she conjured.

"She's saying hello," Debra countered. "Miriam, say hello to your new step-grandmother."

"Just call me Ms. Bex, please."

"Oh," Miriam replied with a slight pout. "I thought she was a nurse."

"Ha!" Sarah quickly recovered. "Sorry."

"Not a kid person, I gather?" Debra asked.

"Best they not get…too attached." Zondra smirked and then clapped her hands twice. "Assistance, please!"

The dour assistant reappeared along with the shop manager, both holding several dresses on large, wooden hangers. The manager cowered a bit as Zondra quickly fingered each garment and found it wanting. With a lift of her eyebrow, she sent the salespeople scuttling back to the storeroom.

Performing a dramatic sweep with her fur cape, Zondra landed in the third armchair, crossed her legs, and stared intently at Sarah. "So, dahling, still writing your…what is it again that you, as they say, *do?*"

"Food writer. Still at the magazine, although I'm a bit behind this week." Sarah shot Debra a look that indicated she'd rather be taste-testing various poisons than dress shopping with a Magyckal sociopath. She glanced at her phone and saw that she had several voicemails. Her editor.

That can't be good.

The shop attendants returned with a new selection in a rainbow of colors and fabrics. Zondra grunted quietly and chose two to try on.

"Now, you two stay right there," she said, entering a dressing room. "I'll need your opinion on which one you think is the most flattering. Well, I'll need Debra's opinion. Sarah, you can have another drink."

"Where would we go?" Debra leaned over to her sister. "She's probably put up a security fence around the perimeter."

"Mom, I'm hungry," Aaron said, sitting on the display window's edge, Albert perched on his shoulder. "Can we go get something to eat?"

Debra opened her small purse and pulled out an apple, two cheese sticks, and a juice box and tossed them to Aaron, who caught them deftly. "Miriam? You want?"

"No thank you," she said, pushing her toy truck over a pair of *peau de soie* dress pumps.

"Wow, you are prepared," Sarah said.

"Not my first time at the rodeo," Debra replied, pulling a roast chicken out of her purse. "For dinner later."

"You have martinis in there?"

"Not today, unfortunately."

Zondra whisked back the dressing room curtain and stepped out wearing a sea-mist green gown with sparkling iridescent pearls covering the bodice and a ten-foot train.

"I don't know." She held up the back of the dress and twirled in the mirror. "It's a bit pedestrian, don't you think?"

The poor assistant looked like she hadn't taken a breath in three hours. "It also comes in forest green." She took a big gulp of air.

"Get me that. I do like a dark green."

The assistant ran her hand over the length of the gown, changing it from sea mist to the darker green. Zondra turned to look at herself, admiring the fit and the beadwork.

"Not bad, but I'm sure I'll have to try some others, of course."

"Albert, no!" Aaron shrieked.

The trio of women turned in time to see Aaron's mini-dragon swoop about the shop and land squarely on Zondra's expertly coiffed head. Sarah was sure that poor Albert was about to meet his demise, but Zondra merely adjusted the dragon to a smart angle and looked at herself in the mirror.

"I hadn't thought about a hat." A grim smile teased her lips. "Perhaps a dragon would be the perfect accessory. After he's been stuffed, of course."

"No! You can't do that!" Aaron protested.

Debra stood and snapped her fingers, retrieving Albert from Zondra's head and back into Aaron's arms. "How about we not terrorize the children, all right? Let's maintain some civility, please." She placed her hands on her hips and glared at Zondra, who was momentarily taken aback.

"I'm…sorry," she said quietly. "Yes, we should…civility. Of course." She turned back to the mirror. "I've never really been a hat person anyway."

"Okay, we're done here." Debra corralled the children and tossed all their belongings in her impossibly small handbag. "I think we've had enough family time."

"But—" Sarah said.

"You'll be fine." Debra kissed her sister on the cheek. "If she does that again I have a feeling I'll lose my you-know-what." She glanced at the kids.

Sarah felt a chill run down her spine. She hugged her sister, then her niece and nephew.

"She's weird," Aaron whispered to his aunt.

"You have no idea, boychik." She gently ruffled Aaron's hair.

"Give me the doll," Debra whispered after Zondra began changing the polish on her fingernails. "I'll be able to sense if Zondra's trying something. I'll send reinforcements."

"No, I'll keep it. You never know."

Debra nodded and quickly guided the children out the door.

"Going so soon?" Zondra said, still facing the mirror. "Ah well. Sarah and I will have a grand time on our own. Won't we, dahling?" She turned her head, but her mirror image remained stationary. The reflection winked.

Sarah sat down, keeping close watch on Zondra, who was watching the children as they left the store.

"Sweet little girl, that Miriam. She reminds me of my sister, Alyce."

"There's two of you?"

"There was. Alyce was older than me and was the star of everything she did." Zondra adjusted the shoulders of her dress. "You know what that's like, don't you? Playing second fiddle to a sister who can do everything better than you?"

"I wouldn't know. Debra and I don't compete."

"Pssh. Please. Sisters always compete. For friends, for grades, for… Daddy. No matter how hard we try, we always come up short." Zondra let out a sharp breath. "It's good that you've coped so well."

"Considering I have my future stepmother trying to kill me, sure."

Zondra turned on her heel. "You're being overly dramatic. It's not becoming." She snapped her fingers. "SHOP!"

The manager appeared in a flash.

"I'm losing interest in this gown," Zondra said. "Do you have anything in imp-skin?"

The manager winked out of sight and reappeared almost immediately with two grey dresses and another that looked like it was made entirely from densely knit spiderweb, which Sarah thought was a little on the nose. Zondra stepped into the changing room, and the dresses disappeared from the manager's hands.

Sarah began to perspire. She scratched nervously at her elbow and fished around her bag for a mint. She found one of Esra's butterscotches and unwrapped it quietly, popping it into her mouth before Zondra could admonish her for eating so close to her dress, as if the sugar could leap off the candy and adhere to the fabric. Her body temperature dropped a few degrees, and she sat back in the chair.

"We're not so different, you and I," Zondra said from behind the curtain. "We will both do what we need to do to get what we want."

"You don't know me at all."

"Don't I?" Zondra emerged from the dressing room like a Cher impersonator on her third encore, one arm raised in triumphant fabulousness. She spun in front of the mirror, admiring herself from all angles. The dress fit perfectly, iridescent grey with bell sleeves and the sheerest of netting by the neckline. "We're both fighters. We just have different methods."

"I'm not out to hurt anyone."

"Afraid of a little challenge? Alyce wasn't afraid. She pushed me to be better. To take what I want. You're getting better too. It's been… surprising. I'm just here to keep you on your toes."

"What happened to Alyce?"

Zondra turned back to the mirror, and Sarah could see a small tear forming in the corner of her eye. She quickly dabbed it and shook her head slightly, taking another quick breath.

"She got in my way." Zondra placed her hands on her hips. "Yes. This is the one. What do you think? Do you think Mummy looks pretty?" It was a statement rather than a question, and Sarah found herself nodding in acquiescence.

"It's very nice." Sarah's voice registered barely above a whisper.

"Maybe someday you'll have a dress like this, no?" Zondra turned to face her. She smiled, the kind that was performed only with the mouth, not the eyes. "You and that beau of yours…Clyde, is it?"

"Colin."

"Ah, yes. Colin. Still holding onto that one, are we? Good for you. I heard you have a tendency to run. Not too fond of the long haul, hmmm? I did that once, and I don't intend to do it again."

Sarah said nothing. Zondra wasn't wrong—she didn't have the greatest track record with men, always finding reasons to end the relationship. One chewed too loudly, another said the word "camera" strangely, and there was the fellow who had a weird relationship with his ferret. Even her career was typical Sarah; it allowed her to be creative and come and go as she pleased. It really was perfect for her, and she realized how much she loved it, although she was beginning to feel that she needed to listen to those voicemails.

"So it looks like this Colum—"

"Colin."

"He could be the one, don't you think so, dahling?"

Sarah's spine stiffened. "It's possible."

"You need to lock that man down. You're not getting any younger, you know," Zondra sneered. "Run off, get married, start a new life somewhere else."

"I'm not leaving my father alone with you."

Zondra's eyes flashed. "Just take off. It's what you want to do, isn't it?" She inched closer to Sarah. "Now, sweetie, you don't want the store. You've been itching to run ever since you came into your, well, let's call them powers, such as they are." She was looming over Sarah, who was inching down her chair.

"I'm learning." Sarah's voice trembled.

"I'm sure. But I think you're a little out of your element. Your mother knew this, didn't she?" Zondra grabbed Sarah's shirt and levitated her out of her chair until they were practically nose to nose. "She was in my way too."

Sarah gasped, then gritted her teeth, her heart threatening to leap from her chest and make a break for it. Swallowing hard, she fought the urge to punch Zondra in the face. She then tried to peel the woman's fingers from her collar, but only managed to move them up to her neck. "You just want power. You don't care about the store. The community."

"What do you know about that?" Zondra's eyes turned dark, and she dropped Sarah back into her chair. "You know nothing."

"I know about the *bareket*." Sarah practically choked on her words. "I know about the Twelve Moonstones."

Zondra laughed darkly. "Such fairy tales!"

"I know who you are, Zondra."

"Then you know what I'm capable of." She reached down and took Sarah's face in her hands. "I will remove you from my way. You, your sister, even your dear, lovely father. I have come too far."

She released her grip on Sarah's face. Sarah looked up at her with uncertain eyes, willing them to focus on the fabric of Zondra's dress, which undulated under the lights of the store.

"That's right. You're a burden. You're useless. You'll never be the Magycian Avi is. Yet he seems to love you anyway. Isn't. That. Sweet. I say that with affection, of course." Another smile lurched across Zondra's face, as if the muscles were tired from the effort and just wanted a cocktail or a nap.

The shop manager appeared, holding a clear clipboard and a small, yellow stick of light. "That looks lovely on you, Ms. Bex. Is this the one?" Her voice was quiet and monotone.

Sarah stood and placed her foot squarely on her bag. She moved her heel a bit until she found the stuffed doll at the bottom.

"Ow!" Zondra said, holding her arm. "What was that?"

"Shopping is a sport, you know," Sarah said, steeling her spine. "Maybe you pulled a muscle squeezing into that dress."

She picked up the bag and slung it over her shoulder. "This has been peachy, Zondra. Hope you can find some matching shoes." She marched to the door, then stopped and turned around. "If you can find any that fit over hooves, that is." Sarah threw open the shop door and left with as much flourish as she could muster.

Sarah got halfway down the block before she realized she was holding her breath. Leaning against the cool stone of the building, she inhaled deeply and felt the winter sun on her face. She dug into her bag to retrieve her cell phone, and with a few presses on the screen, retrieved her voicemails. As she put the phone to her ear, a fire truck raced by, its siren screaming, obscuring the first part of her editor's message. But she heard the last part:

"…budget cuts. We're going to have to lay you off."

TWENTY

S arah sat at the kitchen table with Madison, dipping the small brush into the bottle of "Mermaid Green" nail polish and carefully applying it to the teen's nails with a level of intensity usually reserved for brain surgeons.

"And they didn't give you an explanation?" Colin filled the teakettle at the sink.

"Money. It's always money. The magazine is downsizing. Everything but features and sports were kicked to the curb. I've been there ten years, for fu—" She glanced at Madison. "—Pete's sake. *Ten years*."

"That sucks," added Madison.

"It does indeed suck, my friend." Sarah wiped a bit of smudged polish from the girl's thumb. "And there we go. Not too shabby, I think."

Madison admired her fingernails. "I think you have a new career path."

Sarah got up and leaned on the kitchen island. "Ten years. I was there ten years."

"You going to be all right?" Colin asked.

"Emotionally? Who knows. But financially I'll be fine. I have some savings, so I'll be okay for a while."

"Do you want to stay in the business?"

"I do," Sarah said. "I really loved my job. The food, meeting people I never had to see again, and the writing especially. I worked hard to put some creativity into my columns."

"Something will turn up," Colin said. "You're very talented."

"You could always live here," Madison said with a small, shy smile.

Sarah giggled nervously. "Well, I mean, hmm, uh, I wouldn't, you see…"

"Madison thinks she's being helpful," Colin said, kissing his daughter on the top of her head. "We said we wouldn't bring that up right now," he whispered in her ear. "Who wants a cookie?"

"It's fine. I'm just being weird." Sarah looked around. "What kind of cookie?"

"I think we have a few to choose from. Madison had a sleepover last week, but they surprisingly did not finish everything in the pantry. I was expecting a swarm of locusts."

"You got lucky." Sarah paused, then slammed her hand down on the counter. "Damn it. I just didn't need another change in my life right now." She looked at Colin and Madison. "Sorry. Just having a moment."

"You get two cookies."

Colin walked to the pantry and opened the door, revealing Esra, who had his hand raised as if he were just about to knock. Colin jumped back in surprise.

"Here, try these," Esra said, holding up a bag of Mint Milanos in his other hand. "They are quite good."

"Thank you."

"You are welcome. Are you going to invite me in, or shall I continue as a food dispenser?" Esra winked.

"Sorry," Colin said. "This is an alternate entry into the house that I had not previously considered."

"I understand. I meant to land on your front porch, but it looks like my coordinates were a bit off." Esra stepped into the kitchen and removed his hat. "Sarah! There you are!" He glided over to the table. "Who is your charming friend?"

"Esra, this is Madison, Colin's daughter."

"Lovely to meet you, Madison. Your fingernails are green."

"Sarah painted them," Madison replied.

"And this is something that you desired?"

"Yes."

"All right then. Carry on." Esra sat in a kitchen chair, and his nails become the identical shade as Madison's. "What do you think? Is this my color?" He lowered his glasses and winked at Madison, who giggled.

"Would you like some tea, Esra?" Colin asked.

"Do you have Dragon's Bane?"

Colin looked at the boxes of tea. "I have Earl Grey or some kind of chamomile."

Esra shrugged. "Six of one."

"Esra," Sarah said, "not that I'm not thrilled to see you—"

"Naturally."

"—but what are you, you know, *doing* here?"

"Ah yes. That. Of course. Forgive me, I was temporarily distracted by my young friend's cosmetic ablutions." Esra wiggled his fingers, and his nails returned to their natural shade. Colin placed a mug of tea in front of him. "Thank you. Raya told me that you lost your job. She wanted me to come and check on you."

"I'm fine, Esra."

"Truly?"

"Yes." Sarah bit a Mint Milano in half and sat down at the table. "Maybe it's a good thing? Fresh start?" She chewed, swallowed, and rested her forehead on the table. "I have a lot going on right now."

"You do." Esra sipped his tea.

"With the wedding and the whole 'My father's fiancée may be an immortal sociopath' thing. It's a lot."

"Madison, why don't you go read upstairs?" Colin said.

"But I want to stay here. I know about everything. Right, Sarah?"

"Don't worry. You won't miss anything. I promise. Listen to your father."

Madison let out a big sigh and rolled her eyes, the kind only achievable by teenaged girls who feel deeply and strongly that they have been irreparably wronged. "Okaaay." She gathered her manicure supplies and headed up the stairs to her room.

"She keeps trying to get rid of me," Sarah said.

"Madison?" Esra said.

"Zondra."

"Well, yes. It is in her best interests."

"I don't feel entirely safe."

"That is probably a good thing. You need to be alert. Would it help you to know that you were right about her?" Esra took another sip of tea. "This is good. Are you sure it is not Dragon's Bane?"

"Tension Tamer," Colin said, examining the box.

"Appropriate," Esra replied. "As you feared, Sarahleh, Zondra *is* immortal. Artificially, of course. She has had help from the *bareket.*"

"And we need to get it from her," Sarah nodded in agreement. "If she can connect it with the other Twelve Moonstones…"

"We are in for some difficulties. You have good instincts. Keep your eyes and ears open."

"So I'm right."

"You are on the path. What else is on your mind?"

"How much time do you have?" Sarah said.

"As we have discussed, time is a construct of our consciousness, one that is relative to the observer, as my friend Bert used to say. Others think that the observer actually creates time." Esra took another sip of tea. "For instance, I have a class to teach in exactly thirty seconds. But I will not be late."

"Because you create your own time."

"More or less. And so does Zondra."

Sarah let out a quiet growl, then bit into another cookie.

"Let us think about something else then." Esra reached for his knapsack. "Perhaps some music? I learned a new piece recently. I have been experimenting on the rubber bands with a song from a young man called Sting. It is very good. I think he has a bright future ahead of him." He pulled a large pouch out of his bag and began laying out his bands on the table.

Sarah smiled. "Yes, he's very promising." She picked up her mug and brought it to the sink. Colin put his hands on her waist and drew her in.

"You're not thinking of running, are you?"

"I never run. Only when chased."

He kissed her gently and let her go. She turned to ask Esra if he'd like more tea and found him staring at a small portal that had opened up over the kitchen table.

"What is that?" Sarah's eyes widened.

"I have no idea." Esra stuck his hand in it, and Sarah gasped.

"Esra! Be careful!"

"I am fine," he replied. "Just as I suspected. Hmm, I wonder…"

"Wonder what, Esra?" Colin asked. "I'm not used to portals in my kitchen." He pressed himself back against the counter.

"Nor should you be. It is not a usual occurrence." Esra closed his eyes and began to hum.

"What should we do here?" Colin whispered.

"I'm not sure of the protocol either," Sarah replied.

"It is a Soli-Mirror," Esra announced. "Yes, I am sure of it."

"A what?" Colin said.

"It is a spying device, of sorts," Esra said. "Not used much anymore. Usually, it is created in a less noticeable place. But she just put it right there. That is bold."

"Who, Zondra?"

"Most likely. I think she is trying to keep tabs on you."

"Should we hide?" Colin said, giving Sarah a look.

"I don't know, this is new to me too." She shrugged.

"No need." Esra waved his hand, and the portal disappeared. "It is closed. It was rather clumsily done, to be honest. I think she is getting a little frantic."

"Oh, that's nice to hear," Sarah said.

"It is not necessarily a bad thing. She is more likely to act impulsively. We can use that to our advantage." Esra put his bands away. "No time for music now. I am going take my leave. Thank you for the tea, Colin. You are an excellent host." He opened the door to the pantry. "I will put a quick protective spell over your house as I depart, just as a precaution, you see." He put on his hat and secured his bag under his arm. "Oh, and you are running low on peanut butter."

Esra closed the door behind him, and with the tinkling of wind chimes and a soft "bamf" sound, he was gone.

Colin and Sarah stood in silence, and then he took her hand in his and held it to his chest.

Sarah gave a large sigh. "I have a lot going on right now."

"Yes. Yes you do."

"A lot of weird shit."

"Yes."

"Thank you for holding my hand."

"You want to bail right now, don't you?"

"Little bit."

"That's why I'm holding your hand." Colin gave her a hug. "We'll manage. I promise."

"I just have to somehow steal a *bareket* stone from a woman who is basically a supervillain, return it to the vessel of the Twelve Moonstones, and preserve the freedom of the Magyckal community, which six months ago I didn't even know existed."

"Piece of cake."

Sarah looked up at him. "When you say it, I actually believe it."

There was a knock from behind the pantry door. Colin opened it slowly.

"Hey, I made you these," Dave said, holding out a tray. "Almond cookies. Stop with the store-bought."

"Thanks," Colin said, accepting the platter.

"No problem," Dave replied. "By the way, you're out of peanut butter." He licked his lips with his purple, forked tongue and winked, leaving a puff of sparkly blue smoke in his wake as he disappeared.

"You have a weird family," Colin said, looking at the tray in his hands.

"I know." Sarah ate a cookie. "These *are* good! I need to get his recipe."

CHAPTER

TWENTY-ONE

S arah entered her bedroom with a handful of dress bags. Dropping them on the bed, she exhaled heavily and looked at Raya, who was checking her hair in the full-length mirror. It had been six weeks since the fitting. Zondra hadn't consulted them on the bridesmaids' dresses, and Sarah had some serious concerns. The first was why she and Raya were asked to be in the wedding party but not her sister Debra. She could only surmise that Zondra wanted to keep as large a distance between her and the "sticky children" as possible. The other was the concern that Zondra would put a curse on her as soon as she said "I do."

"They're heeere," Sarah said in her best sing-song. "They're surprisingly heavy."

"What's that smell?" Raya leaned over the pile.

"Danger." Sarah looked at her friend. "You know, I didn't even ask. I think the delivery guy was just glad to be rid of them."

"Should we open them slowly, or just rip them open like a Band-Aid?"

"Why delay the inevitable?" Sarah held her breath and carried her dress bag to the bathroom.

"Are you seriously changing in there? I've seen you in your skivvies before, you know," Raya called.

"I have air freshener in here!"

Sarah emerged a minute later, hands heavy by her sides. Raya looked at her and nearly doubled over in laughter.

"I appreciate the vote of confidence," Sarah said.

"Have you looked at yourself?"

Raya physically moved Sarah over to the full-length mirror. Sarah's mouth fell open, whether from shock or revulsion she wasn't sure.

"What colors are those?" Raya asked.

"Rust, lime green, and mustard yellow."

"What do you call that combination?"

"I don't know," Sarah said. "Afternoon Nausea?"

"The turtleneck is nice. Don't often see that in formalwear."

"I was hoping for a large ruff with tassels. Go look at yours."

Raya opened the bag. "Hopefully mine will be better. She hates me less… Holy mother of—" She slapped her hand over her mouth.

It was the same dress but with a Nehru collar, high waist, and a big bow.

"Oh God, mine's rust, lime green, and mustard yellow too!" Raya exclaimed.

"No, yours is mustard yellow, rust, and lime green. There's a difference." Sarah showed her the tag on the garment bag.

"I'm not wearing this."

"Yes, you are. On we go…" Sarah helped Raya pull the dress over her head. "I dig it with the combat boots."

"They're better for stomping."

Together, they looked at themselves in the mirror.

"We look like the worst girl group ever." Raya twirled, then curtsied.

"We could call ourselves The Cough Drops."

"I'm sorry," Raya said. "But this dress makes me want to…what's the expression? Oh yeah. Cut a bitch."

Raya ran her hand up and down the length of the dress, did it again, and then a third time.

"What are you doing?"

"Trying to alter the dress. Nope. She put a charm on it. It's staying put. Boy, she is determined to be the star of this wedding, isn't she?"

Sarah plopped down on the bed, bouncing twice due to the stiffness of the dress material. "I can't believe this is still happening."

Raya sat next to her. "Believe it, friend."

"I could be dead three seconds after the rabbi says, 'I now pronounce you...'"

"You won't be. We'll all be there." Raya took Sarah's hand.

"That is comforting. Really. But family reunions are going to be super awkward."

"Because of the death thing?"

"No, because I'm afraid she won't like my latkes. Yes, because of the death thing!"

"You're holding it together quite well," Raya said.

"I'm in serious denial."

"Good call. By the way, your latkes are very good."

"Thank you."

"Dave's kugel is better."

"I know."

Sarah turned her head to look out the window, hoping to distract herself from the tears that were beginning to form. It was a lovely day, the sky a clear shade of blue, the clouds light and fluffy, and the tree outside was holding the birdfeeder that her father had installed last spring. Sarah stared at the grooves in the bark, the texture rough and intricate. Each one became a path in a maze, running up and down the length of the trunk. She wondered if bugs ever got lost in that maze, arriving home late with the crumb they had found, much to the disapproving stare of their ant-wife. As she let her gaze wander, she noticed a large squirrel on a branch, confidently nibbling on a plump acorn. The squirrel caught her eye and smiled at her.

"How do you do it?" Sarah got up and paced the length of her bed.

"Do what?"

Sarah gestured around the room. "All this. The Magyck. Dealing with it day to day. Isn't it all a bit much sometimes?"

Raya shrugged. "Dunno. It's all I know." She took a deep breath. "It's like speaking a language. You learn it, you grow up with it, and it comes to you as naturally as breathing. I can no more imagine a life without Magyck than you can imagine one without…what? Laughing? Blinking? What does your spleen do?" She sighed. "You really want to know what it's like for me? Every day I look at the people around me, obsessed with their phones and their social media accounts and their jobs and I think, 'Good Lord, people! Look around you! You're missing it!' I take nothing for granted, and I see things not for what they are, but what they could be. There's sharpness, a crispness, a deep-in-my-soul joy that comes to me every day because I can lock into the power all around me and make things *happen*. There is energy, music, math, color, love, art, and Magyck everywhere, Sarah. You just have to know where to look."

"I wish I could see it that way now. I find it scary and weird."

"You will. And look how far you've come this year. I mean, Rick just flirted with you, and you didn't even bat an eye!"

"Rick?"

Raya pointed to the squirrel, who saluted and ran down the tree trunk.

"Look, you've taken on a lot. Most Magycians are born with their power, so they grow up with it. You, you had it dropped on you in middle age—"

"Hey now."

"—near middle age. Pardon me. I'm just saying when this happens, it's like trying to teach calculus to a parrot. It can be done, but it takes a while."

"I'd rather deal with menopause."

Raya put her arm around Sarah. "You are doing great. You will be okay, I promise. Just take it one moment at a time. Keep practicing, and soon it will be like breathing to you too."

"And you promise Zondra won't kill me?"

"I can promise that if she gets to you, it will be because she went through all of us first."

Sarah hugged her. "Thank you." She disengaged and wiped her eyes. "I'll never get used to the squirrel-flirting though."

"Oh no, that's just weird right there."

Suddenly, a small portal opened in the corner of the bedroom. The crackling noise caught Sarah's attention, and she pointed to it.

"Portal," she mouthed. "Zondra."

Raya nodded in understanding, mouthing the words "Follow me."

"Wow, Sarah, I can't believe how great these dresses are. I can't wait to wear them at the wedding!"

Sarah scrunched her nose and tilted her head. Raya gave her the "let's keep it going" gesture, and Sarah mouthed "Oh."

"You're right, Raya. Such flattering colors too."

They got up and walked quietly to the portal. Sarah knew that Zondra couldn't see them, as Esra indicated that it was audio only. She mimed putting her fingers down her throat.

"I think we need to go over some rudimentary Magyck lessons again, Sarah. You're just not retaining the material."

"You're right, Raya. I'm quite the stupid-head."

Raya rolled her eyes.

"But I'm sure the wedding will go off without a hitch," Raya said. "And then you'll go far, far away, so Zondra will never see you again. Right?"

"That's the plan. Now let's talk extensively about my niece and nephew and their love for a show called 'Phineas and Ferb.'"

The portal closed immediately, leaving a few charges of electricity in the air. Sarah felt the hairs on the back of her neck stand up.

"Well, that did it," Raya said. "Worst conversation ever." She pushed up her sleeves. "Let me teach you a barrier spell so she can't drop another portal here."

Raya went over the procedure, and Sarah followed her instructions, although she wasn't sure if she had been successful.

"Close your eyes. Imagine your house, as detailed as you can. What do you see?"

"There is something that looks like a pink eggshell around it."

"Good. Then you did it right."

"You don't think she's going to catch on that we know about the portals?"

"Nah. Besides, what is she going to say? 'I've been spying on Sarah and now she won't let me'? She's not supposed to be doing it."

"Should we call someone?"

"They'll figure it out," Raya said. "If she does it more than once or twice, the authorities will get an alert. She knows this."

"Esra wasn't panicked either."

"See? You're okay." Raya reached behind herself to unzip the dress. "I need to get the hell out of this thing."

"Mine is starting to itch."

"That's probably the fairy dust." Raya wriggled out of the gown and left it in a ball on the floor. She kicked it with the toe of her boot. "Seriously. Everyone thinks that fairy dust is a good thing, but it's really not. It gets *everywhere.*"

Sarah hung up her dress and put it in the closet, and Raya followed suit, holding up her hand and running a small beam of light over the dress bags.

"Just eliminating the smell. Well, not so much eliminating as hopefully containing."

"After we're done with them, can we just burn them?"

"We can try, but they probably won't."

Now it was Sarah's turn to roll her eyes. Raya wrapped her in another big hug.

"Hey," she said. "How long have we known each other?"

"All our lives."

Raya disengaged the embrace and held Sarah at arm's length.

"Do you think I'm smart?"

"The smartest person I know." Sarah nodded once for emphasis.

"Do you believe I will always be there for you?"

"Yes."

Raya smiled. "And will you always be there for me?"

"Yes."

"Then everything will be all right. We have overcome more than terrible dresses."

"I don't know. They're pretty bad." Sarah shuddered, then chuckled lightly.

"And we're pretty badass." Raya did a turn, checked herself in the mirror, grabbed her coat, and flipped her braids over her shoulders. "I'd better go. I'm running an experiment in the physics lab at school, and if

I'm not there on time, the undergrads might try to test out their kinematic theories again. Last time that happened, two of them went home for spring break three inches shorter." She kissed Sarah on the cheek. "*Soyez courageuse, mon amie.*"

"I will."

Sarah walked Raya to the front door.

"So you promise this will all get easier?"

"Maybe not easier." Raya stepped onto the porch and zipped her jacket. "But certainly more interesting. Bye!"

She jumped the last three steps of Sarah's stoop and hopped into her car. She waved at Sarah as she drove away. Sarah closed the door and leaned against it.

"Things are happening."

TWENTY-TWO

Raya slapped her hand on the bar. "I need a beer! *Un verre de bière*! Whatever's on tap, barkeep!"

Nadav looked at his daughter with a stern expression and a raised eyebrow.

"Want to try that again, *ma fille*?"

"I would like a beer please, Papa."

"That's better." He slid a glass of orange-tinted liquid toward her. "It's new. Let me know what you think."

"I believe we could all use a drink. For surviving the worst wedding rehearsal in history," Sarah said, slinking in her chair and slipping out of her jacket, the mild spring weather forcing her to give up her woolen coat. "I have never seen an officiate cry like that before."

"And Jediziah served in Vietnam. Decorated for bravery. Twice," said Nadav.

"We can't do this. Avi can't do this." Raya threw up her hands. "It's driving me crazy we can't just stop it all!"

Esra was setting up his music bands, carefully placing each one on his toes and fingers.

"Patience, niece." Esra looked around for his sheet music.

"Patience?" Raya took a swig of her beer. "That's your response? Patience? I love you, uncle, but this Zen master thing is wearing thin."

"Raya, please." Nadav's voice was soft, but his eyes flashed with irritation.

"Well, this is awkward indeed," Esra said. "Left all my music prints in the bag. Ah well. I will have to improvise."

He began to play the bands, moving each finger and toe in just the right combination to produce the most beautiful sounds that Sarah had ever heard. They had all walked into the bar stiff and sore, bickering among themselves. But as Esra played, she felt the stress of the afternoon begin to melt. And as she looked around, she could see the pained expressions on her family's faces ease, as if air was returning to their collective lungs. Finally, a blanket of calm enveloped the room, and everyone sat quietly drowning their collective sorrows in rich orange beer and a deli tray Nadav had prepared.

"Just a nosh," Nadav said, placing the tray on a table in the center of the room. "We deserve it."

"I'm sorry, Uncle Esra. I'm just feeling so helpless." Raya began to hum with the new tune Esra was playing.

Esra nodded, the music floating above them like feathers on a scented breeze.

Sarah reached for some smoked turkey and then turned to Nadav. "Do you have any bialys?"

Everyone collectively flashed Sarah an incredulous look, their jaws jutted and eyebrows raised.

"Sorry, I'm not one of those people who lose their appetite in a crisis. Pass the mustard."

"Oh, I forgot to ask," Raya said, shaking her head and handing Sarah a piece of rye bread from the basket along with the mustard. "Did you hear from that travel magazine?" She took a piece for herself and stuffed it into her mouth.

"I did. They want to have me interview for an editor position." Sarah sighed. "I'll set it up for next week, I guess."

"How do you feel about it?"

"Mixed. It would be an amazing opportunity, but how can I go? I can't just take off now, clearly." She tore the crust off the rye.

"So, my dear Sarahleh," Esra said, while experimenting with new chord combinations. "You look tired."

Sarah slumped, dropped the bread on the table, then rubbed her forehead. "I am. And I'm terrified. Shouldn't we all be?"

"We are." Nadav placed some napkins by the platter of food. "We are. But we will prevail."

"You're right, of course. We will get through this." Sarah's hand shook as she picked up a glass of water, and she smiled wanly as Nadav squeezed her shoulder. "Esra, you should write that down," she said, pointing to the bands. "That's beautiful, what you're playing right now."

"I will remember," Esra said, stretching a band and tapping on his temple. "My own creations I always remember. For Led Zeppelin orchestrations, I need some assistance." He looked at her over the top of his round, dark glasses. "Do you still feel like dancing when I play?"

"Only when you play The Spiral Vogues."

"Not that any of us feel like dancing now." Raya slid into a nearby chair and rested her head in her hands.

"Noted." Esra continued to play, although the sound of the music grew fainter.

Sarah leaned her head back against the wall and closed her eyes. As the notes played, they became dots of light, dancing and floating in time to Esra's music. She started to drift away, feeling the music now in her solar plexus, wrapped in the sound created by Esra's expert performance. She barely registered the tinkling of door chimes but opened her eyes halfway to see who had joined them.

The hairs on the back of her neck stood up, and she opened her eyes all the way when she realized it was Zondra's new "security team." Sarah thought she had spotted the two of them hovering in the back of the rehearsal space, but between Zondra's dramatic orchestrations of the guests' every move and staccato screeching at the musicians, she didn't have time for their presence to really register. They sat themselves at the bar, their long coats practically pooling on the floor as they perched on their stools.

"What you got, bartender?" one of them barked. He banged his fist on the wooden bar.

"I'm bored," his companion announced. "I want something new!"

He looked around. "Well, well, well. The Greenberg party. What a charming surprise. Isn't it charming, Nar?"

"Oh yes. So charming, Sinc," Nar sneered. "And precious."

Nadav placed two steins of the orange beer in front of them. "Try this. It's a novo-brew made by a friend of mine in France."

Nar and Sinc slammed their drinks, swallowing them in one long gulp.

"French sissy beer," said Sinc. "Might as well be wine. What else you got?"

Nadav poured two dark, thick drinks into iced glasses and slid them down to the belligerent guests, who sniffed them suspiciously.

"Go ahead, you'll like it," Nadav offered, and as they drank, he mouthed to Sarah and Esra, "Prune juice."

Esra quietly removed his music bands and gently placed them in his bag, never taking his eyes off the two men. He nodded to Raya, who responded in kind.

"Stay alert," he whispered to Sarah. "They are not to be trusted."

Nar and Sinc spun around on their barstools. "So this is where the all-powerful Greenbergs go to relax," said Nar. "No gold dishes. No crystal goblets. Kind of a letdown, actually."

"I agree, Nar," said Sinc, who had slipped off his barstool and was now prowling around the room like a wound-up panther. "Kind of a dump, wouldn't you say? How the mighty have fallen."

"Or they will," said Nar. "And it's about time too." He swiped his arm across a table, sending the glassware crashing to floor, then grabbed a fistful of cold cuts. "Oops."

Sarah knew this duo did Zondra's dirty work, although now she had a sneaking feeling they were working on their own at the moment. She followed them with her eyes, as Esra did, and kept silent. Raya looked ready to pounce, her hand near her hip.

"I think we should do a little redecorating, don't you, Sinc?" Nar waved his hand, and the decorative steins behind the bar came flying off the shelves. Sarah looked nervously at Esra, who remained placid, his eyes now closed, his breathing shallow.

Sinc grabbed a barstool and threw it at Nadav, who stopped it midair, setting it down on the floor with merely a glance.

"Ah, the old man still has it," sneered Sinc. "Let's see what you can do with this!" With a sweep of his arm, he sent Nadav flying across the room, but Nadav did a counterspell, performing a smooth somersault and landing on a table in the corner.

"C'mon," spat Nar. "Let's have a little fun!" He raised his arm to shoot a new spell but froze. Sarah looked at Esra, who had his palm up and was facing the thugs. A soft beam of light emanated from his hand. As she turned to look at the room, she realized that everyone, save for her and Esra, had stopped moving and were locked in a strange tableau.

Sarah rose and walked around the visitors in wonderment. "You slowed time again."

"So, Sarah. What do you want to do now?" Esra looked directly at the men. Even with his glasses on, his stare looked dark and intense.

"You're asking *me*?" Sarah poked Sinc in the arm, his leather coat feeling slightly greasy under her finger.

"Yes. Do you want to get revenge? Do you think they deserve it?"

"What?" Sarah said. "I mean, we can't do that. You're not really suggesting that, are you?"

"No," Esra replied. "I was just checking to make sure you were still yourself. Good." With his palm still extended, he moved Sinc closer to his companion, sliding the man quietly across the floor. "So what do you think we should do?"

"Hold them until we can call someone? We do have law enforcement, right?"

"Anything else?"

Sarah frowned. "I don't want them to hurt any others."

"That we can do." Esra took off his glasses and placed them in his shirt pocket. Sarah always found the color of his eyes arresting. They looked as if they contained tiny shards of sea glass that glistened along in tune with his words and feelings.

"Pay attention now," he said. "I want you to tie them up. Reach out and touch the energy string and move it around them like a lasso."

Sarah did as instructed and was surprised to find a glowing yellow rope appear and encircle the two men, holding them together.

"Good grief. I'm Wonder Woman!"

"Indeed, you are."

Sarah placed her finger on her chin, and without saying a word, reached out to a pale green string and imagined it draping over the men's heads like a scarf, sending with it a sense of peace.

"Nice, Sarah. We cannot change people's minds, but we can offer kindness. Well done."

"Is that what I did?"

"Yes. They will have a feeling of tranquility when we release them. At least for a while. Hopefully, they will cause less trouble in the future."

"But we're still calling the authorities, right?"

"Oh yes. I did that several minutes ago." Esra sat down at this table and replaced his sunglasses. As he took a sip from his drink, he waved his hand the length of the room. As he reached the far wall, everyone started to move again.

"Good job, *mon frère*." Nadav jumped down from the table where he had been perched.

"It was mostly Sarah," Esra replied. "She did the heavy lifting, as they say."

Sinc and Nar struggled under their restraints but soon gave up, waiting patiently as Nadav, Raya, and Sarah began to clean up the room. Brooms and dustpans worked independently, and a beige terrycloth polished the tabletops with its own delicate flourish. Presently, three men armed with glowing clubs strapped to their belts entered the bar, nodding at Nadav as they gathered up the two ruffians.

"You two again," one of the officers said. "Come along, we've done this before. Sorry about this, folks. They've been warned." The officer replaced Sarah's gold rope with their own grey ones. "I don't think the judge will be too happy about you two breaking the terms of your parole." The guards hustled Nar and Sinc out the door, waving to Esra as they left. "Give our best to Avi, please!"

"What will happen to them?" Sarah asked.

"They're repeat offenders," Raya said. "There will be a larger consequence. Either imprisonment or a temporary suspension of their powers. Or both. Depends on the judge."

"I wonder if Zondra will find out."

"I'm sure she will. And I'm also sure she won't be too pleased about her bodyguards being in the clink."

"You mean jail?"

"Sort of," Raya replied. "It's like an invisible box in the justice hall. We call it a clink. That's also the sound it makes if you accidentally touch the walls, by the way."

"I would suggest lying low until the wedding on Saturday," Nadav offered. "Why take the chance?"

"Understood," Sarah said. "The fewer run-ins with her I have, the better. Should I tell my father?"

"He knows," Esra said.

Sarah plopped herself into her chair and brushed the hair from her face. She let out a long sigh. "I could use a good sleep. And a snack."

A cinnamon roll appeared in front of her.

"Thank you, Nadav. Very thoughtful."

They all sat quietly as the bar finished cleaning itself, sipping their drinks and nibbling on the new food Nadav put out. Esra rummaged around his bag, and finding the previously missing sheet music, held it up in triumph. He donned the music bands and began his rendition of "Black Dog."

The door chimes rang as Colin entered the pub. He wore a big smile and placed his hand on the bar as he waved eagerly to the group. Sarah greeted him with a kiss and a long hug, holding onto his waist as she tried to regather her strength. He surveyed the room, then sat on a stool and grabbed a sandwich from the stack.

"Hey, guys, what'd I miss?"

TWENTY-THREE

S tanding in front of the stove in his kitchen, Colin flipped the French toast in the pan and slid it gently onto a plate. "Just like you showed me. A little cinnamon and nutmeg in the egg, and make sure the heat isn't too high."

"Excellent presentation," Sarah said. "Four stars. Would recommend."

"Even though I forgot the parsley?" Colin said. "Which I'm thinking now really doesn't go with breakfast food anyway?"

"It's okay. I always hated it. I appreciate the effort, but it just sits there on the plate like a depressed little tree."

"You miss your job."

"I do," Sarah sighed. "Something will come up."

"How'd that interview go? The one with the travel magazine."

"Very well. They want me to come in and meet the executive editor. But I don't know if I should."

"You should. What do you have to lose? Excuse me for a sec," Colin said. "Madison! Come have something to eat!"

"I'm not hungry!" Madison called back from her bedroom.

"She always says that, and then she gets cranky," Sarah said. "Deb is the same way."

"It's going to be a few hours until we eat again! You get cranky!"

"DAD!"

"Okay, okay." Colin put the plate on the table. "She told me, I guess."

"I have some granola bars in my purse."

"Excellent. Basic and old school. You want to split the last piece?" Colin pointed to the French toast.

"I would, but I don't know if I'll be able to zip my bridesmaid's dress," Sarah replied, finishing the last of her coffee.

"You say that like it's a bad thing." Colin tore the bread in half.

"The only good thing about wearing that dress is being able to get out of that dress when this is all over."

"I'll help you." Colin waggled his eyebrows.

"Don't waste all that romance on me, buddy. We have a sham wedding to get to."

Colin took the remaining food to the sink. "Do you need the bathroom? I just have to shave and throw on my suit."

"No, go ahead. I showered before I came over, so all I have to do is throw on some makeup. I can do that in the powder room."

As Colin dashed upstairs, Sarah gathered her makeup bag and went to the small bathroom to get ready. She applied her makeup lightly but artfully, blinking her eyes in the overhead light while checking her work. Something looked off, so she peered closer. Had her eyes changed color? They had always been something of a hazel-mud green, but now she noticed that the iris was brighter, with little amber flakes around the pupil. She was about to write it off as nothing when she realized she had seen those eyes before.

Her father. Avi had the same eyes. So did her sister. And Aaron. And Miriam. She wondered why she had never noticed before, thinking perhaps it was a side effect of her former otherness, but now the Magyck had changed her outside as well as her inside.

I've got Greenberg eyes.

She stuck a bobby pin in her hair to tame a flyaway curl and wiped a tiny smear of lipstick from her chin. Taking a deep, fatalistic breath, she unzipped the garment bag, pulled off her sweats, and stepped into the monstrosity she was generously calling a dress. It was hot and snug and felt like she was wearing a suit made of bees.

As she was tugging at the fabric, pulling it here and there, trying to make it even a jot more comfortable, a piece of paper appeared in her hand. It was intricately folded, possibly in the shape of a squirrel, or perhaps a swan. She pulled it open. It was from Raya; her elegant script highlighted the letters written in an unusual shade of purple that changed its hue as Sarah read the note.

Sending a car for you.
Keep an eye out for a Model A.

Slenn. A ride with them was basically taking one's life in one's hands, and this was definitely not the dress Sarah wanted to be buried in. But she appreciated the gesture, and it would certainly be more exciting than a limo. She hoped Alvin had taken his Dramamine.

She stepped out of the bathroom, tucking the note into one of the six holding flaps the dress sported.

At least it has pockets.

Colin was already in the kitchen and halfway through a second cup of coffee, confirming her theory that most men can get ready for a major event in less than sixty seconds and look amazing as well. Despite the unjustness of the whole situation, not to mention the couch cover she was wearing, she felt like a very lucky person. That is, until he took one look at her and spit his coffee over the morning newspaper.

"What is that?" he sputtered.

"Wait. It comes with a hat." She pulled the matching hat out of her tote bag. Zondra had given it to her, calling it the "finishing touch."

"Boy, she really hates you."

"Raya's has a big bow on it."

"The hat or the dress?"

"Yes." Sarah took off the hat and stuffed it back into the bag. "I think I'm going to conveniently forget that." She scratched her shoulder. "Oh, by the way, we're getting a ride. Raya arranged for transpo."

"Is this a real car or a Magyck car?"

"What do you think?"

She took a peek out the front window and saw the jalopy pull into the driveway. Slenn had outfitted the car with streamers, and their support dragon was perched in the rear window. Alvin was wearing a purple vest with a little bow tie, and he looked quite pleased with himself.

"They're here." Sarah picked up her purse and slung it over her shoulder.

"Madison!" Colin called. "Let's go!"

Madison came flying down the stairs, her green-streaked hair tied nicely into a single braid, and she looked quite grown up in her simple blue dress, Sarah thought.

"Do we have any more French toast?" Madison asked, craning her neck to look into the kitchen.

"Are you kidding me? Let's go. Sarah has granola in her purse." Colin held the door for Sarah and his daughter, who struggled to put on her satin jacket as they walked outside. Sarah gave her an assist by holding the sleeve.

"What are you wearing?" Madison asked as they walked down the front sidewalk.

Sarah put a granola bar in Madison's mouth.

Slenn got out of the car and waved. "Long time no see!" they said, running around to the other side of the car and opening it for their passengers. "Allow me."

"A Prius?" Madison asked. "How are we all going to fit in there?"

"It's not a Prius. It has a disguise spell. It's roomier than it looks." Slenn looked over their blue tortoiseshell glasses and smiled. They had changed their hair since Sarah had last seen them; it was now three shades of magenta and had a picture of a unicorn carved into it, which flapped its wings just over Slenn's right ear.

"Cool hair!" Madison exclaimed, climbing into the back seat.

"Thanks, kid. You too," Slenn said.

"It smells like cookies in here," Madison said, sliding over to make room for her father and Sarah.

"Yeah, sorry about that. Alvin's got the toots," Slenn replied, pointing to the support dragon.

Madison looked around the inside of the car. "You were right. This definitely isn't a Prius."

"Just one of the advantages of flying first-class," Slenn said, plopping into the driver's seat. "Things aren't always the way they appear on the outside."

"This is going to be cool." Madison grinned at Sarah. "I mean, Taylor takes the El by herself and thinks she's so badass."

Slenn's driving skills hadn't improved in recent months, and as they flew—fortunately, not literally—down the streets of Oak Park and into the city, the three passengers held on to each other for dear life. Madison occasionally let out a squeal, but Colin had taken to gripping Sarah's hand and squeezing his eyes shut, which Sarah found to be an infinitely more sensible reaction.

"Now, Madison, you might see some weird things today. Are you ready for that?" Sarah gently touched Madison's arm with her free hand. "This is not going to be your typical wedding."

They hit a pothole, and even with the seat belts, Colin's head hit the roof of the car.

"Oof!" the three passengers said in unison.

"Sorry!" Slenn waved.

"I'll be fine." Madison shifted in her seat. "I'm more mature than you give me credit for, you know."

"I know."

"Plus, Isabel's stepmom plays tennis, one of Sophia's mothers builds dollhouses, and Kat's mom keeps decorating their living room over and over again. You're way more interesting than that. Weird, but interesting."

Sarah kissed the back of Madison's hand.

After compressing the car to squeeze down a much-too-small alley, causing Colin to nearly vomit, they arrived at the Greenberg store. Sarah had initially been surprised by the choice of location, as she assumed Zondra's tastes required something more upscale. But as Raya reminded her, Zondra would want to be close to the vessel of the Twelve Moonstones as soon as possible. She was claiming her stake. In her mind's eye, Sarah pictured Zondra rubbing her hands together with glee, like a cartoon villain who thinks the hero has been dispatched.

Slenn opened the side door to let the passengers exit.

"Are you coming in?" Madison asked Slenn.

"Nah. Thanks though. I have an art installation I need to finish. Might crash the reception though. I love those little mini-quiches." Slenn kicked the curb with their orange-glittered Doc Martens. "Have a good time. And Sarah…"

"Yes?" Sarah turned around.

"Be careful, okay?" Slenn's sunny disposition gave way to genuine concern. "She's no good, that one. We have your back."

"Thanks. I will."

"That's all I can ask." Slenn's bright smile returned. "See ya later, gators!" They ran around the front of the car and got behind the wheel, flooring the gas pedal and once again catching Alvin off guard. He gave a little burp of smoke as he was pressed against the back windshield.

"Thank you!" Colin waved, then wiped a bead of sweat from his brow.

When Colin, Madison and Sarah entered the store, it was empty and quiet, lit by several large, intricately shaped candles that cast long shadows on the floor. The surroundings were familiar, but Sarah felt a tightening in her chest. She tugged on the collar of her dress.

She spotted Dave standing by the back room door, wearing a sequined, powder blue tuxedo and holding a stack of programs.

"Why don't you two go on back? I'll be there in a minute," Sarah said, pointing to Dave.

She walked along one of the side shelves, running her finger along the displays of magic sets and tricks, boxes, trinkets, and various accessories. She never had much of an interest in any of this as a child, although she picked up some knowledge, but she loved people-watching at the store. Many of them came specifically to talk to her father, who would hold court, his customers and admirers hanging on his every word. She was a little envious too, and she wondered if she had learned to pull a pigeon out of a hat when she was younger, she would have gotten a little more of his attention.

As if on cue, Avi popped up from behind the counter.

"Hello, sweetheart!" He took another box off the counter and set it on the shelf below. "Are you going to go in and get in place?"

"I will. What are you doing out here?"

"Thinking. Thinking and musing and planning." He straightened his tie. "Also, I'm not thrilled about having the wedding on Shabbat, but Zondra was insistent."

"Yes, she is," Sarah said, pointing to her gown.

"Oh, that's a terrible dress. I'm sorry, sweetheart." Avi came out from behind the counter. Sarah thought he had a little more grey in his beard, and he looked a bit tired. "Are you all right? Zondra hasn't…" He seemed to be searching for the right word. "…bothered you too much? I've been trying to keep an eye on her."

"She's been okay." Sarah hated lying to her father, but she couldn't bear to pile on. "She hasn't tried anything. Well, nothing big."

"Look, I know you think this is all madness. But Esra and I have a plan. Do you trust me?"

For a moment, her belief in her father wavered. Years of lies by omission, of believing he favored her sister, followed by him marrying the woman who might try to kill her. But she looked in his kind eyes, and for the first time she knew. Knew she wasn't second best. That he believed in her. A life of protection and spells and secret charms flashed before her, and she stumbled, her father catching her by her elbow. She saw the truth. She stood tall and squared her shoulders.

"I trust you."

"You need to trust yourself too. Can you do that for me?"

"I guess so."

"Your mother would be so proud of you today. I still think of her every day, you know. That will never change. She was my love, and I was lucky to be her husband."

"You can still back out, Dad. It's not too late."

"I'm afraid it is, my darling. The wheels are in motion. Just pay attention. It will be fine. Things will work out the way they're supposed to." Avi hugged Sarah. "What's the line? 'Magic is believing in yourself. If you can do that, you can make anything happen.' Goethe. Nice fellow. Very prolific. Old Benjamin would always advise him, 'Focus, Johann, don't try to do it all!' But he didn't listen. I'm sorry, what was I saying?"

"Trust. Pay attention."

"Ah, yes. I should listen to my own advice. I get distracted."

"Me too."

He gave her another hug. "That's my good girl. Why don't you go in now? Esra will come get me when it's time."

"Are you really sure, Dad?"

"I'm sure. I want to keep you safe. That is my top priority."

Sarah kissed her father on the cheek and headed to the back room where Dave was standing guard.

"Hey," Dave said. "Chin up, kid." He placed the stack of programs on the floor and materialized a shot glass full of a clear liquid. "Here. You might need this."

"Is this some Magyck courage potion? An anti-anxiety elixir?"

"It's vodka."

"Excellent." Sarah downed the shot and handed Dave the empty glass.

"Hang out here," he said, making the glass disappear. "You don't have to go into the main room until the ceremony starts."

"All right." She sat on a folding chair near the door. She felt the cold of the metal even through the burlap-thick fabric of her dress. Taking a deep breath, she looked around at the kitchenette, the vases on the shelves cleared of their occupants. It was quiet, still, and slightly eerie from the lack of life and movement to which she had grown accustomed. She closed her eyes, focusing on the energy strings around her. She looked for ones that were clear and bright but found none. They were there, but they had faded and were moving slowly. There was one though—one small, green string in her peripheral vision, and if she tried to focus too closely, it vanished. So she let her eyes relax as the green string danced in her mind's eye.

And then she heard the music begin.

CHAPTER
TWENTY-FOUR

S arah and Raya peeked through the door of the Crystal Room and saw that it had been transformed. Although still dimly lit and slightly dank, it looked like a Goth fairyland, with flowers climbing the dark, stone walls and clear crystals suspended along the ceiling. Each crystal ball on the shelves had been individually lit, projecting beams of silver, gold, and pale pink. Sparkling webs of silk floss draped along the backs of the chairs and around the mirrored silver fountain, which bubbled with a pink translucent liquid. But despite the warm light of the candles and the people in the room, it felt cold and hollow, giving Sarah a chill from her head to the top of her ugly shoes. She surveyed the crowd. Some faces she recognized, some she didn't, and there were a few guests she thought might not be quite human. They all talked among themselves in a low murmur; the usual wedding gaiety was nowhere to be found.

"I've been to funerals more jazzed than this," Raya whispered in her ear. "Did you grab any of the hors d'oeuvres? I'm starving."

Sarah pulled a second granola bar from her pocket and handed it to Raya. She saw the rabbi milling about, chatting with the guests. "What happened to Jediziah? I thought he was officiating."

"There was a last-minute change. Your father insisted."

The rabbi, who sported a long, silver-blue beard and wore a red and purple *tallit* around his neck and shoulders with a matching *kippah* perched on his nearly bald head, had taken his place under the *huppah*; the canopy had been built with ornate, striped fabric and decorated with small, multicolored crystals and stones. It looked like a fancy sideshow carnival tent. It had Zondra's fingerprints all over it.

The rest of the guests quickly seated themselves, and Avi and Esra took their places next to the rabbi. Esra's suit was made of dark green velvet, his tie a size too big and a little off-kilter. It changed color as he moved; the lights from the candles scattered about the room refracted though the crystal drops and gave the velvet the look of spilled oil on the sidewalk, the colors shimmering and whirling as Esra rocked back and forth on his feet in time to music that only he could hear. Her father looked solemn in his dark grey suit, his normally unruly curly hair tamed by a stiff comb and sheer determination.

He looked miserable.

The music changed, a slightly off-key dirge that sounded like it was trying to be Mozart and failing spectacularly.

"Psssssst! Psssssst!"

Sarah walked back through the kitchenette and into the reading nook of the store, looking for the source of the noise.

"Over here!" Raya waved.

Sarah hurried over to Raya. There was a screen set up in the corner that she hadn't noticed before. Raya pulled her staff from the back of her dress and clasped it in her hand. Taking a wide berth, they crossed around to the side of the screen. Behind it was Zondra, holding a single silver rose.

"There you are," she purred. "I thought maybe you wouldn't come."

"To the wedding or behind this screen?" Sarah said.

"Don't you two look...nice."

"I can make anything look good," Raya said.

Sarah felt her back stiffen, but she was determined not to show fear. "We didn't want to outshine the bride."

"Speak for yourself," Raya sniffed. "What do you want, Zondra?"

"A little emotional support? Perhaps one of your patented pep talks?

I heard they're quite inspiring." She placed the rose on the small table next to her and gently fingered the green brooch on the strap of her dress. "I just want to make sure we're not going to have any, how should I put this...drama? Yes. I like that term. No drama."

She sighed heavily, leaned on the table, and pressed the back of her hand to her forehead.

"Oh no. Never any drama." Sarah looked Zondra in the eye. "You sound a little hangry. Do you want a granola bar?" She pulled out a snack from her front pocket. "Oats and Honey." She dropped her gaze to the green stone.

Zondra's nostrils flared, and she curled her upper lip. "No thank you." She bared her teeth with a smile that was just a little too wide. "I will tell you how it will all proceed. You will smile, you will march up that aisle, and you will keep your mouth shut. Understood?"

"Can I stop for cheese on the way?"

"Sarah!" Raya said.

"I just thought a nice Gruyère would sweeten everybody up." Sarah took two steps back.

"Am I understood?" Zondra's voice was shrill and staccato. "Or are you more stupid than you let on?"

Sarah opened her mouth to protest, but in a flash Raya had extended her staff and was holding it in front of Zondra.

"We don't speak like that to *family*," Raya hissed.

In an instant a burst of light flew from Zondra's outstretched hand, holding Raya in a glowing twist of rope. With the other hand she reached out toward Sarah.

An energy beam wrapped around Sarah's neck, and she felt her throat constrict. She was now hovering about six inches above the floor, her feet dangling like a marionette.

"Listen to me and listen well." Zondra spoke quietly, her voice streaming in a low hiss. "I will not have this wedding ruined by the likes of you. I should have taken you out long before this, but your father pleaded with me not to. And I knew he would never go through with this ceremony if something happened to you. But my patience is coming to an end, Sarah. You *will* walk into that room, you *will* smile, and you will *stay out of my way*." She clenched her teeth. "Or else." Her face softened for a moment in a gross caricature of compassion. "All right, dahling?"

Sarah nodded as best she could, and Zondra released her grip, letting her fall to the floor. Raya remained ensnared. Sarah sat on the floor, gasping for air.

"Keep your bodyguard in line, won't you?" Zondra continued. "I would not waste any tears over a *teacher*." She spat out the word "teacher" as if it was an insult.

"Fine, fine!" Sarah said. "Just let her go!"

After Zondra released the glowing rope from Raya's arms and shoulders, Raya collapsed her staff and returned it to its hiding place between her shoulders, her eyes never leaving Zondra.

"Good, good. I'm so glad we understand each other now." Zondra picked up the silver rose from the table. "Now run along and be good little bridesmaids. Don't want to keep everyone waiting."

With a wave of her hand she dismissed Raya and Sarah, who backed out from behind the screen.

"I could have broken out of that restraint spell," Raya said as they returned to their spots outside the crystal room. "Just for the record."

"Why the hell didn't you?" Sarah rubbed the skin on her neck, which was raw and sore.

"She would have squeezed the life out of you in retaliation."

"Fair point."

Dave grabbed Sarah's arm as they stood next to the door. "You two okay?"

"Just calming Zondra's pre-wedding jitters." Sarah's heart was still beating faster than was comfortable.

"Let me look at your neck." Dave grabbed a chair from the kitchenette table and stood on it. He held her chin in his small, blue hand. "She got you good." He gently prodded at the skin with his index finger, turning her head this way and that. Sarah swatted his hand away.

"Stop being such a *yenta*."

"Stop being such a pain in the ass. Just let me fix it."

Dave waved his hand over the reddened skin and pressed his palm gently against the side of her neck. The welts faded. "There, that should help." He peered at her. "You seem remarkably calm for someone who almost got squonched."

"She can't hurt me, Dave. No matter what happens." Sarah felt her whole body calm down, and she took a deep breath.

"That's very Zen. I still don't trust her farther than I can throw her. Which, given my center of gravity, isn't that far. So, you know, I don't trust her at all." Dave jumped down from the chair and floated it back to the table, pushing it in with a flick of his wrist.

"I'm keeping an eye on her. We all are," Raya said.

"Good, good. Yes, we are." Dave handed Sarah and Raya their bouquets, swatting away the annoyed-looking bee who had taken up residence. "I think we need to start the show now, okay?"

The music changed again, a minor-key processional that sounded to Sarah suspiciously like a death march. Dave slipped inside the Crystal Room and levitated over a chair in the back row.

"Sarah, I just realized something that I need to tell you," Raya said.

"Now?" Sarah asked. All the guests turned to face them as they entered and began the processional. "Step, together, step, together…"

"It's important."

"You're throwing me off," Sarah was determined to concentrate on the one thing she could control in that moment.

"This isn't the Electric Slide, Sarah. Just *walk*," Raya whispered as Sarah adjusted her pace. "I know what Zondra is going to do."

Sarah stopped midway down the aisle and looked at Raya, mouth agape. Raya turned her around by the shoulders and gave her a nudge.

"Keep moving!" she hissed.

As they got into place in front of the *huppah*, Raya took a step closer so she could speak into Sarah's ear without being too obvious. "I know why she has the *bareket* stone."

"It's keeping her alive," Sarah whispered back, looking out among the guests. She plastered a large smile on her face.

"Yes. But it will also allow her to take over control of the Moonstone vessel."

Sarah looked nervously at the carved wooden door behind her, where the vessel containing the Twelve Moonstones was housed. It was slightly ajar, the glow from the stones scattering like a kaleidoscope on the stone floor. The music changed again and grew louder, causing Raya to lean in closer.

"She's going to return the stone to the vessel, probably tonight. Once it's in place it will connect with the *bareket* residue in her body and connect her to the vessel. That will give her ultimate control of the source of Magyck. *That's* why, despite her threats, she didn't kill you. She didn't need to. And this won't be a good thing. She'll be like a Magyckal—"

The music stopped.

"Hitler!"

Everyone snapped their heads to look at Raya, who gave an embarrassed wave.

"Because that's who we *don't* want at a wedding, am I right?" Sarah stammered to the guests.

"Nice cover," Raya whispered.

"Nice Hitler reference."

The music started up a third time. It sounded to Sarah like "The Imperial March" from *Star Wars*, but she knew she was just projecting.

"She had to wait for the right time, when she knew she'd have regular access to the vessel. She needed the right amount of *bareket* powder in her system, and this stupid wedding was the only way she could be assured of having access without getting caught."

Sarah remembered Zondra taking the green capsules and knew that Raya was right. A vivid image appeared in her mind of the coming of a dark time for the Magyckal community, as she realized that once Zondra had control of one vessel, it would be likely she could get access to the others scattered across the globe. All Magycian's lives controlled by the whims of one woman bent on ultimate power. Sarah felt another chill, stronger this time, one that took hold of her insides and turned itself into a chunk of ice.

Zondra began her ascent up the aisle, dressed in a grey lace gown, her white-blonde hair in a tight bun and her face even tighter. Her lips were pursed and set in a determined line as she floated forward, holding the single silver rose.

Sarah imagined her on a throne, wild and fiery, but in reality

Zondra's eyes looked steely and dead. She was inching closer and closer, and Sarah feared the woman might just reach out and—

Everything froze. The lights had stopped flickering, and the guests were as still as if they were trapped in amber. Sarah was the only one who could move. Had she done this? She had done it once before with Esra's help, but he was frozen too.

She quickly realized that she wasn't the only one unaffected. She heard a rustling from one of the chairs and turned to see her nephew Aaron standing, his eyes wide and his arm outstretched.

"Aaron? Did you do this?"

"I don't know, Aunt Sarah." Aaron ran to her and hugged her tightly. "You looked so scared, and I just...I just..."

"It's okay, honey."

"I didn't want her to be too close to you!" Aaron wiped a small tear from his large eyes, looking much younger than his nine years. "But I don't know how long I can hold this."

Sarah gently touched his brown curls, then held his face in her hand. "You did good, kid. Now run back to your seat by your mom. I have something I have to do while I have time."

As Aaron scampered back to his seat, wiping his nose on his sleeve, Sarah knew she had to act fast. She ran up to Zondra and ripped the *bareket* brooch from her dress. As she did, Aaron lost the spell and time resumed to its normal speed. Zondra whipped around and shrieked, her eyes full of fury.

"YOU!" she screamed. "Give that back to me!"

Zondra threw a bolt of silver-black light from the flower in her hand, and Sarah instantly knew where it was aimed. She dashed in front of Colin and Madison, and with all the strength she could muster, she reached out to the energy strings around her and threw up a wall in front of them. The bolt of light hit the field and dissipated.

Zondra tried again with the flower, but it wilted from the vibrations. She threw it on the ground and glared at Sarah, beads of sweat forming on her upper lip. A few of the guests, as well as Nadav, had begun to move toward Zondra, their hands up in various defense spells.

"Stop!" Sarah shouted, her voice cracking. "Everyone, please stop!" She ran her hand over Madison's hair and gazed at Colin. They were unharmed, although Colin looked stunned and Madison buried her face in her father's shoulder.

As she gripped the green stone in her hand, she began to hear that familiar humming sound and instinctively looked around the room for the source. In that moment, she knew she had two choices: keep the stone or return it to the vessel. If she held onto it, Zondra would surely kill her before the others got to her. And if she returned it to the vessel, she would be completing Zondra's mission and Zondra would overtake them all.

Something didn't feel right. Her father had said he and Esra had a plan—but they hadn't yet moved from their spot under the *huppah*. Her mind whirled as she saw Zondra swarmed by a group of guests who had decided to take matters into their own hands. She began pushing them out of her way, trying to get to Sarah and take back the stone. The tight feeling in Sarah's stomach grew more intense. The humming had taken on a dissonant chord, growing louder and louder. She looked at her father, who nodded once.

It's not the real stone.

Sarah realized Zondra didn't have the actual Moonstone *bareket*. Properly charmed with the right dark spell, any *bareket* could, theoretically, be enough to keep her alive all these years, but it would be useless in the vessel. Sarah threw it on the ground, and reaching out to a bright, vibrating string, sent a beam of light from her hand to the stone, shattering it into dust.

A piercing shriek filled the Crystal Room. The crowd parted, and Zondra staggered forward, her eyes red with fury. She raised both arms in the air, and with bold, sword-like strokes, she made cuts in the air with her right arm, sending a surge of white-hot Magyck directly at Sarah.

Before Sarah could react, she was pushed out of the way and fell to the floor. She looked up just in time to see Esra and the rabbi absorbing the energy, the rabbi directing it upward while Esra burst into a cloud of fine green dust.

Sarah screamed.

The rabbi spun on his heels and whirled his hands, collecting the dust into a small, rotating cyclone that hovered in the air in front of him. In the next second, Avi maneuvered the green dust into an energy beam in his hand, gathering strength, and bounced it back at Zondra. It hit her square in the chest, and she looked down at the hole in her torso. Then she stared at Sarah, formed an O with her mouth, and shattered into thousands of small silver shards. The green dust circled around and returned to Avi, reforming into its miniature tornado shape before gently falling to the floor in a light, shimmering cascade. The rabbi collapsed into a chair, his head in his hands. Debra ran to him and put her arm around the old man.

The room was silent. No one knew what to say or do. Slowly, they began filtering out, some supporting their companions as they walked away, and some just quietly fading from view. Soon all that was left was the family, the green dust, and the tinkling of the silver and pink fountain.

Nadav knelt over the dust, his head almost to the floor. Colin got up from his seat and picked Sarah up off the ground and held her in his arms. She wept, hard and deep. She felt her sister, father, Raya, and Madison protectively gather around them, wrapping themselves around each other, the children and Dave snuggling themselves between the legs of the others.

After a few minutes, Dave disengaged and grabbed a broom, sweeping up the pieces of all that remained of Zondra Bex into a gold dustbin and pouring them into the fountain. The liquid steamed and sputtered, then went perfectly still.

"Everyone, sit." Debra waved her family into the chairs. "Aaron, please help Dave, would you? Miriam, stay with me, okay?" She pulled a doll from her small bag and handed it to her daughter.

Colin put his arm around Madison. "You okay, sweetheart?" He wiped a tear from her face as she laid her head on his chest.

Avi and Nadav stood over the green shimmering dust.

Avi cleared his throat. "Many years ago, the world of Magyck was becoming a dark place, with a few individuals craving power over the others." He put his arm around his elder daughter's shoulders. "To combat this darkness, twelve Magyckal families from around the world were selected to be keepers of the Twelve Moonstones, which represented things like hope, joy, and wisdom. Each family that was entrusted with a vessel represented different cultures and faiths. This, they hoped, would spread the wealth of the energy, keeping it from concentrating in one place." He walked over to Aaron and ruffled his grandson's dark hair. "The Greenbergs, obviously, settled here."

Avi sat down on a chair. "There were a few families who opposed the dispersal of the Twelve Moonstones—"

"Like the Bex family," Aaron added.

"That's right. When Zondra tried to steal the *bareket* stone the first time, after Old Benjamin opened the store, she was unsuccessful. My great-great-grandfather took no chances and replaced the stone with another, knowing that Zondra, or another from her clan, would try again. The desire for power was strong in the Bex family. This much I have learned from my good friend Rabbi Shraga." He gestured to the old man sitting nearby. "The rabbi's family suspended the real *bareket* in a protective spell, and the stone was passed down through our guardian family."

The rabbi stood, bowed deeply, and dissolved into a swirl of white light that spun upward and passed through the ceiling.

Nadav stood and slowly walked to Avi, sitting next to him. "When I was a boy," Nadav said quietly, "I kept the stone in a glass jar in my room. I took good care of it, so my father didn't protest. I loved to feel the glow of the stone on my face as I did my schoolwork at night, and the light comforted me when the night was quiet and dark." Nadav took Avi's arm. "One day when I was in my room, the stone glowed brighter than ever before. And then it disappeared. The next day Esra appeared and saved my life."

"Esra was the *bareket*," Sarah said softly.

Nadav stood and helped Avi to his feet. "Come, my old friend. Help me."

The two men stood over the scattered green dust and held out their arms. As it formed into a thin, pulsating river of green, sparkly light, the door to the room that held the Moonstones opened. They guided it into the room, walking slowly toward the vessel. Sarah and the others followed, a silent procession of unity and grief. Nadav lifted his arm, and the green dust moved from their hands and into the vessel, where it slowly coalesced into a smooth, round stone. As it began to glow, the adjoining Crystal Room became brighter, trading the gloom for a sense of wonder and joy.

"In another life, *mon frère*," Nadav said, touching the glass.

Avi gently placed his hand on Nadav's shoulder, and the two of them watched the stone take its place among the others in the vessel.

Everyone returned to the Crystal Room, shading their eyes against the new light. The room was beautiful; the crystals hanging from the wall tinkled with a light tune, the flowers bloomed, and the stone floor and walls transformed into a milky, opaque glass.

"Yes," Avi said. "It is right again."

Sarah felt Colin grab her hand. She turned to him and placed her other hand on his cheek. He looked bewildered, as if the world he was just coming to accept had turned on its head.

Because it had.

Colin took her hand off his face and held it in his other hand and reached out for his daughter to join them. Madison raced to her father's side.

"You saved us, Sarah!" Madison exclaimed, hugging Sarah. "I was so scared, but you just...thank you."

"I will always take care of you," Sarah said.

"We look out for each other," Colin said, holding them close. "We're a team now, aren't we?"

"We are," Sarah agreed, putting her arm around Madison.

"Would you..."

Sarah looked at the *huppah*. "Oh boy..."

"I'm not asking you to marry me. At least, not now."

"But someday?"

"Yes. Someday. Let's play it by ear."

"I can do that."

Colin kissed her before she could set down any other conditions. "Esra wanted to make sure I proposed at some point. He said not to rush you though. You dance to the beat of your own drummer, he said."

Madison clapped her hands in glee and let out a controlled squeal. The three of them hugged again and had a moment of silence for Esra.

"But just to be clear," Sarah said. "We'd have the wedding someplace else, right?"

"I'm on it," Dave said, pulling a clipboard from the pocket of his tuxedo. "I'll handle the whole thing. Your mother gave me instructions years ago, just in case. Now, about the menu—"

"We can discuss that later, I think," Avi said, intercepting his someday-to-be son-in-law. "Now, let's discuss your conversion. It won't hurt. Much."

Colin opened his mouth to protest, but Sarah gave him a little shove from behind.

"He's kidding. You knew my family was weird. Too late now, pal." Sarah started to leave with the others but turned and went back to the doorway of the room containing the vessel of the Twelve Moonstones, giving them one last look. The green *bareket* stone glowed brighter than the others.

"Goodbye, Esra," she said. "I won't ever forget the music."

She closed the door slowly behind her.

TWENTY-FIVE

"I will say, Dave, that you have a way with the crab cakes," Colin said, taking his third helping from the outstretched platter.

"It's a skill. Those little suckers are hard to catch," Dave replied. "They may move sideways, but they pick up velocity." He mimed smashing them with a hammer.

Six weeks after the wedding-that-wasn't and Esra's transformation, and things were just beginning to feel normal again. For the first few days, Sarah felt adrift without Esra's presence. She turned off the radio, preferring to sit in silence. She didn't even hum. But gradually, oh so gradually, she began to hear it again, that soft other-sound of Esra's music in the back of her head, propelling her forward and back into her life. They hadn't sat shiva for him, forgoing the usual Jewish period of mourning for a series of dinners, coffees, and small get-togethers, sharing stories and jokes he had told. Strangely, no one had photographs of Esra, as he had either declined to be in them or dashed out at the last minute, leaving a smudge of green where he had been standing.

But they had memories.

This night, Nadav arranged to close the pub for their private party, and the atmosphere was decidedly brighter than the last time they were all together. Raya was pouring drinks behind the bar in place of her father, who had yet to arrive. Debra was enjoying a leisurely glass of wine at a table, and Sarah was glad to see that her brother-in-law, Mike, who usually eschewed family events, was keeping an eye on the children. Sarah leaned down and kissed Colin on the cheek.

"You want anything to drink?"

Colin, his mouth full, shook his head and pointed to the drink in front of him.

Sarah hopped on a barstool. She had been thinking about Esra all day, and in that moment she wished someone would put on some music.

The bells on the front door chimed as Nadav entered the bar with a boy of about six or seven years old. He was a handsome child, with ebony skin and close-cropped hair. Nadav placed his hand on the boy's shoulder.

"Everyone? Hello?" Nadav raised his other hand to get everyone's attention. "I'd like to introduce you all to someone very special. This is Elian. He is our foster son, and we're very glad he's with us."

Elian smiled shyly, showing off a deep set of dimples in his round cheeks. He turned to look at Sarah, his eyes a familiar shade of emerald green. Sarah forgot to breathe, holding his gaze for a second before he turned and looked up at Nadav with a look of admiration.

"Papa, I'm so happy." Raya jogged around the bar and gave her father a hug. "I didn't know you and Mum had actually gone through with this!"

"We weren't going to. We were worried that we were too old, that they wouldn't choose us. But the agency called us the other day, told us about Elian, and asked if we'd be interested in giving him a home. It felt like the right thing to do. He's new to the Magyck foster system, so they don't have a lot of background on him yet. He just showed up one day."

"Hi." Raya extended her hand to the little boy. "I'm your big sister, Raya."

Elian shook it and giggled. He spotted a brown leather satchel on the bar counter and wiggled up a stool to take a closer look.

"What's this?" he asked Nadav, peeking into the bag.

"It's a very difficult instrument to play. Not many people can do it."

Within seconds Elian had slipped off his sneakers, wrapped the bands around his fingers and toes, and was wriggling them as fast as he could. At first nothing happened, but Elian scrunched up his little face, stared at the back wall, and the notes came. They were random at first, but soon they ordered themselves into a sweet tune, one that Sarah had never heard but would not soon forget.

Avi approached Nadav and touched him lightly on his arm. "Is he…"

"Perhaps." Nadav shrugged. "It doesn't matter. It is right."

"Agreed." Avi slapped his friend on the back. "Mazel tov. Come, sit with us. Have some food."

He brought Nadav to his table, leaving Raya to watch her little brother make music. She smiled and danced to the songs he was making up on the spot. Soon Aaron and Miriam joined them, and Elian lost interest in the music, taking off the bands, sitting with the other children, and playing with Aaron's pet Albert, who was reveling in the attention.

After a while, Avi stood up and clinked his glass.

"One of the great joys in a man's life—or at least this man's life—is being able to spend time with his family. Sadly, we lost a member of our family, and we give a toast to his memory. We miss him dearly. To Esra!"

Everyone held up their glasses. "To Esra!"

"Now that we've had a chance to collect ourselves, I want to share some news about the store." Avi downed what was left of his drink and placed the glass gently on the nearest table. "Now that Zondra is gone, and since she had no heirs, the contract her family made with mine is null. It stays with the Greenbergs. No matter what." Avi walked over to the children and kissed his grandson on the top of his head. "Much fuss was made over who would take over the store once I retired. For a long time it was unclear. I had no idea if Zondra would come to collect, or if I would pass it on. I came to realize, however, that Sarah is not the one who should inherit."

"It's all right, Dad. I'll do it."

"You don't have to. I realized that there is a more appropriate person." Avi kneeled on the floor. "Now, I don't plan on going anywhere for a long, long time, but…Aaron? How would you feel about coming to spend time with me at the store? On a regular basis?"

Debra gasped in joy and quietly clapped her hands.

"What do you think, Aaron?"

"That would be awesome, Zayde!" He hugged his grandfather tightly.

"Can I come too?" Elian said, his voice soft and even.

"I don't see why not. We can always use an extra pair of hands. Right, Nadav?"

"You sure he won't be any trouble?" Nadav asked.

Avi looked at the boy intently. "None at all. I know we'll get along swimmingly. Don't you think so, Elian?"

Elian smiled from ear to ear.

"Will I get to come every day?" Aaron asked eagerly.

"As long as it's okay with your mother and father and it doesn't interfere with your studies, you can come as often as you like."

Aaron jumped up and down, then took Elian by the hand. "We'll have fun. You're young, but I think we can be best friends."

Elian looked at Aaron like he had just discovered a new superhero.

Avi left the boys and sat next to Sarah at her table.

"I know they offered you that editor job at the travel magazine," he said.

"They did, but I can't—"

"But you can. And you must. This wasn't for you. I see that now."

"I guess Zondra was right," Sarah said.

"She might have said it, but she didn't mean it the way I do. You're a writer. That's what you're supposed to do. Food, life, art—it's all part of your story. Esra would agree with me, you know. Take the job."

Sarah rested her head on her father's shoulder. "Thank you, Dad. I will call them tomorrow and say yes."

"Good. Write for yourself. The world will find you."

"Maybe I'll even write a book about us. About...all this?" She shook her head. "Never mind. I know we're supposed to keep it secret."

"Go ahead." Avi smiled broadly. "No one would believe it anyway."

In a few hours, everyone was packing up to go, tired and full of food and drink. Even Dave was done, picking at a few remaining stuffed grape leaves with his index finger talon. Elian carefully placed the music bands back in the satchel and looked up at Nadav.

"May I…have these? I want to make more music."

"Of course, my son. They are yours."

"Their old owner…was he your friend?" Elian asked.

"He was *mon frère*. That means 'my brother.' He would want them to be used. You would have liked him, Elian. He was as big as a mountain and wise as the moon. He had a laugh like the ringing of bells and eyes like a forest."

"You're funny, Papa." Elian slung the bag over his shoulder. It was heavy, and it hit the floor. Nadav picked it up and stuck it under his arm.

Colin came over to collect Sarah but looked at her and frowned.

"What's the matter?" he said.

"I'm going to take the job."

"That's great! Why do you look sad?"

"It's a new beginning. Beginnings are hard."

Colin gathered her in his arms. "They are. But then you get to the cool part. We will work it out, okay? You need to do this."

"I love you. Always."

"I love you too." Colin got his hat and handed Sarah her jacket. "We'll talk more about this later. I'll see you at the house? Madison wants to make dinner. Is that okay?"

"That would be great. I'm really full though."

"I am too. Bring some Rolaids, just in case."

Sarah patted her purse. "I always do."

"Before you go, Colin?" Avi called out to him. "A word?"

"I might be a while," Colin said to Sarah.

"Yeah, you will. Text me when you're on your way home." Sarah smiled and put on her sweater. Stopping before she reached the door, she turned to survey the room.

These people, she thought. These strange, wonderful people. And now that she, too, felt the hum of Magyck pulse through her veins, she knew she was part of something larger than herself.

She was a Magycian.

She stepped out of the pub and into the early spring sunlight, bright and new and fresh. As she walked briskly down the sidewalk, she heard a familiar voice over a crowd of people standing in a small lot at the end of the block.

"And now, for my next trick…"

The man in the lavender suit was there, plying his trade, creating illusions for the skeptical crowd. He hadn't improved much since the last time Sarah saw him. He rolled a large gold coin over each finger on his right hand, and as he tried to make it disappear, he dropped it. Blushing, he picked up the coin and tried again.

As he rolled the coin over his fingers, Sarah discreetly waved her hand, and the coin disappeared. He looked as surprised as his audience did, his mouth agape as he peeked up his sleeve.

"I'll give you that one, pal," Sarah said quietly, chuckling to herself. She put her hands in her pockets, and she noticed a small lump in the left one. Pulling it out, she opened her fingers to reveal a green stone with one word carved into it:

MAGIC

She took off her glove and rubbed her thumb over the script, feeling the smooth surface of the stone, practically weightless in her hand. In the distance, she thought she heard a familiar tune.

> *Happily ever after now,*
> *The colors glow and sing…*
> *Mr. Skye will guide you on,*
> *As stars before you sing…*

She shook her head and looked around but couldn't tell where the music was coming from.

> *Through the groove of space and rhyme,*
> *Dancing Mr. Skye…*
> *Lose yourself and be found again,*
> *Dancing Mr. Skye…*

She continued walking down the street, holding the stone firmly in her hand.

"Got it, Esra. Thank you."

She laughed and even danced a bit, a sense of wonderment and joy in each step as she traveled the neighborhood she had known all her life. She had love, she had her family, and for the first time in her life, she had purpose. No matter what happened, she knew everything would be all right. She trusted herself.

And this time, her car was exactly where she had left it.

Thank you for reading! Did you enjoy? Please add your review because nothing helps an author more and encourages readers to take a chance on a book than a review.

And don't miss more from Jennifer Inglis at
www.jenniferinglis.com

Until then, discover SECOND STAR TO THE LEFT, by City Owl Author, Megan Van Dyke. Turn the page for a sneak peek!

You can also sign up for the City Owl Press newsletter to receive notice of all book releases!

SNEAK PEEK OF SECOND STAR TO THE LEFT
BY MEGAN VAN DYKE

Nothing attracted attention like free booze. The Lazy Mule wasn't usually this popular, or so the locals said, but the promise of free drinks lured every shopkeeper and down-on-their-luck sailor into the dirty, ramshackle building near the docks. Tropical air, thick with humidity and the promise of rain, filled the bar as tightly as the patrons crammed into every nook and cranny.

Tink pulled her braid over one shoulder, careful not to dislodge the sections covering her pointed ears. She rubbed the loose ends between her fingertips, feigning nervousness as she glanced over her shoulder.

Men and women alike clamored toward the far table where a large, blond man regaled the crowd with tales of his crew's success. He was attractive, with bulging muscles, towering height, and a chiseled jaw. But if he made one more crude joke about plundering something, Tink was going to toss her drink at him. *Stupid pirate.* Soon enough he'd stumble and fall, or the rotting table would finally give way. She grinned. That alone would be worth the cost of the trip.

But the blustering first mate of the *Jolly Roger* wasn't her target. No, to get what she needed, only the captain would do. Tink licked her lips as her gaze caught on the equally tall but leaner man with one shining black boot propped on the seat of a nearby chair. He shouted colorful additions to the first mate's tale and called for another round of drinks for all his "friends."

The poor ale Tink sipped turned sour on her tongue before she forced it down. The captain's arrogance knew no end. He traveled from one pirate-friendly port to the next so he and his crew could rave of their accomplishments. At least it made them easy to track.

Tonight, they bragged about their theft of the Heart of Fire, a stunning ruby set in gold. A half-grin pulled at her lips. What would they say when she stole it from them?

Captain Hook, so named for the distinctive metal weapon that replaced one hand, raised a pint in the air. Dark ale splashed over the side. Mugs clinked, rising with cheers from the crowd who joined in the toast.

Finally, *finally*, the captain glanced her way.

Her heart gave an involuntary leap as sinful lips twitched on a strong face. Or perhaps it was his coal-dark eyes that twisted her up inside. He raised his mug, taking a long swig, but his attention never left her.

Perfect.

One look and she'd hooked Hook. A small laugh burst from her lips that she covered by biting her bottom lip in feigned embarrassment.

Before he lowered his drink, Tink twisted around back to her mug warming on the bar. Warm ale and filthy pirates. Every girl's dream night.

She snorted. *Sure.*

Her stomach turned as she rubbed the mug between her palms. This wouldn't be her life. Not anymore, not after tonight.

A woman squealed as a drunkard yanked her onto his lap, nearly sending them both tumbling to the ale-soaked floor. How did she ever enjoy these horrid human bars? She and her cousin Lily used to slip through the pixie doors—the circles of trees, stones, mushrooms, or whatever the elders of old selected—for a little fun in the human world all the time. They'd drink, dance, flirt with whichever handsome human caught their eye, then sneak back home before the elders were ever the wiser. They'd done everything together for as long as she could remember. The elders frowned on such elicit exploits. But really, only allowing them out to trade and gather goods not available in their homeland was, well, boring.

Her chest grew tight. *Had Lily made it home? Was she okay?* The bracelet around her wrist with its broken gem weighed her down. Tink had committed an unforgivable sin—selling her pixie dust—to save Lily from that wretched Captain Blackbeard and his crew. A nastier man never drew breath. *Filthy pirate bastard.* That act got her banned from her homeland, Sylvanna Vale, rendering her unable to pass through the magical doorways. Pretending to be human and hiding her wings was a pain. *By Durin's beard, binding them hurts!* Without the cloak around her shoulders, someone would notice where she'd lashed them to her back, and that…well, best they didn't.

"Hey there, lovely lady." A man brushed against her at the bar, smelling of sweat and sour ale—or something even fouler.

"Hello." *And please go away*, she added silently, barely giving the man half a glance. If he had any wits, he'd leave.

"You here with anyone?"

Somehow his breath was worse than the stench clinging to him. Hanks of greasy hair lay against dirty skin. When was the last time he bathed? Humans were disgusting in general, but this one was something extra.

Tink glanced back at the pirates and stiffened. The captain was gone. *Shit. Where did he—*

The intruder slid in front of her. "I'll put the wind in yer sails if ya raise my mast."

Tink gaped. He did *not* just say that to her.

A burning flush rose from her chest to the tips of her ears. Her lips thinned. She needed to ditch this slob and quick. If she lost her chance to get the Heart of Fire because of this fool, she'd… Her nails dug into her palm. She didn't even know, but something horrible.

His filthy hand latched onto her arm. "Come on." Grime-crusted nails dug into her skin. "I can pay ya."

With one quick move, Tink *accidentally* knocked her drink over. Ale splashed across the man, some of it splattering her as well.

"You bitch!" He stumbled back. The man behind him barked in outrage.

Tink slid off her barstool, aiming to flee, but the man grabbed her arm again. She wrenched it back, her other hand sliding under her cloak, searching for her hidden dagger.

"I'll—" The man paled as a hand closed over his forearm. Clean, black cloth and fine stitching caught her eye.

"You'll leave the lady alone," the velvet voice rumbled just behind her.

Unexpected heat raced up her stiff spine. Captain Hook pushed the man away and wedged himself between them.

"You...you're..." the man stammered before turning and shoving his way through the crowd in haste.

"Good riddance." Hook faced her, glancing over the splatter of ale on the billowing tan shirt tucked into her tight breeches. "You all right, love?"

"I can take care of myself."

His eyes widened.

Shit. She was supposed to seduce him, not brush him off. "But..." She licked her lips before glancing away, then back. "I really appreciate the help."

He tipped an invisible hat, the motion as natural as if he rarely went around without one. "Always happy to help a lady in distress."

"How very gallant of you." It took everything she had to keep the sarcasm out of her voice.

"Can I buy you another drink..." He cocked his head, waiting for her name.

"Tinker Bell." *Oh, Beryl's wings.* She hadn't planned to give him her real one. She grinned through her error and slid closer. "And I do believe you already ordered another round for everyone."

His fingertips, with nails painted a midnight black, grazed the edge of her shoulder before he pulled back. The touch, so brief and fleeting, sent a thrill down to her toes. It shouldn't have. He was a pirate—a notorious one. Worse, her target. But if he was interested, it made her job so much easier. Stealing the ruby was a test, and she couldn't fail, not if she wanted the merfolk's queen, Titania, to trust her. She needed her trust before the queen would even discuss a trade for the black pearl —the only object known to fix anything broken, even her bracelet.

"Tinker Bell." He took his time with her name, and the way he drew out the words melted her more than any drink.

"Just Tink is fine," she added, suddenly warm.

"Aye. Not that swill, Tink." He gestured to the nearby drinks. "The barkeep has a few more pleasurable options."

"Well…" Tink ran her hand down his sleeve. "I think I might enjoy that."

Don't stop now. Keep reading with your copy of SECOND STAR TO THE LEFT, by City Owl Author, Megan Van Dyke.

And find more from Jennifer Inglis at
www.jenniferinglis.com

**Don't miss more from Jennifer Inglis at
www.jenniferinglis.com**

**Until then, discover SECOND STAR TO THE LEFT, by City
Owl Author, Megan Van Dyke**

Tinker Bell, banished from her homeland for doing the unthinkable,
selling the hottest drug in Neverland—pixie dust—wants absolution.

Determined to find a way home, Tink doesn't hesitate to follow the one
lead she has, even if that means seducing a filthy pirate to steal precious
gems out from under his...hook.

Captain Hook believes he's found a real treasure in Tink. That is, until
he recovers from her pixie dust laced kiss with a curse that turns the seas
against him. With his ship and reputation at the mercy of raging storms,
he tracks down the little minx and demands she remove the curse. Too
bad she can't.

However, the mermaid queen has a solution to both of their problems,
if Tink and Hook will work together to retrieve a magical item for her.

As they venture to the mysterious Shrouded Isles to find the priceless
treasure, their shared nemesis closes in. However, his wrath is nothing
compared to the realization that achieving their goal may mean losing
something they never expected to find—each other.

*The swagger and adventure of Pirates of the Caribbean meets the sexy banter of The
Hating Game with a healthy dose of steam in this retelling of Peter Pan that's far
from the Neverland you know.*

Please sign up for the City Owl Press newsletter for chances to win special subscriber-only contests and giveaways as well as receiving information on upcoming releases and special excerpts.

All reviews are **welcome** and **appreciated**. Please consider leaving one on your favorite social media and book buying sites.

Escape Your World. Get Lost in Ours! City Owl Press at www.cityowlpress.com.

ACKNOWLEDGMENTS

Writing is very much a solitary endeavor, but it some ways it's also a team sport, which for me is strange because I don't play sports in any way, shape, or form. Ah, well. Firstly, thank you to my father James Inglis, who provided the support I needed to write this book, even if it was just in the form of, "Did you write today?" Dr. Dan Novy, my long-time friend, lent me the title of Raya's doctoral thesis and I am ever grateful. I appreciate the efforts of my agent extraordinaire, Amy Brewer of Metamorphosis Literary Agency, who understands perfectly my brand of weird and enables it in just the right way. Thanks to Kristen Johnston, a force of nature and unbelievably talented human. Also to my editor, Tee Tate, and publisher, Tina Moss, for believing in my book and handling it with the utmost care.

Lastly, much love and a great big "howdy do" to all the odd, misfit, creative, extraordinary people everywhere. The Magyck in me respects the Magyck in you.

"It doesn't stop being magic just because you know how it works." — Terry Pratchett

Rock on.

ABOUT THE AUTHOR

JENNIFER INGLIS is an author and humorist, and has studied comedy writing at The Second City in Chicago. An alumna of Northern Illinois University, she earned a bachelor's degree in theater arts, and a master's degree in teaching from National-Louis University. She formerly worked as a public school drama teacher, which meant she spent six years being ignored by middle school students. In a past life, she worked in professional theater in suburban Chicago, as a playwright, actor, assistant director, and producer, despite being a classic introvert who'd rather be home reading a book. Jennifer currently lives in Chicago and, when she's not trying to dress up her cat, Daisy, in a variety of fetching hats (and failing miserably) she works as a freelance writer and proofreader.

www.jenniferinglis.com

 instagram.com/jennifer.inglis.writes
 facebook.com/JenniferInglisWriter
 twitter.com/Jennifer_Inglis

ABOUT THE PUBLISHER

City Owl Press is a cutting edge indie publishing company, bringing the world of romance and speculative fiction to discerning readers.

Escape Your World. Get Lost in Ours!

www.cityowlpress.com

facebook.com/CityOwlPress

twitter.com/cityowlpress

instagram.com/cityowlbooks

pinterest.com/cityowlpress

tiktok.com/@cityowlpress

www.ingramcontent.com/pod-product-compliance
Lightning Source LLC
Chambersburg PA
CBHW060609030726
47498CB00005B/1602